This charming debut from Denise M. Colby about a young woman finding her bearings as a rural teacher in 1860s California kept me smiling through the pages. I especially adored Bert the rooster. If you love sweet historical romances with *When Calls the Heart* vibes and tender threads of faith, this story is sure to put a smile on your face too.

—BECCA KINZER, AUTHOR OF *DEAR HENRY, LOVE EDITH* AND *LOVE IN TANDEM*

Denise M. Colby's debut novel, *When Plans Go Awry,* is delightful. Follow Olivia and Luke as they encounter both poignant and humorous challenges that test their best-laid plans. With its charming characters and captivating setting, you'll find yourself hooked from page one.

—KIMBERLY KEAGAN, HISTORICAL ROMANCE WRITER

With a cast of characters sure to steal your heart (including a rooster who steals the show!), *When Plans Go Awry* beautifully touches that deep need within all of us to be loved and accepted. This deeply layered story also reveals a truth we often forget—that innate desire to trust when life has proven to be untrustworthy. You'll walk dusty streets, run from danger (literally), and brave the flood of emotions (and the river!) in this must-read historical romance from debut author, Denise M. Colby. I've waited nearly ten years to hold a copy of *When Plans Go Awry* in my hands, and I am thrilled that the time is here!

—CHAUTONA HAVIG, *USA TODAY* BESTSELLING AUTHOR

Denise M. Colby has woven a wonderful story about two people who are determined not to fall in love. Denise hooks the reader with vivid descriptions of a growing frontier town, along with a realistic depiction of the life of a one-room schoolteacher. Her characters are both charming and frustrating, and she adds excitement as well as tension throughout the story. I look forward to reading more books from this budding author.

—MARIE WELLS COUTU, AWARD-WINNING AUTHOR OF THE MENDED VESSELS SERIES

Denise M. Colby brings to life a must-read historical inspirational romance about the dilemma of women in an era when they had little choice and voice of their own.

Best-laid Plans ✦ Book One

When Plans Go

Awry

DENISE M. COLBY

Scrivenings
PRESS
Quench your thirst for story.
www.ScriveningsPress.com

Published by Scrivenings Press LLC
15 Lucky Lane
Morrilton, Arkansas 72110
https://ScriveningsPress.com

Printed in the United States of America

Paperback ISBN 978-1-64917-391-1
eBook ISBN 978-1-64917-392-8

Editors: Regina Rudd Merrick and Linda Fulkerson

Cover by Linda Fulkerson, www.bookmarketinggraphics.com

All characters are fictional, and any resemblance to real people, either factual or historical, is purely coincidental.

Unless otherwise noted, scriptures are taken from the KING JAMES VERSION (KJV): KING JAMES VERSION, public domain.

Scriptures marked NKJV are taken from the New King James Version®. Copyright © 1982 by Thomas Nelson. Used by permission. All rights reserved.

For Barb & Kaycy
for reading the very first scene and
encouraging me to write more.

And for Ken, my very own hero.
How can I say in so few words
all that you mean to me?

A man's heart plans his way, but the Lord directs his steps.
—Proverbs 16:9 (NKJV)

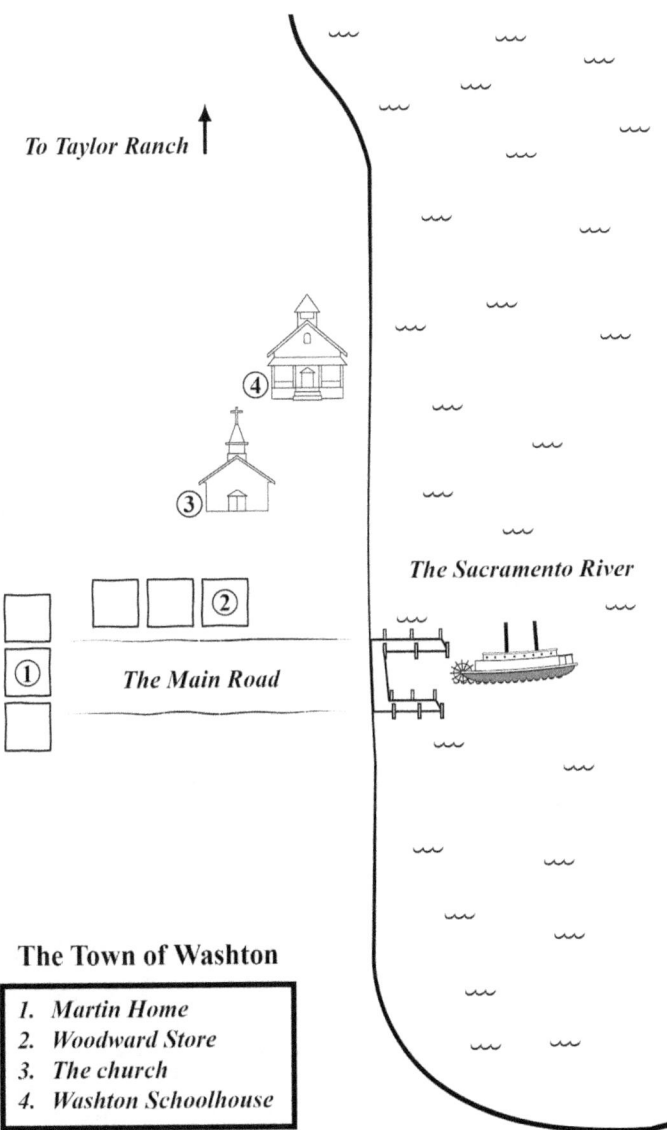

To Taylor Ranch ↑

The Sacramento River

The Main Road

The Town of Washton

1. Martin Home
2. Woodward Store
3. The church
4. Washton Schoolhouse

One

July 1869
Cincinnati, Ohio

Olivia Carmichael placed a single rose between the
two freshly packed mounds, then brushed the dirt
off her gloves. Maybe this would be her new
routine, starting her day with her parents like she did when
they were alive.

A small breeze rustled the leaves from the red oak tree that
offered shade from the heat of the rising summer sun.

A tear ran free, and she caught it with her stained glove,
leaving a dirt smudge on her face. She should've brought an
extra pair to arrive home pristine as always, but there was
nothing to be done for it now. "The house is horribly quiet
without you both. I miss your booming voice, Father, and—"
She squeezed her eyes shut. To lose them so suddenly. And to
such tragedy. Yes, she even missed his harsh and criticizing
words.

Another tear escaped. As she wiped her cheek, the

dampness permeated the fine fabric. "Mother, I miss your confidence and encouragement and how you would drag me everywhere."

She squeezed her covered hands and held back the whimper building in her chest. "Richard and I will wait a while longer to marry, of course, for the appropriate length of mourning."

Speaking of her fiancé, where was he? He had been absent for the past day, saying he had much to attend to. Surely tomorrow, he would want to come to pay his respects. He had admired Father, after all.

And she needed him.

"I will keep your charity alive at church, Mother. No one will forget either of—"

"Miss Carmichael! Miss Carmichael!" Their stable boy ran straight to her, then placed his hands on his knees to catch his breath.

Olivia glanced at his bowed head. "Yes, Tommy? What is it? Are you all right?"

Tommy gulped in a big breath. "Somethin's happenin' at home. You need to get back straight away."

She blinked away her tears as she gave her parents' graves one last glance and then faced Tommy. "Can you tell me what you saw?"

He scrunched his nose. "People came to take away your possessions, Miss. Mr. Jasper asked me to come get ya straight away."

A cold chill crept up her spine, urging her to rush out of the churchyard. "Whatever could this be about?"

"I don't know, Miss, but we gotta hurry." Tommy ran off ahead.

Olivia followed. What now? Could she even cope with

another situation? *Are you there, God? I'm not sure how much more I can handle.*

She rounded the corner to her street and froze. "Impossible." The large double doors to her family estate stood wide open. Two men carried her mother's new sofa down the front steps to a parked wagon loaded with the rest of her family's furniture.

With an unladylike squeak, she rushed toward the commotion. "I insist you cease your actions."

They didn't.

"Excuse me, miss," a man from behind said gruffly.

Startled, she stepped aside until she noticed her father's prized clock in his hands. "What are you doing? That was my father's. Sir! Wait."

The man continued his steps. "Just following orders, Miss."

"*Whose* orders?" she called after his retreating back.

He shrugged and handed the clock to the man standing in the truck.

Footsteps pounded behind her on the brick walkway. She swiveled, then exhaled when Jasper, her family's butler, appeared. But one look at his strained expression, and she knew this wouldn't be fixed easily.

"Miss Olivia! Thank the good Lord you're home."

"What's happening, Jasper?" she demanded.

He glanced around before his eyes met hers. "Not here. Follow me."

A sense of dread overcame her as she followed him.

Once inside, he led her to the same room where she'd left the couch that morning, paused, and then changed directions. They moved toward the kitchen, her favorite room in the house. She'd spent many hours here with the staff as a young girl, eating milk and cookies and babbling, mostly about trivial

3

matters. And lately, not so trivial, like her betrothal and her parents' untimely death.

A glass of milk, as well as a plate of Cook's delicious oatmeal cookies, sat on the table next to some papers. Her heartbeat raced, nearly exploding in her chest.

Father had banished the staff from serving treats three years ago, claiming quite pointedly Olivia had to lose a few pounds to attract a proper husband.

He needn't have worried. Richard never said a word about her eating habits.

But still, she was a grown woman, so milk and cookies hardly appeared these days. Her heartbeat accelerated. The last time had been when she learned of her parents' fate.

Jasper held out a chair. Her stomach twisted when both he and Agnes, the housekeeper, sat across from her at the worn kitchen table. Her hands came together, and she squeezed hard, allowing the discomfort to anchor her.

"Olivia, dear ..." Agnes glanced at Jasper.

Jasper placed his hand over Agnes's. They had served her family since Olivia was ten and had been married even longer. The silent communication between them was palpable. Olivia pressed her fingers harder.

Agnes looked at her with tears rolling down her cheeks.

Jasper took over. "Your father, Miss, he ..."

Agnes nodded. "There's no easy way to say it, dear. Your father was a fraud."

"What?" Olivia's ears rang, and she swayed.

"Easy, love." Jasper reached over and grabbed her shoulder.

The old endearment comforted her. She leaned into him. "I don't understand."

He squeezed her shoulder, gave a hesitant smile, and gestured to the documents. "These papers the men handed over when they arrived explain the d—."

"Scuse me," one of the working men interrupted. "We'll be taking the table and chairs now."

Agnes stood and raised a wooden spoon. "Oh, I would love to flatten you, you ol' coot. Can't you see the miss is in distress? She lost her parents, and now she's losing her home! You can give her five more minutes to sit here on her own furniture before you take it away."

Olivia stared at Agnes. What did she mean, exactly? Father a fraud? And ... and her entire home—gone?

Hands shaking, Olivia unfolded the papers and glanced at the first page. Mouth dry, she held her breath while her brain scrambled to find a possible excuse. Anything that could explain away the accusations.

Had her father truly conned others out of their money?

She stood abruptly and scanned the room. Most of the furnishings were cleared out. She moved to the hallway. Gone were Mama's paintings, the black gold-lined vases the servants filled with fresh flowers every day, as well as her mother's favorite wooden cabinet she'd brought from New York. Everything had been removed.

Oh, Papa. How could you?

A lump formed in the pit of her belly. "Where will I sleep?" she whispered.

Agnes and Jasper approached. Olivia considered the two people who had raised her since she was ten. Wet streaks blotched Agnes' face as both she and Jasper shook their heads.

"I don't understand. Why? How?" Shock merged into anger. "Tell me this isn't happening. That none of this is true."

Agnes placed her hand over her mouth and murmured. "None of us knew."

Her father deceived them all. Accepted in social circles, men sang his praises. Doors were opened to him without question. And Richard. Dear Richard. She inhaled deeply. She must find him. Her fiancé would help sort out this mess. Maybe they could marry sooner.

"Not to mention, he most likely wanted to protect you—" added Jasper.

"Protect her?" Agnes shouted. "That's not protecting. It's even written in the papers, and he's not here to defend himself. And now? We're all affected by his poor choices. We've no job, no referral, no home, nothing!"

"Agnes—" Jasper glared at his wife.

In the papers? Olivia wrapped her arms around her middle. Too numbed by grief to focus on the rest of the world, she hadn't looked at one in days. "What was written about my family?" If the papers wrote about her father's actions, this affected not only her but the entire staff. She'd never felt so helpless. "What will you and Jasper do?"

They both shrugged, but the fear was evident in their eyes.

She lifted her chin. "This is our home. We've lived here for ten years. They can't just take it away, can they?" A sliver of a memory surfaced. When they arrived in Cincinnati, the move west allowed them luxuries they couldn't afford in New York. Her father had instructed her to never mention the conditions they came from. Too young to fully understand then, she knew now what he implied. Society wouldn't accept those who made their money. Had he acquired all they owned illegally?

She gasped. Had Mama known?

Her stomach roiled, and she placed a hand on the nearest wall.

Mama must have.

Olivia closed her eyes. Hurt, dread, and disbelief mingled together. Her father's tales implied a story of inherited privilege. After hearing his version of the truth for years, she had believed him.

She groaned. Was her life a complete lie?

The men brushed by her, carrying the benches and kitchen table. She followed them until they crossed the threshold. She had to do something. She ran through a mental list of acquaintances who might be of assistance. If the story was in the newspaper, she needed to see with her own eyes what it said.

And then her fiancé appeared. He glanced around, dusted his hands, and frowned.

"Richard." She ran to him, hands outstretched. "I'm so glad you came ."

He pursed his lips and put his arms behind his back.

Unease wound its way around her heart.

"Miss Carmichael." He refused to meet her eyes.

Alarm bells rang in her head, but she ignored them. "Did you hear what happened? Will you make these men stop tearing apart my home?"

His eyes locked on to hers but held no compassion. "I'm sorry, Olivia."

She reared back. "Won't you please help?" Why was he so distant? Why didn't he try to comfort her or take charge?

"I cannot help you with your request." He focused on a spot beyond her left shoulder and raised his chin.

She shifted her weight. "But you're my fiancé. You have every right to—"

"May we talk somewhere privately?"

She glanced around the hallway. No furniture remained, and, except for Agnes and Jasper, who stood together near the wall, they were alone. "Whatever you want to say, you can say in front of them. You," she waved her hand to encompass all three of them, "are all I have left."

He cleared his throat. "As you wish."

Agnes stepped beside Olivia and placed a comforting hand around her waist.

"We can no longer be affianced, Miss Carmichael. Your father led me astray, and I agreed to a contract under false pretenses. You may keep the ring as you may need the funds." He dipped his head then executed a perfect pivot and walked out.

Olivia stared mutely at his retreating back.

Jasper growled. "If it wasn't important for me to stay respectable so I might find new employment, I would gladly pummel him and put him in his place. Of all the low-down, callous—"

"Jasper," Agnes warned.

"What?" He now stood on Olivia's other side.

"Not now."

He glanced at Olivia. "Sorry." He touched her shoulder. "He wasn't right for you anyway, Miss Olivia. All of us thought so. It was your father who asked him to court you, anyway."

The turmoil in her stomach moved to her throat. Richard hadn't chosen her of his own accord? Their relationship was a lie too? Richard. Her dear Richard. But he wasn't her dear Richard.

He was her father's Richard.

She held her breath, afraid any movement might toss up Agnes's cookies. That would surely add a fitting layer of humiliation onto what she would forever deem the second worst day of her life.

"Jasper!" Agnes shook her head at her husband.

"Well, it's true. She's better off without him." He shrugged and looked at her, his gaze filled with love and compassion.

Even though her heart lay in pieces, ripped apart by the two men she trusted most, she felt oddly calm. "I think I need to examine the house."

Agnes squeezed her before she let go. "I'm terribly sorry, dear."

Olivia wrung her hands and faced Jasper. "It seems you are the only male I can truly depend on."

Jasper's face shifted between a smile and a frown. "Even so, my dear, I'm not in any position to offer you refuge since Agnes and I lived here with you. Sadly, I also will let you down."

She looked at the two people who had been more family than servants and knew if they were in any position to help, they would. But they couldn't. "Whatever are we going to do?"

OLIVIA SPENT the next week sheltering at Agnes's cousin's house. But she couldn't sleep on a floor pallet forever or take food when there wasn't enough to go around. So, she headed to her friend Margaret Wilcox's house, the location for this month's Ladies Aid Society luncheon.

Her family had supported the Society for years, and they, in turn, would be able to offer her assistance. That necessary support, as well as the prospect of a friendly smile, hot tea, and warm scone, spurred her on.

She stopped at the cobblestone entry, smoothed her skirt, and willed her palms to stay dry. Her hand shook as she knocked.

The butler opened the door with Margaret right behind him, a look of astonishment on her face. "I'm surprised you're willing to appear here after what has transpired." Margaret stepped in front and crossed her arms. "I'm sorry, but you're not welcome."

Olivia's heart sank. "Maggie, please." She glanced at the butler, who stood stiffly, waiting for his mistress's word. "This entire situation is difficult for me. We've been friends a long time, and after these uh ... developments, I need my friends now more than ever."

"We've taken a vote, Miss *Carmichael*." Margaret spat out Olivia's surname. "Given all the recent facts brought to light, we cannot, in good faith, include you in our efforts going forward."

Olivia rose to her toes and peered beyond Margaret's shoulder. The rest of the group hovered nearby, but not one made eye contact. The scent of fresh blueberry scones wafted in the air. She was sure the tea sat in the pot, growing cold.

With one last hopeful effort, her gaze bore into each person, willing them to look her way. "Do all of you feel this way?"

Not a single person moved. None of her *friends* would offer her support?

Pain stung behind her eyes. *I will not cry. Not in front of them.* "I have served faithfully beside you, along with our mothers, for years. Friends don't abandon each other in their hour of need."

"Friends don't lie about who they are," Margaret nodded to the butler, who shut the door in Olivia's face, her past life on one side of the solid, unyielding wood, and her on the outside.

Blinking the sting out of her eyes, she turned and inched away, paying no mind to her direction. The burden of her father's crimes was hers to bear.

Alone.

A sudden coldness hit Olivia's core, chilling her like a bitter snowstorm. She shivered and hunched her shoulders, dragging her feet with each step. Abandoned by everyone associated with her or her parents, this group was her last hope. They were supposed to serve those in need. But now she saw the truth—and it was ugly.

She broke wide open inside. A crevice so deep and wide the anguish burrowed deep in her soul. If this was how God-fearing people behaved, she wanted nothing to do with them.

What would she do now?

In a matter of one week, Olivia had lost her parents, her home, all her possessions, and then, Richard had jilted her.

If it hadn't been for her beloved servants, Jasper and Agnes, she didn't know what she would've done. No, not servants. Friends whom she loved and cared for, now homeless due to her father's actions.

She had no skills to take on employment. And based on the charity group's reaction, no one would hire her anyway. They wouldn't trust her, and she wouldn't trust them. Not in this city, with the knowledge of what her father had done plastered in the *Cincinnati Enquirer*.

The Carmichael name—*her* name—was tarnished, associated with criminal activities.

The tightness in her chest increased, and she squeezed her hands together. She truly was on her own, in a situation she still found impossible to believe.

"Pardon me, ma'am." a gentleman grumbled as he walked around her.

She raised her head and blinked. "Pardon me," she replied, but the man moved on without a backward glance. His retreating form disappeared as he moved down the narrow street. She glanced around. Where was she, and how did she get here, several blocks in the wrong direction?

As she surveyed the area, the wind blew loose trash around her and up against the storefront, drawing her attention to the newsprint taped to the window. She shivered and wrapped her long coat tighter around her middle as the words drew her closer.

Wanted
Women who are willing to travel West and live in rural areas.
Will be trained to teach and civilize the young.

11

Great Need.

Her heart hammered. Was this her answer? She frowned. There was nothing in Cincinnati for her now. No one would notice or care if she disappeared. She bit her lip. The ostracism hurt far more than she wanted to admit.

The notice beckoned another read.

Teach and civilize the young.

Being an only child, she had little experience around children. But she was well-read and educated. Could she control a schoolroom full of students? Would they follow her direction?

She shifted back and forth, pondering her next step. It was brash. Risky, even.

Considering such a permanent resolution should warrant much contemplation. But at this juncture, a hasty, on-the-spot decision would suffice.

Olivia peered at the address on the advertisement, the location only a few blocks away. She smoothed the imaginary creases on her skirt and shifted her hat. Shoulders straightened, she breathed deep and willed her feet to move.

The sunlight peeked from behind the clouds and warmed her back, propelling her forward. As she turned the corner, her steps grew more purposeful. Children played near the building she approached, and their laughter encouraged her spirit.

Never again would she allow anyone to make decisions for her—not man, not friends, not God. With a plan of attack formed in her mind and her emotions more in control, confidence seeped in as she climbed the steps and entered the building.

Two

I'm excited, nervous, and a little scared, but I know my plans are sound, and I won't ever have to depend on anyone again.

—From the journal of Olivia Carmichael

Five Weeks Later
Sacramento, California

"Fifteen more minutes to Sacramento, next stop," the conductor shouted from the back of the railcar.

Olivia scribbled furiously to finish her latest diary entry. The need to finish writing about the past before she set foot in her future drove her to complete the entry before she reached her new destination.

The book, a gift from their teacher, had become a close friend and the safest place to capture her thoughts and opinions. She only had a bit more time to write out everything that had happened during the past few weeks. Events that led her to make a major redirected change in her life from everything she knew. She didn't want to forget, but she didn't want anyone in her new life knowing about her past, either.

Even now, thinking about her parents' accident, followed by the loss of her home and social status, left an aching hole in her chest. She found it difficult to breathe. How could the society friends who gave to charity have no charity to give her? She shook her head. If she pondered it too long, her body would seize up, and she'd be unable to move.

Her new roommate at the training school, Jenny Millard, had found her this way numerous times and helped her snap out of her trance and keep moving forward. Barely. If it wasn't for Jenny, Olivia didn't think she would've survived the first week. But somehow, she found the ability to study, pass her exams, and not let anyone else know she was broken inside. The immense grief would overcome her at odd times. While sitting in class taking a test or in line for the noon-day meeting. The worst was at night. Sharing a room for the first time in her life, the noises, both inside the building they stayed in as well as outside, were new and unfamiliar. Gone were her routines and the people she cared for.

All of it made her head spin.

As the train swerved around a bend, the person next to her jostled her leg, causing the pencil to scratch across the page. She closed her eyes and pressed her lips together to hold back a retort. Additional jerking from the train forced her to pause writing and grip the book tightly to her chest. As soon as the tracks straightened out, she went back to writing. She wanted it all down and out of her head before the next stop. Before her new life began.

The train slowed to an abrupt halt, and Olivia raised her head. The loud commotion distracted her a few moments before she placed her pencil in her reticule. She hadn't paid attention to the five-minute warning, and now there was no time to put her journal away as the passengers around her stood.

"Excuse me." The older lady next to her pushed at her legs for her to move. She stood and stepped into the aisle. Several others were already pressing forward, and they caught her up within their path. She stumbled down a few rows before she stepped into an empty set of seats. Her traveling group passed, and she nodded at them.

"Livvy, where are your things?" Jenny stopped, holding up the passengers behind her.

"I had to move out of the way. I need to go back to my seat. Go ahead." Olivia waved her hand. "I'll catch up with you outside." She pushed her way back through those still exiting, passing those sitting in their seats to travel to the next stop. Grabbing her luggage, she struggled to carry it all down the passageway as she hustled to the exit.

Bright sunlight blared in her eyes, and she halted in the doorway. She blinked, then searched until she saw her group crossing the street straight ahead. She blew out her breath. She'd follow behind in just a bit. After embracing this moment, where all the plans she wrote out in her journal would begin, she wanted to capture this juncture as it would be the perfect first step in following those plans.

LUKE TAYLOR STEPPED out of the Sacramento post office, his new path forward decided and sealed. His mailed reply to Evelyn Watson, the bride he'd picked from the few responses to his ad, was now with the postmaster. He, who had sworn off marriage, was joining the herd to slaughter. Not right away, but soon enough. There was no turning back now.

A lump formed in his throat, and he swallowed.

If all went to plan, she'd be here next month.

His stomach rolled, and he lengthened his strides along the boardwalk as he reflected on Evelyn's letter.

Clear and concise, she'd grasped what he asked for and accepted his terms. She didn't gush over how she would love him or mention any relationship expectations like the rest of the respondents. No, she wrote about handling the chores around the house. And teaching his sisters. Exactly what he wanted.

Why did the other potential mail-order brides think he was lonely and looking for love? They also assumed he had wealth because he lived near the gold mines. But the mines hadn't paid out the way the papers claimed. His ranch's success, one of the largest in the area, was because of his family's hard work.

Luke stopped at the corner, caught his reflection in the barber shop glass, and grimaced. Women expected more than what he could offer. Some have said he was handsome, but he was only a man. A man who took his responsibilities seriously and wanted nothing to do with romantic notions, especially after Sarah, his so-called former fiancée, left him and the girls behind and forgotten. No, for him, marriage encompassed only two motivations—help raise his sisters and provide a woman's influence as they grew.

Something, he reluctantly admitted, he couldn't provide.

He'd marry, but he wouldn't fall in love or deal with someone who wanted to fall in love with him.

He pulled the brim of his hat lower and moved on. A bead of sweat dripped down his back from the late summer heat. In another month, the temperatures would cool off. He couldn't wait.

As he headed toward the train depot, he passed the hotel, then the ice cream shop, grinning at the way the children pressed their faces against the glass as they looked inside. But as he approached the dress shop, his smile faltered. Guilt washed over him. Caroline and Rose hadn't been shopping once since Ma died two years ago. And he hadn't realized the omission until just this moment.

His feet stopped in the doorway. He had no idea how to shop for dresses. Nor any interest. They could wait another month, couldn't they?

"Excuse me." A lady's voice interrupted his thoughts.

"Pardon me, ma'am." He grabbed the brim of his hat and inclined his head. Stepping aside, he allowed room for a lady with an enormous fake bird on her hat to enter the shop. A young girl turned to look at him over her shoulder as she followed her mother inside. He remembered Caroline at that age, and guilt pressed harder against him. She had grown so much this past year, taking on more responsibilities around the house and helping raise Rose. All while handling the death of their ma with strength and resilience.

Was she really almost thirteen? He shook his head. Even though she believed she could handle anything, Luke knew she needed a lady around to guide her.

He crossed the street to where he'd left Admiral, his horse.

Ranching he understood, but parenting and marriage were a different story. Lately, when Caroline's moods swung back and forth like his bull's tail, he'd skedaddle out of the house to tend the cows. At least those he could understand. Womenfolk? He knew nothing about them. Ma had managed all those matters before.

Yes, he was doing the right thing—for his sisters' sake. They needed a ma, and Evelyn Watson would fit the bill. He shifted his hat back and scratched his head. As much as he needed this woman's help now, he wished to prolong the inevitable as long as possible.

He picked up the pace. Now that the railway had connected the entire country, his future steamed forward as fast as the Overland Flyer. The new expansion shortened the time it took to travel West by several weeks. And with those shortened timetables, Evelyn's appearance would arrive faster than a calf chasing his mama.

A shiver coursed through Luke. If only he had more time or didn't need to marry at all. Marrying someone for convenience didn't sit well with him, but he would not open his heart to more pain. People he loved died or left, and he wouldn't take any more risks than necessary.

Cutting through the station, he dodged folks coming and going on that newly arrived passenger train while remnants of smoke puffed out the smokestack. A group of ladies descended and moved straight across the platform, chattering and oblivious to those around them.

A young boy darted in his path. Luke jerked to the left. "Whoa!"

"Sorry, sir," the boy called as he ran away.

Luke acknowledged the apology and then observed his surroundings.

A young lady stood at the exit of the passenger car. Loose strands of blonde hair blew around her face, but she didn't swipe them away. Instead, her eyes darted back and forth before she set her things at the top of the steps.

Why did she pause? Did she need help? A strange protectiveness surged inside him.

She closed her eyes, tilted her head back, and a small smile spread across her lips.

An unbidden awareness engulfed him as everything around him faded into the background except her. Would Evelyn glow like this woman? He swallowed, smothering the spark that struck his heart. He wanted none of this awareness floating through his veins. What he wanted was a wife to manage his home and help raise his sisters, not a pretty lady who would drive him to distraction.

He forced himself to move but couldn't help watching her out of the corner of his eye. Sweat broke out on his forehead. If Evelyn looked anything like this woman, he'd indeed be distracted.

Three

When I get to California, I plan to fend for myself. No father deciding everything for me. No servants to take care of my needs. No more misplaced trust in a fiancé. My future depends on my own independence. Just like our country claimed independence from England, I'm claiming independence from the male species.

—From the journal of Olivia Carmichael

From the steps of the train, Olivia let the warmth from the late afternoon sun seep into her soul and bolster her courage. Everything would be fine. She could feel it.

Breathing in deeply, it smelled ... familiar? How could that be?

She jerked her head back and opened her eyes. Yet only unfamiliar sights assailed her. Porters carried baggage out of the coaches while passengers boarded for the next destination. A handful of women in bright-colored dresses and heavily adorned hats walked along the wooden sidewalk across the street and darted inside the shop facing the train station. Horses pulled wagons in both directions on brick and cobblestone-lined streets.

Olivia let herself relax. She didn't know what she'd expected but was thankful for dust-free roads. Cobblestones were more civilized and less dirty, in her mind. Hopefully, she found Washton the same.

Water sloshed from somewhere behind the train, reminding her of Cincinnati and the Ohio River. The familiar odor must be the Sacramento River. A slew of memories bombarded her, but she shoved them aside. The buildings, the roads, and the people were different.

She sighed. Maybe all these people would not pay her any mind.

"Extra! Extra! Read about the circus in town. Ten cents. Excuse me, ma'am. Would ya care to support a young boy and buy a paper?"

She turned toward the voice and gasped.

A boy with dirty blond hair held a newspaper smudged in black ink. He looked at her expectantly, his grin showing his missing teeth.

She cringed. "I'm sorry. Not today. But thank you."

Disappointment filled his face, and he ran off, his canvas bag full of papers bouncing against his back.

Her chest tightened. The few measly coins left in her reticule had to last till her first paycheck, whenever that would be. Maybe she could purchase one then. She clasped her hands and squeezed, then glanced about. Where did the other teachers go? The hotels were straight ahead. If she hurried, she'd surely catch them.

Pressing her hat on her head, she grabbed the handle of her portmanteau. Her hand slipped. Oh, her wretched sweaty palm! With no time to stash her journal, she tucked the book under her arm and awkwardly lifted the case with both hands. As the journal slid, she squeezed her elbow tight against her side to hold the book in place then lurched from the train.

"Pardon me. Excuse me!" Olivia wove through the crowd, focused on the direction she figured the other teachers must have gone.

A gust of wind blew her hat backward into the air. She immediately let go of her portmanteau as she reached behind. Her journal landed on the ground with a hard scrape, pages opening this way and that.

She swung around and crashed into a solid warm body, the abrupt halt jostling her luggage until it hit something hard.

"Whoa, there, ma'am." The voice had an earthy tone to it, masculine and deep. Or at least that's what it sounded like with her ear plastered against his chest. The vibration tickled her cheek, and her hands grew warm where they rested on his ribs. The sensation traveled to her back where arms surrounded her and held her close.

He felt stable, strong, and secure.

She shivered but not from the cold.

And then, a different sort of panic took over.

THE FAINT SCENT of lavender permeated Luke's brain as his leg throbbed. He glanced down, and his breath hitched. The lady he'd admired from afar was now nestled firmly against him. He flexed his muscles, and his heart sped up. She fit perfectly against his six-foot two-inch frame.

Alarmed, he dropped his arms and stared.

She stepped back and glared.

He blinked. Not the response he expected.

As he studied her, his world shifted. Even shooting

daggers, her eyes shined crystal clear. The color of the sk ... wait—what was he doing?

He checked the hat in his hand. "Excuse me, ma'am. I believe this is yours."

She quickly snatched the headpiece from him. "Thank you, sir."

"My pleasure, ma'am." He dipped his head, but she bent to retrieve the book sprawled on the ground, then turned away from him. stood on her toes and searched the area.

No adulation or fawning. She paid him no mind, and for some reason, the desire to assist her further grew. He cleared his throat and spoke to her back. "The wind can be mighty strong in these parts, especially when trains arrive or depart. You might want to tie the strings a little tighter in the future." He winced. No woman liked to be told how to dress by a stranger. His brain was addled, no two ways about it. Did sending for a mail-order bride make one lose one's mind?

His comments caused her to whirl around, her beautiful blue eyes reflecting a hint of annoyance. Then she slapped her hat on her head and tied the strings, each movement harsh and overexaggerated, until the bow she made secured her hat so tightly, it caused an indentation in her chin. "Like this?" She raised her eyebrows. "Never mind. I really must be going." She didn't wait for a response, just turned and gathered her things.

"Are you looking for someone?" he asked.

Since her back was to him, her answer was muffled. "I don't even know you."

"I meant no offense, ma'am. I do understand hats and ribbons. My sisters have the same problem at times." Why was he still talking to her? And about ribbons and hats?

She stopped, turned, and tilted her head, her voice calm and controlled. "Well, if you have sisters, sir, I'm sure you're aware, sometimes there just isn't time to tie the ribbons."

He laughed—a great big belly laugh. He liked her spunk. He liked that she didn't bat her eyes at him. He liked *her*. "You've stated the truth of the matter. Caroline and Rose are always running late and leaving their ribbons untied."

Her features softened, and the right side of her mouth lifted a smidge. She searched his face. For what? He didn't know.

Though he needed to go, he couldn't walk away without offering his help. His mother had drilled manners into him from a young age, so he reached for the luggage still in her hands. "I won't leave you stranded here. Where's your destination?"

She tugged her suitcase back, her expression wary, which irked him. He considered himself dependable. Then again, he'd want his sisters to exercise caution.

Stepping back, he raised his hands. "I meant no disrespect, ma'am. I know I'm a stranger, but let's pretend I'm a porter or something and can help you get to where you want to go. Then we can each be on our way. All right?"

Her gaze never faltered as he waited for her nod.

"What's the name?" He reached for the handle again and raised his eyebrow.

Before he could touch the handle, she set the suitcase down and crossed her arms.

"Your hotel. The name of your hotel?" He pinched the bridge of his nose. Even he knew asking a strange woman her name in the middle of a train station wasn't done. Of course, asking where she was staying was probably worse, but how else could he get her luggage there? "I just want to help, ma'am. I promise."

She blew out her breath. "I believe the establishment started with an *O*."

"You mean the Orleans?"

"Yes, that sounds correct. You really don't have to help me."

"The Orleans is not far, just two blocks straight down Second Street here." He held her portmanteau with one hand and pointed with the other.

"Really, I can manage myself." She touched his hand before he could pull away.

A fissure of heat traveled up his arm, and their eyes met in surprise.

Her mouth gaped open, and he heard her quick intake of air.

Or maybe that was him.

If he didn't complete this errand soon, his wits might desert him entirely. He strode off, not bothering to wait. Was she alone? And why? If she was married, shame on her husband, because if Luke were her husband, he wouldn't leave her to fend for herself.

Aggravated with his thoughts, he didn't dare look back. He didn't want to feel attraction to anyone. Attraction led to dealings of the heart. And once hearts were involved, one couldn't control the emotions that swirled within the blasted organ.

By picking a mail-order bride, his mind chose someone to share his life and responsibilities with, not his heart. Of course, he loved his sisters, but he was born into that. Loving a wife? That was voluntary. And he planned to keep his heart locked up and the key firmly lost.

Four

After all that has happened, putting my trust in others won't be easy. Thankfully, I have things well in hand. I've learned much these past few weeks about how to take care of myself. I look forward to handling all my responsibilities on my own and can't wait to start.

—From the journal of Olivia Carmichael

Olivia's heart pounded as the man strode off with her belongings. Was he stealing them or truly helping? Should she trust him? Of all the men she'd known, only Jasper had proven trustworthy, and this man looked nothing like her former butler.

Her first chance to handle something on her own, and she failed.

She shook her head. No, she hadn't. And she wouldn't. Not so long as she kept him in sight. She strode along the platform, trying to lessen the distance between them. If only she hadn't paused for a moment of solitude when disembarking from the train.

Here for less than fifteen minutes, and already she'd lost the band of teachers she'd traveled with and her good intentions to be cautious and strong. All her wits had vanished when she'd bumped into this ... this ... man. Not just any man, but one who made her heart flutter and her stomach lurch in a way the train did not.

She should've fled from him immediately.

But then she wouldn't have gazed into those large brown eyes, which held compassion and patience. Something so foreign to her since the news broke of her father's misdeeds. His kindness caught her unaware and made her a bit panicked. No doubt he'd scorn her like everyone else if he ever learned what her father had done. She didn't want to see a look of contempt on his clean-shaven face. Ever.

Not that she'd see him again.

Maybe this entire interaction was a figment of her imagination.

Closing her eyes, she counted to three before opening them again.

He was real, holding her belongings while striding farther and farther away. Olivia swallowed a groan as she rushed to catch him. Wasn't it every girl's dream to be rescued by a handsome gentleman and be swept off her feet?

Not that he'd swept her off her feet. Just her luggage. Now, those fairy tales her mother shared when she was a child played in her mind. The gallant knight and hero, putting others' needs before his own, saving the damsel in distress.

An unladylike snort almost escaped her lips. Barely. Real life turned out to be nothing like those stories. No one would save her because not a single person truly cared.

As she drew near, he glanced over his shoulder and grinned.

Not knowing what else to do, she smiled back.

Sometimes, she wanted to believe in those fairy tales. Life would be so much simpler.

She shifted her thick book to her other hand and imagined her next journal entry. *Today, I bumped into a handsome man who came to my rescue, saved my bonnet, and escorted me safely to my hotel. A true knight in shining ...*

This time, she did snort out loud.

He stopped and turned.

Had he heard? Pretending the unladylike noise hadn't escaped her mouth, she scanned the surroundings. Above his head hung a large painted, wooden sign with the word *Orleans*. Now, she could take control once again. "I appreciate your escort, but it's best if we part here."

"Oh, of course." He held out his free palm toward the entrance. "Your hotel awaits."

She reached for her portmanteau, and their hands bumped. Again.

They burst into laughter, and she quickly covered her mouth. His subsequent smile brought out a twinkle in his eyes.

Ignoring the funny sensation traveling all the way to her toes, she inclined her head. "Thank you, sir. A knight-errant you are for assisting me."

His gaze met hers and held a question. Of course, he had no idea her comment stemmed from her thinking of knights in shining armor and damsels in distress. And she'd prefer not to explain.

"I'd better go." She broke the connection, turned, and strode up the steps, her luggage banging against her legs the entire time. Relief was swift when the doorman held open the entranceway, and she scurried through.

Once inside, Olivia set her baggage on the floor. She pressed her palms together in a composed manner while she caught her breath. The bellman ran over and relieved her of her bags. She willed her rapid heartbeat to slow.

The good manners and the friendliness in her knight's voice attracted her in ways she couldn't explain. She shook her head. These feelings encouraged trust, and she couldn't go there.

No matter how gallant the knight, falling in love was not part of her plans.

If she'd learned anything these past several weeks, it was that people weren't as they seemed. True human nature hid underneath a friendly facade. In fact, her rescuer probably judged her right now. But, oh, how her heart wanted to believe otherwise.

She straightened her hat brim, now creased from the journey, and glanced around the lobby. Near the opening to the restaurant, she spotted a hint of pink and headed toward Violet, one of the four other teachers who'd traveled with her.

"Livvy!" Violet exclaimed, walking the few steps to close the distance between them. "What happened to you? One moment, you were behind us, then another, you disappeared. We grew worried." She glanced over Olivia's shoulder and waved her arm brazenly, grabbing the attention of the other girls.

Of course, each person in the vicinity noticed as well.

Olivia winced. Violet tended to act without much thought. Olivia had reined in her own exuberance these past few weeks. Which hadn't been easy—not when she'd been trained to command attention when she entered a room. Or been allowed to choose her own path and others followed, which was how she created a situation that warranted a rescue from a gallant knight.

She shook her head. Minimizing attention to herself was paramount. Too much came her way after her parents' accident and subsequent fall from grace. Now, she wanted to be left alone.

"I was delayed a little when the wind blew off my hat. Once retrieved, all of you had disappeared." Olivia's face flushed, sure her cheeks revealed the same color as a ripe tomato.

Violet scanned Olivia's head. "I see you retrieved it."

A small smirk appeared at the corner of Olivia's mouth. Then, the confession burst out of her. "A nice gentleman assisted me."

Violet raised her eyebrows, "You met a man already? Without a proper introduction?"

"Well, it would've been quite rude of me not to talk to him. He handed me back my hat." Olivia answered the question before Violet asked. "And no, we did not exchange names. What's the point? We stood in the middle of the train depot, heading in different directions. Perfectly acceptable."

An incredulous look crossed Violet's face. "What's the point? Dearie, attaching myself to a fine gentleman would be what I'm after. If you're not interested, maybe you can introduce him to me?" She wiggled her eyebrows.

Olivia glanced around. "I didn't get any information about him. Who knows where he's from?" Pinpricks trickled down her spine. What if he lived in her new town? What if ... Oh! Her heart thumped. No, she must stay unattached, in accordance with her plans. And for her sanity, she hoped never to see him again.

Then Olivia placed her hand on Violet's arm. "We made a commitment to teach a full year. You don't want to dishonor your contract, do you?"

Before Violet answered, Jenny rushed over. She glanced from Olivia to Violet. "What are you whispering about?"

"We were discussing all the new people we will meet."
Olivia gave Violet a look.

"Don't remind me. What if I'm not what they want?" Jenny
responded. The shyest of their quintet traveling together and
the most insecure, she glanced at each of them. "If that
happens, you'll help me, right?"

Olivia squeezed Jenny's arm. "Jenny, you have nothing to
worry about. You'll see."

"I can't help my thoughts," answered Jenny. "My own
family had to let me go because they couldn't afford to keep
me. What if the same thing happens here?"

Olivia didn't reply but instead looped her arm through
Jenny's and guided her inside the dining room. "I will write
you, Jenny. I look forward to all of us staying in touch." Her
gaze over her shoulder encompassed the group as they
followed. "Which will be easy. However, saying goodbye
tonight. That'll be hard." Ready as she would be, she pushed
thoughts of tomorrow out of her mind. All she had to do was
remain anonymous, focus on her work, and all would go
according to plan.

* * *

LUKE REMAINED until the young lady entered the Orleans hotel.
She'd called him a knight. His lips twitched, which meant he
had a horse named Gringolet. It also meant she was no
different from the women who answered his ad.

He ambled back toward the depot. No, he'd done what any
other gentleman would've done. He'd helped somebody in
need. He hadn't gone out of his way—she ran into him. But his
mother would've had his hide if he'd done anything less than
help. Besides, he would want someone to do the same for his
sisters.

Where did she come from? What brought her here? Was she alone? So many questions, and he had no business knowing any of the answers.

His mouth shifted into a smile as he crossed the street. Whatever her story, she shined brightly as sunshine and as prickly as his bull, Ol' Fred. A chuckle escaped his lips. A sensation he hadn't allowed himself to feel since sickness took his Ma. And all because of a run-in with a pretty lady. His smile faded. William, his best friend, and the town's pastor, would call this healing. Luke called it reckless.

William had lost his own parents in the same flood that took Luke's pa and younger brothers. That's when Will and his sister, Sarah, moved in with Luke's family. A blessing for sure, but then Will left for seminary school, and shortly thereafter, Luke's older brother and Ma got sick. Will didn't experience the helplessness from watching a loved one grow weak and waste away. It's not something to get over quickly. And Luke didn't want to, which was why William's words annoyed Luke. Didn't matter Will spoke as a pastor should and often voiced to Luke, 'God never leaves us' and 'good can come amongst the bad things which happen in life.'

Luke once believed that way, expecting his world to stay pretty much the same. Now he knew sometimes life threw big rocks into the river and changed the flow of things forever. The last boulder set in place when Sarah ran off right after Ma's death.

Left Luke high and dry to mind the ranch and his sisters by himself, breaking her promise to Luke's Ma to marry Luke and help raise the girls. Hurt and confused by her betrayal, Luke dove into work, increased ranch operations, and shut himself off from the world at large.

Of course, he fulfilled his obligations, including attending church each week. William would chase Luke all over his ranch if he missed a Sunday. Therefore, to keep the peace, Luke went. But the discord inside him was so loud, he didn't know where he stood with God or where God stood with him. No one knew his struggle, and he planned to keep it that way.

But today, some long-dormant emotion flickered to life. Maybe the letter to Evelyn triggered something. He wouldn't call what he felt hope. More like another step in the process of life. Simply put, his two sisters needed a ma, a woman in the house to teach them how to be ladies. He'd promised his parents, and he always kept his promises, even when other people didn't.

He gathered Admiral and headed toward the dock to catch the next ferry back to Washton. Martin had called a community meeting tonight about the new schoolmarm, and as guardian of his sisters, he wanted a front-row seat for the discussion.

Thoughts of the blonde-haired, blue-eyed damsel sprang to mind as he replayed their interaction. A hint of a smile lifted his lips as he wondered if he'd ever see her again.

And couldn't help but be a little disappointed he knew he wouldn't.

Five

I'm looking forward to meeting my new students. I've been told several of the children live on surrounding ranches and only a few in town. I wonder what type of schooling they've had thus far.

—From the journal of Olivia Carmichael

L uke guided his horse into the schoolyard full of wagons, the horses loosely staked and eating dried grass. He pulled the reins and patted Admiral's neck. "Well, boy. It looks as if the entire town is here to catch a glimpse of the new schoolteacher."

Dismounting, he tethered Admiral near the others and headed toward the entrance. His curiosity was piqued as well, and he was a little relieved his sisters were the students and not him. Did the teacher look anything at all like he imagined —a stern-faced, never-smiling woman?

Whoever she was, she had a lot to prove. A fierce debate had surfaced over hiring a woman, with the one-person opposition led by James Chapman. James had appeared one day and kept appearing periodically, probably figuring if he stuck around, Washton would let him teach. Luke later found out Chapman was a tutor from Sacramento looking for his own schoolhouse to run. But what James didn't know was a few years back, Luke's ma had convinced the whole town if women could own and run a business in California, why not let them teach? Which was why James's arguments were ignored.

The idea of a Miss for his sisters' teacher intrigued Luke, but he had one concern. Life was rough here, and he didn't think a woman from somewhere back East, a lady for that matter, had ever lived in conditions like these before. Even though the American Women's Educational Association claimed their teachers were well prepared.

It wasn't his place to judge. His job was to build the schoolhouse.

Passing the large glass windows and the strong beams on the wraparound porch, a sense of satisfaction suffused him as he entered the packed schoolhouse, filled with neighboring ranchers and families he had known most of his life.

"Hey, Luke!" a familiar voice called out.

Luke removed his hat and headed toward his neighbor, Gabe.

"How are the girls?" Gabe asked as Luke sat next to him.

"They're good. Excited to go to school and be around other kids their age. They keep telling me they need a woman's influence." Luke cringed at his words and how they sounded.

"That's why you need to get married, boy!" Gabe slapped him on the back and gave a knowing smile. "You know, in a few more years, my daughter Laura will be close to marrying age."

The idea of marrying the young girl, who was close in age to his sister, was intolerable. Besides, he had a bride chosen, even though he wasn't quite ready to share the news. He held in his response and kept his tone affable. "I won't have a lot of time to devote to a wife, but I appreciate the suggestion."

Gabe chuckled. "You were clear that you didn't want any help after your ma and brother passed, so we've respected your wishes. We just want to help, being neighbors and all."

Luke nodded. "I appreciate the offer. As I've said before, I promised my pa I would take care of the girls, and I had to figure out how to manage things on my own." He would never forget the day Caroline was born. Pa had sat twelve-year-old Luke down for a man-to-man with a stern message and the heavy weight of responsibility. It was what propelled him to finally send for Evelyn.

"You've done well, son." Gabe placed his hand on Luke's shoulder, then faced forward as the mayor, Arthur Martin, approached the podium.

The words warmed him from the inside, reminding him of his father. His heart ached from missing Pa's encouragement.

"May I have your attention, please," Mayor Martin's voice boomed across the schoolhouse.

Luke frowned. *Where was the teacher?*

"I'm excited to announce school will start the day after tomorrow," Martin said.

Cheers erupted, along with a few shushes.

"The missus and I will pick up Miss Carmichael tomorrow," he continued.

The strange silence mirrored Luke's disappointment.

Martin added, "This part is important, so listen closely. I called this meeting before she arrives to set the ground rules."

Gabe glanced Luke's way, and Luke shrugged. Something niggled in the back of his mind, but he shook it off.

"We all know what happened to the last teacher." Martin paused. "But it won't happen this time."

"There'd be no need for this meeting, Mayor, if you'd let me teach." James Chapman stood and faced the crowd. "The town has bought into the notion a woman can teach better than a man. I'm telling you, teaching is a man's job. I have experience. I would do a superior job. Put me in the schoolhouse!"

"That's enough, James." Martin raised his hand as if swatting a pesky fly.

"What're you saying, Mayor?" someone yelled from the back. "We can't help if there are not enough womenfolk in town."

"No, you're right, Bart. The last teacher didn't set foot in the schoolhouse before she married—"

"Exactly why I should teach," James hollered. "You can't keep a woman from getting married. You'll have to keep replacing her. Since she can't teach if she's even being courted." He glanced around the room. "Why can't you all see a man is more desirable for the job?"

A chorus of 'sit-downs' bounced off the wooden planks.

James crossed his arms.

Luke shook his head. Not all men embraced change. First, the mines didn't pan out, and then the war came. Women stepped in, doing a better job, in some cases, and maintained those positions, even after the men came home. The world had evolved, and Washton was evolving right along with it.

Martin concentrated on James. "I'm sure you're a great teacher, James, but the town decided before you arrived, we would hire a teacher from the American Women's Educational Association. We have a contract, and we intend to honor that contract. Now, please sit down, or I will ask you to leave."

Reluctantly, James sat, but then called out, "How do you know this one won't get married?"

"I'm glad you asked. Now, listen carefully, everyone. There are rules I expect you all to abide by. So, let's get started. Rule number one: No courting the schoolteacher."

A few small groans erupted throughout the room.

"Rule number two: The schoolteacher signed a contract for a one-year commitment. She can then decide to continue for another school year or get married."

The gentleman behind Luke snickered. "She'll have every man knocking on her door the day school lets out. She'll have so much attention, she won't ever want to go back to teaching."

An image of the young lady Luke met earlier flashed in his mind. If their new teacher looked anything like her, even he would have a hard time staying away—*if* he was in the market for courting, which he wasn't.

"You don't even know what she looks like, Thomas. She may just keep teaching to protect herself from your sorry hide." Wade's comment refocused Luke's attention away from his not-so-exciting impending nuptials.

Laughter broke out from those who sat nearby.

"Rule number three," continued Martin. "Female teachers are not allowed to ride in a wagon or buggy with a gentleman who is not her brother or father ..."

"You going to make her walk everywhere, Mayor?" yelled George from across the room.

"... alone," continued the mayor as he pointedly glared back at George.

More groans.

Luke shifted on the bench. Going through this list added fuel to an already combustible problem. He understood the rules, but he also figured the men would find some way to work around them. He couldn't care less if she decided to marry afterward, but he wanted his sisters to have a qualified teacher last a full school year so they'd move up a grade at the end of term. He would do his part to ensure nothing got in the way of that happening.

Martin raised his hands. "That's it. I appreciate your support in making Miss Carmichael feel welcome. All students can plan to start school on Wednesday. Pastor William, will you please close us in prayer?"

"I'd be happy to, Mayor," Will said as he walked to the front of the room.

After "Amens" were said, Luke raised his head and found his best friend nodding in his direction.

Luke motioned back, but folks around stood and blocked Will out. Raised voices filled the space as they exited the schoolhouse.

Once outside, George appeared alongside Luke and placed his hand on his shoulder. "Luke, you interested in meeting this new teacher?"

"Sure am." Luke caught George's grimace, and he glanced at the others.

"I knew it!" George slapped the person next to him. "You have an in with Martin, so the rest of us don't stand a chance."

"What?" Luke frowned. Then, realization dawned. An awkward chuckle escaped. "Not in the way you're implying, George. I have parental responsibilities. I want to meet her because she will be *teaching* my sisters."

"Sure! You have the perfect excuse." He tilted his head. "Hey, I'll come with you. You need help, right?"

Luke shoved George on the shoulder and laughed.

"All right, all right. I'll leave things be. For now." George waggled his eyebrows.

An idea formed as Luke studied his friend. "I might have to offer her my protection." He inwardly sighed. He didn't have time to get involved. Nor was he interested. But they didn't need to know he had a mail-order bride on her way. And the idea held merit. He could offer his protection and let the town think he was interested. Then their fight would be with him, leaving her free to teach.

George looked at him in horror. "Don't you dare, Luke. None of us stand a chance if you become her protector."

He smirked. "Maybe if you bathed more frequently, you'd have a shot. But remember, she must teach all year, so nothing can happen now anyway."

His friend laughed at the ribbing, but Luke saw a calculated gleam in his eyes.

Time to shift tactics. "I just remembered I need to find Martin. See you later, George."

"Later, Luke." George's voice sounded strained.

His friend's worry was unwarranted. The rules didn't bother Luke because he had no interest in courting. Courting allowed the heart to get involved, and he had no desire for his heart to be affected. Women, in his book, were not to be trusted with one's heart.

He'd stick around long enough to make sure the men left the schoolteacher alone, and then things would go back to the way he liked them—calm and predictable. Should be easy enough.

OLIVIA SETTLED in for the night, the silence in the hotel room a stark contrast to the thoughts swirling in her head. She looked over at Jenny as her new friend slept in the next bed. Was Jenny nervous about the future?

Not able to fall asleep, Olivia pushed her covers aside and rose. Sleep wouldn't claim her until she wrote out her contemplations. Walking on her tiptoes, she reached her valise, released the clasp, and pulled out her journal and pencil.

A gift from her instructor, Miss Beecher, the first day Olivia arrived for training, this journal was one of the few belongings she could still claim as her own. Warmth radiated throughout her body as she carried it back to the bed. When she wrote her first entry, she worried her words would somehow be used against her. But after a few weeks, she found writing, even the most mundane things that occurred in the day, soothed her soul, and her journal had become her one trusted friend.

Careful to not scratch the cover, she gently dusted off the dirt from when she dropped it earlier. Heat engulfed her from head to toe. She couldn't get her run-in with the handsome, gallant stranger out of her mind.

Oh, her behavior! What must he think of her? Had she really called him a knight?

She fidgeted, but the feelings didn't dissipate. She had to purge the memory somehow.

Putting pencil to paper, she wrote from the beginning:

Today, we arrived in Sacramento on the Overland Express. I still can't believe I'm here. Most people never travel this far, yet here I am, nineteen years old and as far west as a person can go. The last part of the train ride through the mountains was beautiful and vastly different than the flat dry land we passed in Kansas. Such a wonder to look out the window and pass things so quickly. My body still feels the rocking motion as if I'm moving. Such an interesting sensation. My ears haven't stopped ringing from all the loud noises either. And I had never been so happy to don clean clothes today.

She paused as a slow smile spread across her lips. Then she continued writing:

I am so embarrassed about what transpired today. The wind blew my hat off, and I collided with a stranger, who then assisted me to the hotel. He was handsome, but more than that, kind, held concern, and he took charge. Much like a knight protecting his lady. I said I would never trust a man again, but if I did choose to marry one day, would my knight be someone I would fancy? And would he fancy me?

She hesitated, her pencil hovering above the paper. Where had those thoughts come from? Shaking her head, she continued.

Something about him made me hopeful, and I have learned hope is a very dangerous sentiment. This is just a pleasant memory. One I won't forget anytime soon. The butterfly feelings in my stomach whenever I think about him? Those I could do without.

Tomorrow morning, I meet the mayor and his wife. I'm so nervous. What if they don't like me? What if word traveled this far west, and they know who I am? Would they still let me teach? I know I must not fret unnecessarily. I truly want no one to know where I'm from or about my past. I plan to take care of myself, work hard, and mind my own business. And by starting over, I'm in control of my destiny. Doesn't matter if I had help today. I would've figured things out on my own. I don't need anyone. Family, friends, or God.

And I'm so thankful I have you to write in, Dear Journal. I don't know what I would've done without you these last few weeks. I'm looking forward to getting into a routine and calmer days from this point on. Wish me luck tomorrow,
Olivia

Six

Even though I'm ready for this part of my life to start, I will miss my new friends and the camaraderie we shared over the past month. The idea of making new friends all over again feels a bit daunting. How do I know who I can trust?

—From the journal of Olivia Carmichael

Luke found Caroline and Rose waiting in the kitchen when he arrived home from the meeting.

"Did you see her?" Caroline asked.

He shook his head. "Nope. She'll be in town by tomorrow night, and you two will start school the day after."

"Hooray!" the girls shouted.

Luke reached over, pulled one to each side, and hugged them both. "What am I going to do while you're at school all day?"

Caroline turned to face him. "You won't miss us. You're always out on the ranch."

"True." He tugged on her braid.

"Hey." Caroline squirmed out of his arms. "I'm too old for that."

Luke stared at his sister. "Since when?"

"Since I'm turning thirteen in a few weeks." She swirled her dress back and forth. "I'll be a lady."

"Don't remind me." His hand rubbed the back of his neck. More like thirteen going on eighteen.

"I'm the lady of the house, and soon, I'll be old enough to go courting."

Luke coughed into his hand. "What did you say?"

Seven-year-old Rose shouted, "Courtin'!"

He cupped Rose's sweet face. "I heard, sweetheart. I just don't agree."

"Mrs. Elizabeth said she began courting at thirteen and married by the age of fifteen. Ain't that right, Rose?"

Rose nodded her head in complete agreement.

"Mrs. Elizabeth is also over eighty years old and doesn't remember where she puts her teeth. Are you sure she had her years correct?"

Caroline huffed, blowing her bangs out of her eyes. "Luke, listen. I know how to tend a house. I already do most of the cooking and cleaning."

"With Jimmy supervising," he said.

She placed her hands on her hips. "He says I'm doing just fine."

When it was a life-or-death situation, she wouldn't argue. But over I'm old enough for courting and being the lady of the household? Evelyn would have her work cut out for her. As much as he wanted to prepare his sisters for their impending new family member, he didn't want to give them too much time to find ways to sabotage the entire thing. He wasn't getting married for his sake but for theirs.

The oven door slammed, and he glanced over.

"See. I have dinner all prepared and ready for us." Caroline's arms shook as she held the pan with a towel and carried the dish over to the table.

He rubbed his hands together. "Then let's eat. Riding into town today made me hungry." He walked over to the washtub and dipped his hands in the bucket.

The front door opened, and Luke's foreman, Jimmy, walked in. "Hi, boss."

The moniker rankled. Even though he was technically Jimmy's boss, Jimmy had far more years of experience and age than him. "Hi, Jimmy. How's the north pasture?"

Jimmy took off his hat and hung it on the peg. "Everything is where it's supposed to be, including Ol' Fred."

Reaching for the towel on the peg, he dried his hands. "Good. Just how I like things. Everybody in their place. It's how we prevent accidents and run a —"

"—smooth ranch operation," the girls chimed in. "We know." They giggled.

Luke sat at the head of the table and grabbed his fork. "Let's dig in and eat."

"*Ahem.*" Jimmy cleared his throat.

He glanced at the man, who he considered an uncle. "Oh, right. Let's pray first." He placed both hands open on the table.

Caroline and Rose placed their smaller hands in each of his and reached for Jimmy's hands on the other end of the table.

Luke bowed his head and prayed the words by rote. "Dear Lord, bless this food. Bless our time on this earth, and bless our loved ones. Amen."

"Amen," Jimmy, Caroline, and Rose repeated.

Luke dug into his meal. He loved his little family. Which at one time was much bigger. The job to keep those who were left safe and together now fell to him. He would do anything for them. Including marrying a complete stranger.

47

* * *

OLIVIA AWOKE EARLY the next morning, rested and thankful to have slept in a bed. She rushed through her toilette, making sure not to wake Jenny. The cold water calmed her racing heart, but when she went to dress, her fingers trembled as she buttoned her blouse.

Jenny stirred. "Is it time, Olivia?"

"Yes, Jenny." She slid over to Jenny's bedside, pulled the blankets, and covered Jenny much like Olivia's mother had when she was a girl. "You can go back to sleep. Get all the rest you can before your meeting."

"Thank you. Good luck," Jenny mumbled.

"Good luck to you too." She placed her hand on Jenny's shoulder.

"I'll miss you," Jenny said sleepily.

"And I, you. Don't forget to write." She gathered all she owned and slipped out the door.

Her mind raced through possibilities as she headed to the stairwell. What if she didn't like any of these people? What if they didn't like her?

"Miss Carmichael?" a masculine voice called out.

Her heart pounded. Who knew her name? Had they found her out? Her gaze landed on an older couple who stood looking at her expectantly from the bottom of the stairs. She continued down the steps. "Yes, I'm Miss Olivia Carmichael."

Both beamed and looked at each other, delight shining in their eyes. "I am Mr. Arthur Martin of Washington, and this is my wife, Christina."

"You can call me Chrissy, dear," added Mrs. Martin.

Olivia's brow furrowed. "Don't you mean Washton?"

He chuckled a fatherly laugh, and Olivia's throat clogged. "Many moons ago, the people of Wash-ing-ton got tired of saying three syllables when they could shorten it to two. We've called it Washton for years now."

She breathed a sigh of relief.

We don't think our first president would've been offended, so we aren't. The town was named after him, you know.

Not knowing how to respond, she grinned. "That sounds sensible."

Mr. Martin's eyes sparkled, and he held out his palm. "Well, Miss Carmichael. Welcome to California. You have no idea how happy we are you're here."

Placing her hand in his, she shook as Miss Beecher instructed. He didn't show any distress by her manly actions. "Thank you, Mr. Martin." She pulled her hand back and made the same gesture to Mrs. Martin. "Pleased to meet you, Mrs. Martin."

When their hands met, Mrs. Martin placed her other hand on top. "Call me Chrissy, please." The woman's eyes bore into hers.

Olivia swallowed. Years of manners propelled her to do otherwise. "Are you sure, Mrs. Martin?"

"Dear, we'll be great friends in no time, you'll see." Mrs. Martin squeezed her hand.

Though she wouldn't be comfortable calling Mrs. Martin by her first name, she would try and respect her request. "I'm looking forward to becoming a part of your community and teaching your children. Do you know how many students I will have?"

Mr. Martin gestured behind him. "Why don't we sit for some breakfast and talk?" Then he took her luggage.

The idea of eating sounded awful right then, but she followed them into the dining room. Her stomach said otherwise as it rumbled from the mixed aromas of bacon, eggs, and biscuits filling the room.

As the server went to place their order, Mr. Martin asked Olivia, "Now, where were we? You had questions?"

Olivia brought the cup of tea to her lips. "Yes. Please tell me more about the children I'll be teaching. How many are they?"

Mr. Martin squinted. "Let's see. If they all came? Seventeen. But many will come only a few times a week. The rest of the time, they will help on their ranches. Every person helps around here. Even children. There's no other way to get the work done."

She swallowed the tea, burning her throat in the process. Would she have to work on a ranch too?

Their food arrived, and all three of them ate quietly. After the first bite, she didn't want to stop, surprised at how hungry she was.

Mr. Martin cleared his throat. "Our schoolhouse is new."

She wiped her mouth with the napkin.

"You'll be our first official schoolteacher."

Her breath stalled. The first? She'd be able to establish the schoolroom the way she wanted. Which meant rules and order too. She shuddered. Discipline would not be her favorite part of this job.

Mr. Martin watched her closely. "I don't like asking this question, but I must. You understand this assignment is for a year-long commitment, correct?"

"Yes, of course." Olivia narrowed her eyes. "Why do you ask?"

He hesitated. "You'll find we don't have many ladies your age in town."

"Oh, I'm not here looking for social engagements. I came to teach, so you don't have to—" Her face flushed.

He chuckled. "That's not what I meant."

Olivia looked from one to the other. "I'm not sure I understand."

The couple glanced at each other. Mr. Martin cleared his throat. "The average ratio of men to women in these parts is a bit uneven."

She frowned. Why was this such a big deal? "And?"

"Well, your arrival will ... shall I say, not go unnoticed." Mrs. Martin interjected.

Not what she wanted to hear, but nothing would change her plans. "Let me assure you, I have no designs on grabbing any man's attention. I came here to teach."

Relief showed on both their faces. "You don't know how delighted we are to hear you say those words," he said.

The older gentleman's smile was full of warmth and compassion, and a deep longing filled her. How long had it been since she felt genuine love and acceptance? To be welcomed unconditionally and made to feel she mattered.

As her lips curved upward, for the first time in a long time, the expression came from her heart instead of the false front she'd been showing the world.

Mrs. Martin motioned to their empty plates. "Do you need to do anything before we leave, Miss Carmichael?"

She shook her head. "No. I'm as ready as I'll ever be."

Mrs. Martin placed a hand over Olivia's and beamed. The warm, friendly gesture reminded Olivia of her younger self when she was naïve about the ugly side of life. "Don't worry. Things will work out just fine. The good Lord has brought you here for a reason."

Olivia jerked back and stood. "On second thought, would you mind if I used the ladies' retiring room first? Then I can be ready."

Mr. Martin's smile dimmed. "We'll meet you in the lobby, then."

As she hurried away, their voices carried.

"She seems perfect for our town, dear," said Mrs. Martin.

"I agree, Chrissy. I just hope she's prepared for a different way of life here."

"We'll just have to pray for her adjustment."

"Your faith, Chrissy, is one of the things I love most about you. You're never one to give up hope."

"That is what the Bible says to do," Mrs. Martin replied. "Hope."

Olivia couldn't hear the rest as she entered the lobby and strode into the retiring room. What did Mrs. Martin mean about the good Lord bringing her here? She'd made this journey happen, not God. And maybe Mrs. Martin still found hope in God, but Olivia knew the truth. Her own hard work had gotten her this far and would see her through. And how different could living here truly be? She'd show them her capabilities, and after a few days, they would see. All would be fine.

* * *

OLIVIA CLUNG to the barge rail and peered over the edge into the dark water below. Her heart hammered as she pictured her parents drowning when their carriage crashed and fell into the Ohio River.

She shivered and gathered her shawl about her with one hand. Even though large bodies of water had never bothered her before, she hadn't been close to one since her parents' deaths.

Mrs. Martin waved her hand back and forth over the railing. "Two rivers merge north of here to form one large one. Sometimes we have floods. We need the waterway, yet the river has a mind of its own sometimes."

"Do floods happen often? When did the last one occur?"

Olivia firmly held her hands together to stay grounded and keep from grabbing Mrs. Martin's arm.

Mrs. Martin didn't seem to notice. "A few years back was the last severe one. After that, Sacramento raised all its streets. The city officials brought in all sorts of equipment and materials, which was quite an undertaking. Some folks in Washton wanted to also, but the work was too expensive, and when voted on, the majority chose to wait."

The barge's river wheel creaked and splashed, making it challenging to hear, but Olivia smiled at Mrs. Martin, then glanced over to the west bank. Several rooftops peeked through the trees near the river.

"Our town isn't grand like Sacramento, but we have a good community. The people are genuine, and we all like living here." Olivia's muscles relaxed at hearing Mrs. Martin's words.

Based on articles she'd read, she envisioned Washton as a rugged, almost barbaric place with wooden shacks for structures. Instead, the sight before her included three-story buildings, a mill operating on the water's edge, and a steeple located farther north.

As they approached the riverbank, she swallowed the lump in her throat.

The way Mr. Martin spoke, the entire town knew of Olivia's arrival. She had wanted to stay as inconspicuous as possible. But now, each and every person would know her comings and goings, her routines, and if they didn't like something, judge her. Could she handle more public scrutiny?

She drew her shawl closer and held back tears. She would need to stay on guard and always maintain control. How would she manage that every moment of the day?

A wave hit the side of the boat, and water splashed onto her face, releasing the tears. She shook her head and wiped the drops from her cheek.

Chuckling, Mr. Martin stepped beside her. "There's even more spray when the tide's high."

Presenting a forced smile, she hoped to hide the tears.

Mrs. Martin appeared on her other side and put her hand on Olivia's shoulder.

The effort had fooled no one. She wanted to hide.

"I know all of this must be overwhelming for you." Mrs. Martin placed her arm around Olivia's shoulder. "I don't know your circumstances, but I do know we prayed and prayed for the right teacher, and God has brought us you."

Olivia held her eyes open, so more tears wouldn't leak out. Her gaze followed the ripples in the water as they came together in the current.

Mrs. Martin patted Olivia's shoulder but didn't speak for a while. "I'll give you time to collect your thoughts. Come, Arthur."

As they reached the other side, Olivia contemplated Mrs. Martin's words. Was God really there like Mrs. Martin believed? If so, maybe He hadn't completely abandoned her. She shook her head. She wouldn't continue that line of thinking. God had left her alone. Richard and her friends abandoned her as well. They judged her. All because of her father's choices.

She would have to build the life she wanted on her own. Whatever happened to her would be due to her own decisions.

Besides, why would anyone care about her?

She breathed in the misty air.

No matter what life threw at her, she would fight to survive. To be the one in control of her destiny and live the new life she planned.

Seven

I was lonely as an only child. I wanted to spend time in the kitchen with Cook but wasn't allowed. Instead, I had to act a certain way, be friends with those my parents approved of, and become affianced to their choice of a husband. I hope I can be of influence to the girls in my school. Teach them how to be independent young women. Be a friend if they need someone to listen. And help them avoid the problems I've faced.

—From the journal of Olivia Carmichael

The warmth from the sun's rays seeped through Olivia's bonnet as Mr. Martin drove the buckboard off the barge, Olivia on the opposite end of the bench, and Mrs. Martin squished in the middle.

He flicked the reins. "Before we take you home, how about we show you the schoolhouse?"

"Yes, that would be lovely."

She gripped the edge of her seat as the horses strained to

pull them on the uneven ground, up the hill away from the water.

At the first junction, they veered right. "Going left takes you to the center of town. This way leads us to the schoolhouse."

Trees, scattered in no particular order, lined the path that followed the river. Rushing water sloshed nearby, and the *clip-clop* of the horses' hoofs and creaks of the wagon wheels filled the air. The sounds were oddly soothing.

Ahead on the left, a tall steeple, high on the rooftop, reflected the bright sunshine. Next to the church sat an open yard large enough to fit a dozen or more wagons and carriages.

A rock formed in her stomach. Would they expect her to attend services? Not since the horrible day when her so-called friends shut the door on her had she stepped foot in a church. Her palms dampened, and she rubbed them on the front of her skirt. No sense in getting hysterical. Maybe church attendance wouldn't be required.

Mr. Martin interrupted her thoughts. "The schoolhouse is beyond the church on this road. On Sundays and special meetings and events, we use both buildings as well as this main yard."

Beyond the church and farther back on a slope sat a brand new wooden building, adorned with a fresh coat of paint. A set of steps led to a large wraparound porch while windows framing both sides of the front door glinted in the daylight.

Mr. Martin reined the horses to a stop. "As I've said, you'll start tomorrow, so let's go over your duties and show you the chores you'll attend to."

She glanced at the pristine building. Waiting would cause her to doubt herself, so she might as well start right away. "Whatever you think is best. I'm ready."

Mr. Martin secured the brake and reins, hopped out of the wagon, and then assisted her to the ground.

While he helped his wife, Olivia lifted her skirts and walked up the steps, counting four. She stopped at the window and peered in, her forehead touching the glass. The cold sensation contrasted with the heat from the full sun.

Mr. Martin chuckled. "Let's go inside and look, Miss Carmichael. Then I will leave the key in your capable hands."

He unlocked the door and then held it open. She lingered on the threshold and surveyed the room. The coziness warmed her straightaway. Several sanded benches in neat rows framed the room, and a new slate board hung on the main wall. A large desk sat beneath the board. The teacher's desk. Her pulse quickened, and her mouth grew dry. She walked over, reached out, and brushed a finger over the ornate design on the front cover of the top book.

"We assumed you would have your own Bible, but we wanted to provide you a brand new one as a welcome gift." Mrs. Martin appeared beside her. "Look inside."

Olivia slowly lifted the cover. Tears formed as she read the inscription:

To Miss Olivia Carmichael—
Thank you for teaching our children.
The town of Washton
September, 1869.

She stood silently and pinched her lips. The ongoing hints of God aggravated her as a constant reminder of his abandonment.

"Beautiful." Her voice wavered. "A thoughtful gift."

"We're glad you like it."

Olivia forced a smile. They were churchgoing folks, and she

didn't wish to offend on her first day. No one needed to know her current relationship, or lack of one, with God. To shift the focus elsewhere, she moved toward the big blackboard and gripped a piece of chalk, then wrote her first words ... *Welcome, Class. My name is Miss Carmichael.*

She set the chalk down and brushed her hands together, sending chalk dust all over her boots. A laugh escaped.

Mr. Martin scratched his chin. "What's so funny?"

His voice startled her, and she gave Mr. Martin a sheepish smile. "I was accepting the fact my boots will always have dust of some sort on them, and I'd better get used to it."

He chuckled. "A hazard of teaching, I would guess."

"It looks that way."

The American flag stood to the right, next to the desk, and grabbed her attention. The recent war had taught her the importance of fighting for freedom. And this job represented her own freedom—a new life free from judgment and censure.

Her heart swelled with hope for the future.

"Is it all to your satisfaction, Miss Carmichael?" asked Mrs. Martin.

"Yes," she whispered, then turned to both of them. "Thank you. I want you to know I take my post here seriously."

Mr. Martin motioned for her to join him at the stove. "Let me show you how things work. You'll be responsible for lighting the stove each morning so the building is warm when the students arrive. The wood stack is there, and more piles are at the back of the schoolhouse. Ask the boys to restock before you excuse them for the day. Then, the wood will be dry in the morning. I'm assuming you know how to light a fire?"

Thankful to have paid attention to this part of her lessons, she nodded. The reality that she was now standing inside her very own schoolroom caused her to wonder how she would've proceeded without her training.

Mr. Martin cleared his throat and gestured toward a chair. "We have an official contract for you to sign, and I need to go over some rules." He handed her a parchment. "There's nothing in here not asked of other young misses throughout the area. You're agreeing to these for the entire school term."

Olivia sat and read over the list, even though she already knew its contents.

- *Teachers will refill lamps and clean lamp chimneys each day*
- *Each teacher will use only one bucket of water and a scuttle of coal for the day's session*
- *Make your pens carefully. You may whittle nibs to the individual taste of the pupils*
- *Men teachers may take one evening each for courting purposes, or two evenings a week if they go to church regularly*
- *Women teachers who marry or engage in unseemly conduct will be dismissed. No courting allowed.*

With no intention of marrying, that last one wouldn't be a problem. A pang of sadness twinged her bruised and battered heart as the gentleman she met yesterday came to mind, but she dismissed the image immediately. Even if she married, her husband could lie, cheat, and leave her to pick up the pieces. She would not put herself in the position to depend on someone else ever again.

She raised her head and smiled confidently. "These are not a problem. Where do I sign?"

Mr. and Mrs. Martin both released their breath and glanced at each other.

Mrs. Martin leaned forward. "You didn't come out here to get married?"

Olivia froze. "No. I came out here to teach."

"We wanted to make sure you understood the length of the contract."

Didn't they believe her? "I came to California to live on my own and teach." Perhaps women who came west were more like Violet than she imagined. She put as much authority into her voice as she could muster. "I guess it might be difficult to believe, even though it's the truth."

A puzzled look crossed Mrs. Martin's face. "You're aware you'll be living with families, dear?"

"I know some communities house teachers in student homes. I wouldn't mind for the first year. I can save funds and get to know my students. But my preference is to live by myself in the boardinghouse." An undeniable pause made her look at both of their faces. "What?"

Mr. Martin shifted in his chair. "Um, Miss Carmichael … Washton doesn't have a boardinghouse."

Mrs. Martin patted her husband's arm. "At least as of today. We keep growing, and the new train station south of town will bring in additional businesses and workers." Her tentative smile showed a hopefulness her eyes did not. "We hope."

Olivia would not be dissuaded. Or discouraged. "Is there a room addition at the back of the schoolhouse? Perhaps I could live there."

He shook his head. "We don't currently have that option either, but it could be something for us to consider if you sign the contract." He cast a look at his wife, then back to Olivia. "Also, your salary is in credits, not cash. You can get anything you need at the—"

"But—" Olivia sputtered. "That's not—"

With a raised hand, he continued, "Hear me out. Your covered expenses include room and board, meals, and a monthly allotment at the general store. Most families have little since our last flood, and several conduct business by trading. Cash money is scarce here. For their children to attend school, parents will help house and feed you. I can tell by the look on your face you weren't aware of this part of the agreement."

The blood pounded in Olivia's ears. No. No, No. This wasn't what she wanted. How would she support herself if she had to rely on others?

She held back her groan. What choice did she have? "For the record, I was not aware of these arrangements, but I will accept them. For now." She searched the room. "Perhaps we might add a room on to the school in the future?"

The Martins didn't say no to her idea, but they didn't seem overjoyed about considering the option, either. With or without the room she hoped one day to have, she needed this job. She picked up the pen, dipped the end in the ink, and signed her name.

Mr. Martin gathered the papers and reached out his hand. "Welcome to Washton, Miss Carmichael, as our first schoolteacher. Congratulations!" He turned toward his wife. "Chrissy dear, is there anything else I'm forgetting?"

Mrs. Martin beamed. "I think we need to take her home now so she can get settled." She looked at Olivia. "I'm sure you're exhausted."

Yes, she could sleep for a week. "I could use some rest."

No sense in giving them a reason to let her go before she had even taught one day. Already, she regretted her words about her room and board.

She held back further conversation as they locked the door and rode over to their home. Somehow, as judicious as her plans were, already she'd run into a few minor setbacks. Who was she fooling? These were major issues.

Her logical, practical approach to protect herself from depending on others—the exact reason she came West—gone the first day. Control over where she slept and how she received and managed her own funds as she saw fit were unavailable to her.

Would anything else go wrong? She couldn't shake the idea that more of her meticulous plans were about to change.

* * *

OLIVIA UNPACKED her valise and portmanteau in the small bedroom of the Martins' home. She shook out one plain black skirt. How smoothly would things go tomorrow? What would the children be like? Would they like her? Would she like them? So many questions only time would answer.

Her meager belongings unpacked, she glanced about the room. A covered seat and a small wooden table sat in the corner beside the bed. A perfect place for her writing. She reached for her supplies and sat in the cushioned chair.

She first wrote to Jasper and Agnes, letting them know she had arrived safely and all was well. Even though things weren't exactly as she planned, she didn't want them to worry. Then she wrote to her new friends. She wondered how Violet, Emilia, Lydia, and Jenny fared. Did they find themselves with families? Or did they have a room attached to the schoolhouse or even a boardinghouse option? She had little time, so she kept her letters short.

Her missives written, Olivia opened her journal and turned the pages to her last entry. She read her words and shook her head. Her encounter with her knight yesterday now seemed a lifetime ago. A small hitch in her heart made her yearn for something not there. She blew the loose hairs off her face and flipped to the next blank page. So many new things to share and document. Her teeth bit into her bottom lip as she raised her pencil and wrote:

I've finally arrived in Washton. The schoolhouse is beautiful with a wraparound porch where I can stand and ring the bell each morning. I have my very own desk and brand-new slates for all the children.

A handful of children ran and played in the field as we drove by. It looked like they were chasing a very large rooster, or perhaps it chased them. Mrs. Martin assured me he was harmless, but I wonder if I'll have to keep my eye on him.

The Martins are kind and are taking great care to ensure my comfort. There is one thing required of me that worries me, but I don't think there is anything I can do. Church attendance is expected of me, as well as reading from the Bible every day in class. I will perform my duties, but I prefer to avoid such things. If God cared, He wouldn't have let my parents die and my home be taken from me. If God had cared, my fiancé and friends wouldn't have rejected me. I came here to get away from the bad memories. And the church people were the worst. They would say one thing but act another. Now, I worry about people doing the same thing here.

Even though I'm a little uncomfortable being around complete strangers, I find it comforting at the same time. They don't know anything about me or my past. I truly get a new start. I guess if I don't want to draw unnecessary attention to myself, I must attend church.

I'm looking forward to my first day of school tomorrow. The time has come to put all I've learned into practice. I'm hoping the first day will go smoothly, and the children and I will get along. Mr. Martin says I could have as many as seventeen students attend at some point. A lot of students for me to teach all at once, but I will give it my all. Wish me luck, Olivia.

She closed her journal and hugged the book to her chest. Over the past month, her journal had become her best friend, the confidant she never knew she needed. No one else she would share her innermost thoughts with.

When the people she trusted abandoned her, she had no one to lean on but herself and now, her diary. She planned to keep it that way.

Eight

Some of the other teachers discussed teaching for a while and then finding a husband. I am resolutely against this course of action. I do not want to be beholden to anyone. No way will I succumb to someone else's choices. I will happily live out my days teaching and managing my own responsibilities.

—From the journal of Olivia Carmichael

Luke filled the shovel with muck and dumped the contents into the wheelbarrow. "I hope Caroline and Rose like their first day of school. And the teacher knows what she's doing."

"What's that, boss?" Working in the stall next to Luke, Jimmy called over the divider. "Didn't catch that last bit."

He didn't want to get into a discussion about his worries. "Nothing."

"If you want my two cents—"

"I don't." Luke cut off a lecture he didn't want to hear. He sighed, took off his hat, and scratched his head. "I'm sorry,

Jimmy. I guess I'm anxious about the girls going to school today. We've been together every day since Ma passed." He waited for the lump to clear his throat. He didn't need to mention Sarah's abandonment and broken promise. And his distrust of women. Two years later, the transgression still ate at him. And the girls still asked why she left without saying goodbye. "I worry about them, that's all."

Jimmy stopped brushing the horse and looked over at Luke. "The girls recognize you'll always be there for them, Luke. They comprehend what they lost. This is a great chance for them to learn. And a break for you too. You spoil them too much."

The left side of Luke's mouth lifted. "Don't remind me. My knowledge about parenting two girls is nil, and I probably have been doing things all wrong. They'll grow up to act like men."

Jimmy shook his head. "You're doing the best job you can."

Luke glanced away, not wanting Jimmy to see his response, even though it was next to impossible to hide anything from him. Jimmy had worked on the ranch since the beginning and helped raise Luke and his siblings. Even before Pa died, they called him Uncle Jimmy, and he ate meals with the family. When Luke's ma passed, Jimmy moved into the house and continued to join them at mealtime, his presence a soothing balm for Luke and his sisters.

As a child, Luke sat and listened to Jimmy read from the Bible, asking a million questions, wanting to grow up to be just like him. But Luke's losses through the years created a thick barrier around his heart. He didn't want any part of the man's beliefs anymore.

"Have you asked God for guidance, Luke?" Jimmy's question confirmed what Luke knew radiated deep inside the man. "Recently, I mean."

Luke owed him an answer, even though he didn't want to. "No. I haven't."

He didn't say anything else, continuing to brush his horse, prepared for what would come next.

Jimmy quoted his favorite verse. "'Be careful for nothing; but in everything by prayer and supplication with thanksgiving let your requests be made known unto God.'"

Luke threw the brush into the crate of supplies, grabbed the milk bucket, and stomped toward the other side of the barn. He didn't need a preaching lesson right now. He needed time to focus and sort his thoughts on his own. That's how he dealt with things.

His parents wouldn't approve. His attitude contradicted the way they raised him, but he couldn't help it. Whenever these conversations arose, his blood boiled, and he didn't want to snap at the man who'd been a father figure to him.

He didn't want to push Jimmy away, but he didn't want to hear what he had to say, either.

His heart, raw and broken, had withered and died like a branch cut off from the vine. Where was God when his father died? And his brothers? What about when his mother got sick? And where was God when Sarah walked—more like ran— away from him after he willingly agreed to honor his mom's last request and marry her? True, he hadn't loved Sarah in that way, but they made a good team. He'd needed her, and she left.

Luke set the pail into place, knowing Jimmy would respect his space. Conversation, albeit different topics, circled them like a rope around a calf. But Jimmy always quietly backed away, knowing he wouldn't get anywhere if he pushed too hard. Made it difficult to stay mad at the man.

"I'm going to go see to the stock. I'll check in later, Luke."

Luke nodded, not knowing if Jimmy saw him or not. Focused on milking the cow, he worked to get his emotions under control. Would this teacher be adequate for his sisters' care? Would a stranger know when Rose got quiet, she needed a hug? Or when Caroline asked too many questions, she was anxious and needed reassurance?

The three of them had weathered several storms together, and he liked their dependence on him. Gave him a purpose, and he didn't want anyone to usurp his role. Even with a wife, he could still control things in his own home. At school, a different story. Who knew what type of influence this new teacher would have? What if the girls didn't need him anymore?

Bessie side-stepped into him and grunted.

Great. He'd taken his frustration out on the cow's udder. "Sorry, ol girl." He placed a calm hand on Bessie's side and murmured in soothing tones. "Settle down."

Working with the animals came naturally to him, and as the cow became placid again, Luke calmed as well.

Milk splashed into the bucket, and the tinkling sound grew softer as the bucket filled. As the rhythm lulled him, he yawned. After being gone most of yesterday, he'd had a late night, catching up on chores.

When did he become so serious and focused on his fears? Yes, his sisters would be independent someday, but did it have to be so soon? The love and the fierce protection he felt for them was what drove him these past two years and gave him something to live for. Did they have to grow up so fast?

With that thought, Caroline and Rose entered the barn, already in their best dresses.

"Time for breakfast, Luke," Caroline called out.

Milk spilled out onto his boot, and he jumped off the stool.

They giggled, and he shot them a frown.

"We don't want to be late. You always say first impressions

are important. And we want to make a good impression, don't we, Rose?"

Rose nodded.

Luke's heart swelled. The younger always followed her big sister's lead. And rarely said much. Not since losing Ma. "Okay, let me finish, and I'll join you shortly."

"Yay!" both girls exclaimed as they swarmed around him, small hands circling his waist.

He squatted to their level, and they each planted kisses on his cheeks.

"Luke. There's nothing to worry about." Caroline acted way beyond her twelve years. "You'll see."

Luke placed his hand on Bessie again to calm her from the girls' high-pitched squeals as they rushed out of the barn with enough noise to rattle a herd. He loved his sisters and would do anything for them. Like driving them to town every day for school. And marry a stranger so they'd have a woman to raise them. He'd promised his parents, and he always kept his promises.

He just hoped this new schoolteacher wouldn't put a hitch into his plans.

A LOUD SCREECH STARTLED OLIVIA, and she opened her eyes. The unfamiliar room and furniture caused a wave of panic until her gaze found her bonnet and cloak hanging on a hook, her brush and personal items on the dresser. Memory resurfaced, and she sighed. She had arrived already, here in Washton.

Last night, the stark contrast between the quiet stillness and the bustling city made sleep almost impossible. Instead of nickering horses and wheels rolling on the streets around her home, shutters creaked, and eerie chirping sounded from unknown animals.

Screech.

Speaking of animals.

Screech.

She jumped off the bed and scrambled for the window. Pushing open the curtains, she looked outside but saw nothing.

Screech.

What a horrible racket. Was it nearby? Distracted, she glanced at her watch while waiting for another outburst. Her stomach flipped-flopped. She needed to get ready for school.

Hints of daybreak spilled in through the clear glass. Hurrying to get dressed, she tied her hair into a knot at the base of her head, hoping the style gave her a more stern, older look. She breathed in deeply, wishing the butterflies in her stomach would go away. Did she smell bacon? She swallowed, hoping her queasiness settled. She didn't want to be rude but didn't think she could eat.

Screech.

If that noise was an animal, it was trying to get someone's attention.

Screech.

Was anyone checking on the poor thing? Ready, she peered at her simple white button-down shirt, plain navy skirt, and dirty boots and laughed out loud. "Does anyone here keep their shoes clean?" No use in shining them. They'd get dirty all over again on her walk to the schoolhouse.

A snort escaped, and she quickly clasped her hand over her mouth. Her simple clothes, smudged shoes, and unladylike noises would horrify her father. He always expected perfection. Correction, he *demanded* perfection. And she had performed most of the time. And even though she missed her father, she loved not feeling powerless anymore.

Olivia fluffed her skirt to shake out the creases, determined to leave the past in the past. "No sense worrying over spilled milk, Grandma used to say."

She'd do just that. No more crying over something she couldn't change.

Opening the bedroom door, she headed to the shared living quarters.

Screech.

Was it in the house? She approached the kitchen cautiously as Mrs. Martin placed food on the table. The ghastly noise didn't seem to affect her.

"Good morning, Olivia,"

"Good morning, Mrs. Martin. Something smells wonderful."

Screech.

"I made a special breakfast for you this morning. Please, have a seat."

"You didn't have to."

Olivia turned and looked out the window, pretending to look for the source of the screeching, hoping the tears forming in her eyes would evaporate quickly. When was the last time someone did something nice for her?

Screech.

Olivia cringed. "May I ask, what is that sound?"

Mrs. Martin carried the conversation as if a terrible racket didn't come from outside. "Well, I know I didn't have to, but I wanted to. For the benefit of the entire town. A well-fed teacher is going to teach better. That's my motto." She saw Olivia hesitate, led her to a chair at the end of the table, and then continued, "And that's Bert. The town's rooster." She laughed. "Bert is privy to everyone and all that goes on around

71

here. He's making so much racket because he wants to meet you."

Olivia gasped. Was this the same rooster from yesterday? She narrowed her eyes, wondering if Mrs. Martin was pulling some trick.

Mr. Martin entered the room and walked over to kiss his wife. "Good morning, sweetheart." He turned to Olivia. "Good morning, Miss Carmichael."

"Good morning, Mr. Martin."

Screech.

He, too, ignored the rooster. "Are you ready for your first day? Would you like me to walk over with you this morning?"

Olivia twisted her finger around a loose piece of hair at the back of her neck. Would he think she couldn't set up on her own? "I believe I can manage. Thank you for the offer, though."

Screech.

Mrs. Martin stood behind Olivia and tapped her shoulder. "I think you need to step outside on the porch for a moment, dear. This won't take long."

When she headed for the door, Olivia followed, glancing over her shoulder at Mr. Martin.

He grinned. "Bert just wants to say hi."

Screech.

In the doorway, Olivia gathered her courage and stepped on the porch. One large colorful rooster stood in the middle of the street, his head cocked to the side, studying her. Bright red, orange, green, and yellow feathers blended from his neck to his tail. He was magnificent.

"We heard you, Bert. Loud and clear." Mrs. Martin leaned over the banister. "Come and say hi to our new schoolteacher, Miss Carmichael."

Bert strutted over. He raised his wings out and screeched loudly.

Mrs. Martin reached for Olivia's hand. "Say hello, dear."

Olivia studied Bert. "Um. Hello."

Screech.

She jumped back.

"Well, now that that's settled." Mrs. Martin headed back inside, calling over her shoulder. "She'll be out after breakfast."

Olivia frowned and followed Mrs. Martin inside. "What did you mean?"

She stopped and faced Olivia. "What? Oh. He's waiting to follow you to the schoolhouse this morning."

Olivia couldn't speak.

Mr. Martin held out a chair for her. "With introductions made, we can now get back to our conversation. If you need anything, send one of the youngsters over. I will drop in near luncheon to see how you're faring. Show my mayoral support and all."

He pulled out his wife's chair and sat in his own. They took each other's hands, then looked at her expectantly.

She blinked.

Mrs. Martin smiled at her. "We hold hands when we say grace, but if you're uncomfortable, you can keep your hands in your lap."

Gulping the lump in her throat, she placed her hands in each of theirs and forced a smile. Mr. Martin bowed his head and prayed out loud while Olivia willed her erratic heartbeat to calm.

The meal went smoothly from there, the three of them eating and talking as if they'd been familiar with each other longer than a day. The Martins treated her as family and acted genuinely happy to have her in their home. Unbidden memories of her own family meals played in the back of her mind.

Mrs. Martin broke through her thoughts. "Best finish your breakfast, dear."

Olivia ate a few additional bites, then glanced at her watch. It was time. She stood, her legs a bit wobbly. "Thank you, Mrs. Martin. Mr. Martin."

Mrs. Martin's warm smile lessoned Olivia's nervousness.

"Remember to call me Chrissy, dear."

"I'll try to remember." Olivia bowed her head. "And thank you for a lovely breakfast. An excellent way to start my first day. I've now had a great night's sleep, a healthy breakfast, and wonderful company. What could possibly go wrong?"

Nine

So many differences in this part of the country. The clothes, the accents, the customs. No servants and no formal rooms. And Mr. & Mrs. Martin truly care for one another. I've never seen a man so attentive to his wife before. My cheeks grow heated whenever they are in a room together.

—From the journal of Olivia Carmichael

M r. Martin followed Olivia to the door, offering to accompany her a second time. The joy radiating from him as he smiled at her was exactly how she wished her father would've gazed at her. He placed his left hand on her shoulder as if to hug her, and the desire to close the distance herself and flee to a corner and weep warred inside of her. The turmoil must've shown on her face, for he let go, shook her hand instead, and acquiesced her decision to go alone.

Mrs. Martin, however, went straight for the hug. Her strong arms enveloped Olivia and squeezed tightly, sharing her encouragement and well-wishes for a good first day. Olivia's heart warmed at the embrace, but she pulled away before she did something crazy, like becoming too attached. Mrs. Martin could easily fill the holes in her heart, and the idea scared Olivia. More than she cared to admit.

Spirit high, Olivia set out through the main part of town toward the schoolhouse, her breath creating rising puffs in the crisp morning air. The sun crested the mountains in the distance, lighting the wooden planks before her. She fingered the two lists in her pocket, one filled with tasks to complete when she arrived, the other with the seventeen names of her students.

She breathed in deeply, savoring the early morning quiet.

Screech.

Olivia jumped.

A bright red blur ran from across the street.

The back of her leg hit the building as she stepped back, preventing her from a quick escape.

Clucking sounds emanated from the rooster as he closed the gap.

Should she run? Call for help? Her arms circled the pail as this animal headed right toward her. It was the animal from earlier. What was his name? Bernie? Bart? Bert!

He stopped abruptly and eyed her. She caught her breath.

There was no time to worry about some crazy bird, for she had to reach the schoolhouse. Leaving the creature standing there, she continued till she reached the end of the street before she glanced over her shoulder.

The colorful animal was following her.

He would've hurt her by now, so she stepped onto the hard ground and headed north along the river. She shivered and pulled her scarf a little tighter. To appear older, she'd pulled her hair back tightly but now wished she left some loose to cover her ears. The temperature had dropped a few degrees closer to the water, adding a briskness and a challenge she didn't expect.

As she passed the church, the schoolhouse appeared in view. Excitement pulsed through her, and she picked up her pace. A young child stood at the top of the stairs, arms waving frantically back and forth. She grinned. Someone was eager to start school.

As Olivia neared, the young girl, possibly eight or nine, jumped up and down. Warmth flowed through her to meet this eager child, and she continued forward till she reached the stairs.

An older boy stepped around the pillar. "Howdy."

Olivia placed her hand on her chest. Her heart wouldn't survive the day at this rate. "Good morning!" Her voice croaked, and she cleared her throat. "I'm the new schoolteacher, Miss Carmichael."

"Hiiiii." The girl said shyly, swaying her body back and forth, her dress flowing around her legs. Such a cute child.

"How do you do, Miss Carmichael? My name's Teddy, and this is my sister, Emily. Ma sent us early to help with whatever you needed." He held an armful of firewood and glanced toward the door.

Olivia paused before answering, her mind a bit fuzzy with how to respond. "What a gracious offer, Teddy."

"I think she wanted us out of her hair as soon as possible," Emily stated matter of factly. "I was so excited 'bout school and meetin' ya, she got tired of all my questions and said we should go and help. I was up early anyways, to finish my chores an' make sure we weren't gonna be late. But now we're early, and maybe that's a good thing so we can help ya and tell ya who is who when they get here."

"Emily." Teddy hissed.

77

Emily looked at her brother, then back to Olivia, clearly unmoved by her brother's admonition. Maybe the girl wasn't as shy as Olivia originally assumed.

Olivia reached the door. "Wonderful. Shall we go inside, then? I'm sure with your help, we can prepare everything much faster."

"Yes, let's!" Emily squealed, then leaped for the doorway.

Teddy lifted his hand. "After you, ma'am."

Olivia gave him an encouraging smile, and his cheeks turned pink. She stepped over the threshold and headed straight for the teacher's desk.

"Can I sit in front?" Emily asked.

"It's *may* I sit in front, and yes, you may," Olivia responded.

Emily beamed. "Yippee." And skipped over to the first desk.

"Emily, watch yer manners," shouted Teddy. He looked sheepishly at Olivia, his cheeks reddening further. "Sorry for yelling, Miss Carmichael."

"Quite all right, Teddy. Let's take a look at what we need to do, shall we?" She pulled one of the lists from her coat pocket. "First, we need to light the stove." In the center of the room, the stove divided the girls' and boys' sides. Olivia strode over, lit the match, and then the kindling Mr. Martin had placed the day before. "Teddy, would you go and fill the bucket from the well?"

"Yes, ma'am." He grabbed the bucket from the stand next to the washbasin and soap then headed to the door.

Screech.

Olivia peered out the window. Sure enough, there in the yard stood Bert, strutting back and forth.

Screech.

Emily approached the window. "Bert is here! Yay!"

Olivia looked at Emily. "You know Bert?"

Screech.

Emily nodded. "Everyone knows Bert. He watches over all of us and takes care of us. Tells us when impor'ant things are happening." Emily acted as if this was completely normal. Maybe it was in California.

"How does he know which things are important?" Children's imaginations were quite creative, but she had to ask.

Screech.

Emily's eyes squeezed shut for a few moments while the rest of her face scrunched together. "I don't know. He just does. Come on, I'll introduce ya to him." And she ran outside.

"Emily, wait." Not wanting the girl to be hurt, Olivia followed Emily through the door.

But before she could stop her, Emily stopped directly in front of Bert, who stood as still as a statue. Watching the animal from the porch was one thing, but standing right next to him? Would he peck the girl? Olivia attempted not to panic. She didn't need a student injured on her first day. It was her job to keep the children safe.

Obviously, Emily had no issue trusting the colorful bird. "Bert, I want ya to meet our new teacher, Miss Car...Carmi." She turned and waved Olivia forward. "Miss C, this is Bert."

Olivia glared at the creature.

Bert glared back, tilting his neck so his right eye watched her, unblinking.

"Ya supposed to say hi to him," Emily whispered.

Olivia turned toward Emily. "I don't think it's necessary for me to talk to him. Animals can't understand people."

"He can! And he's not just an animal. He's Bert. And ya don't talk *to* him. Ya talk *with* him. Come on. Say hi."

Olivia glanced around. The last thing she needed was for other children to run home telling their parents their new schoolteacher held a crazy, foolish conversation with a rooster.

And yet, Olivia didn't want to disappoint this eager student by telling her they already met. Better to be done quickly, whether she believed Bert could understand her or not. She cleared her throat and, in her most proper voice, said, "Nice to see you again, Bert."

Bert made a clucking sound.

Emily giggled. "He said, '*Nice to see ya too.*'" And then she turned to Bert. "School begins today. Make sure to let us know when it's starting time, all right?"

To Olivia's surprise, Bert lowered his head, then strutted to the other side of the field. As much as Olivia wanted to continue their lovely conversation with this unusual animal, she wouldn't allow them to be thrown off schedule. It was imperative she kept things in order and on time. She turned to Emily. "Shall we finish organizing things?"

Emily grinned at her and grabbed her hand.

Warmth flowed all the way to Olivia's heart.

And the entire time they walked to the schoolhouse steps, Emily didn't take a single breath. "I think animals can hear us talk. Do ya think animals understand everything we say? Maybe some animals. Or only the smart ones. How do ya know if an animal is smart? Bert must be very smart ..."

Shy was definitely not the right word for this child. Inquisitive, lively, and enthusiastic all came to mind. Traits Olivia desired to see in all her students. Olivia lifted her chin. "I think today is going to go rather well, don't you?"

The girl stopped mid-sentence and smiled, a cute little grin showing off dimples on both cheeks. Soft brown eyes full of trust gazed back, and in that moment, Olivia's heart skipped a beat. She loved it here. Coming to California was the best decision she could've ever made.

* * *

VOICES AND SHOUTS came from outside as Olivia finished writing on the chalkboard. Her heartbeat pounded, and her palms became sticky from the chalk dust still on her hand.

She brushed her palms together to remove the extra dust, barely catching herself before she rubbed them on her skirt. The white dust would've left a mark. Not the first impression she would prefer to make.

A loud screech pierced the air as she headed for the door to ring the bell.

"Bert's right on time," Emily stated as she followed Olivia outside.

Olivia turned and raised her eyebrow.

"He's telling ya to start school," Emily said cheerfully. "Remember, when ya met him earlier, we asked him to let us know the time for school to start?"

Olivia remembered the conversation but didn't believe a rooster could understand time. A silly coincidence, right? With the children following Bert's direction, she'd let it be. For today.

Some children found their places near the steps, while a young girl with a long braid was chased by an older version of herself, both running toward the schoolhouse. By the patch of trees, two red-headed boys kicked a can back and forth, laughing. And several more students strolled into the yard, waving and greeting one another. They all looked happy. And all were coming to her schoolroom.

She placed her hand on the knotted part of the rope and pulled. A loud metal clang echoed across the field, and she instinctively covered her ears.

The children eyed her reluctantly. She nodded and smiled, as Miss Beecher had instructed, 'Whenever in doubt, just smile as if you have all the patience in the world.' The gesture calmed her own nerves and, she hoped, put her students at ease.

Olivia rang the bell a second and then a third time. The first ring was to alert the children's attention, but three pulls communicated school was to begin.

A squeal yanked her attention to the north pathway, where Bert flapped his wings and chased a few stragglers. She grabbed the railing. She knew it! That rooster would injure students. She stepped down, but a tug on her arm stopped her.

"Don't worry none, teacher. Bert's making them hurry. He won't hurt them," said Emily.

How did a child know if Bert would hurt someone or not? It was Olivia's responsibility. But she waited before acting. Sure enough, Bert stayed a safe distance behind the children. He flapped, screeched, and looked mighty pleased with himself, but he didn't peck or harm them. How many more times would her heartbeat accelerate before the end of the day?

The other nine children stayed in their lines. Not a large turnout, but it would do. Their little angelic faces gazed at her with rapt attention. How would she ever hand out lashings if they disobeyed?

She cleared her throat. "Good morning, children. My name is Miss Carmichael, and I am your schoolteacher. You may call me either Miss Carmichael or Miss C."

No one said a word.

Finally, the young girl with the long braid spoke in a whisper, "Hello, Miss C."

Olivia acknowledged the young girl and then made eye contact with the others.

"*Oof.*" A boy near the back cried out. His hand gripped his side and he glared at the girl next to him, then spoke in a strained voice. "Good morning, Miss Carmichael."

The rest clamped their lips shut. Were they as apprehensive as her, or were they playing a game? She couldn't wait to find out. She was in charge, after all. "All right, children, let's form two lines, boys on my right and girls on my left."

Impressively, they moved without making a sound. Of course, only four boys stood in their line.

A sound from behind halted her next words. She glanced over her shoulder. At the end of the yard, a man helped two girls alight from a rocking wagon.

The children murmured behind her. Should she send them inside now or wait? Not wanting to embarrass the latecomers further, she faced the children. "We will wait for the others to join us."

A prickly sensation tickled her neck, and she rolled her shoulders. Wanting to welcome her newest students, she stole a glance. The large hat, the broad shoulders, and the profile all reminded her of someone, but she couldn't place who. She squinted to no avail, then shrugged. Ghosts. She saw them on her entire journey here. People who looked like someone she knew.

But who would she know all the way out here in California?

And then, like a smattering of puzzle pieces once linked together, the image in her mind became crystal clear. Her heart skipped a beat, and blood pounded in her ears as she fought to stay upright.

It was him.

Ten

I can't get the gentleman out of my head. He was kind and handsome. Where did he live? What a shock it would be to see him again. Not that I want to see him again, nor would there be any chance of that happening. I'm now living in a vast, empty land with a small group of people. Which was exactly what I wanted.

—From the journal of Olivia Carmichael

L uke maneuvered the horses into the yard and looked at the schoolhouse. They were late. The drive took longer with the wagon. He'd have to plan accordingly in the future.

Along the entire way, Luke's mind created scenarios that did nothing for his peace of mind. Would the teacher be old and gray? Motherly? Stern and cranky? Unable to control the children? Would she even know how to teach?

He wiped his brow with his sleeve. Already, the sun was beating down on them.

His sisters sat mutely. Too quiet in his estimation, but their silence told volumes about their nerves. They usually roamed the ranch like bees collecting nectar from a flower, unafraid of anyone or anything. Not the timid girls next to him right now.

"She is pretty," said Rose, awe inflected in her young voice. "Will she like us?"

Rose hadn't talked much since their ma passed, so her question caught him off guard. How was he supposed to answer a question like that?

Always one step ahead, Caroline beat him to it. "O'course, she'll like us, Rosie. We're Taylors. What's not to like about our family?" She turned toward Luke and added, "What's left of us anyway."

His heart lurched, and instinctively, he wrapped his arms around them, one on each side, and squeezed. They were old enough to remember when they were a larger family of seven. Before multiple tragedies struck and shrunk them to three.

The girls looked beyond his shoulder, and he turned to see what they saw.

He cleared his throat. "They're lining up. Now remember, use your good manners and listen to the teacher. It's important—"

"We know, we know," Caroline answered for both of them, as always. "You've said the same thing each morn this week," she added. "We'll be fine. Truly. A tad nervous, but that's all. We don't get a chance to see other kids our age since we live so far from town."

He secured the reins and jumped to the ground, reaching to lift each of them from the wagon. Is that what they worried about? "You won't have trouble making friends. What's there not to like about you both? Come on, let's go meet your teacher. I want to make sure I'm going to approve of her since she'll be spending so much time with you."

They groaned, but he ignored them, remembering full well

what it felt like to be embarrassed by his ma. He gripped each of their hands, and together they walked toward the schoolhouse.

A young woman, dainty, slim, and poised, stood on the porch facing the children. A high neckline with long sleeves covered her arms, while the skirt hung on her without accentuating any shape, the style simple and plain. In his estimation, she didn't look like an Easterner, which was a checkmark in the positive.

He glanced at the girls' clothes, saw the shorter hems, and wrinkled his nose. Yeah, he needed to take them clothes shopping soon.

The teacher's blonde hair, pulled taught and secured to the nape of her neck, looked familiar, but he couldn't think why. He studied her. Did he know her? He shook his head.

As they stepped closer, he pushed his hat off his forehead for a better view. She turned at the same time, and their eyes met. He choked on the air he breathed in.

"What's the matter, Luke?" asked Caroline.

He glanced at his sister and squeezed her hand. His heart beat wildly in his chest. "Nothing. Just realizing how much I'm going to miss you two on the ranch."

"We'll miss you too," said Caroline in a placating tone.

They wouldn't miss him at all. Little stinkers.

He snuck a peak at the teacher again, and his body tensed. There was no way to describe it. Could it be the same young lady he ran into day before yesterday? The one he couldn't stop thinking about?

Her eyes widened, and he broke eye contact, his legs as sturdy as a newborn calf. Maybe she woouldn't recognize him. Oh, who was he kidding? With some sort of connection from their interaction, he *knew*. His options were limited. He couldn't avoid her, nor could he acknowledge any recognition.

The closer he came to the schoolhouse steps, the more his pulse leaped. He climbed the steps, still confirming the fact that the woman he'd met was his sisters' teacher, he was not unaffected by her presence, and he had a mail-order bride coming soon. Now what was he supposed to do?

* * *

OLIVIA'S VISION NARROWED, and her ears rang, blocking out all other sounds. What were the chances he was here in Washton? He, being the knight, the one she couldn't stop thinking about. She blinked rapidly, hoping it was an error. Someone who looked like him. And walked like him. Had a hat like him. A twin, maybe?

She should lead her class inside, but her feet froze in place.

And the closer he came, more of the same tingly sensation from when she first met him traveled through her. Deep inside, she *knew*. Knew, without a doubt, it was him. Her gaze trailed to where his hands held onto two young girls. He was a father and, most likely, married. Of course, he would be married.

She blew out her breath. This she could deal with. In fact, it could be to her advantage.

Not that it mattered. They barely exchanged a few sentences with one another. But ... her knight wasn't *her* knight, and no longer could she think of him as such. Here, real in the flesh, she had no right to think of him other than a gentleman who helped her. A *married* gentleman.

A strong urge to flee crept in again. It was either that or sit down and cry. And neither would work. She needed this job, and giving in to her emotions would not show her best side to the children.

"Excuse me, teacher?" asked one of the girl students.

Startled, she remembered the children in the lines.

"Yes?" Oh, she hoped no one could see the turmoil tossing around inside of her.

"He pulled my braid!" She glared at the boy standing next to her.

Of course, *now* they chose to misbehave. And even if she didn't want to, she must deal with this right away. Otherwise, any authority she had would disappear. Putting on her fiercest look, she raised her eyebrow at the offender and said not a word.

He glared back in defiance, then drooped his shoulders. "I'm sorry, Miss C. It won't happen again."

Without a word, Olivia shifted her focus toward the girl he offended and raised her eyebrow again.

The boy swallowed and looked over at the girl. "Sorry."

The girl smirked.

Olivia raised her chin. So, it wasn't entirely the young boy's fault. Olivia made a mental note to watch this girl closely. From her own childhood experiences, girls were mean. And Olivia vowed then and there to not allow this one to be unkind to anyone in her schoolroom.

Crisis averted, she pasted on a smile, then turned to face the next one.

Closer, the approaching man looked at the ground, which allowed her a chance to study him. Even though he must be older than she first thought, his walk revealed a youthfulness that contradicted his age.

She focused on the girls and the resemblance between the trio. Definitely related.

And their guarded gaze fueled her mouth to curve farther upward, rewarding her with smiles of their own while their hands still clasped each of his.

He raised his head, and their eyes met.

Recognition and wariness were apparent. Still, he didn't say a word.

One of the girls tugged on his arm. "Luke!"

She used the word Luke, not Father or Pa.

He blinked, then turned toward the young girl.

"You're staring," she whispered.

Giggles came from behind, and Olivia angled her head, stern look and all, and they immediately stopped.

"What? Oh." His face stayed neutral. "Hello. You're the new schoolteacher?"

What did she expect? She didn't want him to acknowledge her, did she? "Yes, I am. My name is Miss Olivia Carmichael." She glanced at each girl and eased into a more natural smile. "And who are these two lovely ladies?"

He took off his hat and executed a slight nod. "How do you do, ma'am? I'm Luke Taylor, and these are my sisters, Caroline and Rose." Each girl gave a small curtsy.

Sisters, not daughters.

Olivia planted her feet farther apart to keep from swaying.

The older one, Caroline, looked at her brother with hero worship in her eyes. "Luke's our brother, but he's also our pa. Ain't that true, Luke?"

A tinge of red flared across his cheeks, but his eyes never left Olivia's. "Yes, Caroline. That's right."

Her heart flipped.

He shrugged. "I'm sort of Ma and Pa."

The girls nodded solemnly.

Her heart ached for the loss of their ma and pa and her own. "Pleased to meet you, Caroline and Rose. I'm sorry for your loss." She gave both girls another encouraging smile before looking back at him.

The right side of his mouth quirked up, and her heart flipped again.

"Since I'm Ma and Pa, if there are any issues or concerns, please come straight to me." He squeezed the girls' shoulders.

Both Caroline and Rose glanced at each other and smiled.

How fortunate for those girls he was so protective. A sliver of a wish swirled in her heart for someone to care for her in the same way. Doing everything on one's own brought challenges, to say the least, but being entrusted to the wrong person? That was worse. No, she wouldn't put herself in that position again.

"I'm sure there won't be any issues or concerns, Mr. Taylor." She would ensure little contact with him.

"Please, call me Luke. Mr. Taylor was my pa's name."

What was it with people in this town and informality? No matter how well she knew someone back home, she always used proper names. Considered forward, using given names was not allowed.

Her behavior yesterday flashed in her mind. Could she be found lacking? She didn't need any black marks against her. She swallowed and shoved her concerns aside, addressing the two newcomers, "Why don't you stand behind the other girls, and we'll go in and begin."

She found her most neutral expression possible. "It was nice meeting you." Then, she turned her back on him. "Follow me, class." And led her students inside.

Would anything else unpredictable happen today?

LUKE FROWNED as Miss Carmichael turned her back on him and walked into the schoolhouse.

Caroline put her arms around his waist. "Don't worry about us, Luke." She hugged him tighter. "We'll be fine."

He squeezed her back.

"I like her already." Rose large eyes stared up at him.

91

How could she like her already? They just met. He raised his eyebrows. "Already?"

Rose nodded, her eyes glowing with determination.

"This feels strange for me to leave you two here and not have you back at the ranch. Do you feel it too?"

"Yes." Caroline paused as she glanced around. "But we want to go to school. We need to. You've said so yourself. This is a great chance for us."

He sighed. "How did you get so wise in only twelve years?" He fondly squeezed her shoulders.

"Almost thirteen, and I learned from the best. You, big brother." Caroline poked him in the chest.

He reached his arm around Rose to give her the same big bear hug. "Off with you now, both of you. I'll be back at the end of the day."

They giggled and headed through the door, following the last of the children inside. They turned back as they crossed the threshold and waved. "Bye, Luke. Love you."

"Love you two, too." His mouth hurt from the too-big smile plastered on his face.

He waited, then turned and headed back to the wagon. As he climbed into the wooden seat, he glanced at the schoolhouse. Never did he think the woman he ran into would be the new schoolteacher. And quite literally, he had run into her. His lips twitched as he suppressed a grin.

Why her? The one who brought back to life emotions he assumed were long dead. The one who made him wonder if his mail-order bride would be pretty, like her. Would she be a good influence on his sisters?

His stomach roiled. His mother had believed in this program, and Miss Carmichael came with good recommendations. He knew he needed to give her a chance. But things just got a little more complicated.

Because he hadn't been able to stop thinking about her.

And now, he knew her name.

He repeated the name in his head a few times. Olivia Carmichael. The name fit her. She carried herself in a regal way. As a lady would. Not from around here.

So, where then, was she from, and why did she come to California?

Did she have marriage on her mind? The idea of someone else marrying her didn't sit well with him. And he didn't want her to set her sights on him. He shook his head. Nope. Not him. So why did he feel this anxiousness to see her again?

Disgusted, he set out for the ranch. Halfway home, his mind searched for answers he had no idea the questions for. Was it his sisters' absence? All his decisions had been with them in mind these past two years. But as they grew up, what would he do when they married and had families of their own?

A sharp pang hit his chest.

Lost in his thoughts, Luke didn't remember how he arrived home. He let out a huff as he disembarked from the wagon. Seeing Miss Carmichael again made one thing crystal clear—he found her attractive and distracting. Entering his thoughts was one thing. Seeing her day after day, at school and in town, was completely different. If he didn't have a mail-order bride on her way, he'd be in big trouble.

Eleven

I will enjoy interacting with the children more than their parents.
Adults can be troublesome at times and judgmental about even the
tiniest thing. Children are more accepting, and they don't hide what
they are thinking. It's clear as day all over their little faces.

—From the journal of Olivia Carmichael

Once inside the schoolroom door, Olivia stepped sideways to allow the children to enter, and to catch her breath. Shaking out her skirt, she shoved aside her emotions at seeing her knight again. Her focus had to remain on her students, which now included his two sisters.

She shook her head. How could she take control of her life when situations such as this kept throwing surprises her way?

"Please pick a seat," she directed. "Boys on the right, girls on the left." She mentally repeated their names as she passed by on her way to the front of the room. "Thank you, you may be seated." She faced the chalkboard, picked up the pointer, and began the first lesson.

By early afternoon, Olivia had nearly made it through her first day without incident. She sat at her desk while the younger students read out loud from the reader.

A movement to her right caught her eye. "Yes, Emily?" Olivia asked.

Emily stood and pointed to the window. "Miss Carmichael, Bert's outside. It's time for school to end. May we be excused?"

Murmurs filled the schoolhouse as eleven pairs of eyes watched for her reaction. She glanced at her watch. Sure enough, it was time to end school.

A cry bellowed from the schoolyard.

The children giggled, and she raised her eyebrows till they grew silent. Then she stood and approached the window. Bert sat on the cutoff tree stump fluttering his wings.

He crowed again.

Olivia had forgotten all about the wayward rooster and his caterwauling earlier in the morning. How would he know what time to come back and make a racket? She searched the yard. Maybe his behavior was due to the parents in the wagons. There was no other explanation.

She sighed and turned back. "All right, class. That's all for today. Leave your slates and readers on the desks. See you tomorrow morning."

The kids scrambled out of their seats and grabbed their pails as they left.

"'Bye, Miss Carmichael." One by one they called out as they ran outside.

She waved to their retreating backs, then faced the slate hanging on the wall. Her hand gripped the cloth tightly as she rubbed back and forth on the rough surface. A small tug on her skirt caused her to spin around. There stood Rose clinging to Caroline, eyeing her cautiously. The two girls had their brother's eyes. How she knew what his eyes looked like after only meeting him twice, she had no idea.

"Miss Carmichael?" Caroline asked hesitantly.

"Yes, Caroline?"

Caroline glanced at her sister. "We wanted to say thanks. We had a great first day of school."

Warmth spread throughout her chest. "Why, how sweet you both are. And I agree. It was a nice first day, wasn't it?"

Rose peeked out from behind Caroline's shoulder and nodded.

"I'm so glad you enjoyed school. I will see you both tomorrow?" she asked.

Caroline's eyes shone. "Oh, yes, we wouldn't miss it for the world." She grabbed her sister's hand. "Come on, Rose, let's hurry so we can tell Luke all about our day." They skipped out the door.

Olivia peered out the window and watched them run to the wagon. Mr. Taylor stood leaning against the wagon, arms crossed, until he noticed them running toward him. His lips turned up as he opened his arms wide and scooped them both into an enormous hug.

Olivia's heart lurched. What would it feel to have a family to run to and hug in that way?

Even if she still had family, no one would've permitted such a public gesture. None of her family acquaintances would've done so either. She pinched her lips. All the society rules drilled into her didn't seem to fit here.

She finished her chores and stepped outside to head home.

Bert walked over to her and stopped.

She eyed him and then strode past.

The sun shone low and bright through the treetops as a breeze cooled her face. Wouldn't be long before the sun would set. A rustling sound came from behind, and she swung around. Two beady eyes stared at her from three feet away. The crazy rooster followed her.

"*Shoo!*" She waved her hand. "*Shoo.*"

The bird clucked but didn't go anywhere.

She didn't have any energy to contemplate what he was about. "Fine. Do what you want. I'm going home." Her feet hurt from standing all day, and she couldn't wait to sit in a quiet room and write in her journal.

Bert followed her to the same spot where he'd met her that morning and then disappeared while she continued to the Martins' home. When she arrived, Mrs. Martin ushered her into a chair and handed her a cup of tea, insisting Olivia rest and put up her feet. Every time she rose to help with dinner, Mrs. Martin sent her back to the chair. "I'm preparing a special dinner to celebrate the first day of school in the new schoolhouse. Don't ruin my fun by getting in the way." She hustled back to the kitchen.

Mrs. Martin outdid herself. The savory chicken soup and large chunks of bread and butter disappeared quickly off Olivia's plate. "Would you like more bread, dear?"

"Yes, please." Olivia didn't normally eat a large supper, but tonight, her appetite was enormous. Who knew interacting with children and engaging their minds took so much energy? Plus, she hadn't been around people this much since … well, she'd always had a lot of time to herself, and today had been a long day. But she didn't want to be rude.

"You look tired, Olivia." Mrs. Martin stood to remove the dishes.

A yawn escaped, and she covered her mouth while averting her eyes. How embarrassing to show bad manners. She raised her head once it passed. "Just a bit."

Mr. Martin chuckled. "Children can exhaust you. You'll get used to it, though. We won't mind if you want to turn in early."

Olivia wanted to say 'yes, sir,' but instead stood and reached for a dish.

Mrs. Martin's hand grabbed the plate first. "Oh, no, you don't. You don't need to worry about a thing. You worked hard enough already today. Do what Mr. Martin suggested and turn in."

Olivia placed the back of her hand in front of her face as she yawned again. "I'll take you up on your offer, but just for tonight." She glanced at both of them. "Please know, I have no expectations of you waiting on me each day." Olivia now appreciated the concept of pitching in and doing her share. No longer would she allow someone else to be her servant. "Good night," she called.

"Good night, dear. See you in the morning." Mrs. Martin continued to remove the dishes and headed to the kitchen. If Olivia wasn't so tired, guilt would compel her to help.

She went through her toilette and then sat by the window, journal in hand, unsure where to start. Exhausted, she couldn't structure a complete sentence. Yet she didn't want to forget any details about the first day. No use stalling. Her mind would replay the words over and over until she wrote them down anyway, so she opened the book and placed her pencil on the page.

1869, September 22

> *My first full day as a schoolteacher. I believe all went well. I had eleven students. My feet hurt, my voice is raspy from talking all day, and my eyes see double, but I enjoyed being an authority figure to these children, helping them to learn and grow. The schoolhouse is beautiful. I love all the windows. They brought in the morning sun and allowed a breeze to blow through, which kept the hottest parts of the*

day cool. Otherwise, when the sun rose high, the heat would've been unbearable, and none of us would've been able to focus, including myself.

The first two children I met today arrived early to help. Teddy and Emily. Then the others arrived. May and her sister Sally have blonde hair and wore long braids. Andrew pulled May's braid in line but behaved the rest of the day. John and Joseph are red-headed twins, who had a hard time sitting still and needed recess to run off their energy. Laura and Susannah, the oldest girls and obviously close friends, sat huddled together whispering throughout the day, and then the Taylor girls, Caroline and Rose ...

As she completed the e in Rose's name, her mind instantly flashed to their brother, Luke. He showed respect, not mentioning having met earlier. And he showed outward affection toward his sisters. His actions seemed genuine.

But, still ... others said the same about her ex-fiancé. No one would ever believe the vile words he spewed at her after the truth about her father came out. She still couldn't believe his judgment and the truth of his loyalty.

What if all men were that way? What if they weren't?

Oh, the quandary she found herself in. Would she see Mr. Taylor every day? Did she want to see him every day? Her heart fluttered. She couldn't admit she did. Any interaction with single men was strictly frowned upon. Conflicted emotions stirred inside as she tried to figure out what was safe to write, lest someone see her diary.

But she had to tell someone.

You will never believe who lives here in Washton.

Remember the man I met at the train station yesterday? The one who helped me when my hat blew away?

She cringed.

Turns out he owns a ranch here and his two sisters, Caroline and Rose are my students. I was very surprised to see him, as I'm sure he was to see me. He was distant, yet courteous, which is exactly as he should be.

She shivered. There would be a next time, and another and another. She would see him all the time. A loud sigh escaped her lips. She would stay far away from him the best she could. She yawned, then hurried to finish the entry.

I'm tired and going to sleep now. I have to admit, I'm looking forward to teaching again tomorrow. What a relief to know I like this. Until then, Olivia

She placed her pencil in the case and closed her journal.

Her heart was full. These children were all hers, and it was her job to watch over them. A fierce protection sprung from deep inside her. A responsibility she wouldn't take lightly. She pulled the covers over her body. A good thing she liked being a teacher, given she planned to do this for the rest of her life.

Luke tucked the blanket around Rose and kissed her forehead. "I'm glad you both liked your first day of school."

Caroline leaned against her headboard. "And we can't wait to go back tomorrow, right Rose?"

Rose grinned at Luke, showing her missing teeth. "Yes."

His heart squeezed. Rose spoke more after school today than she had in the past month, her slight lisp not even slowing her down. Both girls described their day in excruciating detail the entire ride home. They mentioned each student, their lessons, and how nice Miss Carmichael was. And he loved every part of their report.

No matter his uncertainty about the way he felt about Miss Carmichael, he silently thanked her for already having a positive impact on his sisters. "Well, let's see how you feel after a few weeks."

"Oh, I will still want to go. There is so much to learn," Caroline answered wistfully.

Luke smiled. "Keep that in mind as you get older. We can always learn something new. Even at my age."

Rose brows furrowed. "What'd you learn, Luke?"

Luke blinked. What did he learn recently? Well, he learned their teacher was the same woman he met in Sacramento. Except he couldn't share that bit of information. He grinned. "I learned I can survive an entire day with both of you at school and not worry. Too much." He tickled Rose till she giggled.

"Time for sleep." He kissed them both again and headed for the door.

"Night, Luke." Did Caroline sound older?

"Night, Caroline. Rose. Love you both." He placed his hands on his heart, then put his hands out in front of him. They mirrored his actions and placed their hands over their hearts. A ritual performed each night since Ma died.

He had had to do something. They were inconsolable. He was, too, for that matter. Especially after Sarah left him on his own. Not knowing what else to do, he gave them the last part of his heart for safekeeping. A reminder for him and them that they held his heart. And because he gave his heart to them, he had nothing left. For God or a wife. Content with that arrangement, he expected Evelyn would be too.

He headed to his study to work on ranch paperwork. Relief swept through him that the girls enjoyed their first day. And from what they told him, he had a good sense of how Miss Carmichael ran the schoolroom.

He had only one concern. Marriage. Not his, but Miss Carmichael's. The only reason he knew of for women to head West was to marry. Did Miss Carmichael come to Washton to marry? Or was she hiding something? Simple questions, but ones he couldn't ask his twelve- and seven-year-old sisters, nor could he come right out and ask Miss Carmichael.

She was wary of him. Of that he could tell. Something inside those sky-blue eyes showed a hint of distrust he couldn't discern. And he had recognized vulnerability in their first encounter. But folks from the East lived pampered lives. He hoped for her sake she had thick skin. Living here would be challenging.

He looked at the papers on his desk. He had read the same entry three times. Energy pulsed through him, and it took a moment to figure out why.

He groaned.

He was looking forward to going to school tomorrow too.

Twelve

My plan is to teach, not be interested in a gentleman. So, I will treat him the same as everyone. Shouldn't be hard at all.

—From the journal of Olivia Carmichael

"Olivia, don't forget your lunch." Mrs. Martin stood at the opened door, holding a tin pail.

"Oh, bother!" Olivia swung around and caught herself, barely, before colliding with Mrs. Martin. "Thank you. I cannot believe I overslept!"

"You've been working hard all week. It's to be expected," Mrs. Martin said.

Didn't excuse being tardy. Not in her book. "Yes, but I have responsibilities. What example am I setting for the children?"

"I think you're setting a great example. And it's important for them to learn grace. We all need grace." Compassion glowed in Mrs. Martin's eyes.

Olivia wished she believed in herself as much as the Martins did. She did not want to let them down. A burden she hadn't expected to experience here. Although, she sensed more a yearning to please them than any external pressure.

She hugged Mrs. Martin, surprising both the older lady and herself. "I appreciate all your support."

"Good luck today. I'm praying for you," she whispered in Olivia's ear.

Prayer was Mrs. Martin's answer to all things. And as Olivia grew more accustomed to hearing her say the words, they didn't catch her off guard so much.

Olivia never had worked so hard in her life. Even though she went to bed early, she'd slept long and hard and had a difficult time waking.

But who knew work could be so rewarding? Teaching invigorated her. Gave her purpose and meaning. And allowed her to tolerate the frigid air which chilled her ears this morning.

She pulled the collar of her coat up, partly to hide her embarrassment for being late. "This can't be happening." She broke into a fast-clipped walk.

Grateful for Miss Beecher's calisthenics, she'd had no idea she'd need them as much as she did.

Her boots clicked as she hurried along the wooden sidewalk. When the walkway ended, Olivia left puffs of dirt trailing behind her. She pushed ahead, even as her muscles burned from the exertion. Almost there. She turned the corner, her sights so focused on the schoolhouse, she didn't see anything until a loud clucking noise startled her.

Bert appeared on her right, strutting alongside her. How did he get so close? She wanted to stop and laugh, but knew if she did, her legs would give out. They must look a sight. A rooster and a lady, walking together side by side.

Inside the schoolyard, she stopped and glanced at her watch. Eight minutes—a record. Her enthusiasm died as she realized she needed a minute or two to catch her breath. So much for saving time. Bent over, her hands on her knees, she gasped on her inhale. A sharp pain radiated from the middle of her stomach to her hip. She placed her hand near her ribs to ease the pain. Those ten days on the train had put her out of shape already. Maybe she should take a long walk tomorrow on her day off and incorporate the calisthenics she learned.

Bert clucked as he strutted over to the tree stump. He hopped to the top and stretched his neck.

Silly bird.

"Hi, Miss Carmichael." Emily hollered, carrying a piece of firewood as she followed Teddy around the corner of the porch.

Olivia waved with her free hand. "Good morning, Teddy, Emily. Thank you, once more, for coming early. As you can see, I forgot to move more wood in, again."

"No problem, Miss Carmichael." Teddy's face turned a hint of pink. "I'll take on this task from now on if yer inclined to let me."

A part of her wanted to object. Would it reflect poorly on her? She wanted to show she could do it all. But in reality, she couldn't. "That would be wonderful. I'm touched by your generosity."

Teddy's face now looked like a ripe tomato. "'Course I don't mind. I wanna help. I wouldn't have offered if I didn't want to."

Her face flushed. "Oh, I wasn't implying ..."

"Ah, shucks, Miss Carmichael. I jus' wanted ya to know you can count on me. No need to worry."

So worried about what others thought, she'd hurt Teddy's pride in the process. Fear of jeopardizing her job got in the way of treating her students with respect and accepting their aid. If she arrived early a few times to open by herself, that might appease any gossip. Or maybe the community would approve *because* she let the children pitch in.

Frustrated with her indecisiveness, she strode inside the building and halted. Then twisted around to face Teddy and Emily.

They beamed back at her.

Why would they assist so much? Suspicion wound around her heart. People usually did things because they wanted something. She did not want to be obligated to anyone.

This had to be addressed right away. "What a great service you are. Both of you. Now, if you expected high marks, I hope ..."

The shock on their faces communicated her misstep.

"We didn't do this to get something." Tears formed in Emily's eyes.

Olivia's heart sank.

"We assisted because we care about our schoolhouse and wanna help. It's what people here do. To be better cit, citi—" She scrunched her nose.

"Citizens," Olivia finished for her. How could she have gotten this all wrong? Oh, how she wanted to start today over. "I apologize. I'm new here, and I needed to make sure things were perfectly clear. In my experience, many people hide their true reasons for their actions."

"But that's deceitful!" Teddy blurted. "Father says our word is the most important thing we have. It's what gives us honor."

"Yes, Teddy, you are correct." She sighed. "Unfortunately, not everyone has a father as wise as yours." She blinked her eyes to hide her emotions. "And yes, Emily, you are correct as well. Helping is a perfect example of being a good citizen."

Both children stood taller.

Unsure how to mend this rift, Olivia placed a hand on each one's shoulder. "I appreciate all you've done. You have good hearts. Why don't you go outside to get some fresh air while I finish writing today's lessons on the board?" She gazed out the open door.

"Thanks, Miss Carmichael." Emily turned and ran outside.

"Ya sure ya don't need my help?" Teddy's eyes gleamed with something Olivia couldn't place.

"Not right now, but I promise if I do need anything, I'll let you know."

He grinned at her and placed his hat back on his head. "Ya do that, Miss Carmichael."

Olivia's eyes followed him as he exited. Who did things only to help? Even the ladies in her church circle back home served because it was expected of them—a duty—an opportunity to look good in each other's eyes.

But here, the Woodwards had taught their children to serve without expecting anything in return. What a different, refreshing approach to life. Were other families in Washton the same?

Her mind rolled this new awareness around as she finished her morning tasks. Children's laughter and shouts grew outside as the time to start drew near. Amongst the noise, a wagon approached. She headed to the window and watched the Taylor family arrive. Her nerves, already unsteady, couldn't handle facing Luke Taylor this morning, so she stayed by the window.

He jumped from the wagon right away and lifted each girl to the ground, hugging and kissing them on the cheek. Olivia's heart fluttered. To have had a sibling or someone else share affection in such an open way.

She brushed her hair off her face and fanned her neck. Maybe she should ring the bell now. Anything to quell the curiosity brewing inside her about Luke Taylor. A man she should not be paying any attention to at all.

* * *

LATER, Olivia dismissed the children and laughed as they ran outside, cheering. After a long first week, she wanted to run outside and cheer as well. Two whole days to do whatever she pleased. Thankfully, the board decided on only five days of instruction each week.

She surveyed the schoolroom. Books stacked haphazardly on a few desks, while a couple of slates lay on the floor. One hung precariously on the edge of the desk. She breathed in, raising her shoulders and arching her back. She should've made the students clean before releasing them, but the busy work would give her time to reflect on this first week and prepare herself for the next.

Cold air blew in the windows as she wiped off the blackboards. The children warned her a storm this time of year could come quickly and be harsh. Brushing the chalk off her hands, she peered out the closest window. The clouds were gray, but nothing to be alarmed about. She resumed her cleaning.

Back home, storms blew in daily. Sometimes a warning cloud or two appeared, but most of the time, the sun shone, then a cloud passed, dropping buckets of water, then the sun sparkled again a few minutes later.

And so far, she'd seen clouds gather and threaten, but not a single drop of rain had fallen since she'd arrived earlier in the week. She glanced out the window again. Maybe today would be different. The clouds had turned darker as the day progressed, giving an almost ominous feeling. Such odd weather.

She sat at her desk to complete next week's lesson plans.

Woohaw, squawk.

She froze, with only her breathing to break the silence.

Bert? Or another animal? She focused on her notes as an eeriness lingered in the air.

Woohaw, squawk.

What a horrible sound, one she'd never heard him make before. Running to the window, she searched outside. There on his tree stump, Bert stared back at her.

"Was that you, Bert, or something else?" she whispered. All of sudden, staying wasn't an option. Would she be attacked? Would she make it home? And if not, how long before the Martins missed her?

* * *

LUKE LOVED the time spent on the trips to and from the schoolhouse. The girls chattered nonstop about their entire day from what they learned to who said what. Although he'd never admit it, he liked the comments about Miss Carmichael best.

According to Caroline and Rose, Miss Carmichael spoke to them kindly and refrained from discipline unless absolutely necessary. The glimpses of her personality told him his sisters were safe in her care. She traveled the aisles throughout the day answering questions while the students worked. She didn't demand absolute silence, and she hadn't used the switch on anyone yet, though many infractions could warrant such punishment.

All in all, he couldn't find anything wrong with the woman.

And there laid the problem. He was grateful Caroline and Rose liked school. They needed a solid education so they would have options for their future, including keeping and running the ranch, if something were to happen to him.

But a part of him wished Miss Carmichael would fail so she would leave.

He squirmed.

Not kind thoughts. But the feelings she stirred in him were unwelcome.

"Rose, I hope Miss Carmichael went directly home," said Caroline. "I don't think she believed me when we told her a storm was coming."

Luke glanced at the clouds. Dark and gray, they blended to form one of those large powerful fall storms the area had this time of year. One that once broken free, would last all night.

He flicked the reins to push the horses home. Maybe he should go back. Not his concern, but something compelled him to check on the teacher.

They completed the curved drive to the front of the house. "Whoa." He pulled hard on the reins.

The girls stopped their chatter, and Jimmy, who appeared out of nowhere, helped them alight. They knew their jobs. He had drilled the plan into them daily for months. But even though they knew what to do, the storms still generated memories he couldn't silence. A helplessness which urged him to act. He wouldn't lose anyone else in his family to a heavy storm.

"You coming straight in?" Jimmy asked.

"No." He shook his head. "I think I'll saddle Admiral and go back to make sure Miss Carmichael doesn't get stuck in this storm."

"We told her," said Rose.

"Yes, Rose, but I don't think she took us seriously," Caroline said.

"Most newcomers don't. She isn't prepared for the danger. You three go inside and do what needs to be done. I'll be back shortly."

"What if she's scared?" Ever since her pa and brother lost

their lives during a storm, Rose would wrap her arms around herself and rock back and forth till the storm dissipated.

Luke smiled at his sister. "If she is, then I'll help her like I help you."

Rose's eyebrows shot to her hairline. "Pick her up and hold her?"

A warm sensation traveled from his heart and his fingers twitched. He laughed to cover the unwanted response. "I don't think she'd appreciate that, but I would wait out the storm in the schoolhouse with her, then give her a ride back to the Martin's. Shouldn't be a problem."

Luke tipped his hat and drove off to the barn. This was the perfect opportunity to speak privately with her. To clear the air between them so the awkwardness would abate. Especially since they would cross paths so frequently. Luke's heart pumped faster. Yes, they needed to discuss things. He had to somehow let her know about Evelyn too. How he would have that conversation without suggesting she had designs on him or vice versa, he had no idea. It just had to be done. He couldn't handle this restlessness that had surfaced since Miss Carmichael arrived in town.

Thirteen

"Bert has been there before, during, and after school every day. He has shooed kids into the schoolhouse when they were late and makes a lot of noise when schooltime ends. Those black beady eyes watch everything I do. I think the sounds he makes mean different things. I'm going to observe and capture the various crows to try and decipher their meaning. Maybe, by keeping track, I can understand him. I believe this creature has taken me quite literally under his wing. And I want to understand why. Am I losing my mind? Of course, only you, dear diary, do I divulge this information. I don't need to make a fool of myself and be laughed right out of town."

—From the journal of Olivia Carmichael

Woohaw, squawk.

Her nerves on edge, Olivia hurried to gather her belongings from her desk. Truly ignorant about the local wildlife and whether she should be alarmed, she began a list of questions she wanted answers to.

Tomorrow, weather permitting, she'd walk around town and get more familiar with her surroundings.

She stepped onto the schoolhouse porch and scanned the area as the awful sound rang out again.

Woohaw, squawk.

Bert sat on the tree stump, flapping his wings. How could something so loud come out of an animal so small?

Olivia lifted her watch. Four o'clock. She didn't know much about roosters, but until she met Bert, she thought they only made their noises when the sun rose.

She blew out the breath she held. "What are you up to, Bert?" She stepped from the porch to the schoolyard.

He strutted toward her in a half circle with one wing extended.

Was he sick? She moved closer to inspect him.

He raised his head and spread both wings. *Woohaw, squawk.*

She jumped back.

His eyes met hers as he waddled toward her.

"I'm not sure what you're about, Mister, but you're making a lot of racket." She hoped no one observed her talking to a bird. "Is there something you're trying to tell me?"

He strutted past, then turned back, his expression saying, 'follow me.' Did her mind play tricks? The need to know sent her after him. When he turned onto her path home, she frowned. Was he walking her home? He slowed, then paced back and forth, clucking and pecking at the ground. When she drew closer, he turned and continued. A chuckle escaped. She was being escorted home by a rooster.

He picked up speed, so she quickened her steps to keep up. He stopped briefly only once at the corner to Main Street to make sure she tagged along, but as soon as he arrived at the Martins' porch, he crowed and flapped his wings. Olivia interpreted this to mean *hurry*. When she stepped on the porch, a deluge of rain fell.

Startled, she swiveled to stare at the bird. His backside hurried away to wherever he went each day. Did he know about the rain? Did he purposely grab her attention to warn her to go home in time? She stayed on the porch and listened to the pinging on the metal rooftop.

"Child, what are you doing out here?" Mrs. Martin opened the front door. "You better get inside before you catch your death."

Confused about what transpired, she went inside, peeled off her jacket, and shook out a shiver. Bert was not some dumb creature. Instead, he acted as her guardian angel.

Her lips lifted on their own. In some ways, she didn't feel so alone. Someone cared, even if it was a silly rooster.

* * *

ON FOOT, Luke led Arabella and the wagon into the barn. Josh, one of his ranch hands, came running.

"Here, take care of her while I saddle Admiral. I need to check something before those clouds let loose."

"Yes, sir," Josh replied.

Luke placed his foot in the stirrup, swung his leg over, and then directed Admiral out of the barn all in a matter of seconds. Thankfully, Admiral was well trained to ride in any type of weather. Dangerous to ride a skittish horse in a storm.

He leaned forward and gave Admiral his head. "Okay, boy, let's hurry."

Thunder cracked off the mountains behind him. Wouldn't be long now before the clouds dumped their fury. In half the time compared with the wagon, he arrived at the schoolhouse. He jumped the steps and grabbed the doorknob. Locked. He pressed his face against the window to peer inside. Empty. No sign of Miss Carmichael anywhere.

He banged his hat against his thigh once, then twice more. Why this compulsion to check on her? Unbidden images from when they met appeared, and the vulnerability he saw in her eyes urged him to investigate further. However, as much as Luke wanted to go to the Martins', neither of them needed to stir up gossip. Besides, if she saw him, he'd have to explain himself, and what would he say?

What a complete waste of time.

He growled as he pressed his hat into place and hurried back to Admiral.

By the time he rode into his barn, all protective thoughts toward Miss Carmichael were long gone. The rain let loose halfway home, soaking him and his clothes till they clung to his body. The only part of him not cold and soggy was his head, his Stetson doing its required job. Frustrated with himself and blaming Miss Carmichael's inexperience for prompting him to do the right thing, he decided he didn't need to play her rescuer. Didn't matter what she might need, she wouldn't be his responsibility.

* * *

THE STORMS OLIVIA had experienced back home blew in and out within an hour, but this one pummeled the area all through dinner and beyond. Brilliant lightning lit the sky, and crashes of thunder shook the small house more than once, while rain pelted the roof with a constant heavy roar. Each boom caused her to jump, and the Martins held a conversation with her to help keep her mind occupied. Now, as she readied for bed, the rain quieted to a soft steady rhythm. Cocooned in her small bedroom, the air felt refreshingly cool.

How she loved this 'starting fresh' feeling. The best way to end her first week of school—a good cleansing to wash away the past. The week wasn't terrible. Just unfamiliar. New experiences, not to mention new people. However, the daily routines formed, the way her students responded to the lessons, and the fact no one mentioned anything about her past, made it a good week.

She let out a long breath.

Teaching was exhausting. But, oh, so exhilarating. Yes, she could do this for the rest of her life. She closed her eyes and all her body tension released. All in all, her plan worked.

She changed into her night clothes, then folded and placed her garments from the day in the top drawer. Shadows flickered from the lone candle on the small table by the chair. Warmth radiated through her as she grabbed her journal and pencil and sat in the worn, comfy chair. Olivia flipped to a clean page in her book and wrote:

So far, the students have shown me respect, and they have each touched my heart in small ways. I'll introduce you, dear diary, to each of them over time. First, there's Adam. At age eleven, he's quite diligent, studious, and wants to learn. I love his eagerness but worry how quiet he is compared to the other boys. He doesn't go outside and play, and his clothes are threadbare and too small. He rarely has food for dinner. I want to find ways to help him without drawing attention in doing so.

She yawned.

Time for some rest. Till Tomorrow, Livvy.

Her heart warmed at using the abbreviation. Never would

she have been so informal before, but her students and the town grew on her, and she liked the nickname Jenny had given her. A sign of change. Growth. Her new life.

* * *

Olivia woke to sunlight shining through the small window. Her viewpoint from her bed, the bright blue sky beckoned, not a cloud in sight. Several birds flew around, their loud, happy chirps blending into a beautiful melody. Perfect weather to be outside.

A groan escaped as she moved her legs to rise. Stiff and sore from standing for hours over the last four days, she pushed to a standing position. Her calisthenic exercises and a long walk would help as well as provide an opportunity to explore her new surroundings.

Dressed in her favorite blue walking dress, which happened to be the only one she owned, she freshened her face, hair, and teeth. The worry lines reflected from the small looking glass on the wall weren't quite as pronounced as they were when she first arrived. Her spirits lifted as she left the room.

Mrs. Martin greeted her when she entered the kitchen, "Good morning, Olivia."

"Good morning, Mrs. Martin."

Mrs. Martin frowned.

Olivia touched her arm. "I'm sorry. Chrissy. Old habits are difficult to change. Life was more formal in Ohio."

Chrissy patted her hand, then went back to stirring the food in the pot.

"It's a beautiful day outside. I plan to take a walk and explore. Would you recommend anywhere in particular?" Olivia placed the water pitcher on the table.

Chrissy peered out the window. "The weather won't stay nice like this as fall closes in, so best take advantage while you can. There's nothing but grazing land as far as the eyes can see once you come to the ranches outside of town."

"I've seen children arrive from different directions, so I thought I'd travel some of those paths."

"Makes sense. Just remember, this is ranch country, so be careful and stay clear of the Longhorns." Chrissy set a plate of food in front of Olivia.

"What are Longhorns?"

"A specific breed of cattle. It's what's raised here, or was. If they aren't full Longhorn, a cow will have part Longhorn in them, and you can't miss them. They have long horns that can span up to seven feet across." She spread her hands wide. "They can be bad-tempered and like to be left alone."

"Thanks for the warning." She had no plans to annoy any of the beasts.

Olivia picked up the teapot and poured hot water into her cup.

Chrissy put her hand on Olivia's shoulder. "Take my warning seriously, dear. You can't outrun them."

"I understand. Don't worry. I don't plan to go anywhere near them. I'm not one to take chances."

She squeezed Olivia's shoulder. "I believe you. But I'll still worry. This area is a far cry from what you're used to. You never know what you'll encounter."

After breakfast, Olivia laced her sturdy boots, tied her bonnet, and grabbed her shawl, then headed out in the same direction she walked each morning. Much later than her usual start time, the town bustled with activity.

An older lady sweeping the boards glanced at her. "Good day, Miss Carmichael."

Her stomach tensed. She hadn't even met the woman. "Good day."

A gentleman secured his horse's reins and tipped his hat. "Howdy, Miss Carmichael."

Olivia acknowledged his greeting with a nod.

After the eighth person called her by name, Olivia realized everyone knew who she was. The joys of a small town. So much for staying anonymous.

At least their eyes held respect and not disdain. So far. She pulled her shawl tighter.

She neared the place where Bert met her each morning, but there was no sign of him. Where did he go when school wasn't in session? Would she see him at all today? She walked on, missing his company, a completely unexpected response.

Olivia shook off the loneliness and drew near the schoolhouse, continued around the back, and approached the river's edge. She always liked water, but after her parents' deaths, her wariness took away the joy it once gave.

She sighed and pushed aside those thoughts. She had to overcome those feelings to move forward. This was a different place now. A fresh start.

A large rock beckoned, so she sat and stared at the water. The soft noise as it splashed on the rocks and tree trunks soothed her. No words were needed to describe how the constant sound calmed her soul.

A tree branch floated by and moved toward the center of the river before another river merged a bit downstream. The wood swirled faster and faster until the current pulled it under. Memories spun around in her mind like the limb, and when it did not resurface, she stood and walked away.

Not far ahead, a large wheel rotated, water raining from the top. Men's shouts came from behind the structure, and she veered left, uninterested in being seen. Eventually, she'd want to learn how the mill operated, but not today.

Her gaze raised to the top of the wheel, and she covered her eyes to protect them from the bright sun. How could equipment be made this size? And how had someone figured out how to harness the power of water? She laughed at herself and the many questions whirling in her mind. When did she become the curious sort?

The warm dry air didn't feel thick like the summer heat in Cincinnati. There was a different sort of rawness of nature here. More natural, not as groomed or structured. She liked it, even if she didn't fully understand it yet.

She navigated her way through some brush, her boot kicking a loose rock on the path. The worn grass held footprints in the dirt. A walkway for folks to and from town, she surmised as she continued, zig-zagging the best she could, even though the path was unclear in some places.

All around her, tall flowers bloomed in unorganized chaos. She leaned over to inspect a bright yellow petal, and a ladybug flew away. She laughed, then glanced around. So much beauty to take in, and most of it unrecognizable to her.

Out of sight from the mill, she pursued her desire for freedom and exercise. A huge grove of tall and imposing trees loomed ahead. They would provide welcome relief from the hot sun. She picked her way through the uneven dirt and rocks and exhaled when she stepped into the cooler air. Dried fallen leaves crunched under her feet as she progressed toward a large tree to rest under before heading back.

When she paused to catch her breath, the loud crunching noises continued. She stood stock still and slowly glanced around.

Crunch, crunch.

Olivia's heart pounded. Why were the crunching noises growing louder?

Crunch.

The unknown creature highlighted her lack of key knowledge. That had to be rectified. Immediately.

The sounds stopped.

She inched her way around the tree and blinked. What a beautiful meadow. Tall trees all along the outside, and in the center the greenest grass she'd ever seen. Colorful wildflowers filled the sunniest side. All delightful, except the large beast who stood in front of her. So close, his hot breath blew across her face.

The mammoth-sized animal lowered and raised his head, his gigantic horns jutting out three feet on each side. His front right hoof scraped the ground.

She gulped, then muttered, "Mrs. Martin didn't fib. Those horns are huge."

More menacing the longer she stayed, the wild animal raised his head a few more times, flaunting those pointy horns and flashing his mean-looking eyes. He stomped both feet with a grunt.

Her heart nearly exploded in her chest as she held back a scream. No time to think, she did the one thing she probably shouldn't.

She turned and ran.

Fourteen

Chrissy Martin frets all over me like a mother would her daughter. I can't say I don't like the attention. I do. Too much. But I need to show her I'm old enough to be independent. She doesn't have to take care of me.

—From the journal of Olivia Carmichael

Luke rode along the river's edge, a short distance from the copse of trees bordering his father's ranch. Correction. His ranch. He shook his head. Seven years later, he still had difficulty accepting he was the adult left in charge.

As he surveyed his land, his chest expanded. He'd been riding the perimeter each week to check fences since the age of thirteen and always enjoyed the silence during the long ride. Today was no different.

Memories appeared unbidden of the pride his pa had when he purchased these acres and built a homestead here. Together Luke, his siblings, and his parents learned how to run a cattle ranch and worked hard to not only survive but thrive in this new territory.

He passed by the chopped-down old oak tree his pa used for his lesson stump. Pa frequently pulled Luke aside to discuss the life cycle of a tree, explaining how tree roots grew deep or shallow, which determined how long a sapling would live. Survival meant weathering specific circumstances, which then imprinted themselves on the rings within the tree during those years. Rain, drought, fire. Each significant event influenced the size of the rings.

"The same could be said about family and land, son." Luke remembered his pa's exact words. *"The soil here is rich, and I intend for our family to grow deep roots here, not just on the land, but with God. We can't survive here without the Almighty. We must trust in Him. To plant ourselves deep in the soil so we stand firm and not get knocked down during the storms that will surely come our way. And believe me, son, at some point, things will go south. Nature can be harsh. But how we endure shows in our character and how we live our life."*

Pa had the roots part right. The connection Luke felt with the land ran deep, and he never wanted to leave. Out here riding Admiral, he still pictured Pa, relaxed in the saddle from sun-up to sun-down, and then Ma holding cold drinks as she greeted them at the end of a long day. An ache spread through his chest. He sure missed them.

Why God allowed terrible things to happen, Luke didn't understand. Pa mentioned storms, but Luke didn't think he meant tempest size. One didn't learn lessons from those, they just hurt. He kept his distance from God and took matters into his own hands now. To control whatever happened in his life. Like choosing a mail-order bride.

He roughly cleared the lump in his throat.

He might be shallow with God, but it couldn't be helped. The wounds were still too raw.

His vision blurred, and he blinked.

What mattered now was building the ranch and surrounding community to secure a future for his sisters. Including hiring a schoolmarm. His sisters would gain a stronger education without sending them away. Relief swept through him that they liked school. And their teacher, Miss Carmichael.

His heartbeat quickened.

She affected him in ways he didn't want to explore. Of course, he would want to know her because of her influence on his siblings. But she drew his interest. *Before* he found out she was Washton's new schoolteacher.

He pulled on the reins, and Admiral tossed his head. "Sorry, boy." Patting the horse's neck, he tried to divert his thoughts. But the image of her standing on the train platform, eyes closed, glowing, filled his mind. What made her want to be a teacher? And why come West? What were her real plans? Every female he'd ever met dreamed of marrying, so was that the real reason she came to Washton? To get married?

A shuffling noise came from the trees, breaking him out of his reverie.

Luke pulled on the reins and glanced around. Jimmy said they put Ol' Fred in the south pasture this week. He saw no sign of the ornery bull, but he gripped the reins. Ol' Fred's temperament made it necessary to be wary, even away from the herd.

He advanced slowly, pulling his rifle from his saddle, his ears open. No loud stomping, only rustling. And a pitter-patter that drew closer. He lifted his rifle as a loud shriek came through the trees.

Luke's stomach dropped. The out-of-place cry echoed in

the meadow and grew louder. Whatever the creature, it was headed his way.

He let go of the reins and squeezed his knees. His horse shifted, but years of working together kept Admiral from bolting. Luke aimed his rifle between two trees, watching for whatever would barge through.

At that moment, a blur of blue appeared. *What in the world?* Admiral shifted again. "Whoa, boy." He clicked his tongue to calm the stallion. And his heart.

Running straight toward him was Miss Carmichael, her mouth wide open, her arms flailing, and her eyes searching the ground ahead of her.

His horse pawed the ground. "Steady, Admiral."

At the sound of his voice, she swung her head up, her eyes wide and full of panic.

Luke willed away his own fear and remained calm. He saw when she became aware of him, then when her eyes tracked the gun he had aimed in her direction.

She pulled up tight, breathing hard.

The sudden quiet allowed Luke to hear the distinct thunder of pounding hooves. She jerked as she heard it, too, turned to look back, then started running again.

Ol' Fred.

Luke kicked Admiral forward.

Her eyes grew as big as his mama's tea plates as he reached over, picked her up, and plopped her unceremoniously over his lap. He gripped the reins tightly and urged Admiral to a gallop. Controlling both the reins and Miss Carmichael, he glanced back.

Sure enough, Fred thundered after them.

Luke headed for the closest shelter—a weathered shack located over three hundred feet away.

He gripped her waist to hold her in place, while her feet

and head dangled on each side. He grimaced. Every gallop had to hurt, if not cause bruises. He hoped they wouldn't be too severe.

She kicked and screamed in protest, her words drowned out by hooves and crunched leaves. Let her howl like a wildcat. They weren't safe yet.

The shack loomed in front of them. Not fast enough. Fred's large hoofs gained further ground, the weight of his long horns not slowing him down. The bull had been itching for a fight since the day he was born. Now that he found one, he wouldn't relent until he rammed them.

They approached the worn, wooden building, Luke yanked on the reins, swung his leg over the saddle, and grabbed Miss Carmichael, flinging her over his shoulder like a sack of flour. He'd apologize later. If they survived.

He smacked Admiral's flank, signaling him to run hard, then carried her inside. The small doorway barely fit them both, but he pushed through, then slammed the door and leaned against the rough surface, Miss Carmichael still in his arms.

He exhaled.

"Put me down!" Miss Carmichael squirmed.

"Gladly." He plopped her feet on the hard ground.

She swayed, and he grabbed her shoulders.

Hooves pounded outside, closer and closer. Luke's eyes met hers, and they both held their breath. He hoped Ol' Fred followed Admiral. Or with them out of sight, lost the desire to fight. Rider-less, his stallion should be able to outrun the bull. He hoped.

The shack shook hard as a horn broke through one wall. Splintered wood sprayed out and across the room. Miss Carmichael opened her mouth. He quickly placed his hand over it and glared at her.

"No sound," he mouthed.

She glared back. Her head dipped a small fraction. Good girl. He moved his hand from her face to her arm.

The shaking stopped, and the pounding turned to stomping and snorting. The shack shook as Fred pushed with his snout. Hot air blew through the newly opened crevices.

Luke held her gaze as they waited. The fear in her eyes cut him deeply, and he put his arms around her protectively, tucking her head under his chin.

More snorts, more stomping, as Fred searched for his prey.

Miss Carmichael clung to him tighter and whimpered.

He covered her head with his hand.

Would Fred charge again? Luke didn't dare take a deep breath. They held their position for what felt like hours. His arms around her, their breathing as one. Completely inappropriate yet warranted at the same time.

After a while, the snorts dissipated. When the sound he heard was his beating heart, he let out his breath and pulled back. Blood pumped through his body, and his ears roared. "What were you thinking?" he hissed. The sound of his voice resonated in the tiny shack. He shook his head to return his hearing to normal. His heart continued to thunder. He needed to back away and catch his breath, but didn't think she was ready for him to let go. Or maybe he wasn't ready to let go of her.

"I ... I ..." Clearly, she was as rattled as he.

Swallowing his anger, he spoke a bit softer. "Miss Carmichael, deep breaths. Take deep breaths." He watched her closely and tried not to remember how she felt pressed against his chest. "That's it. Breathe."

Her face reddened, and she looked away, but he didn't let go of her hands.

Again she swayed, and he slid his hands up her arms to hold her steady. "Are you all right?"

She shook off his hands, backed away, and glared. "Who leaves a creature out in the open where someone can get hurt?"

Good. Anger and fire he could handle. "Creature? Lady, Ol' Fred is a Longhorn bull."

Her head flinched. "Mrs. Martin mentioned Longhorns, but what's a Longhorn bull?"

Luke blew out a breath. "Bulls are a male Longhorn. They are mean and need lots of land to roam. They don't go looking for trouble. But they'll defend their territory if someone enters his space."

"Oh."

"Oh? Why are you so far away from town? You're lucky I was nearby."

Her face contorted into disbelief. Obviously, she didn't share the same opinion.

Her gaze traveled down her person. "Oh, no, no, no," she cried out and brushed her clothes. Frayed and covered in dirt, nothing at this point would help the garment. Yet, she continued brushing. "I'll never get this clean."

Her entire body shook with disappointment. She was worried about her dress?

His annoyance twisted to anger. "If you plan to live here, maybe you should learn a thing or two about the animals."

She swung around, her fists on her hips, and her eyes shooting daggers at him. "I am not incompetent."

He raised his eyebrows.

"Don't look at me that way." She pointed her finger at him as if he'd caused the bull to chase her.

What was wrong with her? He rescued her from a charging bull, and this was how she responded? She should throw her arms around him and hug him.

His heart seized. No, she shouldn't. He didn't want that any more than he wanted Fred to gore him with his horns, so he blurted out the first thought to cross his mind. "You, Miss Carmichael, seem to be in constant need of rescuing." He crossed his arms for emphasis.

Her jaw dropped, and her face turned red. If she were a kettle, there would be steam coming out of her ears.

Maybe he should've used different words.

Rage contorted her face. "I don't need you to rescue me!"

"How would you have escaped a charging bull?" He shook his head, turned to face the wall, and yanked off his hat, his arm shaking. The outcome of said encounter meant either life or death. The idea of finding her mangled body ... He couldn't bear the thought. She had to be more careful. To learn the dangers lurking about and how to survive them.

"But I was running away just fine. And I didn't ask for your help." Her words sounded small and frightened. He didn't care.

"And what about our first meeting? In Sacramento? I rescued you there too. Or did you forget?"

She gasped. "So, you do remember?"

"Of course, I remember." Oh, maybe he shouldn't have said those words, either.

She narrowed her eyes. "You never said anything."

He shrugged. "I didn't know if I should."

"It would've been nice."

He shrugged. "Maybe. But then I would've had to explain to anyone who overheard, including my sisters. I didn't know you were our teacher. I never learned your name."

Her gaze strayed to the ground.

His control back in place, he asked more gently, "May I ask again, what were you doing out here? Were you lost?"

She didn't respond right away, then raised her chin. "I was taking a walk."

He didn't dare speak.

A walk? She took *a walk*! How could she be so careless? She almost got herself mauled, if not killed, because of her ignorance. There's no way she could've outrun Fred. He still couldn't believe *he* outran Fred, and he was on a horse.

He choked back a laugh. "A walk? You were taking a walk." He spun back to face the wall again before he said something he'd regret. He found a knot in the wood to focus on and took deep breaths.

"What's so funny?" she asked.

"Lady, I'm not laughing," he snapped. "It's called releasing steam."

"Oh," she whispered.

Her lame response made him want to strangle her, yet something in her voice caused the guilt to overlay the anger. He paced back and forth, not wanting to apologize. He couldn't think straight. And not all the adrenaline pumping through him was from being chased by Ol' Fred.

And that didn't sit well with him, either.

He stopped in front of her. Even with her hair falling all over in disarray, dirt smudged on her face and arms, and her dress torn and frayed, she was beautiful. His senses never felt so alive.

Growling, he went back to pacing. He needed to keep moving. Anything to distract his mind.

"Are you all right?"

"I will be." He kept pacing, while her narrow escape replayed in his mind. He should praise God and let things be, but the image in his head of Miss Carmichael laying on the ground trampled by Ol' Fred in her beautiful dress and blonde hair all dirty was so strong. He shook his head to make it go away.

"Now what are you doing?" She placed a hand on his arm.

He stilled, and she pulled back, but not before her hand left a searing imprint. Did she feel the electricity that passed between them? He glanced her way.

Her stunned look said all he needed to know.

Loose wisps of blonde hair surrounded her face. Yet she stood proper and straight. Such a contradiction, which mirrored his emotion exactly. Furious at her for being so naïve, and yet grateful she wasn't severely hurt. Someone needed to keep a close eye on her to keep her safe. He couldn't be the one. Yet, he didn't want anyone else to be either.

"Nothing," he muttered. "I'm still a little shaken."

She took an audible breath and nodded.

"I'll admit you scared me, okay? I wasn't expecting you to come running out of the trees." He didn't dare mention her nearness shook him as much. He smashed his hat on his head, stomped to the door, then added, "And I haven't had lunch. I'm cranky when I don't eat."

Opening the door, he peeked outside. No sign of Ol' Fred, nor Admiral. They might have to walk back. He stepped outside and whistled.

"What are you doing?" she hissed as she followed him outside. "Do you want him to come back?"

He knew they'd hidden long enough for Fred to give up and go back to his quiet spot. She wouldn't. "He won't come back unless we provoke him again."

She visibly sighed.

His lips twitched before he whistled again.

"Who are you calling?" she asked.

"Admiral."

She looked at him in question.

"My horse. There's no sign of him. He probably went back to the barn." He headed toward home, but after a few steps, he noticed she wasn't following. Turning, he found her using the door as a shield, the top of her head peering around the side.

He raised his eyebrows.

"I ..." She lowered her head. "... can't."

Fine time to come to her senses about the danger she faced. "He's gone. Nothing else will happen, I promise."

Her gaze met his. "That's not what I mean." Her eyes held a hint of dismay.

He raised his eyebrows, his patience thin as a piece of worn thread.

Her pretty blue eyes grew dark and full of trepidation. An uneasiness filtered through his chest. She couldn't be afraid of him, could she? He'd just rescued her from a charging bull.

As he moved back toward her, she stepped out to the side, held out her hand, and gestured to herself. "Look at me! I can't be seen like this. I ... I'm the schoolteacher. I have rules to follow."

He had tried not to notice, but with her standing there, asking, he looked. And he found her captivating. And yes, the town would be all a buzz if they saw her disheveled this way, even though she'd done nothing wrong.

His gaze landed on a nearby tree.

Would every encounter with Miss Carmichael challenge him?

Out of the corner of his eye, he saw her shift back behind the door. Her discomfort would've been charming if they weren't out so far from the house. He was hungry, she needed to be safe, and he needed distance from her. But she couldn't stay here. He had to take her back to the house.

He faced her and cleared his throat. "So, what do you suggest we do?"

Fifteen

I've never had someone affect me the way Luke Taylor does. When I see him before and after school with his sisters, my heartbeat quickens, and I get butterflies in my stomach. I don't know how to rid myself of these unwelcome reactions. What am I going to do? My job is my priority, which means I must stay far away from him.

—From the journal of Olivia Carmichael

"We aren't going to do anything." Olivia studied the man before her. Did he not understand the danger? "As the schoolteacher, I have rules to follow."

He continued to stand there with his arms crossed, clearly not comprehending the predicament.

"I am not supposed to be here," she spoke each word succinctly. "Alone. With you." Her voice cracked.

Luke grinned, causing the skin around his eyes to crinkle. "Now there is something we both can agree on. You're right, you're not supposed to be here." He shook his head. "But don't worry, nothing will happen."

She gasped. "How can you say that? *I* can't risk my reputation. You go for help, and I'll stay right here." She clasped her hands.

He shook his head again. "Oh, no. I've been raised as a gentleman. And I know you don't know me, but you can trust me. And who knows what type of trouble you'd get into out here on your own? Come on. We need to get back to the house. I'm starving." He reached for her arm.

She pulled away, turned in a huff, and paced. Why did she need his help every time she came near him? And what were those weird flutterings in her stomach, again? Her feet paced faster. She couldn't concentrate. Not with him so near. How easy it would be to let him take charge. But she couldn't. She didn't need him to be her real hero. She only wanted him to be her imaginary one.

Turning, she placed her hands on her hips and immediately flinched. "Ouch!"

"Are you okay?" Concern lined his face.

Bruises had formed where the saddle rubbed and poked, and the pain reminded her of how he manhandled her. Her face grew hot. She couldn't look at him, wanted to be far away from him, but needed his help. How would she get out of this predicament?

She studied him. "How can you think of eating right now?"

He shrugged. "I'm a man. I function better on a full stomach. I plan to eat before we drive back to town." He stepped into the shack and touched her forearm. "You're pale as a ghost. You should sit for a spell, and you've got to be hungry too. Running from a bull can give anyone an appetite."

She pulled her arm from his light grip. "I can't." She vaguely remembered her mother saying something about a way to a man's heart was through his stomach, but she wasn't trying to get to this man's heart. If anything, she wanted to run far from it.

He sighed loudly. "What's the problem, now?"

How could she help him understand? No way could she be seen in a wagon with him. It was completely against the rules.

Rules. Caroline and Rose mentioned he was a stickler for rules. She focused on his eyes, hoping her words made their point. "The rules clearly state I can't be alone with you."

He continued to look at her, his brows pulled together.

Did she really have to spell it out for him? "I could lose my job." Didn't Mr. Martin explain the rules? "I'm not to partake in any meals with the opposite gender. Mr. Martin was quite clear. I don't want to break anyone's trust, and I don't want anyone to find a reason to let me go." She gasped, then pursed her lips together. She said too much.

His lips twitched. "Well, technically you could watch me eat, and you wouldn't be partaking, would you? And then I can drive you back to town."

Olivia pointed at his chest. "You can't drive me back to town! I'll just walk back the way I came." She pivoted toward the door and winced when pain shot up her leg. Didn't matter, she had to get far away from him. Far away from his ranch.

After limping only a few feet, she faltered. That direction would place her in the same set of trees she came from. Toward the bull. Maybe she could walk around. Heading left, the pain in her feet grew. Within minutes Luke caught up and blocked her path.

"I'm going a different way"

"Proceed that way, and you'll have to go through the meadow," he hissed.

His tone ruffled her more than she cared to admit. "Please don't raise your voice at me."

He raised his hands in the air in surrender. "Sorry, but you weren't listening."

"Well … you're being a brute," Olivia retorted

"I'm used to people following my directions," he stated.

"You mean orders?"

"Are you saying I'm bossy?" He closed the distance between them until he stood so close, she saw his nostrils flare and his left eye twitch.

But she held her ground. "That's exactly what I'm saying."

He took another step closer.

His warm breath tickled her cheek. Her heart pounded, waiting for him to fire back, but his eyes searched her face, then landed on her lips.

A not-so-uncomfortable tingle flowed through her.

He smirked, and a small dimple appeared on his right cheek. "I can see the events of today have taken a toll on your otherwise highly educated mind."

She wrinkled her nose at him but didn't respond. So much for him being a knight in shining armor.

He reached out and wiped something off her cheek.

She froze. The contact sparked a fire inside.

He stepped away, and air re-entered her lungs. "It's not safe for you to walk back to the Martins'. First, walking through my ranch is too dangerous, and second, I don't think your toes will last." He pointed at her feet.

Olivia leaned over and lifted her skirt. One boot was scuffed and ripped open, the other missing. No wonder they hurt. Her stockings, now tattered and torn, exposed her ankles. Horrified, she lowered her skirt, then smoothed out the fabric of her soiled skirt.

He was right. She couldn't walk home. Her shoulders sagged. Could this day get any worse?

"Now, about a ride home. I think it would be perfectly acceptable for you to ride with me—"

She stared at him in horror. "How can you say that?"

He waved his hand in an open gesture. "Hear me out, please."

She opened her mouth, and he cleared his throat. Then he softened his voice. "For someone who listens to her students, you sure have a problem listening to me. You like to interrupt. What I wanted to say was Caroline and Rose could ride along with us, making things perfectly respectable."

Olivia chewed on the inside of her lip. He was trying to help. But he couldn't truly understand how important solving her own problems and keeping this job was to her.

"Well?" He tilted his head and raised his eyebrows.

Olivia let out a long breath. "I think given all the circumstances, as long as we're not alone, that should suffice."

He rubbed his hands together. "Good! Let's head back and get some grub then."

She narrowed her eyes at him, "If you need to eat in order to drive the wagon, by all means, I will watch you partake in a meal." She quickly added under her breath. "I still think you are bossy."

He grinned as he headed toward her.

"What are you doing?" she squeaked as he bent over and placed an arm under her legs and another arm around her back. "Put me down this instant!"

He dropped her feet to the ground.

"Ouch," she cried out.

He lifted her again and carried her across the field. "I didn't think you would be able to walk. Don't worry. You won't lose your job, I guarantee it."

How he could promise, she had no idea. The desire to get this over with kept her mouth closed.

He kept his eyes straight ahead, his breath never changing, as he carried her with little effort. As they crossed the pasture, he shifted and drew her close to his chest. With each step, their bodies bounced into each other, and she became more attuned to him.

This handsome, strong man, who rescued her the first day they met, rode toward a charging bull to protect her and now carried her because she lost her shoe and her feet hurt. He wouldn't do this to be polite, would he?

This could only mean one thing.

He cared.

Maybe not specifically for her. But he was a caring man. The town respected him. And his sisters adored him.

What a rare find.

Her body warmed all the way to her toes.

A cool breeze blew across her skin, countering the warmth. Losing her job was now not her only concern. A new burden emerged. One more detrimental to both her immediate plans and her future. She could lose her heart to this man, something she promised she'd never do.

"Relax, I'm not going to hurt you." He shifted his arms again, holding her with care and a gentleness which belied his tone.

Too late.

Her heart was already lost.

* * *

LUKE HELD Miss Carmichael tightly to his chest as he headed toward the house.

Bossy? She thought he was bossy? *Well, that's calling the kettle black.* She was the difficult one, not him. He had no choice but to raise his voice at her. She didn't know things, but Luke did, and she needed to listen to him. He sounded childish, but seeing a woman act so foolishly, and then be so quick to get defensive, burned his hide.

Why was he so riled? Why did he care? His sisters adored her, but deep inside he knew there was more. Irked by his troublesome thoughts, he focused on the need for someone to protect her from future trouble. And who that might be? Not him. No, sir. Someone else would have to keep an eye on her.

He shifted her in his arms.

"This is so embarrassing," she murmured.

"Trust me, there's nothing to worry about. No one will know."

"I will know."

He grinned. No matter what he said, she countered. He hated to admit he liked the fiery temper underneath the polish. "Yes, you will know. But your feet will thank me later."

As she shifted and glanced at her feet, awareness coursed through him. He could carry her all day, she fit so well. Completely improper and unwanted, he slammed the door on those thoughts and grasped for something else. Anything.

Of course, questions came to mind. If she didn't want to marry as the Martins claimed, then why had she come west? Eastern schools employed women, didn't they? Someone had hurt her. Her demeanor showed a tough outer shell. She would walk through fire coals if she had to, but underneath was a lonely person. She worked hard to make sure no one noticed. He sensed a vulnerability deep inside, and he was a sucker for the vulnerable—had this innate drive to want to take care of them. She had the perfect opportunity to trap him, although he had the perfect reason he couldn't be trapped. "Why are you so afraid of losing your job?"

Her blue eyes found his. "I'm not really afraid."

He raised his eyebrows.

She broke eye contact. "I need this job. I have ... plans."

Aha. Her plans must include marriage after all.

He carried her through the next copse of trees. As much as he needed to hurry and get to the house, his body slowed to savor this unique time together. Reminding him of his ma, Miss Carmichael didn't ask for help and had a mind of her own. No batting eyelashes at him or throwing herself into his path. In fact, she acted as if she wanted to get as far away from him as possible.

He chuckled.

Her gaze found his again.

"Don't worry, I want you to keep your job as much as you do. My sisters love you. They would kill me if I caused your departure."

Even though she clung to him, she must've believed him, for he felt her shoulders relax. Earning her trust meant something. If only he could trust himself. And ignore their hearts beating in harmony.

He had to remember his purpose here. To help her keep her job. The best way to do that was to put her down and stay away. But he couldn't take those actions till he arrived at the house.

Far on the horizon, the roofline of the main house arose, and relief flowed through him. He couldn't get home fast enough. As his steps gained momentum, he didn't know which drove him more—hunger or self-preservation.

Sixteen

Things are different here, but the loneliness remains. Still, I would rather be lonely than have people treat me with disdain and contempt, which was even harder.

—From the journal of Olivia Carmichael

"Did you know Miss Carmichael is all alone?" Caroline asked as they drove back from taking Miss Carmichael to the Martin's.

The girls never questioned Miss Carmichael's disheveled state when Luke arrived at the ranch house, holding her in his arms. After he said, "She met Ol' Fred," they each took a hand, led her to the washroom and helped her wash while he ate. Then he hitched the wagon behind Arabella, and they all piled in to drive her home.

"Yep, she moved here by herself to teach."

"No Luke. It's not the same thing. She's *completely* alone," Caroline held his gaze.

Luke frowned.

"No ma or pa or brothers or sisters. All gone. She's an orphan, which is worse than us."

"How do you know this?"

"She told us while we helped her. Said she understood what it was like to lose a ma and pa. Don't you see? She came here because it was sad for her to stay."

Losing a parent, he understood, but moving clear across the country?

Caroline grabbed his arm. "No one should be *all* alone. She needs a big brother like you, Luke. If we didn't have you, we'd be all alone too."

Rose leaned over, her head bobbing in agreement.

"Can we adopt her into our family?" Caroline pleaded.

The horses veered left, and he righted them, his heart beating double time. He glanced at Caroline and Rose. They both smiled at him, waiting. "The fact you're both concerned about Miss Carmichael is thoughtful."

Caroline shrugged. "We really, really like her."

"Well, I like her too."

"You do?" they both cried out in unison. Caroline's hands gripped together at her chest while her face held a dreamy look.

He did a double-take. "What? No, that's not what I meant. Not like that. I like her as your teacher. I think she's done a good job so far, don't you?"

Rose's head bobbed again, but Caroline's face fell. When he glanced at her again, she narrowed her eyes. Her perception grew as she aged, but she barked up the wrong tree. A romantic at heart, Caroline desperately wanted Luke to fall in love and marry. One reason he stayed clear of females. But Miss Carmichael had her contract, so she was safe, wasn't she? He had to only converse with her about school-related topics. Of course, he could square away any doubt if he'd tell the girls about Evelyn. Soon enough, Evelyn would be here, and then they would adjust.

But for now, the urge to avoid any changes to their lives stood paramount. The girls would go to school, he would run his ranch, and Miss Carmichael would teach.

He guided the horses around the next bend, and he pondered Caroline's revelations. Miss Carmichael didn't have a male champion besides Mr. Martin. Could she drive a wagon? Shoot a rifle? Or ride a horse? All necessary skills to survive in this area. Someone had to teach her. His mind ran through the list of men who would have time, but the married folks had their hands full. And he didn't trust the single men.

"You say somethin', Luke?" asked Rose.

Startled, he looked over at Rose and winked. "Just talking to myself again."

She searched his face, then turned to Caroline.

He grinned as his idea grew, and he formulated a basic plan. He'd discuss the details with Arthur and ask him to teach her what she needed to learn. Then he wouldn't have to worry, and he could stay far away from her, knowing she'd be safe.

THE STEAM RISING from the hot water inside the galvanized bathtub filled Olivia's lungs. Finally, a chance to unwind and sooth her aching muscles. Worried she would be fired for her escapade today, she expected Mr. Martin to be furious. Instead, he cheerfully greeted them at the door. and when Luke left, Mr. Martin pulled him into a bear hug and thanked him for looking out for her.

She had no idea the Martins and Taylors were close, but the trust Mr. Martin had in Luke was evident. Why Luke could guarantee she wouldn't lose her job now made sense.

Still, she worried, even though the Martins made no negative comments as they listened to the details of her adventure. Thankfully, he'd omitted the parts where he carried her both on his lap when he rescued her and through the fields to his home.

Sharp pain made her flinch as she pulled her dress over her head. Hurt radiated into areas she didn't know could hurt. Gingerly, she stepped into the warm water.

"*Ahh,*" she murmured as she lowered herself into the tub. "What a day."

What an understatement.

The entire experience highlighted one thing quite clearly. This was not Cincinnati. Out here, creatures were wild and dangerous.

Too tired to move, she laid her head back and contemplated her next journal entry.

Dear Diary,

What an exciting day.

No, won't do …

I had the pleasure of running into Mr.

No, not those words either …

*Every day I'm learning something new about this place.
Today I learned the animals here are big and scary. I met a
bull named Ol' Fred. He didn't like me in his space, so he
charged, making me need to be rescued by Mr. Taylor,
again, who lectured me about my walk.*

After her bath, Olivia sat in her comfy chair and wrote. Her pencil marks grew darker.

I was not at fault. I was minding my own business. His bull came after me. Why is it every time I see Mr. Taylor, he needs to rescue me? Oh, what he must think? And why do I care so much?

I will admit only here how nice it felt to be held in his strong arms. Embarrassed, yet cared for. I haven't had someone care about my well-being in a while. And craving more is a problem. I need to control my feelings when he's around. He cannot be my shining knight. And I don't need him getting any ideas. I won't lose my teaching position, no matter what. But still, to have someone care fills a deep hole. Is he just being nice? Or could he truly care?

She slammed her book closed, placed it on the side table as if on fire, and then crawled under the covers.

The next morning, when Olivia rolled over, pain radiated up her back, down her legs and her arms. She wanted to pull the covers over her head and pretend yesterday never happened, but she couldn't move. Squeezing her eyes shut, the images appeared anyway—the bull running toward her, Mr. Taylor swooping her up and over his saddle, their word exchange, and how he carried her to his house.

Her cheeks burned when she remembered how he held her. Not even Richard had handled her so familiarly.

Enduring the pain, she curled into a ball and covered her head. Could she stay in bed all day? Wait, what day was it? Her heart filled with dread. Sunday. She moaned as she rolled over again, careful of her bruised body and her vulnerable heart. She and God were not on speaking terms, and she never wanted to be again. But she had to go to church, for obvious reasons.

"Oh, no!" She lifted herself to a sitting position, her body protesting the quick movement. *He* would be there!

Would it be too much to hope he wouldn't attend, given her much-needed distance between her jumbled feelings and the man who caused them? She frowned. Didn't his sisters say that Pastor William was Luke's best friend?

"Ohhhh." She flung herself onto her back, covering her face with the blanket again.

If she didn't appear, questions would arise. And she had to set an example. A bitter laugh escaped. She would be expected, and gossip would occur if she didn't. They would be aghast, anyway, if they knew how many months since she last set foot in church.

Reluctantly, she rose to get ready. Her need for the job and avoiding drama outweighed the desire to avoid the next few hours.

"Are you awake, Olivia?" Mrs. Martin tapped quietly on the door.

"Yes, Chrissy, I'm awake." Still uncomfortable calling her Chrissy, she forced the words out to not offend her host.

Mrs. Martin called through the door, "How are you feeling?"

Olivia's heart warmed at Chrissy's concerned tone. "A bit sore. I'm moving a mite slower than usual."

"I expected as much. Breakfast is about ready. We'll need to leave soon after we partake."

"Thank you. I'll be right there."

She would go and play her part. And, while the pastor spoke, she'd use the time to observe the families and learn more about her students.

Ignoring her aches and pains, she dressed quickly, then

joined the Martins at the table, followed by their walk to the church.

Amongst the parked wagons and horses, people greeted one another. Mr. Martin guided them through the churchyard, stopping every few feet to make introductions. She answered questions and paid attention to their responses, ensuring their satisfaction with her answers. So far, so good.

Chrissy squeezed her arm. "We need to take care of something. Do you mind heading inside and waiting? We'll be in shortly to take you to our seats." She walked off with Mr. Martin.

Olivia stood alone, the weakness in her legs barely holding her upright. Her skin crawled as multiple sets of eyes watched her every move. Squaring her shoulders, she took a deep breath and headed to the entry of the whitewashed building. In the entryway, people gathered in small clusters, chatting with one another. They smiled her way as she squeezed between them. How many people could fit inside one small building?

She found an open space to wait for the Martins.

"There you are." A few minutes later, Mrs. Martin joined her. "I'm sorry we left you. We had to set up the reception area for after the service." She tugged on Olivia's hand. "Now, come with me. I have some folks I want you to meet."

Olivia stayed close behind Mrs. Martin until they stopped alongside a tall gentleman wearing a small bowler hat and a shorter woman whose arms flew all around as she spoke. She recognized them instantly as Teddy and Emily's parents.

"Olivia, I'd like to introduce you to Mr. and Mrs. Woodward. Barbara and Jacob, this is our schoolteacher, Miss Olivia Carmichael. Emily and Teddy are their children."

Both Mr. and Mrs. Woodward faced her with broad smiles and reached out their hands.

She placed her hand first in Mr. Woodward's, then Mrs.

Woodward's. "You have such lovely children. What a pleasure to meet you."

"Oh, the pleasure is all ours. Emily talks nonstop about how wonderful you are." Mrs. Woodward tittered at her own statement.

Mrs. Martin touched Olivia's arm. "Of course, you've already met Luke."

Olivia froze. Inside the small circle stood Mr. Taylor. How had she not seen him? Her face burned hot, and her stomach felt like the leaves Ol' Fred trampled on. Etiquette dictated she address him, so she dug deep inside for confidence and reached out her hand. "Hello again, Mr. Taylor."

His face expressed shock as he stared at her hand. Finally, he placed his hand in hers. "Good morning, Miss Carmichael. I hope you're well this morning."

A spark tingled up her arm. She wanted to pull her hand away, but he held firmly, his gaze boring into hers as he raised his brow. They held their position a few seconds more before they both dropped their hands.

Warmth flooded her face as Olivia glanced back at the Woodwards. But Mrs. Woodward kept talking. "We'll have you over for dinner soon, Miss Carmichael. We'd love to get to know you more. The children have nothing but great things to say about school."

"Thank you," Olivia replied, focusing on the boisterous woman instead of the aggravating Mr. Taylor. "They're a joy to have in class, and I appreciate the help they provide each morning. Thank you for sending them early each day."

Mrs. Woodward swatted her hand in the air. "Not a problem at all. Helps me out as well, if you know what I mean." She threw a large wink to the group.

As the others chuckled, Olivia's heart filled with gratitude. For this opportunity, for the people she met, and for her students. But as her heartbeat fluttered loudly in her chest, there was one person she was not grateful for. She couldn't wait to take her place in a pew far away from the distracting man.

* * *

LUKE COULDN'T TAKE his eyes off her. As he listened to the exchange in front of him, he was in awe. No one would ever know yesterday she had run from a bull, been jostled upside down on a saddle, and gone home with a broken shoe and a torn dress. He smothered a smile.

What a conundrum.

Here, she stood and conversed, straight and confident, calm and demure. But he knew differently. Underneath all the veneer, she had strong opinions and knew what she wanted. And he wanted to see more of that side of her. But now wasn't the time or place. She needed to make a good impression on the community, and he wanted that for her.

Out of the corner of his eye, he saw James Chapman at the back of the church, staring at Miss Carmichael. James was harmless, but he should warn Miss Carmichael all the same. Inevitably she would make a mistake here or there, and James would have no scruples about drawing attention to them. The man still wanted the teaching job for himself.

Luke tuned back into the conversation, looked at her, and grinned.

She tilted her head.

He leaned in. "I have something I need to talk with you about."

She frowned.

Will rang the gathering bell.

"We'll talk afterward." He didn't want to leave her side.

153

"Come, Olivia, we sit over there." Chrissy pointed to the row of pews on the left. "Luke, as always, great to see you." She hugged him.

He lifted her hand and kissed her knuckles. "You're looking lovely this morning, ma'am."

She playfully swatted his arm. "Oh, go on, you."

He grinned and headed toward his seat in the front right pew between the girls.

Caroline leaned over. "What were you talking with Miss Carmichael about?"

Luke glanced at his sister and saw hope in her eyes. "I wasn't talking at all. She met the Woodwards."

"Is she all right after yesterday?" she whispered.

He nodded. "Seems so."

Caroline scrunched her nose. "Didn't you ask her?"

Luke sighed. "No. But she didn't look any different than she normally does."

"Luke," she hissed. "You're impossible."

He shrugged, then faced the pulpit where Will stood on the raised wooden platform.

William raised his brows at Luke as he addressed the crowd. "Now that I have everyone's attention. Let's begin."

What a lovely diversion Miss Carmichael was this morning. Normally he'd go through the motions, but today dawned differently. He bit the inside of his cheek. As much as he welcomed the diversion, he didn't like where his thoughts were leading. To distract himself, he focused on William's words, something he hadn't done in a long time.

And what a pickle. Either sit in the pew and open himself to God's message or keep thinking about a blonde-haired, blue-eyed schoolteacher. He'd rather face Ol' Fred again. Of course, those thoughts made him think of Miss Carmichael. Again.

Seventeen

Today, I found myself in church. Someplace I thought I would never set foot in again. I'm immensely relieved to have found everyone cordial and kind. The pastor's delivery was smooth, his diction precise, and he had a warmth about him that made me want to listen to what he had to say. However, I have felt so abandoned by God that even if I spent a whole week sitting in church, it wouldn't make any difference.

—From the journal of Olivia Carmichael

The wooden church bench was unforgiving on Olivia's sore body as she listened half-heartedly to the pastor. She wasn't here to mend her relationship with God, she was here for her job. That's what mattered, which made attending church bearable. She could survive the rest.

At the conclusion, the pastor invited Mr. Martin to speak.

Mr. Martin stood and addressed the congregation. "We want to welcome our new schoolteacher, Miss Olivia

Carmichael, to Washton." Appreciation shimmered in his eyes as he glanced at her. The congregation clapped.

Olivia wanted to hide under the wooden bench.

He opened both arms in a welcoming gesture. "Please join us outside for a welcome reception so you can meet her and say hello."

Olivia peered at Mrs. Martin, who leaned over and patted her hand. She ignored every urge to flee, stood, and put on a happy expression like her life depended on it.

As the congregation filed outside, Mrs. Martin led Olivia to the chairs under an enormous oak tree. Sunlight filtered through the multi-colored leaves, which shaded a large area of the yard. A train whistle blew, and she peered in the direction of the sound, far across the river. Someone nearby stated the water level was high for low tide, and it indeed seemed fearsome and full. How much higher was high tide? Didn't the Martins mention floods?

She shivered.

Past experiences with the Ohio River were devastating. She could only imagine what damage could happen here. She glanced at her schoolhouse, which sat farther from the church, closer to the river. Would she and her students be safe?

* * *

Luke stood by the porch and watched as Chrissy introduced Miss Carmichael.

Arthur Martin strode up beside him. "She fits in well, don't you think?"

Luke nodded. A group of parents gathered around her and shook her hand enthusiastically. Her interaction with others and the grace she showed, impressed him.

"I think she's exactly what this town needs." Arthur

nudged him. "You going to tell me what really happened yesterday?"

Frowning Luke faced his mentor and friend, "What do you mean, what happened?"

"She was quite shaken."

"I was shakin' in my own boots. Being chased by Ol' Fred is no laughing matter. As for your other question, there's no doubt Rose and Caroline like her and are enthusiastic about going to school every morning." He shifted his focus to Arthur. "But—"

"You don't think she's good enough? She carries herself affably and is well-spoken. Something we lack in this part of the country." Arthur studied him.

"It's not that." Luke glanced back to where she stood. "There's something about her. She's not from around here. There's a lot she doesn't know. Our land is wilder than what she's used to. Will she survive?"

She stopped and turned toward them as if she knew they discussed her. Her eyes met Luke's and held.

Arthur cleared his throat. "You know your ma came from a genteel background. She adjusted and thrived for many years until other factors took her. And so will Miss Carmichael. I don't think she would've moved here if she wasn't prepared."

Luke eyed Arthur cautiously. "She just seems so naive. I think she needs lessons."

"For what, exactly?" Arthur narrowed his eyes.

"Can she ride a horse? Drive a wagon? Shoot a rifle?"

"You want her to shoot a rifle?" His eyebrows shot up.

Why wasn't Arthur taking this conversation seriously? "She needs to be able to protect herself. Ma knew how to handle anything on the ranch. Her strength, her skills, and her abilities were assets. Just at the end, the sickness ..."

Arthur studied Luke. "I think, in time, Miss Carmichael will learn what she needs to. You're a little more than concerned for her, Luke. Is there something else you're not telling me?"

Luke resettled his hat. "No, sir. I guess the bull situation yesterday rattled me up good. She didn't even know what a bull was. Had never seen one before, and she ran."

"Well, now she knows."

The man replied almost too calmly, in Luke's estimation. He balled his hands into fists. "You do know, I almost shot her when she came running through the trees. She had no business walking around the ranch freely. She didn't know where she was or the potential dangers lurking around. Even Rose knows better, and she's seven."

"I think yesterday made a large imprint on her. She'll be more careful in the future." He studied Luke further. "You seem interested in her welfare."

Luke only let his shoulders move, unwilling to show too much. "I know how hard it was to get a teacher here, and Caroline and Rose have already gotten attached. I don't want anything to jeopardize their happiness."

Arthur grinned and patted him on the shoulder. "I'm sure that's all, then. You keep telling yourself that." He walked away.

Disturbed by Arthur's comment, Luke fought the urge to watch Miss Carmichael. But as he searched for his sisters, he found Miss Carmichael alone at the refreshment table. He switched directions, but before he reached her, James appeared. Luke observed from a distance, wondering what the scoundrel would do. Her eyes widened and face paled, and before he checked his actions, his feet moved in their direction, automatically stepping in to rescue her once more.

* * *

THANKFUL FOR THE MARTINS' thoughtful planning, Olivia found the social was the perfect place to become acquainted with the entire community. All were quite welcoming and accepting. Each interaction added a new layer of confidence she needed.

At one point, she caught Mr. Martin and Luke Taylor huddled together, eyes on her, which she found oddly comforting. However, another gentleman hovered nearby, the same one who stared at her before church. Was he someone's father? Had she upset the student, who had gone and complained? Scenarios played in her mind to explain his scrutiny.

A prickly sensation settled on the back of her neck as he approached. "So, you're the new teacher?"

"Yes. I am Miss Carmichael," She held out her hand, expecting him to introduce himself.

His eyes narrowed, but he didn't move. Why didn't he shake her hand? Why did he study her as if she were a bug to squash?

She fought back a sense of unease. "Forgive me, but do you have a student at the school?"

He glared. "How old do you think I am, ma'am? No, I do *not* have a student. I'm just a concerned citizen."

If he wasn't a parent, what was he about?

His dark eyes narrowed. "I want you to know, I will be watching. Closely. And when you mess up, I'll be there."

Olivia's blood drained from her face. Did she hear him correctly? Did he know her father? She glanced around, then counted to five before speaking, determined to brazen this out. "I'm not sure what you mean. I assure you I am adequately trained for the job. And if there is—"

"You're a woman doing man's work." He crossed his arms.

Before she could muster a clear response, he turned and walked away. Miss Beecher prepared her teachers to face opposition to a woman teaching, but Olivia hadn't expected a personal attack. What did he have against women? And what did he mean by, 'I'll be there'?

All the fears about her planned future roared back, but before they took root, a familiar male voice spoke from behind. "Don't pay James any attention."

She swiveled, then peered into familiar brown eyes full of compassion. Had Luke seen what transpired? And when did she start thinking of him as Luke? Her face flamed.

"He's upset he didn't get the job," he said.

Someone else wanted her job? "Was he supposed to have the job?"

"Nah. From the beginning, the town decided to have a woman teach. But he's determined to prove us all wrong." He nudged his head in the direction the man had gone.

Olivia forced a smile. "I appreciate the information and will make sure to do my job well so he cannot complain. Thank you, Mr. Taylor." She turned to walk away.

Luke touched her arm. "Hey. I meant what I said. He came over here searching for something and wanting to cause trouble, but he's harmless. Don't let him bother you."

She patted his hand, giving herself as much assurance as him. "I'll be fine. I appreciate your concern."

She held her chin high, but shook inside. One thing was clear—her plans could unravel at any minute, and it was up to her to protect herself. Why was it, no matter what she did, there was something to thwart her path?

Eighteen

I met so many people at church. All were pleasant except for one. This one man, James Chapman, said the strangest things. But besides Mr. Chapman, the worst is over. I'm becoming a part of this community and will give my best as their teacher. I have to. I don't have any other choice.

—From the journal of Olivia Carmichael

Olivia arrived, with Bert in tow, at the schoolhouse early enough Monday morning to write the first lesson on the chalkboard and direct Emily to place the readers on each desk. First week jitters out of the way, Olivia welcomed the second week of school and getting into a routine.

Outside, horse hooves and creaking wheels filled the air. She checked her watch. Odd. Bert hadn't given his cue yet.

She placed the chalk in the tray, brushed the dust off her hands, and rushed through the front door to have the children line up. A few men gathered at the bottom of the steps. Bert stood off to the side, his wings wide as if holding them back. As she stepped fully onto the porch, all of them looked at her expectantly.

She retreated inside and touched her hair, making sure the small bun at the base of her neck wasn't out of place. Doubts from the past arose. But she quickly shoved them deep inside and catalogued arguments to defend her position. She didn't think anyone was unhappy, but she had read people wrong before.

Pushing her fears aside, she placed her hands clasped behind her back and stepped out to face the men, ready to deal with whatever may come.

To her surprise, they all stood dreamy-eyed, hats held to their chests. As she surveyed their faces, she recognized a few she met at church yesterday. Others, she had never seen before.

No one said a word. Not knowing what else to do, she forced a smile and acknowledged them. "Good morning, gentlemen. Is there something you wish to speak to me about?"

The one closest to the porch stepped directly to the top step. "Miss Carmichael, let me introduce myself. My name is George Henly, and I wanted to say you are prettier than anyone I've ever seen. If you ever need anything, anything at all, I'm yer man. Jus' holler, and let me know. Okay, Mz. Carmichael?" Mr. Henly stroked his mustache as he wagged his eyebrows.

Olivia's mind recoiled as she squeezed her hands tighter. He bowed, turned, and headed back down the steps. Unsure how to respond, she stared as he walked away and missed seeing the next man approach until he stood directly in front of her.

"Goo' morning, m'am. I'm Wade Schreiber. Pleased to meet you." His Adam's apple bobbed, and his face turned as red as a tomato. "Thank ye, tha's all." He swiveled around and hurried to the others, taking two steps at a time.

One by one, the others approached her and introduced themselves. They addressed her cordially, saying nothing about *why* they were there.

Her body tingled, and her vision blurred. Could they *like* her?

No. What an absurd thought. Schoolteachers weren't allowed to court, and Mr. Martin made sure to point out to her that everyone knew the rules. Her mind searched for answers. Could this be a trap put forth by the gentleman who challenged her yesterday? He had said he'd be watching her. Was this a test of some sort?

Her knees weakened, and she placed a hand on the banister. Why, why, why? She scanned the area. Was someone watching and waiting? What if she lived here on her own at the schoolhouse, undefended, like she had requested?

"Are ya okay, Miss Carmichael?" The gentleman in front of her gripped his hat.

She pasted a smile on her face and took a deep breath. "I apologize. I'm not used to so much attention. I'm a mite overwhelmed." She tried not to encourage him, but at the same time, didn't want to be rude.

"It's okay, ma'am. My name's Thomas. Thomas Anderson. It's nice to make your ack ... ackwayntince." He stood straighter and grinned as if he was pleased with himself.

She tilted her head to the side. "Yours, too, sir."

As he stepped aside, the line had continued to build. How much more of this could she endure? And where were her students? She had class to begin.

Out of the corner of her eye, she saw a wagon approach. Was this the man to humiliate her or to witness and judge her demise? She didn't want to look, but she didn't want to stand there, waiting. She stole a peek over her shoulder and inwardly groaned. It was the Taylors' wagon. What would Luke say about all this? Would he know this was not of her own doing? Surely, he wouldn't report this to Mr. Martin and get her fired?

Her pulse jumped.

Or was he here to join them?

* * *

LUKE PLANNED to drop his sisters off at the corner as he'd done since the second day of school. Mostly, so he could turn around and get back to the ranch and his chores faster, but also so he would see as little of Miss Carmichael as possible. Much safer that way. At least that's what he told himself. "The way of things," he stammered.

"Did you say something, Luke?" asked Caroline. The girls rode in the back of the wagon and sat on their knees, looking over his shoulders.

"Nah, I was mumbling to myself," he replied.

"You've been doing that a lot lately," Caroline teased.

He reached back and tugged on her braid. "I guess I have a lot on my mind."

He never did get to talk with Miss Carmichael at church yesterday about how she fared from the bull incident. And what he'd witnessed between her and James bothered him.

Caroline tugged on his arm. "Aren't you going to stop, Luke?"

"I thought I'd make sure Miss Carmichael is all right after meeting Ol' Fred Saturday."

The girls raised their eyebrows at one another.

"And to make sure you two are behaving yourselves," he added.

Their eyes grew wide, and something pricked his conscious.

"You are behaving yourselves, right?"

"Yes, of course we are." Their voices were higher pitched than usual.

They didn't look guilty, but something in their demeanor made him question their answer. His mind was all too happy to find some reason to keep driving.

As he turned the corner to drive into the schoolyard, he noticed several wagons and horses. "Is it usually this busy?"

A muffled "No, why?" came from behind him.

He slowed his wagon and parked.

Both Caroline and Rose leaned out to take a look, holding on to the side of the buckboard. "Why are there so many people here? Did something happen?"

Concern engulfed him. "I don't know. Let's go find out."

He helped his sisters debark and took Rose's hand, then glanced around as they headed toward the schoolhouse. Several single men who lived throughout Washton stood by the schoolhouse porch.

"They're talkin' with Miss C," said Rose.

"I can see that." His stomach tightened, and he squeezed his hands.

"Ouch." Rose cried out as she tugged on his arm.

Luke cringed and relaxed his hold. "Sorry, sis." The pain in her eyes added to his torment.

He should probably leave.

But he glanced one more time at Miss Carmichael, and his protective instincts kicked in. Her stance reminded him of the first day he saw her, standing on the train. But this time there wasn't an angelic look on her face.

Caroline nudged his arm. "You need to help her, Luke!"

"I'm seeing that," he growled.

Bending, he gave them each a hug and kiss goodbye. "Okay. Go play with the other kids and have a good day at school."

"We will," they chimed in unison as they ran off to join the other children. Bert clucked at them and circled around to face outward, as if protecting the students from impending harm.

He'd have to thank Bert later. For now, he had to help Miss Carmichael.

Luke neared the porch. What were these men about? Somehow, he knew Martin's rules would incite this type of behavior.

The need to keep distance ran out the barn door, while a larger need to protect surged through him. He'd met her first. That gave him the right to safeguard her, right?

He stomped forward, determined to pull her away from the men.

She glanced his way, and her eyes grew wide like a rabbit caught in a fox hole looking for a way out. He took his hat off, forced a smile, and spoke quickly. "Miss Carmichael, if I could have a minute of your time, I need to talk with you about Caroline and Rose." He softened his facial features to not scare her further.

She studied his face. "Of course, Mr. Taylor. I have a few more minutes before I need to call the students in." She faced the other men. "Excuse me, please, I need to *work*. Nice to meet all of you." She headed inside.

He followed her all the way to the front of the room, by her desk, words filling his brain with what he would say. Artwork hung from clotheslines, and a few lunch pails sat on the side wall near the water bucket. The place felt so domestic and homey.

Once she approached her desk, she swiveled around and made eye contact.

At a complete loss for words, only one kept repeating over and over again in his brain.

Mine.

* * *

NERVOUS AND THANKFUL at the same time, she didn't know which to convey first, so she opted for neither. "What can I do for you, Mr. Taylor?"

He glanced at his hat in his hands. "You know, you can call me Luke. Everyone does. My father went by Mr. Taylor, and I'm not him."

Olivia considered his request. As much as she didn't want to, he'd been nothing but kind to her, and so she decided to honor his appeal. "Okay, Luke. I'm assuming you didn't come in here for me to learn your Christian name?"

Luke chuckled. "No, ma'am. I did plan to ask how my sisters were adjusting to school. But when we arrived, and I saw your face, you looked like you wanted to get away from all the attention."

Head bowed, she gazed at her toes, peeking out from under her skirt. She hadn't done a good job hiding her emotions. Well, she had done nothing wrong.

She lifted her head and caught rich brown eyes watching her. Oh, how she could come to depend on this man. But how needy he must think of her. She wanted to show him her capability to be strong, so she chose to focus on the first part and ignore the latter. "Your sisters are doing quite well." Her lips curved naturally, letting the adoration she felt for Caroline and Rose show. Then she added, "They are sweet girls and get along well with the other children."

He chuckled. "They received our ma's gift of friendliness, for sure. Sometimes they can be too friendly, especially with strangers. I don't want them to be scared of people, mind you, but I would like them to be careful. I'm not sure how to point that out without bursting their bubble that the world is a safe place."

"The world is not a safe place, Mr. Taylor," she responded without thinking.

He frowned. "You say that as though you've had personal experience."

This was not information she wanted to share with him, or anyone. The school board would never let her live by herself here at the schoolhouse if they had a reason. She narrowed her eyes. "I don't know what you're implying, *Mr.* Taylor."

He held up his palms. "I'm not implying anything. Your comment—"

"You don't know anything about me, so please do not judge me or accuse me." She shot back.

"Now wait a minute," he protested. "I was not judging. I never judge. That's not my style. I heard what you said and asked for clarification."

Surprised, she didn't know what to say. She cleared her throat. "My apologies. This morning has been uncomfortable for me." She waved her hand toward the door. She hoped he would let the matter drop.

His gaze bore into hers, then he altered his stance.

"All you need to know is, I'm trained and will teach your sisters to the best of my ability, and I am and will be an upmost citizen in your community. You have nothing to worry about. I do owe you a thank you for your assistance the other day when I came across your bull. I promise to be more careful in the future." She would not list out all the other times he'd come to her rescue. Already she owed him too much.

"Now, if you'll excuse me, I must ask you to leave so I may

start our lessons." She walked past him and stepped outside to ring the bell. Thankfully, all the men had left. Her hand reached for the rope and pulled.

My word, what will happen next?

* * *

She just gave him the cut? And what did she mean by, 'the world is not a safe place'? He glanced at his watch and winced. He had taken more of her time than he intended.

Obviously, she had been dealt a bad hand. What wasn't obvious was why he wanted to help her so much. It wasn't to pry or use the information against her. Why the fear in her eyes? What would take the apprehension away? Several scenarios swirled in his brain, all making him sick. Between his upbringing and having sisters to protect, he never had any inclination to behave in a rude manner, but some men didn't share those principles. He could only imagine what a young beauty such as Miss Carmichael could attract. Especially all alone. His sister's words echoed in his ears. "She's all alone, Luke. No family."

As he exited the schoolhouse, he placed his hat on his head and glanced in her direction even though she couldn't see him. "Have a nice day, Miss Carmichael. Thank you for your time."

He chuckled as she mumbled, "Thank you, Mr. Taylor."

The yard was now empty, but this morning's visitors would be back. With few women around, the local men swarmed anyone new, and even with the mayor's warning, they would follow her around and preen like Bert. She needed to protect herself. He told Martin that yesterday. Today, the need became more urgent.

Of course, now he didn't trust any of the men in town for

the job, except himself. He inwardly sighed as he climbed into the wagon. Why did he have this driving need to watch out for her? He groaned out loud and let his head fall back as he tried to ignore the excitement brewing inside of him at the thought of spending additional time with the feisty schoolteacher.

Nineteen

*I see how a woman could get swept away with offers of marriage.
I'm thankful for Mr. Martin's rules. Some of the men look at me as if
I'm something they want to devour, and it puts me on edge.*

—From the journal of Olivia Carmichael

L uke drove straight to Arthur's office on Main Street. After parking the wagon, he marched right over to the yellow-painted structure and swung open the door, reluctantly catching the attention of Mary Ellen, Arthur's assistant.

"Good morning, Mary Ellen." He removed his hat as he approached her desk.

Face flushed, she focused all her attention on him. "Good morning, Luke. What brings you in this morning? I haven't seen you in a while."

"I need to talk with Arthur." He ignored her last statement since he purposely stayed away from Mary Ellen as much as possible. She'd been one of the females who'd been trying to catch his eye over the past year, and he didn't want to give her any encouragement.

She leaned over her desk and batted her eyelashes. "He's in his office. Go ahead in. He'll be happy to see you."

"Thank you." He strode down the hall, knocked on the open door, then poked his head inside. "Hi, Arthur. Do you have a minute?"

Arthur stood and waved Luke inside. "Hi, Luke. Come in."

Luke closed the door behind him.

"Ah, so this is a private matter. Take a seat. Tell me what's on your mind. This isn't about your advertisement for a mail-order bride, is it? Don't know why you won't find one the old-fashioned way."

Luke closed his eyes for a moment before he sat in one of the two leather chairs facing Arthur's desk. In all the turmoil, he'd completely forgotten about Evelyn. Guilt overtook him, and he lost some of his bravado.

Focused on his hat in his hands, he chuckled. "I wish I never mentioned my plans to you. Necessary for family, you know."

"Only you would think marriage necessary, Luke. You told me because someone needed to know your plans, just in case. And you know I'm not one to judge."

Luke did know. They shared the same loss since Luke's pa had been Arthur's long-time friend. After his death, Arthur took Luke under his wing, and even though he gave Luke the space to be his own man, he was always available to listen and offer advice when asked.

"For your information, I replied to one of the ladies, but haven't heard back. If all goes well, she'll be packing her things and on a train within the month. But that's not why I'm here. I'm here because of Miss Carmichael."

Arthur raised one brow.

"Don't mix the two topics. My future bride's name is Evelyn, and she's very interested in raising Caroline and Rose."

Arthur chuckled.

Luke ignored him. "I won't say any more on the matter. Instead, I came to continue our conversation from yesterday. Miss Carmichael needs a protector, sooner than later."

Arthur studied Luke. "Ah, yes. Why a protector? What gives you the idea she is not safe?"

"I'm worried she'll be pressured into marriage, like the last teacher."

"Can't. She signed a contract. But keep explaining. What happened to bring you hustling in here this morning?"

"No one cares about your rules or a slip of paper. When I drove the girls in this morning, a group of men were introducing themselves to her, dressed in their Sunday best. When I got closer—"

"Did you join the line too?" Arthur smirked.

"Arthur, I'm serious." Luke crossed his arms. "Those men made her uncomfortable."

"Luke—"

"What if she was at the schoolhouse alone, and someone made advances she couldn't stop?" He shouldn't suggest such a thing, but he wanted Arthur to take this seriously.

Arthur was quiet for a few moments, "I think Miss Carmichael is fully capable of taking care of herself. Together, the men will hold each other accountable. Most of our men here are harmless. I appreciate your concern, Luke. But I'd be careful. People may think you're claiming dibs for yourself."

He ignored the suggestion. "Harmless?" asked Luke.

"Okay, there are a few who concern me." He frowned. "And I worry when she's alone. But since she's staying with us currently, we're watching out for her."

"Whose house does she go to next?" asked Luke.

"After us, she moves to the Woodwards'. I trust them to protect her too."

Luke examined his hat again. Why did he care so much? Was he blowing this out of proportion? Arthur had her best interest in mind. He couldn't shake the sense something was wrong. "I know what I saw, Arthur. Fear. I got the feeling something has happened in her past."

"What do you mean?"

"I don't know. Just an instinct."

"You and your instinct, Luke, gets you in all sorts of trouble." Arthur sat still, absorbed in thought. "Yet, in most cases, it's right."

Not wanting Arthur suspicious about her for any reason, he continued, "I don't know if my instincts about her hiding something are correct. With no father or brother responsible for her, you're, in essence, her family. I felt you should know. You can't be with her all the time, so at least teach her to protect herself."

Arthur's hand stroked his chin. "An interesting idea, Luke. And something I already considered based on your comment yesterday. Today's situation brings more credibility to my idea. I'll talk with her tonight. Come see me tomorrow, and I'll let you know the plan."

"Thank you, sir," Luke said, as he stood.

"Oh, don't go 'sir-ing' me." He, too, stood, then stuck his hand out. "Good to see you, son. Say hi to Jimmy and the girls for me."

Luke shook Arthur's hand. "I will. Thanks for hearing me out." He saw himself out, passing Mary Ellen without a glance. He'd done his part, and now Arthur Martin would do his. His job protecting Miss Carmichael was complete.

At least that's what he kept telling himself the entire drive home.

* * *

AFTER DINNER, Olivia rocked back and forth in the chair on the front porch, enjoying the fresh fall air, while the Martins sat side-by-side in their porch swing. These moments spent with them soothed her and filled an emotional hole in her heart. Yet, inside she knew she must mention what happened this morning at the schoolhouse.

She now knew the list of rules was not only meant to prevent her from certain activities, but it was also to protect her. Which meant something else entirely and she needed to know why.

"I had several visitors at the schoolhouse this morning. Why would a group of single men introduce themselves to me at school?"

Chrissy gasped, then exchanged glances with Mr. Martin.

So, there was something. Olivia charged forward. "At first I thought I might be in trouble."

"Trouble?" Chrissy stopped the swing. "What type of trouble would you be in, my dear?"

"I would hope none, but I don't know," Olivia answered honestly. "The entire situation was surreal. As if they wanted my favor, but I know the rules clearly state otherwise. I would assume they all know this."

Mr. Martin visibly sighed. "You're right. They do."

Mrs. Martin cleared her throat. Loudly. Then glared at Mr. Martin.

Mr. Martin didn't look at all surprised. "I didn't want to scare you off, but I realize now you need to know. And I promise to raise this with the men again."

Olivia had heard this area was considered wild for women. Stories were shared of men who proposed quickly without courting and then left their new wives at the homestead while they headed back to the mines or other jobs. She thought the tales exaggerated. Until now.

"Arthur, by the look on her face, you're frightening her. You need to tell her all of it." Chrissy reached for Olivia's hand.

Olivia's stomach tightened.

"Well, we have a problem in these parts," Mr. Martin cleared his throat. "There are more men than women, and as soon as someone new appears, the men pursue her. The next thing anyone knows, all those offers coerce the lady into marriage."

Her stomach dropped. She wouldn't ever be safely on the shelf here. The men wouldn't leave her alone, even if she had signed a contract. Some of the comments she received this morning now made much more sense.

Mr. Martin stood and paced, "When our first teacher arrived, the men overwhelmed her the moment she came to town. Basically, she became betrothed before we even met her, let alone got her into the classroom. And school rules dictate—"

"Young ladies may not teach if they're married." Olivia finished for him.

"Correct. We made sure no one knew you were here until we met you, and you signed the agreement. The night before we met in Sacramento, I held a town meeting and explained all the rules. I thought that would be enough, but I think curiosity got the better of folks as the children sang your praises." He chuckled lightly.

Olivia processed what Mr. Martin said. "The children are saying good things, then? No one is unhappy with me?" Hope surged in her heart.

Chrissy squeezed her hand. "Whatever would give you the idea people were unhappy, dear? You need to have more belief in yourself and God's plans. You're here for a reason, you know."

Olivia blinked. She wasn't here for any reason other than this is where she chose to be. But she wouldn't be rude and say so. The Martins had been nothing but kind to her.

"It's nice to know the children are happy. I've heard them mumble a few things during lessons, so I wondered if they went home and complained."

"Oh, I didn't say the children haven't complained." Chrissy laughed.

Olivia frowned. "But?"

"What I *said*, dear, is the children are happy with you. They like you."

They like you.

Olivia hadn't realized how important those three words were until she heard them.

Her fingers tightened on Chrissy's hand. "Thank you for telling me."

"Oh, Olivia, take a look around you. You can tell by their faces."

"Excuse me." Mr. Martin cleared his throat. "To get back to the topic at hand. With all this attention from the men folk, I'm afraid you may not have the freedom to walk around unescorted. And I don't know if the room addition you asked for would be wise before you learn some basic skills. Have you ever shot a rifle?"

"No!" The idea of handling a gun terrified her. "Why would I need to shoot a rifle?"

"Driven a wagon?" he asked.

She spoke a little more softly. "No."

"Can you ride a horse?"

Olivia gripped Chrissy's hand tighter at the thought of

climbing on a horse again. "I'm sure riding a horse is not necessary," she whispered.

"Actually, my dear, it is. And I have a plan. Be prepared for some lessons of your own after school this week."

Olivia kept silent. She would have to handle whatever was asked of her, especially if it meant she would ultimately be independent. If she could leave her previous life behind and move west on her own, she could survive anything.

Her mind drifted to the morning, and she shivered. All those men had made her uncomfortable. Except for one. Why? Because Mr. Taylor hadn't used his proximity for any personal gains, and instead, found a way to extricate her from the fray. A habit of his to be there at the right time. But she couldn't depend on him nor show weakness in his presence.

She needed the upper hand.

Maybe the lessons Mr. Martin mentioned would help her be able to do that. She would learn what was necessary to stay self-sufficient, safe, and keep her job in the process. And then, she'd never need to be rescued by Mr. Luke Taylor again.

Twenty

I don't want a repeat of this morning. I was terrified and uncomfortable. I can't afford to be distracted. My life depends on staying focused on my plans.

—From the journal of Olivia Carmichael

Olivia cautiously peeked around the building. To her relief, no wagons, horses, or scores of men stood in the field next to the schoolhouse. She heard a loud crackle behind her and jumped. Bert stood, flapping his wings and clucking at her.

"*Shh,*" she said. "Oh, why am I talking to you? You don't understand anything I'm saying."

Bert folded his wings, ducked his head, and cackled.

"What? I was making sure it was safe to proceed."

He scooted around her, leading the way toward the schoolhouse. Of course, it was clear for him, but was it harmless for her? Bert continued a few paces, turned, and squawked.

"Okay, okay, I'm coming," she hissed at him. "If anyone asks, I'm not following you." She raised her chin and jetted past him. Bert clucked as he scurried past her, so she let him lead. Every few steps he'd stop and look over his shoulder.

Once at the schoolhouse, he waddled over to the tree stump, jumped onto the top, and crowed "*Cock-a-doodle-doo*."

"Bert! No!" She had had enough undue attention yesterday.

He flapped his wings, but thankfully crowed no more.

Her boots echoed in the quiet as she entered, then preceded to open the windows to let the brisk morning air cool the room. She faced the blackboard and wrote the lessons for the day. Loud to her ears, the scraping of the chalk reminded her that neither Teddy nor Emily had arrived. Their absence should've bolstered her, but it didn't.

She had requested they take a few days off, allowing her full responsibilities for preparing for the day. But even though this was what she asked, the loneliness permeated the schoolhouse. Only the faint sounds of Bert's clucking brought a small amount of comfort that she wasn't alone.

Not much later, a loud crow amidst shouting erupted in the yard. She ran toward the open window. Bert stood on his perch, flapping his wings and squawking. A small cluster of students stood nearby, a look of horror on their faces, while Susannah, the oldest student, had a protective hand on Sally's shoulder.

Teddy held back a growling Andrew, while May held her fists high and shouted at him. "You're a bully, Andrew. Stop picking on my sister!" Nine-years-old, May constantly lashed out at anyone who came near her younger sister, Sally. Olivia suspected she did the same at home.

"Am not." Andrew pointed at Sally. "She started it." A young leader at ten, Andrew had a tendency to see things with no gray area in between.

"*Nuh-uh.* You did. You said I wasn't any good at ball. Meany," Sally cried, tears streaming down her face.

Susannah whispered something in Sally's ear, but Olivia couldn't make out the words.

Andrew threw his hands in the air. "But it's the truth. Teacher says we're to always tell the truth." He looked at Teddy. "She came at me. We aren't supposed to hit each other." He glared back at May. "But I'll hit back if I have to, even a girl."

Olivia picked up her skirt and ran out the door. "Children, please." She hurried off the porch steps and across the yard. "Andrew and May, come with me. Susannah, please look after Sally. Everyone else, line up."

The children hustled into their positions as she led the duo to the side. Andrew and May continued glaring at each other, then May stuck out her tongue. A lead weight pitted in Olivia's stomach. Even with authority, she hoped not to have to use the discipline stick. She swallowed and chose her words carefully.

"Yes, one should not lie, nor hit. But Andrew, one should not point out another person's faults either. Sometimes, we need to keep our opinions to ourselves. What is the point in saying what you said? If you're frustrated, then all you're doing is trying to make the other person feel bad because you feel bad. So, in a way it was mean for you to say those words to Sally. Do you understand?"

Andrew scrunched his face. "But how do you know when it's okay to say something and when it's not?"

"What a great question, Andrew. It's not always easy. But we shouldn't judge each other. Judgment hurts. Do you understand?"

Andrew breathed deeply, then swallowed. "Yes, Miss Carmichael."

She focused on May next, who held a smug look on her face. "May, one should never hit another, either. Ever."

The torment on May's face broke Olivia's heart. "Unless one deserves it!" she yelled.

Olivia kept her voice calm. "When does someone deserve to be hit?"

"When they are hitting you first," May answered without any pause.

"I didn't hit you," yelled Andrew.

"Did so," she yelled back.

What should she do? Both fought. Both made a mistake. The rules state quite clearly arguing during recess required lashings, but weren't lashings the same as hitting? And after this interchange, how could she strike either of them?

She wouldn't be any better than what May claimed.

Who decides what's deserving behavior and what's not? And why was she making this complicated? She had a job to do, and whether she liked some parts or not, she needed this job.

Olivia grabbed each by the arm. "I'm disappointed in your behavior. Both of you. You will sit for a time in the corner while I get the rest of the class's lessons started. And then," she swallowed, trying to keep her voice steady, "there will be lashings."

Andrew hung his head while May narrowed her eyes in defiance. Olivia had no choice. If she didn't set her boundaries now, it would be harder to keep order during class. Maybe this experience would encourage the children to behave well enough she wouldn't have to dole out lashings again.

Why did the sense of control always seem out of reach? She couldn't control the men wanting to court her. She couldn't control her student's feelings. She couldn't control the outcome of her parents' deaths. So many things a person couldn't control. Like how her father's choices affected her life.

And no matter what she did, she had to live within the rules someone else made. It wasn't fair.

She didn't want to have to enforce rules she didn't make. All she wanted was to teach quietly and mind her own business. Why couldn't life go as planned?

LUKE PARKED the buckboard in front of Arthur's office and secured the reins, stifling a yawn. He laid awake most of the night staring at his ceiling, restless. Whenever he closed his eyes, he saw big blue eyes with a hint of fear in them. A person had to have experienced something horrible to know that type of fear.

Even his sisters mentioned how distracted she was after all the men finally left, although who could blame her? Caroline mentioned Miss Carmichael tried to write on the blackboard with the eraser instead of chalk, and at lunchtime, she gathered the bucket of wood shavings instead of her own lunch pail.

He didn't want to be, but he was worried about her. He'd like to say it was as simple as caring for a neighbor, but what he felt was more. Somewhere, in the short amount of time he'd known her, she'd crawled under his armor, and now he couldn't walk away. He wanted to protect her. But what from?

He hoped Arthur had some answers.

"You were right, Luke. Yesterday's events spooked Olivia," Arthur said as Luke entered his office. "Have a seat. I have an idea."

Luke sat and crossed his arms.

Arthur looked at him steadily. "I think she needs a protector, and I think it should be you."

Luke narrowed his eyes and shook his head. "Arthur, I—"

"Now don't get your feathers ruffled," said Arthur. "Any other man I would consider can't afford the time away from their ranches with their children already missing chores due to school. Yes, you have a ranch to run, but we both know Jimmy can handle things." He held up his hand halting Luke's protest. "You would be perfect because you don't have a wife to be home for—yet—and you're a parent, so you have a vested interest. I trust you, Luke. Only you. I know you would never do anything untoward."

Luke uncrossed and recrossed his arms. The words meant a lot to him. To have men in his life who knew him. Trusted him. "I ..." He looked away and his heartbeat galloped in his chest. He'd have time with Miss Carmichael. But, should he? He glanced back at Arthur. "What about your rules? Aren't the other men going to see this as breaking them? You know, when I came here yesterday, I had no intention—"

"Oh, I know you had no ulterior motive, which makes you perfect for the job. You care for your sisters deeply and want to make sure their teacher stays safe. No one here knows you have a mail-order bride on the way, but if they did, it would help."

"No. I don't want anyone to know yet. I have yet to hear her decision on my offer." He shifted in his seat. "And I don't want the girls to know and have time to sabotage my plans."

Arthur chuckled. "Okay, then. We will have to do this another way. But some people might get the wrong idea. And I'm okay with that because I know the truth. I'll announce Miss Carmichael is allowed to spend time with you and your sisters and give my permission for you to teach her how to ride and shoot."

His mouth went dry. "Don't you think people will think I'm courting her?"

Arthur nodded. "They might. There's only one way to dispel the notion, and you're not ready." He winced. "And ...

maybe if it looks like you have a claim on her, the other men will drop their cause."

Luke's head swam. "Don't you think this plan would encourage others to not play by the rules?"

"I don't think so. Especially if I have given my blessing. And they know we're close. They wouldn't cross both of us. I think it's the best way to protect her and for her to learn the skills she needs. You don't mind spending time with her, do you? You said yourself you weren't interested in courting her."

Luke sat stunned. Well, shoot, he had said those words, because, well, that's what he should say. Needed to say for both of their sakes. The way things should be. But when he was around her, his heart betrayed that line of thinking.

Could he spend more time in her company and not be affected?

There was one more person to consider. "What about Miss Carmichael? She won't like this. She's a stickler for the rules, and this job is important to her."

"She's made it very clear she has no intentions of ever marrying. I think eventually she will, but in her eyes right now, it's not an option. I don't think this will be an issue." Arthur grinned, the matter resolved in his eyes.

Luke blinked. She didn't plan on *ever* getting married? He didn't know a single girl who didn't dream of finding a beau to marry one day. What female declared that?

One who had been hurt by someone, that's who.

Still, to choose to live on her own? Women weren't allotted much in the eyes of men, even though, in California, a woman could own a business. What happened to make her not want a husband? His protective instincts reared. Who hurt her—and how?

"Don't say anything." Arthur headed for the door. "Come with me, and we'll take care of this right now."

What was Arthur up to? Curiosity won out as he followed Arthur out to the street and then to the Rooster Café. Luke counted at least fifteen men as he entered, many of whom were at the schoolhouse the day before.

"Arthur!" Several men near the door raised their hands in greeting. "Hi, Luke."

Luke lifted his hand in response. And then waited.

"Hey folks," Arthur called out. "Listen."

The place quieted immediately.

Arthur put his hands on his hips. "I understand some of you went to meet our new schoolteacher yesterday."

Several pairs of eyes grew wide.

"For every action, there's a reaction. So, given your move yesterday, I'm now assigning a family as hers, so to speak. Rules still stand. No courting. But she's now a part of the Taylor family and can be seen coming and going with Luke, Caroline, and Rose."

Dead silence.

"Luke will be teaching her how to ride and shoot. This is fully sanctioned by me. If you see them together, it's nothing." He turned his head toward Luke and nodded.

Luke caught the 'we're done here' nod and headed toward the door.

"I could make her a part of my family. Why does he git to?" Harry slurred out.

The hair on the back of Luke's neck prickled. He turned and faced the town drunk, who stood in the corner, leaning heavily against the wall.

Then, Chester stood. "I could teach her things. I haven't had a job in over a month and have the time. You don't even have to pay me." Luke cringed at his wicked smile. "A service to the town." Tall, smart, and handsome, Chester was lazier than a lizard lying in the sun too long. No way would Luke allow Chester anywhere close to Miss Carmichael.

Another man stood, but Arthur cut him off before he spoke. "There's no way I'm going to let any of you yahoos be responsible for her. Not after your little display yesterday. So, get those fancy notions out of your heads."

Groans and protests filled the room. "*Ow*, come on. We didn't do anything wrong, Mayor. We just wanted to introduce ourselves."

Arthur took two steps farther inside the cafe and glared at the men. "Actually, you did do something wrong. You frightened her. So, no, absolutely not. And you will not complain, either. Luke here is the best option for several reasons." He lifted his hand and held up three fingers. "He's a parent, he's trustworthy, and he's not interested in finding a wife."

Luke winced. How pathetic he sounded. Even though true, mostly.

He appreciated the few "Yeah, right" comments he heard in the din.

"We all got to 'elp in her ed-u-c-a-shun." Harry interjected.

"The decision is made gentlemen. I've prayed and am at peace with my decision."

No one could argue when a man 'had a peace' about his decision. People trusted Arthur and his faith. Luke had just been given a complete blessing for Miss Carmichael to be under his protection.

He was pretty sure Miss Carmichael didn't want this anymore than he did. So, for both their sakes, moving forward quickly would be best. Should be pretty simple. All he had to do was teach her to shoot a gun and ride a horse. No problem.

Luke held back a grin. He wouldn't let anyone know how much he looked forward to the prospect.

Twenty-One

*I never expected the overwhelming love I feel for my students. Each
one is different and special in my eyes. I never paid attention to
children before. The idea of doling out lashings to any of them is
harder than I thought possible. But how else will I keep order if I
don't discipline? I don't look forward to the day I have to use the
switch. Hopefully, it won't be soon.*

—From the journal of Olivia Carmichael

Olivia sat on her bed, her face in her hands, sobbing.

"Child, whatever is the matter?" The bed dipped as Chrissy sat next to her.

She gulped in air to stop her tears, but a sob escaped anyway. She felt horrible for giving lashings to Andrew and May, but what else could she have done? She had to follow the rules. But she never expected how doing so would affect her. It took every ounce of her resolve to hold herself together until school ended.

She didn't want to be seen as weak nor give anyone a reason to fire her. Why was this so hard?

"Tell me, Olivia," Chrissy insisted. "Whatever it is can't be all that bad."

She tried to find something other than the truth and latched onto the first plausible reason. "It ... It's nothing. Just a bit of homesickness."

Chrissy placed her arm around Olivia. "Ah. I understand. I'm sure things are different here. You must've left friends and family behind. I can't imagine doing what you've done. You're very brave."

Olivia leaned into Chrissy and cried harder. She *was* homesick. Various sounds and smells drifted through her mind, and the yearning in her heart ached with the need for familiarity. For her mother's piano playing, taking cook's meals in the kitchen, and laughing with friends before her circumstances changed.

But she didn't feel brave. Not the way Chrissy stated. She made Olivia out to be someone noble who put others ahead of herself, which was far from the truth. Her decisions, her actions, were to protect herself.

"I didn't have any choice," she blurted out and then burst into more tears.

Chrissy hugged her tightly and hummed. Olivia recognized the hymn immediately as one she remembered from her childhood. She sobbed more.

"Oh, my sweet child. I'm sorry to upset you further. I was reaching out to the good Lord in song to comfort you. God wants us to worship Him in all things, even when we're sad. But since it hurt more, would you mind if I prayed instead?" she asked.

Olivia held her breath. A hiccup escaped.

No one had ever asked permission to pray for her. Prayer

was private and not discussed, wasn't it? And did she want prayers? Would they even help, if God had abandoned her?

Her head rubbed against the older woman's shoulder with her answer.

"Dear Lord." Chrissy pulled her close to her side. "Our dear Olivia has so much sadness in her heart. Please wrap Your arms around her and fill her with Your love. Help her to see she's not alone here. That there are people here who care. And show her You care and will help carry her through this difficult time. Amen."

Silence engulfed the room as an odd peace filled the air. Olivia kept her face averted, embarrassed to have such an intimate prayer spoken out loud.

Chrissy didn't seem to mind. She just held on to Olivia and breathed deeply. A few minutes later she released her snug hold and ran her fingers through Olivia's hair.

The tugging and tingling flooded her with memories of her mother, and silent tears dripped down her face.

"Now, why don't you tell me about your ma and pa?"

Olivia flinched. Could she share without revealing too much? Even a little? Recollections filtered through her mind. "There's not much to tell. They both died in a carriage accident."

Awkward silence.

"Are you an only child?" asked Chrissy.

Olivia used the back of her hand to swipe her face. "Yes."

"Were you and your parents close?"

Olivia trembled. "I always thought so. I had what every little girl desired—a lady's education and a lovely home." A home abruptly taken away. Seeing families together here, and knowing she would never have a family again, left a hollow spot.

Chrissy continued to finger comb Olivia's hair. "I'm sure

your parents left provisions for you. What made you decide to sell to come west?"

How should she answer? Her father was an underhanded man of business? She didn't dare mention his sins, lest they pass judgement on her by association, much like her church family did back home.

Her sadness turned to anger. At the situation. At her father.

"I didn't sell anything. It was all taken away." She hung her head and said a little less forcefully, "As I said earlier, I didn't have a choice."

Olivia folded inside herself, waiting for the judgmental comments. To be pushed away. Instead, Chrissy squeezed and held her.

A small fissure of warmth flowed from the contact to her heart.

"It's obvious to me you have more to share, but I won't push you. Whenever you're ready, Olivia. I'll be here to listen and be a friend."

She'd never be ready. Not because she didn't want to, but because it wasn't safe. Where would she go if the trouble from Cincinnati followed her here?

Chrissy filled the silence. "I hope, in time, you'll feel comfortable to trust—if not me, then God—to help you through your hurt." She looked affectionately at Olivia as she rose from the bed. "I need to prepare supper, but know when you're ready to talk, I'll be here. You don't have to carry your burden alone. I'm here for you, Olivia, and I won't judge you, Neither will God. I do believe God brought you into my life like He brought me into yours."

Olivia sat stunned as a multitude of emotions warred inside. Could she trust Chrissy Martin? Her actions supported her words, and she had shown herself to be trustworthy. But, why should God get the credit? His lack of help *was* the reason Olivia had to come here in the first place.

A small seed of strength straightened her spine. Her own actions are what rendered results. Not some prayer or dependence on God. And she'd prove it. To everyone, including herself. And then Chrissy would see what Olivia knew.

* * *

AFTER SUPPER, Olivia sat on the porch swing rocking back and forth. The crickets' chirps filled the cool night air. Her tears long dried, she hugged her shawl tighter around her shoulders.

The screen door opened, and Chrissy appeared in the doorway, a tea tray in hand.

Olivia stood to help.

"Thank you, my dear. Beautiful night, isn't it?"

Olivia took her seat again. "Yes, yes it is."

"Are you feeling better?" Chrissy poured tea into two cups and sat in the adjacent wooden rocker.

"Yes." Her cheeks flamed as she focused past the porch to the street beyond. "Thank you for earlier."

"Don't mention it. I meant what I said. We can talk anytime. Even after you're no longer staying with us."

Olivia shoulders sagged. She didn't like the idea of living with different families throughout the school year. Would each family be as friendly and hospitable as the Martins?

"You plan to never marry, correct?" Chrissy asked.

The question startled her out of her thoughts. "Well, yes."

"May I ask why?"

"Do I have to have a reason?"

Chrissy studied her, then nodded. Which told Olivia she really didn't understand.

Chrissy sighed. "I do believe God designs some to never marry."

Why did Chrissy bring God into every conversation? She frowned. "God doesn't make people marry or not. People make those choices for themselves."

Chrissy didn't flinch at Olivia's accusatory tone. "I don't believe that, dear. God makes us all special and unique. He has a plan for each of us, whether we want to believe it or not."

Olivia pondered the words of this lovely woman, who was fast becoming a mother figure, if she allowed it. She swallowed the lump in her throat. If God *did* have a plan for her, why did it include destroying her life? He wasn't a very nice God to allow those things to happen.

Chrissy's lips formed into a smile. "You are a strong woman, Olivia. Don't let anyone tell you differently. But here in Washton, we look out for each other, depend on each other. Our only way to survive this harsh land. Don't shut people out. If you're so set on taking care of yourself the rest of your life, you'll need to learn how."

Olivia looked at her and raised her eyebrows.

"If you're going to live on your own, you'll need to be able to shoot a rifle, ride a horse, and drive a wagon."

Olivia shuddered at the thought of getting on a horse again. "Why? I've made it this far."

"Oh, but Arthur and I disagree with you."

Olivia brows furrowed. "Why?"

"You yourself have said you can't depend on any one person. Which means, in the case of an emergency, like a flood, a fire, or if, God forbid, one of your students gets hurt, you'll need to take care of the situation. Alone." She emphasized the last word. "Things, unfortunately, are not always civilized here in Washton. And as our town grows, more danger can intrude. And not only the four-legged kind."

Chrissy continued, her eyes never leaving Olivia's. "Mr. Martin met with folks today, and they agreed you should be taught basic skills." Chrissy leaned forward and patted Olivia's hand. "Never fear. You'll have the best teacher."

Olivia shifted, uncomfortable with what she might hear next. "Mr. Martin?" she asked.

"No, silly!" Chrissy touched Olivia on the knee and laughed. "Luke."

"Luke?" Olivia stood, and the front of the rocker bounced against her calves. "I ... I don't know if that's a good idea." She grasped for a reason, any reason. The contract. "What about my contract? I am not supposed to spend time in a single man's presence, alone."

"To be honest, several of the men already want to get to know you more than they should, so any of them would put you in a dangerous position. Arthur wants to protect you. And Luke has a vested interest in your safety because of his sisters, who, by the way, are expected to be there with you, so you won't be alone. There really isn't another man Arthur trusts more than Luke."

Olivia stepped to the banister and tightly gripped the railing. "That man infuriates me. He catches me at my worst. I don't like exposing any weaknesses to him."

Chrissy chuckled. "Then I suggest you learn quickly. The faster you learn, the shorter the lessons. He seems anxious to get them done quickly as well."

Olivia turned, her brows scrunched.

A smug smile crossed her lips. "Mr. Martin tells me he wasn't too happy about the assignment, either."

Was that supposed to make her feel better? *Ugh!* This man should not affect her so.

She gripped her hands together.

"I can see you're mulling over the idea. I suggest we pray

and see what the good Lord says. And while we're at it, we can pray for the means for your lodging at the schoolhouse too. That is what you want, correct?"

Before she could stop her, Chrissy prayed out loud. Right there on the porch.

Mortified, Olivia squeezed her eyes shut before she saw anyone, wishing the moment over quickly and not listening to a single word Chrissy uttered. When she said *Amen*, Chrissy raised her head and beamed at Olivia. "Things will work out, dear. You'll see. Nothing to worry about."

Olivia *did* worry. She worried about a lot of things. Her job, her students, and her future. And because she would never marry, she did need to be able to handle herself. Mr. Martin's idea was wise, even though it meant she'd spend extra time with Luke Taylor.

Why was she so hesitant? Was it pride? No, her pride had already been shredded to pieces, and she didn't fear hard work.

The sense of control? If so, she would be more in control once she learned these skills. So, why did she want to say no?

She inwardly gasped.

Her heart.

The organ in question pounded loudly in her chest, and a flush came over her body. Dipping her head to her chest for privacy she vowed to herself. She could not, would not, allow her heart to become engaged. She'd focus strictly on the tasks at hand. She could do this. She *would* do this.

She pulled back her shoulders and gave a curt nod.

Chrissy grinned.

They both might agree on the benefits of these lessons, but to prove herself the one in control, Olivia knew she would have to make sure neither God nor her heart would be involved.

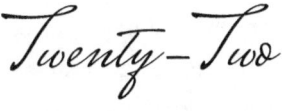

Twenty-Two

Why do I have to ride a horse? Walking is a perfectly good mode of transportation. I don't like horses, and they don't like me. If I have to get on a horse, someone is going to get hurt, and most likely, that someone will be me.

—From the journal of Olivia Carmichael

Luke leaned against the wagon in the schoolyard, waiting for school to end so he could start Miss Carmichael's first riding lesson. His sisters would stay and chaperone. He had argued having an audience would only embarrass her, but Arthur wouldn't budge. Arthur had stressed the importance of there being no question of impropriety.

How he got himself into this mess, he had no idea. Well, he did know. He shifted his stance. Martin trusted him. And he trusted himself more than anyone else. Which meant teaching her was his responsibility.

Although a side saddle was the accepted norm for a lady,

here in California, sitting astride was much more practical. His sisters could ride both ways. Not knowing any details of Miss Carmichael's preference or experience, he brought both types of saddles with him. But to sit astride, she needed to wear pants or a riding skirt. He had no idea if she owned either.

As the time grew near, he unhitched the horses and pulled out the gear from the back of the wagon. Children's voices filled the air as they piled out of the schoolhouse, leaped off the steps, and scattered in different directions.

Bert strutted around, pecking at some of their feet, then wandered over to the tree stump, jumped to the top, and crowed loudly. Focused on watching the rooster's display of dominance, Luke didn't notice his sisters approaching until tiny hands circled his waist.

"Hi, Luke." Caroline squeezed his stomach. "You won't believe what Miss Carmichael said today."

He raised his eyebrows.

"Miss Carmichael's afraid of horses."

"She is?" He glanced over and saw their subject creep toward them. Instead of a smile, there was a look of pure terror on her face. This may not go as he hoped. He patted his sister on the shoulder. "I appreciate the warning."

Miss Carmichael stopped a few feet away and glanced warily at the horses.

"Ready for your lesson?" He added as much encouragement he could muster.

She nodded absently.

He had his work cut out for him.

The girls climbed into the wagon, and he touched Miss Carmichael's hand. She was so focused on the horse that she didn't even flinch, even though he felt a zing of energy simmer between them.

He tugged her closer to the horse. "I want you to meet Arabella."

"What a beautiful name." Her wooden reply contrasted with her words.

"She's a beautiful horse. I picked her for you today because of her temperament."

She turned her head sharply, her eyes narrowed. "What's that supposed to mean?"

The girls giggled in the background.

Good. Feistiness he could work with. He bent his knees and looked directly into her eyes. "It means, she has a gentle beautiful spirit, so she won't frighten you."

She glanced back at Arabella. "Oh."

He cleared his throat and continued. "When you walk near a horse, talk to her in soothing tones."

"Why do I need to talk to the horse?" she asked, raising her hand to touch Arabella's neck.

"Because you'll want to reassure her. Otherwise, she'll sense your fear."

She stiffened. "I'm not afraid."

Great, he just reminded her of her fear. "Miss Carmichael, please. Just do what I ask."

She scowled at him.

"You need to learn to ride, correct?"

She pulled her hand away and glared at him. "I didn't choose this. Why do I need to ride?"

Luke sighed, pulled off his hat, and ran his hand through his hair. Teaching a reluctant rider was next to impossible. He watched her pet Arabella as Arthur's words echoed in his mind. He needed to find a way to make her want to learn.

He put his hat back on his head. "Look, Miss Carmichael, if an emergency came up—"

"What type of emergency?"

"*Any* emergency." He reached deep for additional patience. "And you need to get help fast. You would need to ride a horse."

When she didn't respond, he turned and faced her more fully. Her brows scrunched together as she stared at the ground.

"What if there were no horses around?" She spoke so softly, he had to lean in. "I don't even own a horse or have the means to own one, let alone keep one—"

"Olivia!" At this rate, they would never get her on a horse.

She placed her hands on her hips. "I did not give you permission to use my Christian name."

Using his 'talking to a spooked horse' voice, he said, "Please forgive me, Miss Carmichael. Mr. Martin asked me to teach you to ride, and he's asked you to learn to ride. This was not my idea. Do you want to tell the Martins tonight how the lesson went, or do you want to explain how uncooperative you were? Now quit stalling and let's get this lesson over with." He stormed around to the other side of the horse.

She eyed him suspiciously through the dangling reins.

The girls piped in, "Come on Miss Carmichael. You can do it."

She jumped, then gazed over her shoulder, her face radiating the affection she had for his sisters. His heart clenched. What he wouldn't do to be on the receiving end of that smile.

He cleared his throat and focused on tightening the reins.

She swung back, her smile now forced. "Put in that context, I wouldn't want to jeopardize my job."

Always the job with her. Luke didn't know whether to be thankful she'd become the teacher or not. If she hadn't taken the job, he wouldn't be standing here in her presence. He glanced at Caroline and Rose. His sisters wouldn't be excited about school, either. And they would kill him if he did anything to hurt her. "I don't want to do anything to jeopardize your position either, Miss Carmichael. We are on the same side here. So, are you ready to truly begin?"

"I suppose so. Since it means that much to you."

Oh, believe me, it does, he wanted to say, but he answered her with, "You have no idea," instead.

* * *

OLIVIA LIKED ANIMALS. From a distance. As a little girl, she enjoyed watching horses pull carriages and begged her father to let her learn to ride. Her parents told her she needed to be older. She pleaded over and over and finally, her father relented.

But her one riding lesson turned into a complete catastrophe. Her father hired one of his employees to teach her with a semi-lame, untrained horse. The horse threw her, and when she landed, she broke her leg. She stayed in bed for the rest of the season and promised herself she would never go near the beasts again.

Now, here she stood, next to one. *Never say never, Olivia. I never thought I would move far away, nor work a job that required me to ride a horse. But here I am. I can do this. Just as the other things I've learned, I can do this.* She sunk her teeth into her bottom lip and briefly wondered if her trepidation came from the horse or the man teaching her to ride the horse.

"Ready to get on?" Luke's strong voice rang in her left ear.

She jumped and quickly covered her mouth to hold in her shout, but the movement caused her to bump into his chest. He placed his hands on her shoulders. Heat radiated down her arms.

"Whoa, there. I got you," he whispered.

She whirled around. "I am *not* a horse."

He furrowed his brow. "I never said you were." He studied her face. "What did I say?"

"You said, 'Whoa there.'" She fisted her hands and glared. Much easier to be mad at him than to admit whatever it was she felt when in his proximity, so she let the anger take over. "Aren't those words you say to a horse?"

He laughed out loud. "Oh, honey. That's what all us ranchers say to everything."

She stomped her foot and crossed her arms. She knew she looked childish, but she didn't care. "Now you're laughing at me."

Pulling his hat off and hitting it against his thigh, he studied the headgear before answering. "I'm not laughing at you, just at your thinking." He grinned and his entire face lit, which left her with an unsettled stomach.

Better to stay mad than feel those butterflies again. "That is laughing at me." She swiveled and walked away.

He grabbed her upper arm and turned her around. To her satisfaction, he no longer grinned, but his eyes were clouded and stormy. "Doesn't matter. We need to get on with your lesson." He motioned with his hand.

She sighed. He was right, of course. She didn't want to be here right now but making things challenging wouldn't help either of them. "You're right. The faster we do this, the faster we're done." She approached Arabella, allowing the anger to still brew beneath the surface. Anger made things easier to forget her fear.

The horse stepped sideways.

He came and stood at her right. "You'll need to calm down first. She can sense your emotions."

Great. Now the horse would judge her.

"First we need to fix your seat."

She placed her hand on her lower back. "My what?"

"Seat. That's what we ranch folk call the saddle on the horse you're riding. The saddle needs to be secured correctly, or you and the saddle could fall right off. And we wouldn't want that to happen," he said dryly.

"No, we would not." She sobered. "Maybe I should learn to drive a wagon instead?"

"Oh, we'll get to that lesson too. But in these parts, you'll need to ride horseback to cover more distance faster."

She'd like to forget the saddle part and just go. Far away. Far away from him.

Luke pulled on the leather ties beneath the horse. "Now see how the cinch is pulled tight? This keeps the saddle from going upside down. Once it's tight, you can mount. Step into my hands." He kneeled, laced his hands, and held them out to form a step.

She held in her groan and bit her bottom lip again with her teeth. Could she handle more contact? What if her skirt lifted? No, she couldn't. At this rate, she might draw blood soon. "Um. Is there another way?"

He squinted at her with those dashing brown eyes. The unsettled feeling in her stomach jolted and pinned her in place.

One side of his lips quirked. "No. This is how it's done. Just put your left foot in my hands, and I'll give you a boost."

Olivia held her breath and placed her foot into his cupped hands.

He shifted his body. "Hold my shoulders while I lift you."

Distracted by his closeness, she acted without thought. The next thing she knew, she rose into the air. She squeaked and gripped his shoulders hard. "Put me down, put me down," she cried out.

"Okay." He unceremoniously dumped her into the saddle, his hands holding her legs in place.

Stunned, she didn't move.

The horse fidgeted.

"Whoa, girl." Was he speaking to her or the horse?

"Miss Carmichael, you need to relax."

She spoke through clenched teeth. "I am relaxed."

The horse nickered and flicked her head.

"No, you're not. Arabella can tell. Take a deep breath. Relax your body. You're gripping too hard." His voice remained calm, but the urgency was clear.

Olivia closed her eyes, willing herself to relax. Slowly, she dropped her shoulders and relaxed her legs. The horse bent to graze.

"Better," said Luke. "Now that you're in the saddle, how does it feel?"

She opened her eyes and peered to each side. "The ground is a long way down."

He chuckled, the sound in stark contrast to his earlier frustration. He bowed his head, and all she could see was the top of his big brown hat.

She wrinkled her nose. "What's so funny?"

Slowly he raised his head until she saw underneath the brim. The gleam in his eyes told her he found this amusing, but something else lurked there as well.

"Your expression is what's funny." He smirked. "It's clear you've never sat on a horse before, and you're frightened."

"Well for your information, I *have* been on a horse before." Warmth radiated throughout her body when she saw the surprised look on his face. "But I fell off, broke my leg, and never went on one again." Then she raised her voice. "And I'm *not* scared!"

He raised an eyebrow.

Why couldn't he understand how hard this was for her? "Okay. So maybe I'm a little scared." She couldn't stop herself. "I had nightmares for months. I've never let myself be in situations where I'm not in control. Control is good. I like to be in control. And it's more challenging to stay in control when perched on top of this very large animal."

Much to her dismay, he didn't help her get off. Instead, he handed her the reins.

"Ah. But you *are* the one in control. The horse will follow your command and sense what you feel. If you feel fear, she feels fear. If you show trust, she will completely trust you. She will follow you wherever you take her. You two can become one if you allow it, and she will never leave your side. She'd even protect you, if you let her."

He said this last part in a whisper as their eyes met.

The horse shifted, and her body moved to match the sway.

Approval shined in his eyes. He broke the connection to look over Arabella and then back at her.

"Yay!" yelled Caroline and Rose. "You did it!"

"You're a natural." He winked.

Again, the horse shifted. Olivia moved her body to match. Joy flooded her limbs all the way to her toes. She grinned back at him, his eyes dancing like they did the first day they met. A fissure of fear tried to break through the joy, but she couldn't pull her gaze away. Maybe she didn't have as much control over things as she thought.

Twenty-Three

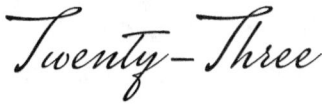

Good thing I have decided to never marry. No one would want me as a wife. I don't know how to cook or sew, I talk to roosters, anger bulls, and can't ride a horse.

—From the journal of Olivia Carmichael

Luke closed his mouth. Where did those philosophical words about trust and friendship come from? And what exactly was he trying to say?

She didn't react negatively, so maybe his words weren't as awkward as he thought.

He checked her seat one more time. "Much better. Already you can see Arabella trusting you. Now stroke her neck. Tell her she's a good girl."

Olivia tentatively leaned over and touched Arabella's neck. "Good girl, Arabella. We girls have to stick together, right?" she cooed, turning her head toward Luke. "Like this?"

Luke stood still, watching her connect with his horse.

"Do you think she can understand the words I say?"

He chuckled. "I'd like to think so. Many men have had long conversations with their horses."

A cute little dimple appeared on her right cheek as she smiled. "Do you have conversations with your horse, Mr. Taylor?"

"I told you, Mr. Taylor is my father. Call me Luke. And yep, sure do."

A spontaneous laugh filled the air. Something flared to life inside him.

She patted the horse again. "Oh, Arabella, if only you could talk. I'd love to hear what you and Mr. Taylor have had conversations about."

Luke ignored her inquiry. "Now that you're saddled and ready to go, I'm going to walk you back and forth to the fence one time."

She gripped the reins and blew out a breath. "Okay."

"You'll do fine. Just holler if you get scared or anything." Luke instantly knew he had chosen the wrong words. Miss Carmichael pulled on the reins and clenched her legs, making Arabella jolt sideways and run into him.

"Whoa. Careful, girl." He first soothed both horse and rider, then bent to pick up his hat.

In that split second, Miss Carmichael yanked on the reins again, forcing Arabella to step back. Panic flitted across Miss Carmichael's face as Luke reached for the harness. She screamed and Arabella bucked, knocking him to the ground.

A heavy weight rammed onto his chest, knocking his breath out and pinning him down. He heard lots of shrieking, but he couldn't maneuver anything since his arms were completely immobilized.

When the noise stopped, he focused on his breathing first. He still couldn't inhale deeply, and his arms pinched to the point the tingling sensations went all the way to his hands. He opened his eyes and saw nothing but white. Relief swept through him that Miss Carmichael was sprawled across him and not his horse. He heard a nicker, then a snort. A wet muzzle nudged the right side of his head, and the shrieking commenced.

When he opened his mouth to yell, layers of cotton stuck to his lips. He puffed a ruffle off his lips, and then bellowed, "Miss Carmichael! Miss Carmichael, please! I need you to calm down."

Giggles grew louder as Caroline and Rose reached them.

"I can't calm down. Did you see what that beast did? She threw me off. She doesn't like me. I told you this was not a good idea."

"Miss Car—"

"—I'm never going—"

One arm broke free and Luke pulled the material away from his face. "Olivia!"

Silence reverberated across the field. Tears streamed down her face. With his free hand, he reached and wiped away one on her cheek. "I'm sorry." Pitiful, but all he could think to say.

She blinked and looked away.

The girls tugged her off of him. "Miss Carmichael, are you okay?"

He knew exactly when she realized she was lying on top of him, on the ground, in the dirt. She scrambled to get her feet underneath and pushed hard on his stomach. He held back a groan, not wanting to spook her further.

She sniffled. "Y ... Y ... Yes, I'm fine. I think."

While she shook off the dirt from her dress, Luke took inventory of what body parts could move. The tingling in his limbs subsided. He cautiously twisted his body and pushed himself onto his knees. He wanted to say 'Don't worry about me, I'm fine,' but appreciated his sisters' help in distracting Miss Carmichael.

He searched for his hat, which had fallen off during their tumble.

"Are you looking for this?" Miss Carmichael stood far away from Arabella, her chin raised.

He cleared his throat. "Thank you."

"You called me Olivia." She stated quietly.

Dusting off his hat, his eyes didn't meet hers. "Yes, yes I did." He glanced at her. "You went off like a banshee, and I couldn't get your attention." His eyes implored hers. "I'm sorry if I came across too forward."

She stood there, blonde hair blowing in the wind all loose around her face. She looked ... beautiful. He tried not to pay attention to how much he liked her this way.

"Well ... I ..." She gulped. "I told you this would never work. Riding a horse is not for me. I'm sorry for being so difficult."

Luke chuckled. She wasn't getting out of this that easily. "Falling off a horse is never easy."

Her mouth opened but no sound came out.

"You just get back on and try again."

She shook her head and pointed at Arabella. "Oh. no. I'm not doing that again."

He sighed. "Miss Carmichael."

"You can call me Olivia."

All thought left his brain. "What?"

"I give you permission to call me Olivia." She stood there all innocent-like.

He narrowed his eyes. Was this a ploy to get him to forget the lesson? "Okay, Olivia."

The grin that appeared on her face caused him to forget what he needed her to do.

Arabella snorted, and he automatically grabbed the reins.

He glanced over at Olivia and winced. "You have to get back on again."

She shook her head.

"Trust me, it will be easier."

Her lip trembled. He understood. Trust was not an easy thing for her.

"You'll only sit on her for a minute. Then you can get right off," he spoke softly.

She sunk her teeth into her bottom lip as she shifted her gaze between him and the horse. The fear of getting back on after being thrown, he understood. He might've been five years old at the time, but he remembered.

He also knew if he didn't get her on the horse now, she never would. She couldn't leave today afraid. He needed her to enjoy riding. Somewhere, in his mind, he pictured them galloping together across his ranch, the girls trailing behind. The wariness in her eyes told him he might never get the chance if he didn't earn her trust right now.

And he wanted her trust. More than anything.

OLIVIA LOWERED herself into the metal tub and let the hot water soak her sore body. Except for a few scrapes and her bruised pride, she survived her first horse lesson. Heat flushed her face as she remembered her mortification when she fell on top of Mr. Taylor, screaming. How did he stay so calm? What an infuriating man. She hated how he pushed her. But she had to admit, she got back on the horse and overcame her fear.

After a hard scrub, the dirt finally washed off her arms. Dressed for bed, she grabbed her journal, sat by the window, opened to the last page, and wrote about the day. After writing the excruciating details of her horse lesson, the pencil hovered near the next open space. She had more to say, but should she write her thoughts out? Release them to the world? What if someone read them? What if her feelings changed? So many what-ifs, yet she couldn't keep them inside, either.

The pencil moved on its own as Olivia allowed her thoughts to flow freely.

Luke catches me at my worst, and I feel so helpless. I don't like feeling helpless. He always acts calm and assured, like a rock I can lean on. I've never had this type of encouragement before. My father didn't have the patience, and the men of my acquaintance in Cincinnati didn't teach ladies to ride astride.

Luke's honesty and determination are infectious. I don't want him to see me as a failure. And so, I sat on the horse. When he helped me off of Arabella the last time, he held onto me tightly for longer than necessary. Was he afraid I would fall over or run away? Or was it more? I can only ever admit this here. I thought I would fall over, but not because of the horse lesson. There's a small part of me that wants to explore these feelings, but I can't. What am I going to do?

Her thoughts released from cluttering her mind. She closed her book and lifted the mattress, carefully placing it in her safe-keeping spot. Never had she shared such personal details in her journal. She hoped, by writing them out, she'd act normal the next time she found herself in Mr. Taylor's presence.

Twenty-Four

I'd take one hundred riding lessons with Luke if it meant I didn't have to attend the ladies Bible gathering this weekend. I barely survive attending church each week. How will I make it through this? I just couldn't stand the rejection all over again.

—From the journal of Olivia Carmichael

Olivia hurried across the wooden planks of Second Street, her eyes downcast and her stomach in knots. Focused on placing one foot in front of the other, she rammed into someone as she turned the corner.

"Pardon me, Miss Carmichael," the man said.

She rubbed her arm. Of all people to catch her off guard. "Good day to you, Mr. Chapman." She inclined her head and kept moving. He seemed to be wherever she was, watching her like a hawk who watched for mice, ready to pounce.

Well, she wouldn't allow him the satisfaction of finding anything to report on her. Not today. Agitated, she welcomed the distraction.

It was fleeting, however, as she approached her destination. Her heart leaped, keeping pace with her feet as the memories, forever etched in her mind, replayed over and over, like the clucking Bert made when he walked. The women's facial expressions, the harsh words, and the slammed door at Margaret's house on that fateful day cautioned her that not everyone could be trusted.

With the fear held at bay, she reminded herself that Washton folks had shown themselves different than her so-called *friends* in Cincinnati. But what if they found out about her father and wanted nothing to do with her? Would they respond the same way?

Raw and ugly, the hurt still sat heavy in her chest.

She scanned the small one-story homes as she passed, reminding herself this was a different town, with different people, and a different door. One she now stood in front of, ready to join a group of ladies from the church for a Bible study. For the second time this week, she was partaking in something she said she'd never do again.

The door opened before she could knock.

"Olivia! I'm so glad you're here." Mrs. Timbly greeted her with a warm smile and a hearty laugh. "Please, come inside."

Olivia's response came out as a squeak. "Hi, Mrs. Timbly."

"Just come right in." Mrs. Timbly waved her inside. "We waited for you to start." She led Olivia into her front room and whispered. "I'm looking forward to getting to know you more."

Olivia cringed. Her plan to not let anyone close unfurled more each day. All she could do was smile as Mrs. Timbly led her into the kitchen, where several ladies sat at a large table. Relief flowed through her at the sight of Mrs. Martin and the vacant chair next to her.

Mrs. Timbly's outstretched hand held a tea pot hovered

over a mismatched cup and saucer as Olivia settled into her seat. "Would you like some tea, Olivia?"

"Yes, please." Olivia tuned in to what the women discussed, observing their faces to see if anyone seemed bothered by her attendance. Tension eased from her body as they all smiled and nodded a hello. She picked up her cup and took a sip.

"Olivia, dear, you haven't answered the question."

Olivia blinked. "Oh, I'm terribly sorry." Her face flamed. Not the impression she wanted to give at all.

"Are you feeling all right?" whispered Chrissy. "You look tired. Are you getting enough sleep? Did Mr. Martin's snoring keep you awake last night?"

The ladies chuckled. They all seemed so kind. She wanted to believe they cared. But dreams and real life were separate things. She couldn't allow herself to think otherwise. Not anymore.

"I'm sorry, I'm not sure what's come over me. I think I'm still getting used to living far from home." At the mention of home, she inwardly cringed.

"I'm sure you miss your home and family, Olivia. Do you have much family where you came from?" asked Mrs. Timbly.

Olivia's eyes found Chrissy's as she wished her words back. "Not anymore."

"We can be your family now," a voice to Olivia's right murmured.

Olivia blinked rapidly as Chrissy's warm hand touched her arm. "I *did* hear Mr. Martin's snoring last night, but the noise didn't bother me."

Chrissy's eyes sparkled. "Maybe it's a good thing you'll move to the Woodwards' home soon."

"Although, with all the kids in our house, the roar won't be much better," laughed Mrs. Woodward.

Everyone joined in to share the joke.

The idea of moving every three weeks to a new home didn't thrill Olivia. But this was how Washton paid her, so she didn't have much of a choice. The Woodwards seemed like a good family. They worked together to manage the general store, with their home situated directly above.

She turned to face Mrs. Woodward. "I'm very much looking forward to getting to know you and your children better." Besides Teddy and Emily, the Woodwards' youngest son, Jack, was an adorable four-year-old who asked Olivia several times already when he could go to school too.

Mrs. Woodward clasped her hands to her chest. "I know we will be fast friends."

Later in the day, Olivia sat with the Martins in their wagon, headed to the Taylors' ranch for another horse lesson Luke arranged yesterday when he saw her home. Nerves strung tight, her dry mouth and her clenched stomach made it difficult to focus on anything other than her fear.

"What did you think of our gathering, Olivia?" Chrissy asked as they passed the meadow where she had her run-in with Ol' Fred.

"Everyone was kind," she responded, focusing on the dirt road ahead.

Out of the corner of her eye, she caught Chrissy's smile. "I do hope you will be a regular attender."

She had only considered the one time. Now they wanted her to be a regular?

Her stomach tightened further. She fought back the pain as she faced Chrissy. "Um. It's all so overwhelming. I ..."

Chrissy placed her hand on Olivia's arm. "Say no more, dear. We've got plenty of time."

She nodded, her vision blurring. Chrissy's demeanor never changed, no matter how much Olivia pushed back. She had been nothing but courteous and encouraging. Could Olivia trust her?

They drove under a large wooden sign hanging between two large oak trees with the burned-out words *Taylor Ranch* on it. Her hand gripped her middle. As they approached the house, Mr. Taylor and his sisters stood on their porch. The girls waved enthusiastically.

"Oh, I'm so looking forward to spending time with those two this afternoon." Chrissy waved back and yelled, "Yoo-hoo!" She then added softly, "And to watch you ride a horse, of course."

Olivia winced. She pasted on a smile as the girls ran toward the wagon to greet them. The next thing Olivia knew, they all stood in front of the barn. It was time to ride, whether she was ready or not.

* * *

Saddled and ready to go, Arabella snorted and flicked her head as Olivia approached. She remembered to talk to the horse as she neared. "Hi, girl. Remember me? You aren't going to throw me off today, are you?"

The horse nickered again, turning her muzzle into Olivia's shoulder.

"You must've made a good impression yesterday. She likes you," Luke said as he came to stand next to her. He glanced her way, his eyes watchful. "Ready?"

Her heart leaped out of her chest. Was it man or the horse? She pressed her lips together and gave a curt nod.

He led her to the mounting block and held out his hand as she stepped on the solid wood. She swung her leg over the saddle, letting her body glide as the horse shifted under her.

"Impressive! You're doing great, Olivia."

She glanced at him, raising her eyebrow.

He shrugged as if he had done nothing wrong. "You did give me permission to use your name."

"Yes, but I wouldn't think you would say it in front of them," she whispered, motioning her head in the direction where both the Martins and the girls leaned on the outer fence. She waved at them.

They all waved back.

Luke chuckled. "They're family. It's fine."

"They might be *your* family, but they aren't mine," she retorted and immediately regretted the outburst.

Luke spoke softly, "They consider you family."

Olivia didn't respond, but focused on remaining upright on Arabella. Maybe if she had learned to ride astride as a girl, she wouldn't have fallen off and broken her leg.

"Okay, now we move a bit." Luke led her slowly around the pen. "You're doing great." He glanced over his shoulder and winked. She looked down and saw her ankles showing. Her entire body felt on fire. She tried to cover them, but her skirt edges were too short.

The horse shifted. Olivia bounced her backside against the hard leather and hissed.

"When the horse walks, let your body move in synch along with her," Luke directed.

Her lower half slapped hard against the saddle. "Ouch."

Luke pulled Arabella forward so he could be closer. "Don't try so hard. Just let yourself go," Luke whispered.

Never would she have the luxury to 'let herself go'—not if she wanted to survive. Taking deep breaths, Olivia relaxed as much as she would allow herself, imagining the horse's legs as an extension of her own.

"Yes. Keep doing what you're doing," he murmured.

She glanced at him the same time he looked at her. A

moment passed before the cheers from the sidelines broke through.

"Great job, Miss Carmichael!" yelled Caroline.

"You are on a horse!" squealed Rose.

"And doing a great job, isn't she?" Mr. Martin stated as a father would praise his daughter.

Olivia bit her lip. Maybe they did consider her like family.

"She's a natural," Luke added, looking back at her. "Who would've known?"

Olivia couldn't help but laugh. The movement caused her heels to kick the horse's sides, and Arabella sped forward. Startled, Olivia clamped her knees tight, then made herself relax.

Arabella calmed immediately.

She stayed on, and the horse listened to her. The thrill of that small victory caused her to sit straighter in the saddle and filled her with a newfound joy. A joy full of love and peace.

Mighty pleased with herself, her gaze took in the entire paddock filled with new friends cheering her on, the stunning beauty of the trees, and the colors of the land beyond the fences. This place was so different from the world she came from. Unfamiliar, yet inviting.

She grinned to no one in particular.

Never did she expect to find any sort of happiness here. A place she would want to call home. A peaceful sigh escaped, and she caught Luke gazing at her. Large brown eyes searched hers. What for, she didn't know. But she could get lost in those eyes for eternity.

All movement stopped, and Olivia noticed the mounting block.

Disappointment wound around her heart, but it didn't matter. This one occasion of contentment was more than she had had in months. She would cling to the memory for a long time to come.

Luke reached to help her gain her footing on the block. "Next time, we'll take a long ride around the ranch."

She faltered. "Next time?"

His lopsided grin created funny feelings in her insides.

If her well-thought-out plans had anything to say, there shouldn't be a next time. But she liked riding Arabella and being outdoors in this wilderness. And, she liked Luke.

His eyes captured hers while he still held onto her waist.

Could she keep her feelings in check during the next time? There would only be one way to find out.

Twenty-Five

There's something delightful about being outside on a horse—riding, hearing the birds chirp, and breathing in fresh air. Not to mention a handsome gentleman to share it all with. He truly is a knight in shining armor, and I don't feel so alone anymore.

—From the journal of Olivia Carmichael

Luke nearly fell into the joy and contentment sparkling in Olivia's sky-blue eyes. His chest filled with pride at her determination to get back on Arabella and ride, and how she handled her accidental kick. The urge to saddle Admiral and take her for a long horseback ride flowed through him, which was why he suggested doing so for their next lesson.

"You mean we'd roam free out there?" She flung her arm in a wide arc.

Amused at her nervousness, he grinned. "Yes. That's your next lesson, but not today."

She exhaled and gave a tentative nod.

Arthur cleared his throat. Luke fought off the warmth singeing his neck. He released his hands from her waist and helped her step off the block. "You did good."

She beamed at him. "I did, didn't I?"

Caroline and Rose ran over. Each grabbed one of Olivia's hands.

"You did it. You did it." Rose jumped up and down.

"It's fun, isn't it, Miss Carmichael?" Caroline asked.

Luke watched Olivia focus on his sisters and share in their excitement, their own connection all but forgotten.

A hand covered his left shoulder. "Nice job, Luke. After what happened yesterday, I wasn't sure we would get her on a horse again. Good of you to schedule another lesson quickly."

"I agree. Come with me to put Arabella in her stall?" Luke asked.

"Sure." Arthur followed Luke into the barn. "You know, that's the happiest I've seen her since she's arrived."

Luke rubbed the back of his neck, not knowing what to say.

"You two make quite the couple." Arthur stroked his chin.

Luke blew out a breath. "Arthur, don't get any—"

"I know, I know. Just ... " He shook his head.

Luke looked over his shoulder before he whispered. "Remember, I have a potential mail-order bride coming soon."

"Yes, I know." Arthur sighed. "You know how I feel about this, Luke. I want more for you."

Luke turned away and fiddled with the bridle. "I need help with the girls. That's enough."

Arthur gazed outside the barn door, then back at Luke. "There's someone out there who is doing a marvelous job with the girls. And they love her."

Luke didn't need to be reminded how attached Caroline and Rose had grown to Olivia. "I know. But she's their teacher."

"She doesn't have to be *just* their teacher." Arthur smiled and winked at him.

Luke startled. "Wait. Aren't you the one who was discouraging any interest in the lady so you could have a teacher last the entire school year?"

Arthur held up his hands. "I know, I know. But she's become like a daughter to me. What can I say? I care about her, and I care about you. Anyone with eyes in their head can see there's something between you two."

"You're reading into things, Arthur. There's nothing there. There can't be anything there. We both have our loyalties elsewhere."

"Well, then you need to tell her about ... what's her name again?"

"Evelyn."

"Right. You'll need to tell her about Evelyn. Before her loyalty adjusts, and you break her heart. I wouldn't want to see that happen. More an order, than a request. Understood?"

Luke clenched his teeth and nodded. How was he to introduce that topic? *In case you were interested in marrying me, I need you to know I have a mail-order bride coming,* seemed a bit pretentious. But Arthur was right. Something *was* brewing. He desired more time with her. And the more time they spent together, the more an interest might develop. He couldn't let that happen.

Arthur clapped him on the shoulder. "Sorry we can't stay for refreshments, but we need to head back home."

Luke absently shook Arthur's hand, his mind sorting through scenarios of when to tell Olivia without his sisters overhearing. He stayed in the barn to brush and feed the horses after they left. The quiet worked against his peace of mind. Only halfway done with her lessons, anticipation for the next one flooded his senses. Too much so. And something he couldn't continue when his mail-order bride arrived.

Arthur was right. He needed to tell Olivia about Evelyn. And soon.

* * *

"Good morning, Emily. How are you doing this morning? Ready for school?" Olivia entered the Woodwards' kitchen ready for the day. She had moved into their home after church Sunday. Although leaving the Martins' proved difficult, the Woodward family had gone out of their way to make her feel welcome.

Emily held two pails. "I have our lunches ready!"

Olivia choked back a cry. "You made my lunch? What a wonderful surprise." She shifted her gaze and waited for the burning in her eyes to subside.

"Did I do something wrong, Miss Carmichael?" Concern laced Emily's voice.

Olivia dabbed the wetness from the corner of her eye then strode over to Emily. She put an arm around her. "No, not at all. Actually, I'm quite touched by your thoughtfulness. These —" she waved her hand in front of her face— "are happy tears."

Emily leaned into her and hugged Olivia's middle.

"You will spoil me by helping out so much." Olivia walked to the rack next to the door, where their overcoats hung. She grabbed the smaller one and held the garment open for Emily. "You'll work me out of a job."

"Never, Miss Carmichael. You're the bestest teacher ever!" Emily stated emphatically as she placed first one arm, then another into her coat.

Olivia hoped her student's faith in her would continue

when she gave out this week's assignments. She fastened her own coat, then opened the door.

"Good morning," Barbara Woodward called out in her Irish lilt, as she walked into the main room and gave Emily a big motherly hug. Then she reached for Olivia in the same way and squeezed her tightly.

Tears formed in Olivia's eyes all over again, and she gently hugged Mrs. Woodward back to hide them. Why was she so weepy this morning?

As Mrs. Woodward pulled away, she whispered, "May God be with you both today."

Before Olivia could respond, Jack, Emily's four-year-old brother, tugged on her skirt. "Can I go ta school too?"

"Your time will come soon enough," Mrs. Woodward said to her youngest as Olivia made a mental catalog to give Jack his own personal lesson sometime this week.

Each member of the family had specific chores in the store and at home. All organized and quite effective, they treated one another with much respect. The tight space to fit their family of five didn't seem to bother them as the two boys bunked in one room, and Olivia shared a room with Emily, who now slept on an extra pallet full of blankets and hay squeezed in the corner.

Being an only child, Olivia found the experience overwhelming, yet refreshing. Mrs. Woodward ran the household efficiently, making the chaos work. Olivia might learn a few tactics to use in the schoolroom.

Teddy stood at the bottom of the outside steps waiting, having risen early to do store inventory with Mr. Woodward. The three of them walked through the alley and then onto Main Street, heading to the schoolhouse.

As they stepped onto the wooden planks, Emily asked, "Do you like living with us?"

"Emily," hissed Teddy. "Such a rude question to ask."

Olivia placed a hand on his shoulder. "It's quite all right, Teddy, I don't mind the question." She glanced at Emily. "I enjoy your family very much. And you're quite the hostess."

Emily glowed.

Teddy shook his head.

Never having lived above a store before, Olivia *did* find the experience both fascinating and scary. The only general store in town and considered the heart of Washton, she found herself smack dab in the middle of everything. If someone didn't make a purchase, they came to collect their mail or play chess in the corner by the barrels. She would've loved the buzz of activity before, but now the exposure to undue attention unsettled her nerves.

Emily chattered the entire way to the schoolhouse. She only stopped when they found Bert at the corner, ready and waiting for them.

"Good morning, Bert." Emily curtseyed to the rooster.

He clucked and crowed loudly then proceeded to walk alongside them, scanning the sides as if he alone could protect them from predators lurking in the shadows. Olivia found the action quite comical, but she didn't dare laugh. She made that mistake once before, and Bert didn't stop squawking at her for over half an hour.

How the rooster came about his duties, Olivia had no idea. And where did he go at night? But since he couldn't speak, she didn't waste the time asking. Since the townsfolk accepted him, antics and all, so did she. In fact, she found the town's attitude toward him something to be admired.

In no time, they arrived at the schoolhouse.

"I'll get the wood, Miss Carmichael," Teddy shouted. He ran around the building to the wood pile.

"I'll get the slates out." Emily hustled to the top step and opened the schoolhouse door.

Warmth radiated through Olivia's body. With their mother's helpful spirit, she loved the eagerness Emily and Teddy brought to their tasks. In fact, the entire family's servant posture was refreshing. Where did this honoring come from?

Her one observation was the family prayed. Before each meal, at bedtime, and even in the morning before chores. God wasn't seen, yet the family invited the Lord into every circumstance.

Prayer was a private matter in her world, never spoken out loud or in the presence of others. She found it slightly unnerving hearing them talk to God as if He was in the room.

Her gaze followed Emily as she ran to the door to greet the other children, who piled into the schoolhouse with a level of noise that would distract even the most focused person. Once settled, they spent the next few hours on their studies. The deafening hum resumed as they left for home.

Teddy, Emily, and Olivia headed toward the store. After helping with dinner and chores, Olivia sat on the bed with her journal in her lap. She missed the window chair at the Martin's but would make do anywhere, thankful for a small amount of private time to write before Emily came to bed.

After listing out the day's affairs, she laid across the bed in an unladylike fashion and absently wrote what had been at the forefront of her mind all day.

I feel I'm assimilating here with a solid routine. I find myself wanting to trust people, but I'm afraid. I vowed I would be cautious and never fully trust anyone again. But how does someone care and not trust? I have watched the Woodward family trust God in everyday occurrences. They talk with Him several times a day as if it's the most natural thing in

the world. When I think about opening my heart, the
nausea which overcomes me is too much. Yet I feel drawn in.
I want to start trusting again. In the Woodwards, the
Martins, in Luke, and in God.

A deep sense of relief overcame her. She went back and reread her words and gasped. She had been so careful not to reveal her feelings. But these thoughts cried to be released, and she wrote the words without thinking.

Never had she thought she'd find acceptance and peace again. She never wanted to trust again, and yet, she'd written in her journal, plain as the color of her clothes she now donned.

And the lightheartedness growing between her and Luke Taylor? Her heart thumped. The emotions scared her, but it felt oh, so wonderful too.

But what about her well-thought-out plans? Could she adapt them yet again? Her lips curved as a sense of spontaneity engulfed her. Maybe finally something good would happen.

Twenty-Six

*Washton townspeople work hard. They live off the land. They barter
with their neighbors. They help each other. There isn't a lot of coin.
People must depend on themselves and one another to survive. Such
a different way from how I was raised. Refreshing, yet alarming. I
have no idea how to do anything.*

—From the journal of Olivia Carmichael

After school the next day, Olivia sat at the
Woodwards' kitchen table, working on her
correspondence. She had been woefully neglectful
in her promises to write, including to Agnes and Jasper, fearing
penning her news in some way could curse all she had gained.
But now, as she addressed each one, she realized her folly and
yearned for tidings from all of them.

Were Agnes and Jasper happy in their new positions? Did
anyone notice her absence? Was her father's misdeeds finally
old news? And her new friends. Was Violet still teaching, or did

she find a husband right away? Had Emilia found the adventure she wished for? And Lydia. She wasn't sure what Lydia was all about, but she hoped she found what she wanted. And Jenny. Had she found a family who accepted her and showed kindness to her?

Mr. Woodward entered as Olivia signed the last letter. He poured himself a cup of coffee from the pot warming on the stove. "Would you like some, Olivia?"

"What? Oh, no thank you, I'm fine."

He pulled out a chair. "And how was your day today?"

She set down her pen. "As smoothly as can be expected with twelve children in one room."

He chuckled as he sipped his beverage.

"And how was your day today? Did you sell out the store?"

He shook his head. "Hardly. What a guessing game it is to keep inventory of items people need without them staying on the shelf for too long, which we then have to discount." He held his mug near his mouth. "The joys of owning a store." He sipped. "But it makes life interesting. Since the railroads connected the states, and with our new station opening soon, we don't have to wait months when I order things." He reached into his pocket. "I see you're handling correspondence. I happen to have a letter for you as well."

Olivia recognized the handwriting immediately. "From my friend Jenny." She hurried to break open the seal and unfold the paper. A loose sheet fell to the floor.

"Good news, I hope?"

Olivia bent to pick up the paper. "She doesn't say too much." Her stomach clenched. "She's been transferred to a town called Vallejo." She glanced at Mr. Woodward. "No bad news is good, wouldn't you say?" She turned her attention to the newsprint. "Oh, look at this. She sent me an article from a San Francisco newspaper."

"The *Californian*?"

"I'm not sure." She scanned the page. "It doesn't say."

He shook his head. "Doesn't matter. What's the article?"

"The title reads 'The Celebrated Jumping Frog of Calaveras County,' written by a Mark Twain."

"I've heard of Mr. Twain. He travels in the local area and writes about the people he meets.

"Like the articles I read back home."

He continued to drink his coffee. "I heard he passed through the area a few months ago."

"Maybe this story is about someplace nearby." Her lips lifted while she read the entire story. When she finished, she picked up her letter to Jenny. "I need to add to the letter I wrote her."

"You already have something more to say?"

Olivia chuckled. "I want to make sure she knows I received hers. We roomed together at school and became quite close. I've missed her."

He watched her scribble additional lines. "Would you like me to take your letters with me after my break?"

"Yes, would you?" She re-sealed her letter and settled it on the pile. "Why is your store the mail drop?"

He placed his cup on the table. "Well, after our post office flooded for the third time, they didn't build another."

Olivia blinked. "Was the post office close to the river?"

"Yes, farther down the street, near where those railroad tracks are situated." He pointed toward the south of town. "After the third time, the government advised against rebuilding. Since my store sat in the center of town, we added space to sort and store the mail. Once a week I travel to Sacramento and deliver letters and pick up any incoming mail. Works well for me. More people come to the store. You should come to Sacramento with us on

Saturday. Bring your letters yourself. You can explore the city."

Should she go with the Woodwards and cancel her lesson with Luke? The thought of not seeing him warred with the desire to visit Sacramento. A city trip won out. "I'd love to join you."

She was rereading the article again when Emily walked into the room. "What're you two talking about?"

"Your pa has invited me to go with your parents to Sacramento on Saturday."

Emily gave her father a pleading look. "Can I go, too, Pa?"

He tugged on his daughter's pigtail. "Not this time, pumpkin. Maybe you can accompany us next time."

Emily frowned but then tilted her head to the side. "What are you reading?"

Olivia folded the paper and laid her hands over it. "Something I plan to share in class tomorrow."

"Oh, a surprise!" Emily clapped. "I love surprises."

Mr. Woodward set his cup in the sink and tapped Emily on the head. "Well, then, I look forward to hearing more about it from you after school tomorrow."

Olivia laughed along with Emily. Indeed, Emily would come home and tell the family the entire story. Probably twice over.

She couldn't wait to share. And she couldn't wait for Saturday.

* * *

AT THE END of the next school day, Olivia rose and clapped three times. "All right children, may I have your attention, please? I have a special treat for you."

Murmurings ran throughout the room. Adam, who soaked

up every word of her lessons, watched her closely as he sat forward at his desk, his hands folded on top. Joseph and John jabbed their elbows at one another but stopped as she pulled the article out of her book and unfolded the paper.

Several pairs of eyes studied her curiously. When the whispering subsided, she held up the newsprint. "How many of you know what a newspaper is?"

All the students stood, except Adam. He looked around sheepishly and then slowly came to his feet. Her heart broke. How could she help him? Would special assignments made for him help? Or would those add to his embarrassment?

"Why'd you ask about a newspaper?" Caroline asked.

Her attention snapped back to the entire class. "Excellent question. Have any of you *read* a newspaper before?"

A few sat back on the benches. "What I read is always old news," Susannah whispered.

She had their attention. Olivia smiled at Susannah. "Old news is still news and a good way to practice your reading. Did you know besides news, newspapers publish stories."

Several schoolchildren stopped wiggling, eyes facing forward.

"Have any of you ever heard of a fun story in the newspaper?"

The rest sat, eyes round with curiosity.

Olivia continued. "An author by the name of Mark Twain has been traveling near here, and he wrote about his travels. His stories have been published in a San Francisco newspaper, and my friend sent this to me by post. I want to share it with you."

She moved her chair to the center by the stove and read aloud. The children scooted forward, and as she adapted her voice for each character, they scooted closer and closer. By the time she finished, the children clapped and laughed.

Bert crowed loudly from outside.

Olivia stood and gave a mini-bow.

A man cleared his throat, and all the noise stopped.

Olivia's head swung toward the door.

In the doorway, Mr. Chapman stood, shaking his head. His arms were folded across his chest, disapproval all over his face.

Olivia inwardly groaned. This wasn't the first time he'd appeared, waiting to catch her making a mistake. Why couldn't she go about her business and not be judged? And why couldn't he go about *his* business and leave her alone?

Nothing could be done now, so she turned to the children. "That's all for today. Time to pack your things and go home."

"Aww." The room filled with protests.

"Will ya read us another story soon, Miss C?" Adam asked. His eyes sparkled, and his grin reached ear to ear.

She loved seeing his smile, knowing she helped place it there. "I would love to. I'll see what I can find."

Cheers erupted around the room as the children wiped their slates clean and stacked them on the desks as neatly as their tiny hands were able. Chairs scraped the floor as they tucked them under their desks.

Mr. Chapman continued to stand in the center of the exit, requiring the children to squeeze by him to leave.

Olivia turned her back on him and wrote tomorrow's lessons on the board.

Boots tromped on the porch outside. "Well, hey there, James. What brings you to school today?"

Olivia's heart lifted. Leave it to her Knight to appear at the right time. She glanced over her shoulder and watched Luke crowd the vile man.

Mr. Chapman pushed off from the door frame. "I was just leaving. There isn't any real teaching going on here. Once this town has realized that fact, I'll be ready."

Olivia's heart sank. Why was there always someone, somewhere trying to make someone else fall? Would she ever be at ease? Having to stay alert all the time exhausted her energies. But how else could she guarantee not to be displaced?

* * *

Luke faced James, but out of the corner of his eye, he saw Miss Carmichael's shoulders droop.

He narrowed his eyes. "Nothing will change, James. Accept it and move on."

"We'll see." James shrugged and slid out the door. Once in the yard, Bert followed him, squawking and pecking at his heels. The man glared at the bird and continued walking back toward Main Street.

"Excuse me, sir," Teddy said as he walked in a hurry past Luke. Luke's gaze followed Teddy to the woodpile then back inside where the boy placed the wood on the stack next to the stove. He glanced at his sister Rose, who stood at the front, wiping the bottom half of the board, while another girl wiped the top half. Other children circled Miss Carmichael, eagerly asking her questions.

The children didn't just like her, they thrived. He watched as Miss Carmichael patiently took time with each student. His heart pounded. She was exactly what they all needed. Resourceful, diligent, and caring. He couldn't help but be proud.

Caroline appeared at his side. "Did you hear the story about the frog?"

He swallowed the yelp he almost yelled for her startling him. "I have not. What story is this?"

"One from the newspaper Miss Carmichael's friend sent."

"Oh." So, Miss Carmichael had a friend outside of town. Interesting.

He glanced her way again. As if he could see what other secrets she hid. The desire to know more about her troubled him.

A horse's whiny outside reminded him why he was there. He pushed off the wall and walked over to where she held court. "Excuse me, Miss Carmichael. I'm here for your next lesson."

Their eyes met, her long lashes making her eyes appear larger. A slight blush appeared on her cheeks.

Luke gulped.

No, he shouldn't be troubled at all.

Oh, but he was.

He hurried outside and headed straight to the horses.

He still hadn't told her about Evelyn. When she was near, all thought fled or the timing inappropriate for him to say the words "By the way, I have a mail-order bride coming." But time was running out. He had to say something today. As soon as she joined him for her lesson. If he could find the right words.

The children had exited the schoolhouse and dispersed already, so he adjusted the stirrups one more time while waiting for her to join him. He heard the door open and footsteps sound on the porch, then halt, so he turned, and all thought left his brain. The slit skirt he recently saw in Mr. Woodward's store looked magnificent on her. Or maybe it was the glow on her face as she looked at him.

He gulped. Whatever it was, he couldn't take his eyes off her. His heart galloped at full speed as she stepped off the porch and approached. "I'm ready to begin, Mr. Taylor."

Her formalness amused him. "I told you, Mr. Taylor is my father. You're supposed to call me Luke."

Her smile held a hint of laughter, the little minx. She

ignored him and headed toward his mare, stroked her neck, and spoke in a soft and loving voice. "How are you doing today, Arabella? I've missed you. Are you ready for our lesson?"

Luke wished to be the recipient of her kind words instead of his horse. He pushed on the crown of his hat. "Let's get in the saddle. Sunlight is wasting." He lowered to one knee and cupped his hands.

She set her boot in his palms, and he lifted her as she easily swung her leg over. "Nice job, Olivia."

She narrowed her eyes at him, the left side of her mouth lifting.

He broke eye contact and hustled over to mount Admiral.

"Wait, what are you doing? Aren't you going to guide my horse?"

Luke glanced over his shoulder. "Remember what I said last time?"

"But ... but—" Her eyes darted side to side, and she gripped hard on the reins, her knuckles turning white.

He leapt into his saddle and directed Admiral to her left. "I'll ride alongside you to start."

She relaxed her hold, as Luke took the lead rope in hand and clucked his tongue.

As the horses strode around the schoolyard, he spoke in soft tones. "Relax. Move as one. That's it." He slowed as she rode ahead, her backside swaying nicely in tandem with Arabella.

He swallowed, reigned in his thoughts, and again drew alongside her. "No one would ever know you've had minimal experience riding a horse. You're doing great."

A shy grin returned along with the same flash of joy he saw on Saturday. "I'm learning quickly, don't you think?"

He would jump over Ol' Fred to see this smile all the time.

"I do think you've been a quick learner for horseback riding. Let's see how well you do at rifle shooting next week."

She sputtered, and he squeezed his knees. Admiral shot forward, removing him from earshot. Only then he remembered he hadn't mentioned Evelyn, again. He inwardly groaned. If only he could say the words in the same way. Blurt them out and then run away.

Twenty-Seven

I'm much looking forward to Saturday's visit to Sacramento. My first time there was so quick and overwhelming. Of course, one can't forget my encounter with my Knight, who as you know by now, is Luke Taylor.

—From the journal of Olivia Carmichael

Olivia struck out on her own, her heels thumping on the boardwalk as she glanced inside the different establishments' windows. Sacramento bustled with activity, and the energy filled her with an acute yearning inside her chest, ready to break free.

An hour all to herself to do with as she pleased.

Not that she hadn't enjoyed spending the morning with Mr. Woodward at the Sacramento post office, learning about how the mail came in and out by rail and river in the area. The information gleaned from the excursion would be a great lesson to share with her students and was well worth the time.

The number of letters sorted through this office, especially since the trains came in from the east weekly, boggled her mind. After observing the fascinating process of communication, she could understand how letters became lost if people moved or didn't have the right address.

She strode across the cobbled street onto the wooden sidewalk. Train horns whistled in the background. A family hurried past, the young lady's swinging elbow just missed colliding with Olivia's hip. As she passed the ice cream parlor, sugary smells wafted outside. A hint of regret overcame her knowing she couldn't enter. Such an odd rule for a female schoolteacher, but since she didn't have any spending money to waste away on frivolities, not a huge disappointment. Even though a scoop of vanilla sounded divine.

A pang of loneliness thumped in her chest. She expected today's trip to be a welcome respite from her newfound acquaintances, but now alone, she almost wished Luke was with her. Why did her thoughts turn to him? Could she trust him and let him into her heart? She stopped at the corner. Mr. Taylor made her go soft and desire things she shouldn't want.

Crossing the street, she raised her foot and her shoe caught, grasping her foothold before falling flat on her face. She shook out her skirts, hoping no one noticed her stumble, all the while stealthily studying the sidewalk. The offending wooden planks were unusually high. She'd have to raise her knee twice as much to make the step.

This was what Mr. Martin referred to when he mentioned all the unique changes the city had made after the last flood. Something about raising the ground higher with sand and silt. They raised the walkways higher too.

She stepped cautiously forward and proceeded around the corner onto what the sign called J Street. A massive door to a shop opened, and a man exited. The extra-large door had two to three feet left above the man's head. In fact, all the doorways to the establishments she passed were the same height. Was that a west thing or a result of the sand raising as well?

A group of ladies heading the other direction nodded their acknowledgement, while loud male guffaws filled the air from down the street. A sense of uneasiness filled her. She had gone for walks in Cincinnati, but her father always had a servant follow her. A layer of protection she had taken for granted. The hole in her heart for all she lost grew a smidge larger.

She stopped at the next window to study the colorful displays of candy sticks. Of course, now she wished for discretionary funds, even a small amount, so she could purchase delicious treats for her students. Her mouth watered from the sweet smell.

Then, much to her dismay, her stomach growled.

She pulled herself away from the temptation and continued toward the source of the toe-tapping music. As she approached, a yell came from inside, "and stay out." The door flew open, and a young man shot through the air, crashing into the street, his hat thrown after him, landing at his side. Why men visited these establishments when their families waited at home for them, she had no idea.

Out of curiosity, Olivia turned her head to look through the open door. Tables and chairs sat haphazardly around the piano in the center. A clear path to the back revealed a long wooden bar pressed against the far wall. A woman dressed in loose clothing sat on one end while men stood nearby leaning against the taller table. One man—*No!*

The sour taste in her mouth traveled down to form a boulder in her stomach. Every noble thought twisted into lies. She thought she knew him. Trusted him. How could she be so naive?

For a man, who looked much like Luke Taylor, stood in the saloon, holding a bottle in his hand. As she glared at the back of his head, he turned her way, and his eyes grew large when he spotted her.

Olivia had no reason to feel anger and disappointment, but she did anyway.

Something kept her rooted to the spot, even though she should move for no other reason than a lady shouldn't stand in front of a saloon without asking for trouble. But the connection between them wouldn't let her pull away.

She had to sever the link. Her job depended on her living a trustworthy life, and frolicking with saloon-visiting men brought all sorts of trouble her way, no matter what the mayor might say. What would the other families think? She couldn't control misperceptions, so she had to manage them.

Her sense of preservation finally took over, and she hurried farther down the boardwalk, her vision unable to see any other storefront she passed. The only image in her mind was that of Mr. Taylor in that seedy place.

* * *

WHY HER, of all people to see him here? A few choice words popped into Luke's head, even though he never swore. The disappointment in her eyes was evident. He couldn't let her go without an explanation.

He set down his half-drunk bottle of soda water, pressed a coin onto the bar, tipped the rim of his hat to the keep, and headed for the door. Searching both directions, he veered left after he caught sight of her rounding the corner.

What could he say when he reached her? How does one explain why they were in a saloon in the middle of the day? Which he was. But not the reason she would assume. "Miss Carmichael, hold up!"

Her back rigid and her strides short and quick, she picked up her pace.

His long legs ate away the distance, but as he drew near, she dashed into a door. He grabbed the closing door and followed her in. He halted. Then blinked. The time allowed him to digest what type of shop he'd walked into.

He grabbed his hat off his head, hoping to appear smaller. Walking into a woman's dress shop with his six-foot one-inch frame was like letting Ol' Fred loose in the Woodwards' mercantile. Ignoring all the lace and frilly stuff, he focused on Miss Carmichael, who had swung around and faced him.

"What are you doing?" she hissed.

Good question. Glancing at the frills, he felt way out of his element. He chased her in here because he needed to explain, but they couldn't talk here.

Then an idea formed.

"Miss Carmichael," he said in his most manly voice possible. "I tried to catch you before you did your shopping to ask for your assistance in selecting a few items for my sisters." Luke exhaled, proud of his idea. She wouldn't believe him, but the others in the shop would.

Miss Carmichael raised her eyebrows, tilted her head, and, as he hoped, played along. "I would be happy to. What did you have in mind?" Higher pitched than normal, the hard glint in her eyes contradicted her tone, but she kept a plastered smile on her face.

Luke stepped toward her, honesty spilling out of him. "It's been too long since they received new dress. Caroline has grown several inches over the past year. They'll need something to get them through the winter months and keep them warm on the wagon rides to and from school."

"You want *me* to pick out dresses for them?" Her horrified expression caught him off guard. Didn't women like to shop?

243

He didn't understand her reluctance. He wasn't asking much, such as courting.

Whoa. He needed to stop that line of thinking and lock it away. Forever.

She looked at him expectantly.

"Yes. You're female. You understand these things. I have no clue about patterns and types of—" He turned and fingered the garment right next to him trying to figure out the word he wanted.

"Material?" she finished for him.

"Yes! See, you know these things. I don't. I would probably pick out the opposite of what they need." He warmed to the idea. "I'd like to take home new dresses for them as a surprise for how hard they've been working in school. Will you help?"

She peered beyond his shoulder then back at him. Her eyes shone brighter, and he knew she conceded.

The shopkeeper approached.

"Whatever the lady decides, can be put on my tab, please. I'll just wait outside." Then, he'd get the opportunity to explain himself when she handed him the packages. What little he could say, at least.

Twenty-Eight

I felt honored he asked me to purchase dresses for the girls, but a lot of anxiety as well. What if I chose wrong? What if the girls didn't like them? This was important, special, and intimate. Am I in too much over my head?

—From the journal of Olivia Carmichael

The realization Caroline and Rose had no mother to make or buy dresses for them melted her anger away. And she couldn't say no in front of an audience. No one would understand.

The relief on his face, though comical, distracted her from her wrath. And with the outrage peeled away, the hurt exposed left her feeling precarious. Mr. Luke Taylor was not the man she thought.

Now, what should she do? Not that it mattered. He wasn't courting her, nor did she want him to be. Or did she?

She stood staring at the closed door once he left, then turned to the articles of clothing next to her, running her fingers over the fine material. She loved the stiffness and crispness of freshly pressed cotton. Oh, wouldn't it be nice to have a new dress? What fanciful thinking. She had no need for a new dress. And no money. She shook off the unbidden memories of how she used to have new dresses on a regular basis.

"May I help you find what you need?" asked the clerk, who still stood next to her, waiting.

Olivia quickly released the material, as if caught with her hand in the cookie jar. She straightened her shoulders and faced the woman. "Yes. I'm sure you heard the gentleman." The term tasted all wrong on her tongue knowing what she now knew. "I need to purchase dresses for two young ladies. I think a child size medium and a lady's size four would be about right." She continued providing material and design requirements, hoping her choices would suffice for the coming winter weather. She had no idea how cold the temperature dipped in these parts.

The shopkeeper wrote down everything then went through the curtained doorway to look for the requested items.

Olivia exhaled. Now she would have to see him again when she left the store. Her heart pounded. She couldn't shake the image of him in that saloon.

She would do this for Caroline and Rose, not for him. Never having sisters of her own, something special brewed in her heart for these two. They were kind, eager to learn, and well-mannered. How she'd love to be an influence in their lives long-term.

She swallowed a lump in her throat. What about the promise to herself not to get involved with her students? Involvement meant caring, and caring meant losing control of one's emotions and being open to disappointment. She wouldn't care. Couldn't care. But couldn't she be fond of them? She was their teacher, after all.

"Here we go." The clerk walked back into the main room carrying a multitude of dresses in several colors.

Weeding through the selection, Olivia chose a white and lavender floral design for Rose and a magenta and purple flock for Caroline. The style was more mature, and the colors would contrast nicely with her fair complexion. She asked the clerk to wrap them for purchase.

Satisfied with her selections, Olivia hoped the girls liked the dresses as much as she did. But doubt crept in as she stepped outside and turned to close the door behind her.

"Let me help you." Luke tugged on the box under her arm. "I see you found dresses."

The tug on the box caused her to wobble. She swiveled around, and her hands landed on his chest as he took the box from her. She stopped breathing as she gazed into his eyes. Movement caused her to focus on the package in his hand and she immediately stepped away and cleared her throat. "I did. I hope they won't be disappointed." She cringed. She disliked the lack of certainty in her voice.

"Why would they be disappointed? They're just clothes."

She shook her head. He didn't understand. "What I meant is, I hope I got the sizes correct, and they like them."

"I'm sure what you picked is fine. They're not expecting anything, so they will be happy to receive any new dress. What did you get for yourself?"

She raised her chin. "I didn't purchase anything."

Luke frowned. "You went into the shop. Why then, did you go inside in the first ... Oh!"

Her body tensed and she raised her chin higher. "I was running away from you, remember?"

A tight guilty smile crept up at the corner of his mouth.

Could he look any more handsome? She waited for an explanation, anything to hint she misinterpreted what she saw.

He tucked the package under his arm. "Yes, I remember. You weren't headed for the dress shop, then?"

A heaviness descended throughout her body and she shook her head. "I came today to window-shop and explore, but there seems to be a lot desired when there are saloons situated on every street right next to other establishments."

A look crossed his face, but she couldn't identify it. Hanging out in a saloon was deplorable in her book, and even though an explanation couldn't change her lowered opinion of him, she wanted one.

She boldly held her position, waiting.

"You won't believe me."

Probably not, but oh, how she wanted to. "Try me."

* * *

Luke had nothing to hide, but he couldn't say what she wanted to hear. "Yes, you found me in the saloon—"

Her palm flew in front of his face. "It's not any of my business."

He chuckled uncomfortably. "Yes, yes, it is. I don't like you thinking bad about me."

She bit her lip. "It's not my place to judge."

"But you did." He narrowed his eyes. "As much as it caught me off guard to see you standing there."

She frowned. "What do you mean?"

"What are you doing here? Did you come alone? Who knows you're here?"

She crossed her arms over her chest. "I moved across the country all on my own." She wouldn't mention there were other teachers with her. "I'm perfectly capable of walking around town."

He raised his brow. "Forgive me for disagreeing."

She bristled, which he expected, but it didn't deter him.

"Need I remind you of when you took a walk on my ranch and met Ol' Fred?" He crossed his arms, pressing the package into his side.

Fire sparked in her eyes. "Don't change the subject. I can walk around Sacramento if I choose."

He was willing to accept her annoyance. "I wonder about the truth in your statement. I find you in need of rescuing. Often." He said the last word slowly, to emphasize his point.

She glared at him.

He glared right back. "Fine. You feel you are safe. I'll leave you be. Thank you for your help picking out dresses." He hustled off, spurs clanking on the wooden planks. Even though he recently drank half a bottle of soda water, his mouth felt as parched as the ground on a hot July day. But he didn't dare step into another establishment with her eyes burning a hole in his backside.

As he turned the corner, he strode a few more steps then halted. What was he doing? He couldn't leave her. Not when trouble found her often. He flung his head back and groaned. He needed to go back. Wanted to go back.

He counted to ten before moving, but the sidewalk where he left her was empty. He clenched his jaw. Worry for her burned inside him. When did he become so protective? When did she become so important? Gripping the box tighter, he stomped in the other direction, his boots and spurs thudding and clanking along.

The sounds didn't fit into any rhythm, much like his desire to see her safe and keep her near, and an innate need to run far away from her. The two contrasts gave him a splitting headache.

His conscience won out, so when he turned onto *J* Street and saw her in the distance, his relief made him ignore his public manners. "Olivia!" he shouted, his focus solely on her.

She, along with the two she stood next to, turned around, surprise on their faces.

"Olivia." He said again as he got closer.

"Hello, Mr. Taylor."

Startled at her tone, Luke finally spared a glance to see who she stood next to.

"Hello, Barbara. Jacob." He acknowledged the Woodwards with a handshake and a nod.

Olivia's lips pressed together as mischief danced in her eyes. "What did you need, Mr. Taylor?"

What a fool. She hadn't needed him after all. He *should* feel relief.

But instead, he felt lost and adrift.

He didn't like the feeling, not one bit.

He glanced at the Woodwards then back at her. "I saw you earlier and wanted to make sure you made it home safe. If you excuse me, I have more errands to take care of before the last barge crosses. See you all in town." He lifted his hat and walked away with as much grace as he could muster.

"See you back in town, Luke," Jacob called out.

Luke looked one last time and waved. Yes, he would continue to see Miss Carmichael. Every single day. He sighed. In too deep, he couldn't afford for them to be friends anymore, nor, after seeing him in the saloon, would she want to be, which was for the best. He just didn't like seeing the disappointment in her eyes, knowing he was the one who put it there.

Twenty-Nine

I wish things could be different. I found him in a saloon of all things.
He said he had a reason, but he never told me. Would it matter?
Some things are unforgivable. I should know better than to judge,
but I can't help it. I'm so disappointed. I knew this would happen.
He, too, isn't as he seems.

—From the journal of Olivia Carmichael

Olivia woke with the sunlight warming one side of her face. She rolled over and groaned. As she opened her eyes, she found herself where she'd fallen asleep, sprawled out on the bed, her journal open in her lap. Relieved to find her pencil, she turned to her last entry.

A noise came from the other side of the room. "Oh, good, you're awake. Good morning, Miss Carmichael." A small head peeked through the narrow space of the partially opened door.

"Good morning, Emily." She swallowed, her mouth feeling like cotton.

Emily looked at her curiously. "Why are you still in your clothes from yesterday?"

Olivia lifted her journal. "Well, it seems I fell asleep while writing in my journal."

Emily's eyebrows grew closer together, "Is that what you've been scribbling in every night?" She didn't give a chance for her to respond. "What do you write?

She shrugged "Events from the day to help me remember things."

Emily tilted her head. "Why would you want to write down things you did all day? Can't you remember?"

Olivia fidgeted with her book, thinking how best to explain. "Good questions. Remember to ask one at a time."

"Sorry." Emily shrugged, not looking one spot of sorry.

Olivia's heartstrings tugged for her most curious student. "I like to document things so I can look back later and reflect on them. Also, someone in the future might want to know how we did things in 1869."

"Is it a book, then?"

Olivia laughed. "No, not completely. Although I could see how it would seem like one."

"Sure sounds like a book." Emily tilted her head the other way.

"Why?" Olivia asked.

"Well, you're writing stories about your day, right?"

"I guess my words could read like a story. But sometimes I describe my thoughts about things. To help me get the right perspective. May sound funny, but it's as if I'm having a conversation with myself, only I'm writing it out."

"Like when you talk with God, and it looks like you're talking with yourself?"

"Well, I'm not familiar with conversing with God in that way, but—"

"Why not? Mama says we need to talk with Him all the time. So, if you didn't want to speak out loud and wake everyone, it would make sense to write out the words so God could see what you had to say."

How can an eight-year-old comprehend praying to God? And yet, Emily made the concept seem so simple.

"Writing out thoughts to God," she whispered.

"I think doing so is a great way to practice my penmanship. Maybe Mama will let me have a piece of paper so I can spell out my thoughts and prayers to God too. Would you help me, Miss Carmichael?"

Olivia didn't have the heart to disappoint this special young girl. And, as a guest in their home and Emily's teacher, she could only see an upside to helping her. "Yes, I'll be happy to assist you."

The girl threw her arms in the air and headed to the door. "Yippee! I'm gonna go see if I can find paper right now. I'll need a big piece as I have a lot of thoughts."

Olivia chuckled. "Yes, I believe you do. And God will soon know every single one."

She turned back. "Mama says He already does, 'cause He knows our heart before we even do."

Emily's words hit Olivia's chest hard and stayed there. She repeated the words in her mind a few times, while waiting for the sweet girl to come back. She'd been so careful to guard her heart. Had God known this all along?

The door swung wide as Emily ran into the room. "I got my journal page."

Her enthusiasm warmed Olivia's heart. "Why don't you have a seat and share with me what you want to say in your journal."

"What do you mean?" Emily asked.

"What types of things are you going to write about?"

"Don't I describe whatever comes to my brain?"

Olivia grinned. "Yes, that's the gist."

"How do I start?"

"Well, some people say, 'Dear Diary,' or give their journal a name."

"I'm going to start with 'Dear God.'" Emily held her pencil to the parchment.

Olivia's breath caught. "That would work too."

Olivia watched while Emily wrote 'Dear God. Thank you for today. Thank you for my family and Miss Carmichael.' Then she stopped and scrunched her eyes together tightly.

"What are you doing, Emily?" Olivia asked.

"I'm checking my heart to see if there's anything else God wants me to say."

"Oh, that sounds ... helpful." Olivia would ponder things before she wrote. What if she 'checked her heart' in the same way?

A scratching noise drew her attention back to Emily. "Did you find something else to say?"

The girl didn't answer right away. Then she looked at Olivia, her face lit with pure joy. "Yep. Wanna see?"

"Oh, no. A journal is your own private book."

"But you said, others would read yours and know what you did?" Emily protested.

"Yes, I did say those words. But I meant when I'm no longer around." Olivia shook her head. "I wouldn't want someone reading my book now."

"Do you scribble embarrassing things in your book?" Emily whispered.

"No, just private thoughts, and privacy needs to be respected."

A look of disappointment crossed Emily's face. "Oh. But I want someone to read mine."

"Why?" asked Olivia.

"Because God wants others to know what He's told me. I concentrated really hard to hear God speak to me, and this is what He said so far." Emily held out her paper.

At one time, Olivia had felt God's presence, but this past year, she couldn't hear Him anymore. She assumed He had abandoned her. But had He?

Emily drew the page back. "Wait. There's more I need to jot down." Emily hunched over her paper.

Unshed tears filled Olivia's eyes. Oh, to be a young girl, protected by her family from the outside world, innocent and able to believe so firmly. She peered over at Emily, who stayed engrossed in what she wrote. How nice to trust one hundred percent that God was with her all the time.

Events fluttered through Olivia's mind as she remembered what caused her to doubt God the most. When her parents died? Or when the creditors came and took all her belongings? Or when her fiancé cast her aside? Or was it when her friends shut the door in her face? Alone each time, she had to do everything on her own. Plain and simple, God wasn't there when she needed Him most.

Olivia glanced at her watch. "Oh, look at the time! Emily, you should go see if your mama needs help in the kitchen."

Emily finished the sentence and swiveled a dazed look at Olivia. "What, Miss Carmichael? I was concentratin'."

Olivia's lips curved upward. "I said 'Time to help your mama with the chores.'"

"Oh, yes." She shifted her body around. "Thank you, Miss Carmichael, for helping me start a journal. Did you want to read what I wrote?"

"Oh, no, Emily. Remember, privacy means for your eyes only. A place to put your thoughts and feelings and keep them to yourself."

Emily looked at her brown paper full of lead markings. "Hmm. I guess that makes sense. Of course, God sees everything, whether it's inside your heart or written down words. So, I guess it doesn't matter if someone sees what you wrote or not, because if the most important Person in the whole world knows, then it's okay for anyone else to read it." She slid off the side of the bed and walked toward the door, leaving her journal paper behind. She stopped at the door. "Miss Carmichael?"

Olivia turned to face the young girl. "Yes, Emily?"

"I think God wanted me to talk with you about what you write in your journal."

Olivia frowned.

"He wants you to know He's always there for you, no matter what, even when you don't think He is." Emily walked out the door.

Olivia stared at the empty doorway, then at her journal. Did God really know her heart and her thoughts? Could He be there with her now?

Did she truly want the answer?

* * *

EMILY'S WORDS replayed in Olivia's mind as the congregation around her sang through the last hymn. Maybe she was not the only one who struggled and doubted God. She had assumed everyone else had the world figured out. But did others put on happy faces like she did so people couldn't see the turmoil underneath?

As inconspicuously as possible, she glanced around at the faces around her.

The song ended, and she faced forward, heat creeping up her neck.

"Please turn to Psalm 73," Pastor William called out from behind the wooden pulpit.

The sound of crinkling paper filled the room. Feeling the need to do something, Olivia lifted the church's Bible next to her and did the same.

"Psalm 73 was written by Asaph, one of David's musicians." Pastor William's voice boomed throughout the room.

She searched for the starting point but caught the words in verse three, *"For I was envious at the foolish when I saw the prosperity of the wicked."* She bit her lip and scanned the rest. *"Verily I have cleansed my heart in vain, and washed my hands in innocence. For all the day long I have been plagued, I have been chastened every morning."*

These were words in the Bible? Olivia shifted the book in her lap and read the verse again, letting the words wash over her, trying to understand. When her parents died, each day was a hardship. She had felt punished for something not her fault. Plagued. And had tried to act the way God wanted her to, and she still lost it all, while those who judged her carried on.

Where *was* God? Why did those things happen? Did the person who wrote these words in this Psalm feel the same way? Were the answers here, in the Bible?

She read on, hungry to know more.

Her heartbeat sped as certain words jumped out at her. *"When I thought to know this, it was too painful for me."* Carrying the entire weight of responsibility on her shoulders had been *painfully* difficult.

"Until I went into the sanctuary of God; then understood I their end."

What did those words mean? She didn't know how to interpret them on her own. She frowned and glanced back at Pastor William.

"The Sanctuary of God is wherever God is, sitting in communion with Him. Asaph finally went *to* God in God's sanctuary." He paused for emphasis. "You can't avoid God. You have to go to Him, and I don't mean here in this building. You go to Him wherever you are. In your home, in your garden, while riding your horse, cooking, chores. Everywhere. He's waiting for you."

Olivia's stubborn heart argued. *I don't want to go to Him. I've gone to Him, and He has done nothing for me. He's left me to fend for myself.* And yet, her mind argued back, *when she had no options left, a new path appeared.* Not the path *she* had planned, but a path nonetheless.

Olivia's heart twanged oddly as she read the last verse. *"But it is good for me to draw near to God: I have put my trust in the Lord God, that I may declare all Thy works."*

Stunned, her mind challenged her heart to believe.

God was trying to get her attention.

He had been all along.

* * *

THE WOOD CRACKLED in the fireplace, sending sparks up the brick chimney while warming the main room at the Woodward home. Olivia sat with her back straight in a hardback chair.

Mr. Woodward held the family Bible open and read the verse Pastor William preached on in church earlier in the day. "Teddy, what did you get out of Pastor William's message today?"

Teddy scrunched his brows together deep in concentration. "Pastor William talked about needing to turn to God, and I feel like I do, but how do you really know?"

"A good question. One not easily answered." Mr.

Woodward turned to Emily. "How about you, pumpkin? You studied the verse in children's class, right?"

Emily beamed as if she had the correct answer. "Yes, Papa. Miss Brown shared we can talk with God everywhere we go. We can invite Him into our hearts and up here." She pointed to her head. "Miss Carmichael even helped me this morning have a conversation with God on paper, ain't that right, Miss Carmichael?"

They all turned and looked at Olivia.

She squirmed in her chair. "Correct, Emily."

Mrs. Woodward's eyes glowed. She grabbed Olivia's hand and squeezed. Then she turned back to her husband, signaling him to continue.

Olivia swallowed. Never had she discussed a Bible verse so in-depth before. What she remembered of the church in Cincinnati included a scripture or two and then what committees were available for service projects. But here, the focus was on having a relationship with God. All a tad disconcerting.

"Miss Carmichael, did you hear what I said?"

Olivia pulled her gaze away from the fire, her swirling thoughts trying to form some sort of words. "I'm sorry." She gave a wobbly smile.

Emily walked over to her and placed her hands on Olivia's, where she held them squeezed together in her lap. "I said you prayed, and God answered your prayer and brought you here to us."

Olivia peered into this precious young girl's face, while the power of Emily's words washed over her. All this time she thought she was the one in control, she who found the job, and she who worked hard to get here. Could this be God's response to her prayers all along?

259

And would there be other things God planned that were different from her own?

Luke came to mind, and she shook her head to cast him aside. Even if marriage to Luke was God's plan, she couldn't marry him—not if she didn't trust him. However, a faint glimmer of hope stirred in her heart. Tired of shoving the hope down, the swirling thoughts connected into another branch of possibilities.

Did she have the courage to follow where it might lead?

Thirty

*Why was I so quick to judge Mr. Taylor? I never liked being judged
by others. I'm not any different than those who turned their back on
me in Cincinnati.*

—From the journal of Olivia Carmichael

After dropping the girls off at the schoolhouse, Luke
drove the wagon home. So much had changed in
such a short amount of time. He noticed the girls'
absence more and more, his ranch had grown to the point he
needed to hire more help, his feelings for Miss Carmichael
confused him, and Evelyn would be on a train to California any
day now.

Luke frowned.

He hadn't seen a letter from her since he wired the money.
Wouldn't she write back? What if she didn't come at all?

The weird stabbing pain appeared in his chest again, and
he rubbed his fist against his sternum. Ignoring the ache, he
managed the team as they took the corner, then repositioned

his hat and flexed his fingers. What would he do if Evelyn changed her mind? A strong strain of relief flowed through him as well as an image of Miss Carmichael standing at the front of the church, flowers in hand, and a big smile on her face.

He blinked, then glanced around, anywhere to see something else, and found himself staring at the blue sky.

Talk with me. A distant voice in his head called out.

He searched for something else to focus on.

Parts of Sunday's sermon replayed in his mind. The words from the Psalm knocked another hole in the wall around his heart.

Talk with me. The voice grew stronger.

"Go away!" Although a part of him enjoyed the quiet, his sisters constant chatter kept him from having these types of conversations with himself.

Talk with me. The voice practically screamed in his head.

He pulled on the reins. Was that his conscience, or God? Or could they be the same? Luke pulled his hat low and berated himself. The fact he had to ask. He shook his head. At one time, his relationship with God was crystal clear. Now, he didn't know. Yes, he sat in church each week and said prayers at night with his sisters, but when was the last time he talked with God?

He sucked in a breath and blew it out, hard. "All right, God. I'm here. I'm listening. What do You want?" He didn't mean to sound harsh, but the awkwardness was too much.

Flicking the reins, he set the horses moving again and shortly thereafter entered the drive to the ranch.

Talk with Me.

The team could do this part in their sleep. He slackened the reins as they headed around toward the barn. *All right, God. I know we conversed at one time, but since my parents died, I've had so much responsibility and worry on my mind. I know it's an excuse.*

Things are less rosy these days. Life is hard, God. And scary. So much loss. And You didn't make things any easier. Why should I talk with You? What good would it do? I couldn't anymore. The hurt ran deep. I know it's not right to shut You out, and I'm sorry, God. I'm not sure what else to say, so I'll stop with that. Amen.

Luke's heart pounded so loudly, he could hear the thumping in his ears. Why did he let himself release these deep thoughts? As the hammering lessened, a tiny seed of peace hovered around him, and he didn't feel so alone.

He jumped off the wagon to unhitch the team. He had work to do.

Hours later he stood in the same place, hitching the team for the second time that day. He'd told the girls to walk to the Martins' after school, and he'd pick them up there.

Saved him a whole heap of time and trouble.

He didn't have the heart to face Olivia and see the disappointment in her eyes. For he couldn't explain his reasons for being in a saloon.

The extra time to get chores done before dark and to take care of errands in town made life more organized. Something he hadn't felt since a certain schoolmarm showed up. Yes, her anger was a good thing. It kept him far away, and his life a little less chaotic.

Less bright as well. The thump in his chest appeared again.

The wagon rolled to stop in the small yard of the livery. He disembarked, then unhooked the horses, and walked them inside. After seeing to the horses, he strode up the boardwalk. First to the general store for supplies, then the smithy for the new wheel and harness he ordered.

"Hey there, Luke. Good afternoon," Jacob Woodward called out as Luke entered the store. The sorted mail sat stacked in the cubby holes built into the wall of the store. "Here's your mail." Jacob placed a pile of letters on the wooden counter.

"Also, the rest of your supplies are ready to be loaded. I'll have Teddy start."

"Thanks, Jacob. I left the wagon at Stevie's." He picked up the pile on the counter.

Jacob stopped at the doorway to the back and faced Luke. "One letter is addressed in a feminine hand." He grinned. "Do you have an admirer?"

Luke kept his face devoid of any reaction and hoped his shaking hand didn't betray him as he looked at the stack. "I've been waiting for some business news for a while. I appreciate you having everything ready for me." He raised his hat and waved the mail in his hand. "I'll see you next week."

Mr. Woodward stayed in the doorway watching him. "Aren't you interested in your news? You have been waiting." He gave a cheeky grin.

So much for hoping he'd not notice.

Luke grinned back, infusing as much bravado as possible. "I've waited this long, postponing a bit more won't make any difference. Thanks again." He turned and walked out the door.

He traveled a few paces, then turned into the alley, out of view of the store and prying eyes. Leaning against the wooden building, he looked at the first piece. The address written in feminine script on the first envelope did tell Luke it was real ranch business. He moved it to the bottom, glanced at the next envelope and froze. Here it was. His future written with words on a slip of paper. For some reason he felt like his cattle might when the chute closed and boxed them in.

What a dreadful thought.

No. This is what he had decided on. He must stay the path.

He flipped the envelope over and tore open the back, sweat from his palms dampening the delicate paper. Only a few lines to read.

Mr. Taylor,

Thank you for selecting me to be a surrogate mother to Rose and Caroline. I purchased a ticket on the noon train with the money you sent. I should arrive on the Tuesday train two weeks out if all goes according to plan. I look forward to meeting you and your precious sisters.

Evelyn

Luke held still, his gaze unmoving at the post in his hand. The cattle chute door was firmly locked. He flipped the paper over a few times for good measure, just in case his eyes deceived him. Nope, Evelyn was coming. And soon. He rested his head against the wall and closed his eyes trying to imagine his future. He couldn't. Only another face appeared.

He had two weeks to prepare his sisters, get things ready, finish Miss Carmichael's lessons, and walk away.

He couldn't turn back now. He would marry Evelyn and would have the marriage he planned. One where he wouldn't lose his heart. Which was ironic, because he had already lost it.

A layer of sadness crept in, and he wondered if the sorrow would ever go away.

* * *

A STRANGE SENSATION overcame Olivia as she faced the dilapidated house in front of her. Adam lived here? Adam, her hardest-working student, had not been present this entire week, and no one knew where to find him. Never in a hurry to leave each day, Adam responded well to instruction and listened intently to the lessons. Deep inside, she knew without a doubt he wouldn't miss school unless something monumental occurred. She wandered to the outskirts of town after class on a Friday to find out why.

Maybe she had Sterling's directions wrong. But it wasn't hard to misinterpret the words, "You'll know the house when you get there. At the end of the lane."

She surveyed the yard and shivered.

Empty and quiet, the entire road was so ... so ... desolate. Did anyone actually live here? She covered her nose. Her stomach roiled at the horrific smell as if an outhouse was exposed in the yard. Maybe one was. She couldn't see in the shadows. The yard looked like a graveyard at night as the sun sunk behind the trees.

A sense of unease slithered through her body.

She stepped gingerly over the broken step and onto the weathered porch. Breathing in some courage, she knocked loudly on the warped door. She knew several of her students lived in poverty, but she had no idea any of them lived like this. She assumed all boys got dirty and tore holes in their clothes. But maybe with Adam, there was more to it.

Not one to surrender, her knuckles made contact again with the rough, splintered wood, although the gaps made it difficult to get a solid sound. Was Adam inside sick? Sickness would prevail in conditions like these. Then a horrible thought occurred. What if she was expected to stay here for some time?

She gasped and gagged from inhaling the strong odor. Her eyes and throat burned. Surely Mr. Martin would not allow that to happen. Did people in town know how bad these conditions were? And if they did, why hadn't they done anything?

She shifted her feet. Why did she have to care so much and stick her nose in other people's business? Her plans were to stay indifferent.

A noise came from inside. She held her breath, not

knowing what she would be facing. As the door creaked open, a woman, who looked as old as the building, snapped at her. "What do ya want?"

"Sorry to bother you, ma'am. I'm Miss Carmichael, Adam's teacher. This is Adam's home, correct?"

"Ya, so? What do ya want?"

"I'm concerned about Adam missing school this week"

"Well ya needn't be. He's fine."

Olivia shoulders relaxed. What a relief. She hadn't realized the worry that plagued her. "What great news. May I speak with him?"

"Nay, he's not here."

"Do you know when he'll be back?"

"Not till Christmas."

"Christmas!" Olivia raised her voice. "Whatever do you mean?"

"We sent him to work in the silver mines. Much money to be made. He left with the other men a few days ago."

Olivia gaped and tears burned her eyes. Unladylike, but she couldn't hide her shock. Mr. Martin shared stories of families who came for the gold rush back in the '40s, but they never made much so they worked odd jobs to squeak by. Then when there was no work, the men headed back to the mines.

"What about his education?" Olivia sputtered out.

"Oh, he don't need nah education. He needs ta work." The woman sneered.

"But, he's just a boy," Olivia insisted.

"Ma'am, I don't know where ya are from, but round here, it don't matta what age ya are, everyone's gotta work. There's no free-loading." She swung the door shut.

Olivia stuck her foot against the wood to hold the door open. "But getting an education would improve his options for his future."

"His future's helping us family, and he knows it. Now ya git and leave me be. I don't have time to yammer." She slammed the door, pushing Olivia's foot out of the way.

Olivia stood there as her heart broke into a thousand pieces. Mindlessly, she turned and walked back toward town, not paying attention to anyone or anything as she crossed the main road.

"Hey Lady! Get out of the street," someone yelled.

Squawk, Squawk!

Olivia turned and came nose to nose with a team of horses. Unable to move, she closed her eyes as a huge weight knocked her over. Pain shot along her side and on the back of her head as she rolled and came to an abrupt stop. "*Oof.*" Her breath escaped.

Shouldn't getting trampled by a horse hurt more?

Her eyes squeezed shut, she raised her head and bumped her nose against a soft surface. A pleasant mix of leather, dirt and soap filled her nostrils. With extra effort, she opened her eyes to face two big angry brown eyes glaring at her.

How did she avoid the horses and get run over by a bear of a man instead?

Thirty-One

Emily said God helps us through the bad stuff because we have Him in our hearts. I hope He helps Adam. Wherever he is.

—From the journal of Olivia Carmichael

He had sworn to stay away. But here he was, lying on the ground in the middle of the street, glaring at her while he waited for his heartbeat to slow enough to speak. Why was she a danger magnet? The impulse to strangle her warred with his concern for her well-being.

Squawk! Squawk! Bert flapped his wings and waddled over to protect his mistress. He stopped a foot away and ducked his head near hers. The way this bird took to Olivia flabbergasted Luke. In a strange way, it had become a comradery of sorts in that they both wanted to keep Olivia safe.

"Miss Carmichael! What were you thinking?" He shut his eyes and counted to three, then opened them again.

Her gaze darted all over until it landed on him. "I ... I ... can you get off of me, please!" She squirmed. A promising sign, right? "This isn't proper," she whispered.

"How else could I have kept you from getting run over." He hissed through clenched teeth as he lifted himself up. He reached to grasp her hand and help her to her feet. "Are you hurt anywhere?"

She looked at his hand and promptly placed both of hers behind herself to push up. The rebuff stung, although it was for the best. He didn't need any more physical contact. But then, she wobbled, and his hands shot out on their own accord.

Squawk! Bert pushed between them, and Luke let go.

"Thank you, Bert." Her pointed comment directly hit his pride as she brushed the dirt off her skirt. Luke stepped back. But then she held out her arms, bloody and cut, and it took all his might not to put his arms around her to offer comfort. To her or himself, he had no idea.

Luke reached for his hat, but his hand caught air. He broke eye contact and frantically looked around till he found it a few feet away in the dirt. Seeing the Stetson there in the middle of the street riled him so much it's a wonder steam didn't come out of his ears.

Dust whirled around his legs as he stomped over. He didn't care. Both he and his hat were covered in dust anyway. He bent over, picked up his hat, slapped it on his leg a few times and firmly planted the band on his head.

Taking a calming breath, he turned to face this woman, who tossed his emotions around so completely he didn't know what to do.

But she was limping away from him, in the middle of the street.

"Hey! Where do you think you're going?" He ran after her.

She glared over her shoulder but kept hobbling along and didn't say a word.

He touched her arm and stopped her, turning her to face him. "Hold up."

She glared at him, tears streaming down her cheeks. He gulped back his words and searched her face. Jagged scratches framed her beautiful face all along her hairline, and strands of hair fell from the neat and tidy bun she usually wore. Without thinking, he reached to push hair behind her ear and wipe the blood off her cheek. She flinched, and the idea she feared him made him feel like the worst sort.

"I'm sorry, Miss Carmichael. I didn't mean to hurt you. I saw you in front of those horses and reacted. Didn't you notice you stood in the street right in their path?"

Her dazed gaze looked beyond Luke, and she shook her head. She acted as if the weight of the world sat on her shoulders.

"What distracted you?"

She glanced back, her eyes filled with deep angst.

What happened to affect her so?

Fists tight, his nails dug into his palms. A good reminder to keep from reaching out. Because all he wanted was to wrap her in his arms and tell her all would be okay.

But he couldn't.

A wonder he didn't draw blood in his palms as he stood waiting for an answer.

In some ways, he hoped she wouldn't speak.

He didn't think his heart could handle whatever she told him.

* * *

OLIVIA BREATHED in and out slowly to calm her erratic heart. She didn't know if her heightened awareness came from the scare with the horses or the closeness Luke's rescue brought them.

271

Deep dark brown eyes, albeit softer now, pleaded with her to share, which made her want to unleash all her burdens.

She was so tired of dealing with them on her own.

She inhaled. Her dry mouth choked her, and she doubled over, coughing. He patted her back while her body spasmed. So much dust in this place. As the fit subsided, she straightened and pasted on a smile. "Thank you."

His lips twitched as he tilted his head and stood silent.

She swallowed. "Do you know Adam Holberson?"

He scrunched his eyebrows together. "The young boy who stays afterward with you most days?"

"Yes, him."

He nodded.

Olivia looked away. Her heart ached for the boy with his love for school, who now had the burden to work in a mine to help his family. She couldn't understand how a parent could send an eleven-year-old boy away, not caring for his safety.

She blurted out, "He's gone."

Luke froze. "What do you mean, gone?"

Throwing her arms around, she paced, causing a dust storm around her boots. The imagery mirrored the turmoil in her heart. "I haven't seen him all week, and I was worried. So, I went to his house—"

"You went to his house? Alone?" Luke exclaimed.

Olivia flinched, knowing now why he would react that way. Her insides warmed at the concern in his voice. When was the last time she had someone who cared what happened to her? "Yes, I went alone. What was I supposed to do?"

"Ask me to go with you." The surprised look on his face must've matched her own.

"You really would like me to ask you to go with me to visit my students?"

"Well ..."

"You don't really want to be my babysitter."

"It's not that. Just going out of town by yourself was not smart."

Olivia opened her arms in frustration. "How was I supposed to have known?"

Luke put his hands on his hips. "You ask somebody."

Olivia copied his body posture. "I don't have anybody to ask."

Luke's face turned grim. "You ask me."

"We are back to this again? You haven't been around all week. You've been avoiding me."

Luke stiffened. "I wasn't avoiding you. I've been—busy."

She narrowed her eyes at him. "You've been avoiding me, ever since the day in Sacramento. Please know I don't expect any explanation, by the way."

Luke gritted his teeth. "Not here, though. Come with me."

He led them farther down the street, Bert clucking behind them. They should've attracted attention, but no one was around, apparently trusting their schoolteacher with Luke. Why? Because Arthur Martin claimed it was okay?

Luke stopped at the schoolhouse and motioned for her to sit on Bert's stump. She complied.

He paced a few steps and wrung his hands before he spoke. "One of my ranch hands disappeared after payday. I went there, asking around to find him. I promised his family." He shook his head. "Which has been harder than I thought."

The pleading on his face erased any doubt he told the truth. "I wasn't drinking. Only soda water."

She rose and approached him. "You don't need—"

"Yes, I do, Olivia." He grabbed her hands, then let go quickly. "I want to. I don't want you to think less of me."

"I don't." She responded without thought, the words ringing true in her heart.

He narrowed his eyes. "But you did. You judged me." He shook his head. "I didn't like it."

The words struck her heart much like Ol' Fred's horns had gored the shack weeks earlier. She grabbed his calloused hands. Rough, strong, and gentle all at the same time. This man had watched out for her well-being since she set foot into town. "You're right, and I should know better. I've been judged myself, and it felt horrible. I shouldn't have judged you. I was wrong."

He blew out a long breath. "Well, thank you." He tilted his head to search her eyes. "Are we good to move on from this? Leave it in the past?"

"Are things truly ever left in the past?"

Did he growl? "We should leave them there, yes."

Yes, they should. The energy to keep dealing with the past drained her. "Is that why you avoided me?"

He glanced away.

He had! "I do understand why."

"You do?" His eyes grew wide.

"Yes. You're tired of looking out for me." Then, more softly, she added. "And I got your hat all dirty. Again."

Luke chuckled. "True, I don't like my hat in the dirt." He hesitated. Then he spoke so softly she had to lean forward. "I don't mind spending time with you."

"You don't?" Olivia disliked sounding so hopeful. Distressed in fact, since she prided herself on her sense of control.

He shrugged, then grinned, and her breath hitched. "Someone needs to keep you safe. For some reason, trouble sticks to you like this dirt sticks to our boots.

Olivia frowned, then glanced at her boots. The dirt here stuck helplessly to the leather. Did trouble stick to her the same way? The only reason why he helped? She had hoped it was more. She stepped back. Her heart was too far engaged.

Luke raised his brows.

She forced a smile. As much as she wanted to disagree with his statement to rile him, she didn't have the heart anymore. "Things happen to me all the time, and I don't know why."

He masked his surprise at her words. "Uh ... maybe because you walk into situations without realizing first what they are." He held his hands in a surrender gesture. "I can see on your face you want to get mad at me. Don't. Hear me out."

She bit her tongue.

"You don't have to live life on your own Olivia." He reached for her hand. "You are a determined lady. And no one wants to take your hard-earned independence away from you. Don't you ask your students to help one another?"

Why could she not trust this man? He'd been nothing but kind and patient with her. As much as she wanted to not depend on anyone, she couldn't live life on her own. And she liked having a friend who cared. She had guarded her heart to not have friends. She hadn't expected to have any.

"Are things here different from where you came from?"

She glanced at her small hand in his large one. Warmth traveled up her arm. Was he trying to say something more? She gazed into his eyes.

"Let the town help you. Let me help you." He looked distressed and dropped her hand, as if he had just realized what he'd said.

He paced back and forth. Unsure of his intentions, she followed his movements.

He stopped and pushed his hat brim. "Let *God* help you."

She blanched.

He paced again. "Sorry. I didn't mean to preach." Luke kicked the dirt. "I'm one to talk." As if he struggled with his own advice. A pea-sized pearl of hope fluttered to life in her chest. Maybe they weren't so different.

Facing her, he asked, "Are you sure you want to live all by yourself at the schoolhouse?"

No, she wasn't sure.

But she wouldn't change things now. Not after all the planning for building the room addition next weekend. And not with her emotions see-sawing, creating a queasiness in her stomach she didn't know how to squelch.

"I would feel better if you knew how to work a gun. I could teach you. We could use the targets the girls use."

His words brought her out of her stupor. "The girls know how to shoot?"

"Yes, ma'am. Everyone around here learns at a young age. It's important to know how to protect yourself and others. And be safe. Something may happen in your schoolhouse, so you should know how to handle a rifle to protect yourself or your students."

The queasiness in her stomach threatened to boil over. But she told herself to trust him. "Okay. But not until after next Saturday, with the add-on and all. There's a lot to do beforehand."

"Another week?" His eyes narrowed. and he glanced to the sky. "Okay, then." He stood all business-like, as if stepping off the see-saw altogether. Then he dipped his hat and walked away.

A sense of unfinished business and an urgency to chase after him filled her.

Refusing to move, she let her mind sort through her thoughts as he turned the corner.

She gasped.

She never did tell him what happened to Adam.

* * *

OLIVIA HEADED HOME in the other direction, climbing the stairs and entering the Woodwards' apartments. Thankfully, no one was home as she didn't want to have to explain the dirt and cuts. She cleaned herself at the kitchen sink, then went to the room she shared with Emily. A jumble of emotions ached to get out, the need to write filling her with purpose.

She sat on the bed, her journal on her lap, opened.

Why do I always find myself needing Luke Taylor's help? Of course, being tackled by him was far better than a team of horses, but still, he catches me at my worst. What he must think of me! And yet, he treats me as if he cares. I'm so confused. Does he see me as more than his sisters' teacher? Do I want him to? He's so strong and steadfast. Yes, I appreciate his fast thinking and his protection, but I cannot come to depend on him. It will only hurt more when he breaks my trust.

And what can I do about Adam? My heart breaks for him. I know I wasn't supposed to care for my students, but I do. Who knew teaching would take more of my heart than I ever thought possible? Oh, the thought of small Adam working in a cave. Is he cold? Does he have a book to read? Is he getting enough food? So many questions, and no place for me to get answers. I wish I could do something. I feel so helpless. And I made a promise to myself I wouldn't feel this way again. What do I do?

She stopped writing and studied her words, surprised at the thoughts she put to paper. It read like a letter. But to whom?

Immediately her mind went to the conversation with Emily. Did she just write to God? How did one know? Did this count as a prayer? She hoped so. For Adam's sake, more than any other, she sure hoped so.

She glanced at her page. Then added one more line.

God, please watch over Adam.

She whispered the words on her heart. "I hope you are listening, God. Not for my sake, but for Adam's. Amen."

The front door slammed open. "Miss Carmichael?" came a shout from the front room. "Miss Carmichael, are you here?"

"I'm in here." She placed her journal on the nightstand.

The door creaked as Emily stood in the doorway. "There you are! We thought we heard feet, but we weren't sure so I volunteered to check."

Olivia rose from the bed. "Is something amiss?"

Emily furrowed her brows, obviously thinking why she came charging in so fast. "Oh, yeah, Mamma wanted to know if you would be joining our family Bible reading tonight."

Olivia's heart lifted, happy to be regarded as one of the family and included in their treasured time together. A few weeks ago, she would've passed, but she wouldn't say no after the day she had. "Count me in." Their type of faith was so new to her, and she still didn't fully understand.

Emily beamed. "Great, I'll tell Mama." She darted back the way she came.

Later, as Olivia sat in the family's sitting room, Mr. Woodward held open the family Bible and read Proverbs 3:5-6: *'Trust in the Lord with all your heart and lean not on your own understanding; in all your ways submit to Him, and He will make your paths straight.'* This verse tells us we need to make sure when we pray, to pray for God's will, not our own. We can ask

God for anything, but some things we pray for, we won't receive because it's not His plan for us. We need to trust Him, even when we don't understand."

"Father, is this the same thing when I really wanted the special doll I saw in the catalog you order from, and I prayed really hard for five days, and it still never came?"

Mr. Woodward's laugh reverberated throughout the entire room. "Yes, Em. A perfect example. Do you think God wanted you to have the doll?"

Emily shrugged.

"Did He want to keep you from getting a doll?"

"Nooo," she answered slowly.

"Was the doll expensive?" he asked.

"I don't know. I couldn't read the words yet."

They all chuckled.

Teddy leaned forward. "If it was too expensive, it could've made our family not have funds for food."

"Good example, Teddy." Mr. Woodward nodded.

"None of the other girls would've had a doll like that as well, so they would've felt bad," added Mrs. Woodward.

"So, it was better if I didn't get the doll?" Emily frowned. "Except for me. I was sad."

"Yes, yes you were. But was the toy something you needed or wanted? God gives us what we need, not necessarily always what we want."

Her eyes grew wide. "Ohhhh. Now I understand." Then her nose scrunched together. "I think."

Looking pleased with the discussion, Mr. Woodward continued. "This is a simple example to show when we pray, we need to pray for all things, but our hearts need to be open to *His* understanding, His plans, not our own. We can ask for things. But God knows what we need much more than we do. He sees things and knows things we don't."

Olivia struggled to wrap her mind around the concept. Was there a right and wrong way to pray? When she'd prayed in the past, she heard nothing. So, what was she doing wrong? Taught to keep prayers to herself, should she share her prayers instead?

Their relationship with God made the Martins, Woodwards, and the Taylors different from anyone she'd known. Their actions stood out. Never had she seen so much trust in God before. It seemed a little awkward and peculiar but also refreshing and inspirational. Something she wanted.

But could she trust God again? Had she ever really trusted Him in the first place?

After readying for bed, Olivia stared out the window. Her mind a jumbled mess, unable to organize her thoughts. She gathered her journal, then sat down and wrote from her heart.

Help me, God. I'm not sure what I need to do. Have I been approaching this all wrong? Are you really there for me? I guess I'm asking for Your help. Please reveal to me something to help me understand. Thank you, Olivia.

The awkwardness eased, and a peace overcame her. She sat, waiting.

What now?

Thirty-Two

Moving into my own space is what I wanted, but I never expected to feel a connection to these families. Do I want to live by myself my entire life? And when did I start having a conversation with You about things, God? I still don't know if You'll answer me, but I don't feel so alone anymore.

—From the journal of Olivia Carmichael

Olivia rose early the following Saturday morning to help Mrs. Woodward prepare food for the schoolhouse room addition build workers. Last night she replicated Cook's apple pie to the best of her ability. The smell of baked apples had reminded her of all the times she stood on a kitchen chair and helped Cook bake. The recollection had made her smile while the pang in her chest for all she lost had shrunk. Now, she was making new memories. Something she never imagined would happen.

"Let's put all of these boxes by the door. Teddy and Jacob

can carry them to the wagon for us," Mrs. Woodward said over her shoulder as she pulled biscuits from the oven.

Olivia placed the cooled rolls in the box. "Great idea. These boxes are heavy with all this food."

"Yes, they are. Are you excited to have peace and quiet with your new room?" Mrs. Woodward covered the food with a few towels.

"I am. But I'll miss cooking together and feeling a part of your family." She'd miss other things, but she wouldn't list them out. Mrs. Woodward would never let Olivia leave if she knew the doubts Olivia harbored.

Mrs. Woodward placed a hand on Olivia's arm. "You know you can come back to stay whenever you want."

Olivia squeezed Mrs. Woodward's hand. "I know your offer stands. But Emily needs to sleep in her own bed. And I don't want to be a burden to anyone. Like Mr. Martin has explained, I plan to be a teacher here a long time. I need a place of my own."

Mrs. Woodward nodded. "I know. You've stated your position before."

She shrugged. "My plan all along was to live by myself in a boardinghouse. But there hasn't been one built yet, so this is the next best thing."

"So, you say. Living by yourself in the schoolhouse by the river is not the same, and you know it." She sighed. "But you're a grown woman, who can make her own decisions. You'll have to have meals with us every Thursday as you promised."

The Woodwards had asked her to come on Thursdays, and the Martins had requested her to come every Sunday. She appreciated the invitations. Although learning, she didn't know how to cook. A boarding house would've included meals.

After seeing how many of her students lived, Olivia

couldn't bear to add herself to their responsibility, so she had suggested to Mr. Martin the idea of an added room. At least until a boarding house was built, which wouldn't be until after the railroad station opened.

For now, she would live alone in an add-on room at the back of the schoolhouse.

She should be ecstatic. It was everything she had asked for.

But after living with warm and kind people for the past two months, it would be an adjustment. And, after today, all her goals would be met. All those plans she'd focused on, now complete. Accomplished. So, why did she feel so out of sorts?

"Time to leave," Mrs. Woodward yelled out to the entire family. "Everyone carry something to the wagon."

Ten minutes later, they drove into the schoolyard. The men unloaded the boxes of food, while Olivia and Mrs. Woodward followed them to the wooden table. She was thankful to have a job to do, helping feed all the workers.

She couldn't believe the entire community would be here today to build on her new room. Sure, many would come for the social aspect, thankful to have a reason to get together. Based on what she'd heard, there hadn't been an event like this in ages. Yet, for them to give up an entire day for her needs felt disorienting. To accept her in this way, so unexpected.

The excitement had grown all week long. None of her students had been able to concentrate on their schoolwork.

Neither had she, for that matter.

She gave up yesterday when some of her students presented her with a special gift—a handmade quilt for her new room—made by them. Speechless, she was grateful the men delivering fresh-cut wood to the schoolyard drew the attention away from her, allowing her time to gather her emotions. The present filled one of the holes in her heart.

Now the sound of sawing wood filled the air, amid hammering and shouts as the men worked together to form a square shape in the field by the school building.

"Good morning, Miss Carmichael." Two of her students, Robbie and Griffin, stopped to greet her, then ran to the table and snatched a treat. When no one told them "no," they grabbed a second one and ran off.

Screech. Bert strutted toward her from across the yard.

"Hello to you too, Bert." She grinned at how she could converse with him now and read his movements.

He strutted off toward his tree stump, jumped on top, and moved his head back and forth. Her heart warmed. Even on a non-school day, he kept watch over the schoolchildren. In some ways, they were partners, looking out for one another.

Chrissy Martin waved, hurried over, and hugged Olivia. "It's so good to see you."

A deep peace overcame Olivia as she hugged her back. "You too."

"You're our guest of honor. There are plenty of others who can help with the food. Go have some fun."

Olivia shook her head. "This is all so much. I need to keep myself busy."

Emily ran over and grabbed Olivia's hand. "Miss Carmichael, come play with us? We need you to pitch."

Chrissy clapped her hands together. "Perfect timing, Emily."

Emily beamed at Chrissy's praise.

"But—" Olivia protested.

"Go. Have fun." Chrissy laughed. "I'll be here when you get back." She called out as Emily pulled Olivia where the kids gathered on the open field.

"What team am I on?" Olivia asked.

"Both." Emily replied.

The game of baseball was a favorite of her students, and she'd pitched for them at recess many times. She enjoyed the freedom of swinging her arm around. In Ohio, young debutantes were not allowed to play baseball, or anything else, but were expected to sit demurely on the sidelines, looking pretty. Another piece in the puzzle of this new freedom she found herself in.

"Yay, Miss Carmichael," little Robbie yelled over the other children's cheers.

Teddy handed Olivia the ball. "Everyone is in position."

Griffin walked to the home plate to bat. "Throw the ball right about here, Miss Carmichael." He called out as he moved the bat to his side.

She nodded, then took a step forward and released the ball gently.

Smack!

Cheers erupted from the sidelines as Griffin ran around first base as fast as his legs would carry him. When the other team threw the ball over the second baseman, Griffin stopped with his foot on the wood shavings, huffing and puffing and wearing a big grin on his face, showing a competitive streak he hadn't shown before.

The ball came back her way. She picked it up and faced home plate.

There stood little Robbie, ready to bat, his face all contorted as he stared at the ball. She stepped forward and released it, holding her breath as he swung.

Robbie missed.

Groans came from the sidelines, where the rest of the team waited their turn. Robbie's face crumbled, and her heart ached. "That's okay, Robbie. You still get two more tries," she shouted.

He straightened, and his small hands squeezed the bat. She adjusted her movements to throw more gently.

285

Robbie swung with all his might as the bat connected to the ball in a solid *whack*. Cheers rose around her as both Robbie and Griffin ran to the next base. The other team shouted directions to throw the ball back to Miss Carmichael—and fast.

The game continued until everyone had a chance to bat. Pride filled Olivia as she watched her students play and have fun together. She enjoyed the camaraderie and the opportunity to get to know them better.

"Your turn, Miss Carmichael." She turned to where Griffin held out the bat.

She shook her head. "That's okay, Griffin. I don't need a turn." There was no sense making a fool of herself in front of the entire town.

Griffin pressed the bat into her hand. "Please, Miss Carmichael. We want you to."

Robbie, Sterling, and Emily joined Griffin, smiling. The hope etched over their faces gave her pause. She blew out a breath. "Oh, all right." Her body, filled with pinpricks, moved on its own accord as she gripped the bat. "But someone needs to pitch slow, so I won't miss and make a fool out of myself."

"I'll pitch for you, Miss Carmichael." A voice came from behind. She turned and found Teddy's hand outstretched. Blotchy red spots appeared on his face, and he didn't quite meet her eyes.

"Thanks, Teddy." She spun on her heel and moved to the square. Her quick glance at the men showed them still working. Hopefully no one else watched. She raised her chin to Teddy.

Teddy went through the motions and threw the ball.

Woosh! Her entire body swung in a complete circle as she missed the ball. Her heart thumped loudly in her ears. Above the pounding hammers, she heard, "You can do it, Miss

Carmichael." She pushed her sleeves farther up her arm and gripped the bat again. To her far right, two men sat on the roof, hammer in hand. Frozen dread filled her body, rooting her to the spot. She shook her head. Her mortification would be complete if Luke Taylor saw her. For some reason, she didn't want him to see her fail.

Teddy threw the next ball low and farther away, but Olivia swung anyway and missed. Her face heated.

"Sorry, Miss Carmichael," Teddy yelled. He took two steps closer.

"It's not you. It's me. I've never swung the bat before," she yelled back.

Surprise flittered across his face, and he took two more steps forward. "Let me throw from here."

Her ears rang. Too determined at this point to care, she braced herself to swing, no matter what. As the ball flew toward her, she gripped the edge of the bat so hard a sharp prick pressed into her finger. She ignored the pain and moved her arms, leaning all her weight into her swing.

Bam!

Her body vibrated as the bat made contact with the ball, then flew out of her grip. She gathered her skirts and ran toward first base as fast as she could. Vaguely, she became aware of shouts. Were they cheering or laughing? Yelling run or to stop? Did the ball go far or out of bounds?

She ran to the base, which was difficult while wearing a heavy skirt and corset. When her foot reached the sawdust, she stopped and placed her hands on her knees to catch her breath.

Several small hands patted her on the back. "Yay, Miss Carmichael! You did it!" Their loud yells drowned out the rapid beating of her heart. She wrapped her arms around them and laughed out loud, enjoying emotions she'd never known before. Acceptance, love, and family.

Imagine her surprise when she found herself glancing at the roof again, hoping a certain someone had been watching all along.

* * *

Luke held his hammer mid-air for the fourth time to watch the game.

When Miss Carmichael glanced at the roof, he immediately studied the nail in his hand and swung the hammer a few times. Counting to five, he stopped and took in the scene from his unobstructed view. It was obvious she'd never swung before, but she didn't let it stop her from trying. Her determination was one of the things which drew him to her.

"I see you can't take your eyes off our new schoolteacher." So engrossed in the game, he didn't notice Will kneel beside him.

He frowned. "For your information, my sisters Caroline and Rose are playing, and I'm watching them. Miss Carmichael just happens to be in my line of sight." Thankfully, his voice stayed even and cool when he said her name.

"Well, you might not be, but I am. I can't take my eyes off her. She's something. And the town seems to like her. Perfect wife material, don't you think?" Will nudged his elbow into Luke's ribs.

A surge of possessiveness reared inside him, and he scowled. The idea of her marrying anyone made him want to claim her himself. But he couldn't do that. "You do know she plans to never marry."

Will sat quietly for a moment, studying Luke. "Oh, I see!"

Luke held perfectly still. "What?"

Will grinned. "You like her."

He glared at his best friend. "Your point?"

"I've made it."

"You're acting childish. I'm her friend. Martin asked me to keep an eye on her, and I take my job seriously. So, of course I'm looking out for her." Why did he feel a need to defend himself? "I saw you talking with Green's daughter earlier. Anything you care to announce?" Luke knew his actions were also childish, but he couldn't help himself.

Will's dumbfounded look filled Luke with giddiness. "W-what makes you say that?"

Luke smirked at his friend.

Will laughed and raised his hands. "Okay, brother. I'll be quiet."

Luke pointed his finger at Will. "You started it."

The two men stared at one another, then let out an uncomfortable chuckle.

"All right, all right. I won't keep pushing. But I haven't seen you pay attention to anyone like this since—"

"Don't say it," Luke warned.

"Luke, we always avoid talking about Sarah every time we're in a room together. But we need to address the topic."

"We aren't in a room, Will. We're out here in the wide-open space on a roof."

Will sighed. "Don't state the obvious, Luke."

He hoped his silence would discourage Will. He needed those memories to stay stuffed deep inside and never see light.

Will didn't take the hint. "Even though I would've been fine with you and my sister marrying, neither of you would've been truly happy. I know you both. And care about you both. Yes, she hurt you, but it took a lot of courage and strength to do what she did. You need to forgive her so *you* can move forward. You didn't love her, and she didn't love you—not in the marrying kind of way."

"Who needs love in a marriage, Will?" Luke growled out.

"Or love in any relationship? Love gets you nowhere, just pain. Sarah and I worked well together. She knew the ranch, the life, and the girls loved her. They needed her. We all did. And she left us. Everyone leaves."

"I'm still here, Luke. And what about Caroline and Rose?"

"You sound like Jimmy."

Will's lips twitched. "Jimmy is a wise man."

Luke took a calming breath. Sitting on a roof was a dangerous place to be when upset. He cautiously looked over at his friend and saw acceptance and compassion in his gaze. Luke didn't want either one. He wanted to stay angry and keep his distance.

"She hurt me, too, Luke. But I've forgiven her like you need to. Don't you get it? Awful things happen in life, but God's love will see you through. You know she loved Michael. Did you really want a wife who pined after your dead brother?"

Luke placed a fresh nail in place and hammered it into the board.

"I know that sounds harsh. But it's the truth. You said you needed Sarah, but we can't expect one person to meet all our expectations. What you really need is God."

The denial sat on the tip of Luke's tongue. "It's not that simple, Will." The nail bent instead of laying flush. He growled. "You wouldn't understand."

A hand touched his shoulder. "Is this why you've pushed me away?"

Luke pulled out the nail and started over with a new one. Why did Will have to bring this up now? And why were his eyes burning?

Will squeezed Luke's shoulder. "Man, I've missed my best friend. I've given you the space I thought you needed, but all we created was a larger gap. When I lived on the ranch, we were inseparable." He raised his hands, palms out. "I know, I know. A lot has changed since then. I went away for a few years, but I came back like I planned. Let me in, Luke. More importantly, let God in. Together we can help heal the hurt you've been carrying around all this time. You're missing out on what God has planned for you."

Luke swallowed. "You know, it's not fun having a pastor as a friend. You talk too much."

Will laughed, reminding Luke of the bond they once had. "You know I speak the truth. Both your parents would say the same thing. Don't turn your back on God."

Luke's gaze searched his friend's face. He gave a tentative nod. Without another word, both men turned their attention to the game in front of them. A piece of armor around Luke's heart chipped away. He reached over and placed a hand on Will's shoulder and squeezed, mimicking his friend's action earlier. "Thanks for never giving up on me."

Will grinned.

Luke wanted to say more. Will *was* his best friend, had been for years, but circumstances changed the day Will's sister Sarah walked out of both of their lives, leaving Luke's trust shattered.

He knew Sarah's actions had hurt Will too. Her running off with a peddler created plenty of gossip for the new pastor who had returned shortly after the debacle. It couldn't have been easy standing in front of church each week not knowing where she ran off to, with rumors of her bad behavior circulating around town. And yes, he realized *after* Sarah left, his love for her was strictly platonic, and it was best they hadn't gotten married. But it didn't change the fact he'd lost so many people he cared for. Which hurt.

The bat flew out of Miss Carmichael's hands. She grabbed her skirts and ran to first base. Loud cheers floated from the ground and the children surrounded her with hugs and attention. In the chaos, her face lit with joy, reminding him of the day he first saw her in the train doorway.

An urgent need burned inside him to tell Will about Evelyn and his struggle with his feelings for Olivia, but he hadn't shared his heart in so long, the words wouldn't come out.

Thirty-Three

My new room is awfully quiet, and I can hear many unfamiliar sounds outside. I thought I wanted to be alone, but now I don't know. I miss the sense of family. And what will Bert do without walking me to school each day? One good thing is my time is reduced in the mornings to reach the entrance to the schoolhouse.

—From the journal of Olivia Carmichael

L uke sat in church between his two sisters as he usually did, with Jimmy on the other side of Rose. Week after week, their small family settled in the same pew, and week after week Luke allowed nothing to penetrate the wall he'd erected around his heart.

Until today.

A chink in the armor was missing, thanks to yesterday's conversation with Will. The current breach stirred emotions Luke had worked hard to ignore over the past two years. Rattled and unsettled, his senses were on high alert. They had to be for him to hear the heavy thud of Will's boots on the hardwood floor as he walked down the aisle, signaling the start of worship.

When Will reached the front, he held open his Bible. "Please turn to Romans 8:26-29, and read with me."

Book bindings creaked, fine paper crinkled, and wooden pews groaned. Luke heard each sound, much like when a traveling band warmed up before a performance.

Will cleared his throat. "Starting with verse twenty-six: *In the same way, the Spirit helps us in our weakness. We do not know what we ought to pray for, but the Spirit Himself intercedes for us through wordless groans. And He who searches our hearts knows the mind of the Spirit, because the Spirit intercedes for God's people in accordance with the will of God. And we know that in all things God works for the good of those who love Him, who have been called according to His purpose.*"

The words boomed through Luke and lodged in his heart, holding significant meaning, even though he didn't fully comprehend why. An urgent sense to escape rushed through him. Would anyone notice if he got up and ran? He shifted on the hard bench.

Caroline nudged him. Her gaze collided with his, and she nodded her head pointedly to the front.

He pinched his lips and faced forward. His movements must've been more than he thought for his sister to correct him.

Thump! Will closed his book, then glanced at Luke wearily. "Growing up in Washton, we've all experienced trials or watched other families carry heavy burdens. I'm sure there were times when you've all wondered where God was at that moment. You might've felt abandoned, alone, hopeless or all three. Discouraged to the point of not knowing what to pray for, or if your prayers would ever be answered.

What Paul wrote in this letter is when we are weak and vulnerable, unable to form words to pray, the Holy Spirit intercedes on our behalf and prays for us. Which means God still hears our prayers."

Will looked over at Luke. "I don't know about you, but I'm relieved to know two things. One, God never leaves me. And two, when I don't know what to pray for, God knows. Reassuring, isn't it?" He paused and smiled, his gaze landing on the rest of the congregation.

Luke squirmed and placed his damp hands on his knees.

Will continued. "But let me ask you this. Why do we feel we're alone if God is still with us?

Will's gaze landed on Luke again, and a small, resigned smile appeared. Then he scanned the crowded church. Luke wiped his hands a few times on his trousers and swallowed.

"When there's a crisis, we want answers to our prayers right away. When we don't receive them, we feel unheard, lost, and left alone. But we aren't alone. Nowhere in the Bible are the words 'if you believe, life will be easy.' That's a lie the enemy wants you to believe."

"Look again at Verse 28. 'God works all things for our good.' No matter what we're dealing with, God has the situation work out for our benefit." Will chuckled. "Maybe not the way we want, but the way God does. He wants us to be more like Him. What better way to do that than to use our trials to mold and shape us? Are we willing to let God mold us or do we reject Him entirely?"

Luke stared at his boots while every single word pierced additional holes in his armor. He clung to the spark of hope found deep in his heart. God never left? Was Luke then, the one who moved away? Had he turned his back on God? A horrible sense of shame crept along his neck. What had happened to the faith he was raised with and thought he had? He never meant to lose it, but he did.

The thought made him sick.

I'm sorry, God.

Immediately the despair and desolate feelings he carried around for so long dissipated. He tried to hold onto them like an old, ratted shirt that should've been discarded years ago, but the antiquated sentiments didn't stick around long enough for him to catch them.

He glanced at both sisters sitting on either side. His hands involuntarily reached for theirs and squeezed. Surely God wouldn't let anything more happen to their family, but if He did, Luke had to have faith they would be okay. For them, he needed to learn how to trust God again.

His gaze lifted to Jimmy's, who watched, approval shining in his eyes. Luke swallowed, and Jimmy grinned. This man never gave up on him and had been a solid rock Luke's entire life. Why did he not see what Jimmy had repeatedly pointed out to him? *Because you're stubborn like Ol' Fred.*

His lips lifted, his heart lighter than it had been in a long while.

The hairs on his neck raised, and he glanced over his left shoulder. Miss Carmichael observed with open curiosity. He quickly faced forward, his heart beating double time. No matter what, he couldn't think of Miss Carmichael in any other way than a friend. A responsibility only, no matter what his heart might say. And he needed to tell her about Evelyn. He would do so after their picnic and rifle lesson today. Then he would fade away from her and move forward with the plans he had put in motion and had no idea how to change.

* * *

Olivia sat on a blanket under the shade tree by the schoolhouse, contemplating the sermon while eating a piece of cheese. Could God have been with her all this time? She would've never dreamed she'd find a town like Washton and the people who lived here. Yet, she couldn't imagine being anywhere else.

"You're quiet, Miss Carmichael. Is anything the matter?" asked Caroline.

She brushed crumbs off her dress while the right words filtered through her mind. "No, dear. Why do you ask?"

"You seem distracted," Caroline replied.

Her lips twitched. "Well, to be honest, I'm a bit nervous about firing a gun."

"You'll do fine Miss C. If I can, so can you," Rose piped in.

She pulled on Rose's pigtail. "Thank you for your vote of confidence. The thought of shooting some poor, unprotected ..."

A loud squawking noise appeared on her left.

"What about the loud, not-so-poorly unprotected animals?" Luke interjected as he sat on the blanket. He grabbed the plate Caroline handed him and dove into the food as if he hadn't eaten in days.

Never did she think she'd be defending the fowl. "Bert may be loud, but we should never hurt him. He's quite helpful, isn't he girls?"

The girls giggled while nodding profusely.

Luke chewed, then swallowed. "What? Don't you get tired of hearing him squawk all day?"

The girls giggled some more and shook their heads.

A shadow fell over the blanket. "Care if I join you?" Pastor William asked.

"Not at all." Olivia made room on the blanket and

assembled an additional plate of food. "What a lovely message today."

She caught Will's glance to Luke, who chewed his food with lots of gusto. Will sat and picked at his plate. Curiosity got the better of her. "You two have known each other a long time, correct?"

Will's gaze flashed at Luke, who kept eating. "Yes ma'am, we have. Luke's ma took me and my sister, Sarah, in when our parents died during the flood of '62."

"The same flood that took my brother Thomas and Pa." Caroline's voice was tinged with sadness.

Olivia placed her hand to her chest. "Oh, my. So much tragedy." She noted Luke continued to pick at the crumbs on his plate.

Will sighed. "Yes, tragedy in multiple ways." He hesitated. "Sarah and I moved in with the Taylors, and Mrs. Taylor quickly became Ma to us, especially when Sarah and Michael, Luke's younger brother, became attached." Will laughed. "It was obvious from the beginning they only had eyes for each other."

The group grew strangely quiet. Even the girls. Their faces crestfallen. Olivia hadn't been introduced to anyone named Sarah since she arrived. What weren't they saying? "What happened to your sister, Will?"

Luke pulled a grass blade out of the ground and split it apart.

Will tore apart the food in his hands. "I wasn't here. But Michael caught some disease. He didn't get better, then Ma caught it …" he squinted at Luke. "I left for seminary so I could come back and take over as pastor here when Pastor Kenneth moved on. Sarah and Luke were left to take care of the family. They did all they could to help save Michael and Ma, but she only got weaker. After Ma died, Sarah left."

Words left her. She wasn't the only one who had lost much. Several questions fought to be released, but she held her tongue. She peeked at Luke from the corner of her eye. There was something else. When no one spoke, she dared to ask, "So, is she okay?"

The two men shared a look.

"Sarah left without saying goodbye." Caroline raised her chin a notch. "Ma asked her to be our ma." She looked at her brother. "And Luke our Pa. But Sarah didn't want us."

Olivia's entire body froze. Her heart pounded in her chest. These poor girls. To be so rejected. And Luke. Had he wanted to marry Sarah?

Will leaned forward, eyes focused on the girls. "She never wanted to hurt you. I know her leaving was hard, and not the right way to go about it. But ranch life was never what she desired. She has written, and she's doing well. She met someone and is married now."

Luke finally spoke, his gaze never leaving Will's. "When Ma asked me to marry Sarah in Michael's place, I agreed, because it wouldn't be right for Sarah to be under the same roof as me with Ma gone." He swallowed. "I was willing to do anything for Ma, anything she asked. Even though I didn't understand at the time, Sarah knew staying was not the answer. So, she left." He looked at his sisters. "But it was hard. We ..." he reached for their small hands. "felt abandoned."

Will dipped his head.

Some sort of fog lifted, and Olivia understood. Luke had guarded his heart and tried to control the world around him like she did. Her affinity grew for this man, who protected and cared what happened to her.

What had Pastor Will said today? The Holy Spirit prays for us when we can't? He knows what we need when we don't? She glanced around at the members of their picnic, and a warmth flowed all the way to her toes. Maybe coming to California really wasn't her plan but God's plan all along.

A movement caught her attention. Without any word, Luke rose and walked to the wagon, his shoulders slumped. For all the times he'd lectured her about asking for help, maybe he needed someone to rescue him too.

Will excused himself, but not before he thanked them for the food. Olivia and the girls finished clearing the remnants of luncheon when Luke waved her over to the tin cans he placed on the fence.

"Luke's a good teacher, Miss Carmichael. You'll learn in no time." Caroline hugged her waist tightly before sitting on the blanket next to Rose.

Olivia's whole body tensed as she approached the makeshift shooting gallery.

"Now stand in front of me, right here." Luke pointed to the dirt patch in front of him. She moved forward, and he stepped in close to her.

She shivered.

"Are you cold?" he asked.

She held her breath before she turned her head, and found herself looking right at his chin. She swallowed. "Um ... no." Her gaze lifted.

Big brown eyes searched hers, his right brow raised in question.

She swallowed. "Just a bit of nerves." Which was the truth. In more ways than one.

He pushed back the brim of his hat. "There's nothing to worry over. We'll start on the rules of using a gun."

"Rules? Don't you merely point and shoot?" She lifted her hand as if shooting a gun.

His chuckle reverberated deep inside her heart. *Focus,*

Olivia. You have a plan. Besides, he wasn't struggling being in such proximity to her.

"In order to be safe, you need to know the rules. How to carry, how to hold, load, and fire. All of them." He waited for her to acknowledge his words. "They could mean the difference between life and death."

Their eyes locked on one another.

She couldn't stand the tension and broke the connection. "Okay. I get the rules are important. So, fire away."

He laughed.

"What did I say?"

"Your wittiness comes out naturally when you relax. I like it." He cleared his throat and got a strange look in his eye. "You know, we need to talk after your lesson."

She blinked. And her heart sped out of control.

He held the gun up. "Let's get back to this first. Always point the gun down. This is so if the gun goes off accidentally, the bullet won't harm someone."

As he talked her through step by step how to handle the rifle, she tried to concentrate. But knowing they would talk and not knowing what about made it difficult to focus.

"Now you've learned how to care and load a gun, we can fire your first shot. Stand here, and I'll help you hold the gun for the first time."

Olivia hoped she hadn't missed anything important. She glanced over at Caroline and Rose still sitting on the blankets. Patches of light filtered through the branches of the trees, lighting their faces like a patchwork quilt of light and dark shadows.

They giggled and waved at her, unbothered by the scene in front of them.

The need to chat about something rose inside. "Is this how you taught Caroline and Rose?"

He froze.

The girls answered for him. "Yes!"

Startled, he tipped his hat in their direction, then placed his hands on her shoulders and turned her toward the target.

Tingly bursts traveled throughout her arms. Ignoring those feelings, she sucked in a big breath of air, pulled back her shoulders and lifted the gun into position.

Thirty-Four

I'm admitting here that my heart flutters when I'm near Luke Taylor. Do you think he likes me? Or is all this protecting and caring because of his sisters? I see something in his eyes when I catch him staring at me. And I hope it's what I think it is.

—From the journal of Olivia Carmichael

L uke studied Olivia's stance and tried to stay focused.

Get through the lesson. Then they'd talk.

He pointed to the target. "See the fence post and the tin can sitting on top?"

"Y-Yes." Her voice shook.

"You're going to knock the can off the fence."

She lowered the gun and frowned at him. "You must be joking."

Doubt showed all over her face, which made him more determined. Without thinking he wrapped his arms around her, lifted her hands still attached to the rifle, and leaned in close to help hold her in position. "You hold the rifle here."

Loose wisps of her hair tickled his mouth, while lavender scent invaded his nose. He almost forgot what he was saying. "Unhook the safety, look through the view finder, and find your target. Hold steady and fire when ready."

He didn't dare move as he waited for her to pull the trigger.

Her body shifted. The recoil of the gun pushed her back against his chest. A loud tink was followed by a muffled thud as the can hit the dirt.

His chest expanded, and their closeness immobilized him. He didn't want to let go.

"I did it!" Olivia said softly. The thrill of hitting the target pulsed off her. "I really did it."

She spun around in his arms, her eyes alight with joy. In that moment, she looked happy and content, as she deserved to be. Her grin drew his attention to her lips. The need to kiss her filled his thoughts.

Cheers erupted from Caroline and Rose, breaking the trance. He stepped back, his nerves on fire. Never had he been so drawn to a woman. But he was the lowest cad even entertaining such thoughts.

"Yay, Miss Carmichael! We knew you would learn quickly," the girls yelled.

She stepped away from Luke and waved.

Her absence caused a panic inside. He quickly grabbed more ammunition and handed the reloaded gun to her. "Why don't you try all on your own now."

He couldn't run, and he couldn't hide. To keep from reaching out, he crossed his arms, hoping to fight off the urge to hold her again. No use. He had tried to keep walls around his heart, but now seemed a useless exercise. As she eagerly went through all the motions to shoot the target, his heart revealed a new directive.

No longer did he want a loveless marriage. Although he

kept a neutral look on his face, an all-out war wrangled inside of him. What would he do now?

* * *

OLIVIA TOOK several tries before she hit the target on her own, but the energy coursing through her motivated her to keep going. She loved the concentration needed to shoot straight. She alone controlled the aim, and, after each pull of the trigger, she determined where to shift, right or left, up or down, to be more accurate.

The only thing countering her joy was the look on Luke's face as time passed. Was he unhappy with her? "My arm is tired, but I'd like to try one more time." And to put off the conversation Luke wanted to have.

He shrugged. "Set the safety on, set the gun there on the stump, and go ahead and put the cans on the fence so you can try again. The more you practice, the more precise you'll get."

After resetting the targets, she placed herself back into position. She lined up her sight, pulled the trigger, and knocked both cans off in consecutive shots. When she lowered the rifle, she grinned.

"Yay, Miss Carmichael!" yelled Caroline.

"Okay, that's enough for the day." Luke's set shoulders scared her. He dropped his arms and stalked toward her. "Time for us to talk."

Her mind raced in so many directions, it was a wonder she could walk in a straight line. Did she do something wrong? Was she being fired? Or did he want something else? Only one possibility stuck, but doubt consumed her.

She followed him to Bert's large tree stump. "Please, sit."

Her heart thumped double time as she slowly sat and straightened her skirts. Anything to keep from looking at him.

"This sounds serious." Was he going to declare himself? Did she want him to?

"Well, it is. Um. I need to tell you something. I haven't told anyone yet, except for Mr. Martin. I feel you must know as we've gotten to know each other pretty well over the past month." He glanced away, looking unsure.

Olivia straightened her shoulders, knowing her decision. Time she trusted again. Put the past behind her. "Yes, Mr. Taylor, Luke …"

"Let me finish, please, while I have the nerve." He let out a long breath. "I've found myself attracted to you, since the first day we met."

Warmth swept her entire body. Her entire body screamed to jump around.

"Hey, Luke!" Three men galloped toward them from across the schoolyard. Concern appeared on his face as he turned toward the newcomers. The girls stood up from the blanket, fear lining their faces.

"Sit next to Miss Carmichael." He called to them as he strode in the men's direction.

The girls came and sat on the stump alongside her as she fretted over what type of emergency needed his attention. Hopefully not the ranch. Could something have happened with the Martins? She circled her arms around each girl and placed a kiss on each head, hoping the news was not as bad as she feared.

She recognized the men as they pulled their horses to a halt. Jimmy from the ranch, George Henly, and Wade Schreiber.

"Luke, you sly dog you." Mr. Henly glanced over to Olivia and winked.

An acute uncomfortable sensation overcame her. She held the girls more tightly.

"You've been holding out on us." Wade smirked as he settled his horse. The horses looked exhausted.

Why had they ridden so fast to tease? None of this made any sense.

Jimmy, leaned over and handed Luke a piece of paper. A telegram. "These two brought this to the ranch first. They're sayin' there's a woman named Evelyn waiting for you in Sacramento. She arrived on the 5 o'clock train. Says she's your bride."

* * *

LUKE'S GAZE shot to Jimmy's. No. This could not be how Olivia found out.

Caroline and Rose tugged on his arms. How had he not heard them approach? "Luke. What's going on?"

He couldn't look at Olivia. He hadn't been able to get the words out and now... By the shy smile she gave him a moment ago, she probably assumed he was going to say something else entirely.

"It looks like your brother has found himself a wife." Wade grinned.

Luke heard a gasp at the same time the girls shrieked, "What?"

He hung his head. What had he done?

"Didn't tell anyone, did you?" The two men burst out laughing.

Luke raised his head and glanced again at Jimmy. Jimmy shook his head. Jimmy's horse shifted, and he expertly settled him. Luke wished Jimmy could settle Luke's heart, too, but too late. His heart was out of the barn, so to speak, and getting trampled at this point. Nothing good would come from this now. If only he had trusted God instead of taking the reins himself.

He swallowed. "Jimmy, would you escort Miss Carmichael to her room and take the girls home? I need to take care of this."

"Luke, you can't be serious." Jimmy eyed him shrewdly.

George smirked. "Oh, he's serious. Martin must've been aware. The reason why he would let him near Miss Carmichael and not any of the rest of us, ain't that right, Luke? You've had a bride lined up all along."

He wanted to punch his friend. "Thanks for the message. You can leave now."

"Oh, no. This is getting good." He lifted his head and peered to Olivia. "I'd be happy to escort you home, miss."

Luke's hands formed into fists. "Now..." A hand clasped his shoulder.

"I've got this, Luke." Somehow during the exchange, Jimmy had dismounted. He walked to Olivia and offered his arm. "Miss Carmichael, Caroline, and Rose. Let's see you all home after I hitch my horse to the wagon." He led his horse over and secured the reins.

"Hitched!" The other two men laughed out together.

"Luke's getting hitched, all right. Can't wait to see who Luke's *hitched* himself to." George grinned. "I think I need to go to Sacramento for some supplies. Don't you, Wade?"

"Enough!" Jimmy's tone brooked no argument. "You delivered the message, now back to whatever you do during the day. Time to leave Luke alone."

But their laughter grated on Luke's nerves as they rode away.

"Luke, this is all a misunderstanding, right?" Caroline asked. She and Rose stood at his side, confusion evident in their faces.

What could he say? "I'm afraid some of this is and some isn't. I don't have time to explain right now. I need to go meet Evelyn. We will talk when I get back."

The stricken look on Caroline's face before she ran over to Olivia and threw herself into her arms tore at him. Rose stood stock still, tears in her eyes, staring at him, before doing the same.

A large boulder sat in Luke's stomach as he watched Olivia place her hand on Jimmy's arm, then glance at him. The questions and hurt in her eyes pierced his heart. He had fenced himself into a pasture full of muck of his own making.

Time to follow the path he had laid out for himself. Even if it was one he no longer wanted.

He strode to Admiral and mounted, then left his family, his heart heavy. As he neared the ferry dock, the guilt consumed him. But nothing could be done except settle into the mire for good.

* * *

"No, no, no. Luke is supposed to marry you, Miss Carmichael." Caroline furiously shook her head as she watched her brother ride away.

Olivia wanted to mimic her, but instead she gave the girl what she hoped passed for a smile. "I don't think that was ever our plan, Caroline. I'm your teacher, remember?"

Jimmy's kind eyes held Olivia's. "You okay?"

Olivia tipped her head. What could she say? She barely held her emotions in check as he escorted her to her door. She wanted to be alone to process this news in peace. How had she misread things so completely?

"I don't understand." Rose held one of Jimmy's hands, tears streaming across her face. "What's Luke done?"

"I'll tell you what he's done—he's messed everything up." Caroline stood on the other side of Jimmy, her arms crossed. Pity showed in her eyes when she looked at Olivia.

Olivia summoned strength from somewhere deep within her. "Why are you looking at me as if someone died? I can't marry your brother. I'm your teacher, remember? Not only did I sign a contract, I have no plans to marry. Why do you think the town added on this room?" She motioned to the walls surrounding them. "Your brother knew this." She glanced at their sad faces. "Come here."

She opened her arms, and they both plowed into her and squeezed hard. She placed her cheek on Caroline's head. "He's been acting the gallant hero to protect me from all the other men. And his actions worked. We had you all fooled too." Right now, her feelings didn't matter, but she hoped this speech would help convince herself as much as the girls.

She peered at Jimmy standing there, hat in hand, eyes searching her face. "Truly. I'm okay."

He gave a small smile. "Ma'am, I'm glad to hear it. I'll take your words as they are. Besides, I know God is the One in control." He glanced outside the direction Luke went. "Whatever this is. Honestly, it's not you I'm worried about. That boy has not had his head on straight since his ma passed. I had no idea he had concocted this idea."

"What do you mean, Uncle Jimmy?" Caroline asked. The girls let go of Olivia and moved toward the strong, confident man.

He shook his head. "It means your brother is a fool, and we'll need to pray for him the entire drive home." He raised his hand and pulled on the brim of his hat, then faced Olivia. "Thank you again for being such an example of grace."

She didn't know if it was grace or not, but she did need to be alone before she lost control. "Thank you for seeing me home." She waved to the girls. "Don't be too hard on your brother. He believes he's protecting you all." And himself.

The same way he planned to sacrifice himself with Sarah. Nothing she could do. She closed the door and sat on her bed, stunned. The idea of marriage to Luke should have never been allowed to enter her mind.

Foolish heart.

The sharp pain reminded her of her childhood, when she hoped her parents would spend time with her, but they always had other plans. And her ex-fiancé, Richard, who, in the end, had made it clear he was marrying her for her father's connections and not her.

She knew better than to trust.

Why had she allowed herself to hope again?

Thirty-Five

*How do I deal with these feelings? I don't want to be in love with
Luke. I can't. He sent for a mail-order bride! And never said
anything to anyone about it. I know he didn't owe me any
explanation, but it still hurts and makes me so angry. We had no
official relationship. I just thought ... How could I be so foolish. God,
if you are there, please help me. What do I do now?*

—From the journal of Olivia Carmichael

Luke bypassed Main Street altogether to avoid
running into anyone as he headed to the water's edge
to board the ferry. What he wanted to avoid had
happened, and nothing would change things now. He'd be in a
loveless marriage of his own making within the next twenty-
four hours.

He paced back and forth as the barge crossed the river.
Anything to disperse the tense energy flowing through him.
For a while, he wondered what Evelyn looked like. Now he
would find out. Looks weren't crucial to him, but he needed

something mundane to focus on and keep his mind far away from Olivia Carmichael.

How unfair for his new bride. He hadn't even met her, and yet his thoughts betrayed her.

He ground his boot heel into the wood floor. Why did life have to be so complicated?

A train whistle echoed in the valley. The ferry docked as steam spilled out from the train engine. Luke coughed his way up the ramp as a second hiss of steam billowed around those who loaded and unloaded cargo.

People milled about as Luke stopped to search the platform. He had no idea how to find her. The temptation to turn back around and say he never found her tempted him, but that was a coward's choice. The only solution was to look up. He glanced at the cloudless blue sky. *God, help me through this.*

He closed his eyes and reset his mind. When they opened, a lone petite woman faced away from him, her hands resting on the depot railing. Dressed simply, in tailored clothes, her hair tucked into a small blue hat. A small pile of luggage sat to the side, more than what a passing traveler would carry. She searched for someone. Could that be her?

Somehow, he knew it was.

He shoved aside any doubts and marched in her direction. His chest felt hollow, making breathing difficult. As he approached, he shoved aside his negative attitude and pasted on a smile.

She turned his way and beamed, her eyes crinkling with relief. Her hands pressed against her heart, and her face changed to one of adoration.

He stopped mid-stride and dropped his jaw.

It was her. His mail-order bride.

Evelyn.

And she was old enough to be his ma.

She rushed to him, her hands outstretched. "You must be Luke."

He had enough time to close his mouth, swallow, and dig deep inside for the manners his ma taught him. He grabbed his hat and set it to his chest. "I am, ma'am. And you ... you're ..."

"Yes, I'm Evelyn, and I know I'm not what you were expecting." Did she sound happy? "But before you get all honorable on me, please hear me out." She placed her hand on his arm. The touch motherly, rather than wifely.

He cleared his throat. "Evelyn, there's nothing you need to say. We made an agreement, and I intend to keep my part ..."

"Nonsense." She interrupted him and squeezed his arm. Would constantly interrupting him be a bad habit of hers? "You don't want to marry me any more than I want to marry you."

Luke frowned. "You don't want to marry me?"

"You mean to say, after seeing me, you still would go through with this marriage?" She scoffed and *tsked* at him before she pasted on a motherly smile and patted his arm. "I knew you were a man of honor and that I could trust you."

He shook his head and put his hat back on. "Ma'am, Evelyn, or whatever your name is—you're not making any sense. If you didn't plan to marry me, why did you answer my newspaper ad? Use the money I sent? Agree to my terms if you never intended to carry through?

She patted his arm again. "You'll see in time, dear. But for now, I need your help to get my luggage together. As you can see I have quite a lot."

Eyeing the pile next to her, Luke didn't know whether to laugh, scream, or go to his knees and weep. How would he explain her to his sisters? To the men in his employ? Mr. Martin? Jimmy? To Olivia?

Olivia's hurt expression flashed before him.

Evelyn tilted her head. "Are you all right, dear?"

Instead of answering, he walked to the pile and gathered the smaller pieces of luggage under his arms.

"You didn't answer my question." She followed him and placed a bag in her arms.

Luke didn't stop loading what he could. "I'm fine, I need to rent a wagon to load all of this. Then we can be on our way."

"I can't wait to meet your sisters. Caroline and Rose. Did I get their names right, dear?" She asked.

He rather wished she didn't call him 'Dear.' The moniker made him feel ten years old. "Yes, Caroline and Rose are their names. Caroline is the older one at twelve, and Rose is seven."

She smiled. "I know you care about them. It showed in your letters and now in your face when you say their names."

"Well, ma'am." She was his elder and it felt odd to call her Evelyn. "I do care for them. They're all I have, and I would do anything for them."

"Including marrying an old lady, such as myself."

Luke lowered his head and focused on his boots. How did one not lie but not admit the truth, either? "Yes, including marrying you."

When he raised his head, her eyes sparkled with mirth.

She saw right through him, and he had just met her. And he was truly chastised, like she *was* his ma, which completely terrified him. He glanced at the smithy. "I'll get us a wagon so we can head home."

Home. Today. With Evelyn. To his family. And she never planned to marry him.

This was even worse than anything he could've imagined.

As the ferry crossed the river, Luke and Evelyn sat on the wagon seat in awkward silence. What a fool he'd been. No wonder her words sounded mature and wise—because she was. He studied her as she studied the landscape around them.

Why? Why had she pretended to be a mail-order bride? What was she running from?

He needed answers. But how did he start?

He cleared his throat. "My ranch is north of town, alongside the river. As I mentioned in my letter, we raise cattle for milk and meat. I've learned new ranching techniques to cut costs, allowing me to invest in more cattle."

She dipped her head. "You're a competent young man, Luke."

He squirmed.

"I would think a landowner such as yourself would have no trouble whatsoever finding someone to marry. So, why did you advertise for a mail-order bride?"

She was asking *him* questions?

Before he could respond, the ferry docked. He took fifteen minutes to maneuver off and onto the road. He flicked the reins and opened his mouth.

"Well?" she asked.

"I needed someone who would be a proper mom to the girls."

"*Tsk, tsk*, Luke. Those poor girls."

Did she actually cluck her tongue at him? He gripped the reins hard. *He* didn't need a ma—the girls did. So why did he feel he was bringing home a ma for himself too?

Nothing about this situation sat right. And why was he answering her questions, when he had his own she must answer?

But she kept right on talking, "I'm sure a young lady here would have no problem being a mother to your sisters."

None he would consider. Except one, now.

Evelyn studied him before she turned and faced forward. "Neither of us have been forthcoming, Luke."

She made no sense. "Look, I know you misled me by not revealing your age, but how was I not forthcoming with you?"

She waved her hand at him. "You said you were looking for a wife and a mother to your sisters. But what you *really* wanted was a housekeeper and mother hen. Someone to teach and show the girls how to become grown women."

He shook his head. "Anyone willing to step into that role would live in my house, under my roof. I'm a single unmarried man. The only option for me was to take a wife. And it was your letter I accepted. But first, tell me why? Why the charade? What benefit does this arrangement bring you?"

She glanced away. "I have no intention of marrying again."

"Whoa." Luke yelled as he halted the horses and glared at her. "What?"

"You heard me."

"You don't plan to marry?"

She shook her head. "Once was enough. No offense."

"Then why answer my ad?" Luke asked, exasperated. *And waste my time.*

"What I want to be is a governess. Or a housekeeper, or a nanny. I don't have family of my own. And I want one to take care of. To feel needed and have purpose. Your ad provided the perfect solution. You listed duties for a housekeeper and a nanny. With no mention of marital relations or specific requirements within the marriage. I hoped once we met, you would agree. I read between the lines. You didn't really want a wife. Not yet, anyway. But if I wrote that in a letter to you, you would've passed over me."

Luke swatted his hat on his leg. "Of course, I would have. I expected to marry and move on with my life." He didn't mean to sound so harsh. His insides were churning, like a cow headed to slaughter.

"Notice you did not say you *wanted* to marry."

"Most marriages are made of necessity. There's not *want* about it."

"I know," she whispered.

Luke glanced at her. She bowed her head, hands in her lap.

Lost in thought, she shook her head. "I decided long ago if I had the chance, I wouldn't let someone else make that mistake. I don't know why, but when I saw your ad, something called to me. Somehow, I knew I was being led here. The good Lord has made our paths cross, and I think I can help you."

"Don't bring God into this. He's done nothing but take away from me."

"You're hurting, Luke. God knows you search for something, but it eludes you as you look in the wrong places."

Luke grabbed the reins and flicked them.

Who did she think she was, lecturing him about God? He didn't need to lean on God. And he didn't need her interfering in his life. She didn't even know him.

He focused on driving the team toward his ranch. They both sat in silence.

Was he in the middle of one of those silly plays his sisters put together? Nothing made sense. How did he get here? And what was he going to do? Before long, the wagon traveled under his ranch's sign and into the circle drive leading to the house. When he stopped the horses, he jumped from the wagon and hurried around to help Evelyn debark.

The door opened. He heard the girls' giggles, and then complete silence.

He still had no idea how to explain this, whatever *this* was.

He turned to face his family and found his sisters on the steps, Jimmy standing behind them. Luke saw the second Jimmy noticed Evelyn. He swiveled an astonished look at Luke. Luke shook his head and shrugged.

Evelyn spoke before Luke could say anything. "Hi there,

dears. You must be Caroline and Rose. I've heard so much about you. I'm Evelyn, and I'm going to be your housekeeper and governess."

Caroline and Rose didn't move.

Luke blew out his breath. Yes, he was confused too.

"Caroline, Rose, this is Evelyn. She'll be staying and helping out. You will respect and obey what she says. Are we clear?" He looked at Evelyn and then back to his sisters, "She'll help you with ... ahem ... women things."

Caroline looked horrified. "We don't need her Luke. We've been doing fine on our own. And if someone were to stay with us, then we prefer Miss Carmichael." She glanced over to Evelyn. "No offense, ma'am."

Evelyn beamed. "None taken. I completely understand."

"You do?" Luke didn't dare laugh out loud at the startled look on Caroline's face, even if it was comical. This entire situation played like a farce.

Evelyn marched across the yard to approach the girls. Not much taller than Caroline, she grabbed a hand from each of them and looked them directly in the eyes. "By no means am I looking to take the place of your mother. What your brother is trying to convey is as you mature, you'll need an elder lady around to make things all right and proper, since all of the adults on your ranch are men. You do want to be considered respectable, correct?"

The girls paused, looked at each other, then nodded.

"You'd also be helping an old lady out by letting me feel needed. I don't have a family or anyone to take care of. I'm hoping I'm needed here." She glanced over her shoulder at Luke. "This frees your brother so he can do what he needs to do. And maybe that could include some courting, like this Miss Carmichael you've mentioned."

Luke's entire face went hot. How did Evelyn sum up

everything he'd been trying to figure out for months in the few minutes she'd been here?

The girls searched Evelyn's face, then their own features lit up.

Uh-oh. Somehow the women just joined forces.

"There, there, dears. I can see we're going to be great friends." She raised her head and faltered. "Can you introduce me to this handsome gentleman behind you?"

"This is Uncle Jimmy," Caroline stated.

Rose grabbed his hand. "He takes 'are of us."

"Ma'am." Jimmy held his hat in his hands and stared at Evelyn, his gaze frozen for longer than necessary.

"He's not really our uncle, but that's what we call him. He's taught us all we needed to know about cooking and cleaning, so we know how to tend house." Caroline glanced over her shoulder. "Ain't that right, Uncle Jimmy?"

Jimmy didn't say a word, but kept staring at Evelyn.

Rose pulled on his sleeve. "Unca Jimmy, say something."

"What?" Jimmy blinked and faced Caroline.

She crossed her arms and raised her eyebrows.

"Oh. Forgive me, ma'am." He kept his eyes downcast as he grabbed the rim of his hat.

Luke had never observed Jimmy speechless. What had gotten into him?

Evelyn addressed the girls. "So, tell me, who is this Miss Carmichael?"

Luke shrugged. "Their schoolteacher."

"A special friend." The girls answered at the same time.

Evelyn faced Luke, her expression clearly stating she understood who Miss Carmichael was to him. Even if he did agree, it didn't matter, not after what happened earlier in the day. Trust didn't come easy for her, and today, he broke her confidence. A sure mess he had no idea how to fix.

He pulled Evelyn's luggage out of the wagon and overheard Jimmy tell the girls, "Why don't you girls take Miss Evelyn inside and show her around?"

"Luke?"

His head bobbed his consent without looking their way. At least they still asked him for permission. He couldn't lose their trust as well.

He lifted one of the smaller trunks.

A hand entered his peripheral vision, lifting the other end. "Luke—"

"Don't say anything, Jimmy," Luke hissed. "This plan is all mixed up, but I'll figure something out."

Jimmy chuckled. "Maybe it's time you let God figure things out. He's known from the start what His plan is, but you're the one who keeps trying to control the reins."

"I'm not controlling anything." He shook his head. "None of this was my plan."

Jimmy glanced over at him and raised his eyebrows.

Luke ignored him and, carrying the trunk by himself, headed toward the door.

Jimmy spoke behind him. "She's something, isn't she?"

Luke turned to his mentor and friend, who had the goofiest smile on his face, and then it became clear. He exhaled, threw his head back and closed his eyes. God knew what He was doing. Luke needed to get out of the way. "Let's get all this luggage inside before the girls conspire against us."

Jimmy laughed, a gruff, rusty sound Luke hadn't heard in a while, and the two of them carried what they held inside. Voices came from the kitchen, so they headed there, stalling in the doorway.

"Where will you sleep tonight, Miss Evelyn?" Caroline asked.

"She can have her pick of the three empty rooms upstairs.

I'll take these bags and place them in one of them. Once you get settled, you can decide which room you would prefer."

The girls' jaws dropped, and their eyes bugged out.

Caroline was the first to find words. "But Luke, those are—"

"It's okay, Caroline. Time for some changes around here, don't you think?" They didn't need to scare Evelyn tonight. If she decided to stay, there'd be plenty of time to tell her about the family members they'd lost and the battles they'd fought to eke out a living here.

"Thank you, Luke. That would be wonderful." Did she have a glow in her smile?

He was fifteen again, chest puffed out, all because he had her approval. He turned around to carry the luggage to the bedroom, but Jimmy blocked the doorway, staring like a rabbit frozen on the trail. Luke nudged him and he blinked again. Then they both turned and stomped up the stairs.

Neither said a word as they placed Evelyn's belongings in Sarah's old room. Luke rose after setting the trunk on the wooden floor and glanced around. Not a thing remained of Sarah's, but a lot of memories flooded his senses. But they weren't his memories of her as much as his brother and her together. She had lost a lot at a young age, first her parents, then her fiancé. Now, he could see reminders and why she needed to escape. The realization filled in another hole in his heart, which thumped hard in agreement.

"I'll leave now," Jimmy declared as he quickly moved toward the door. "I'm heading to the bunkhouse. I should sleep with the other men tonight."

Luke raised his brows.

"She's a grown woman. Someone my own age. Doesn't feel right to be in the same house." Jimmy faced Luke. "She was your mail-order bride?"

Luke gazed at his boots.

Waiting for a reprimand, Jimmy chuckled instead. "A little old for you, don't you think?"

Luke shrugged. "She never planned to marry me."

Jimmy *har-har'd* loudly. "She said that?"

Luke joined in. With a chance to absorb all that had happened, it was comical. And even more so watching Jimmy's interest in Evelyn.

"You plan to still find a bride? One closer to your own age?"

Immediately Olivia sprang to mind. "I don't know. There's only one person I would consider. And after today, I don't think she'll ever speak to me again."

Jimmy placed his hand on Luke's shoulder. "All you can do is try, and let God do the rest. His plans are always better than our own. Besides, He does work in the miracle business, you know."

"I know," Luke responded, warmth filling his heart in more places. At this rate, he'd have a whole new heart by Christmas.

Thirty-Six

God, I want to trust you, but again, I've been betrayed. How do I get
Luke out of my mind—and heart?

—From the journal of Olivia Carmichael

Olivia moved woodenly around the schoolroom.
Thankfully, no one was the wiser to her struggle.
Or so she hoped.

When Caroline and Rose arrived, they ran and hugged her,
saying they missed her. They quietly took their seats, and the
school day began. Nothing more.

Had they met this new woman? Had she and Luke already
married?

Olivia gave her head a quick shake. She wouldn't think
about him. He wouldn't be thinking of her.

She glanced around her schoolroom and frowned.
Susannah was absent again. She had missed classes every day
this week. After what happened with Adam, she worried
anytime one of her regular students missed more than a day.

Susannah often came to school with bruises and her dress was mended in odd places. When asked, Susannah told Olivia it was her animals, but in her soul, Olivia feared there was more to it.

By the end of the day, she imagined all sorts of scenarios, none good. What if something happened because she didn't reach out soon enough? Worrying about someone else helped keep her mind off Luke.

She placed the book she read on her desk. "Has anyone seen Susannah this week?"

Her students shook their heads and averted their eyes.

What did they know but wouldn't share?

Asking for Luke's help sprang to mind but was out of the question now.

"I'll check on her after school. Does anyone know where she lives?" Olivia asked.

Several children lifted their heads, their eyes bugged out in surprise before they refocused on their slates. Olivia brushed the concern aside. She wouldn't let anything stop her. She was an adult and the teacher. Someone needed to check on Susannah, so why shouldn't it be her?

She reached into her drawer and pulled out the candy Mrs. Woodward had given her. "Anyone tells me where she lives will get my thanks and this piece of candy."

Several hands went in the air.

* * *

LUKE HAD the girls walk to the Martins' house after school to give him more daylight to finish ranch chores. And coward that he was, a convenient excuse to avoid running into Miss Carmichael.

He still hadn't figured out what to say, and he didn't think she was ready for any explanations.

In the meantime, Evelyn had familiarized herself with the ranch house overnight. She sure knew her way around a kitchen. Her biscuits at breakfast were wonderful. Her kind words set a tone only a loving grandmother could do. And she had already won over Jimmy. He grinned and lingered long after breakfast to help with the dishes. Evelyn didn't seem to mind. Maybe she was what they all needed to bring change in their household.

Luke now knew he went about things all wrong. He cringed. Facing the situation head on was the only way to deal with it.

He arrived at the Martins', set the brake, and jumped off the wagon seat.

Caroline met him at the bottom of the porch steps, her voice frantic. "Miss Carmichael asked about Susannah today, Luke. She hasn't been at school again, and Miss Carmichael was worried. We heard her say she would go check on Susannah herself, but no one told her how dangerous Susannah's pa was. No one told her. You have to go after her, Luke."

He knew by now, if one of her students needed checking on, Olivia would go, with or without help. And she'd be walking into a situation she knew nothing about. Given the way things were between them, she wouldn't have asked him even if she wanted to. She'd have no idea about Susannah's pa.

Walt, who could be put in the same category as a bull, would not take kindly to a woman telling him what he should do. The man's wife mysteriously disappeared several years ago. She was a quiet sort, timid when out in public, yet neighbors said they could always hear her yelling a mile away. She either snapped and ran off, or he buried her in the backyard. Those were the rumors. And both caused people to be jumpy around him.

"All right. I'll check on her."

Relief flashed across Caroline's face, and she hugged him. "Thank you, Luke."

Maybe this was the opportunity he had been looking for.

* * *

SUSANNAH'S HOUSE stood on the opposite outskirts of town from Adam's, dilapidated and worn in similar fashion. Self-preservation screamed to turn around, but Olivia's heart told her not to leave until she had checked on her pupil.

She stopped at the yard, which had six round mounds in the front, held her posture rigid, then marched to the door.

Her hand shook as she knocked.

"What do you want?" yelled a scratchy deep male voice.

"Excuse me, sir. Its Miss Carmichael, Susannah's teacher. I wanted to check on her. Is she here?"

"You're wasting your time—here and at school. Women folk don't need no schooling. All they need to know is how to cook and clean and have babies. Now git! You shouldna be teachin' yerself. Ain't right." The voice grew louder.

Olivia fumed. Of all the pompous things to say. She leaned into the splintered wood. "I'd still like to see for myself. May I speak with her?"

"Nah, but you can see me!" The hairs on the back of her neck raised. Deeper, harsher, this came from behind her.

She didn't dare look.

Putting as much boldness into her voice as possible, she yelled back through the door, "I'm not leaving, sir. Not until I get the chance to talk with Susannah."

All of a sudden, the door yanked opened, and an average-sized man stood in the doorway. Dirty, smelly, with mean-looking eyes. He glared at her. "Lady, if ya don't leave righ' now, you're agreeing ya want to stay, and Burl here will be mighty happy to oblige ya."

Burl? Olivia stepped backward and bumped into a hard body. The stench made her want to gag.

Rotten and missing teeth showed when the older man grinned. "Meet my son, Burl. He's had his eye on ya, Miss School Teacher. Thought ya too uppity for him, but now I see you're pretty and feisty. He needs someone like ya. Ya'll challenge him to keep the upper hand. Ya'll make a great wife for him."

Dirty hands wrapped around her chest, pulling her flush against him.

Olivia stomped on the large boot next to her, then slammed her elbow into Burl's stomach.

The action did what was intended. He let go.

She scampered around the large man and stopped.

Luke stood there, his narrowed eyes focused on Burl.

Burl growled.

Olivia swung around and planted her feet solid on the ground.

Burl froze, then hissed. "Luke Taylor, this is none of your business. Miss Carmichael is mine."

She put on her strictest teacher voice. "Let's get something straight. I'm a person, not a piece of property to be grabbed and held against her will."

Burl's brows furrowed.

She softened her voice, pushing all sense of reason into her words. "You won't keep a wife this way, Burl. You want a woman who will stay of her own accord."

The older man came out of the house, his face contorting. "Ya're standing on private land, Luke. And since it's my land, what I say goes." Spittle flew out of his mouth. "She is Burl's, fair and simple like."

Olivia scrunched her eyes closed.

"If you hurt Miss Carmichael, you'll have the entire town at your door checking into your business. Is that what you want? Think about it. Martin considers her a daughter. The children love her. You don't think those families would sit by and do nothing?"

Susannah's father hesitated a few seconds, but then he broke out into another hideous smile. "James wants her job anyways and would do better at it. Womenfolk belong at home. We'll take good care of her here." A rifle appeared in his hands.

What she wouldn't give to have one herself. He wouldn't have any idea she could fire such a weapon. She'd delight in the element of surprise.

An angry roar came from somewhere inside the house. Both men flinched, darted their eyes and braced themselves. What could possibly startle these hard men?

"Burl. Leave Miss Carmichael alone." Susannah appeared in the doorway with a fierce look and a broom she held like a baseball bat. "Papa!"

Her father raised his hands, his palms turned out slightly as if to placate her.

Olivia's mind couldn't quite grasp the reaction of these grown men. If Olivia wasn't mistaken, they were afraid of Susannah.

The older man gave a small nod, and Burl backed away. "Sorry, miss. I do think you're pretty."

She lowered her arms and took a step back. Right into another male. This time the arms were gentle and warm. "Let's slowly walk away and go someplace we can talk."

Memories of yesterday popped into her head. She wiggled

free. "You've said enough." She brushed off his arms and faced Susannah. "Are you okay? I was worried when you weren't at school this week."

* * *

LUKE'S HEART stopped beating as Olivia brushed him aside. He glanced at Susannah. "Could you give us a few minutes?"

"Doesn't look like she's too keen on speaking with ya. But I'll wait."

He pulled Olivia over to where his horse grazed. "Olivia, please let me explain some things."

She spun around. "You have no right to use my name. None. Especially with a new *bride*." She shook her head. "You shouldn't even be here."

He hunched and met her gaze directly. "Look at me. I *do not* have a bride. And I'm here because *you* are."

She frowned, then placed her palms on his chest and pushed. He didn't budge. Just waited. Even angry, she was the most beautiful woman he'd ever laid eyes on.

"Please explain yourself, sir!" Her fists now sat on her hips.

He had one shot to get this right, and needed to tread carefully. He searched for the right words. "Impressive how you stood up to Burl and Walt."

Her foot stopped tapping. At least she hadn't walked away, yet.

"Caroline sent me. She was worried something would happen."

"In our training, we were taught how to defend ourselves. I never thought I'd have to use any of it, though." A look of wonder crossed her face.

"You surprised yourself?"

A tip of a smile played out on her lips.

"Miss Carmichael?" Susannah appeared from behind. "Why did you come?"

Olivia swung around. "I was worried about you."

Susannah smiled, pleasure showing all over her face. "No one's ever cared enough for me to come check on me before, so thank you. I stopped comin' to school 'cause I was the oldest one there. Seemed silly for me to get some learnin' now, when it wouldn't help me anymore. Papa plans to marry me off soon. I wanted time with my animals before I left."

Luke didn't fully agree with her logic, but it wasn't his place to say anything.

"You're all right then?" Olivia asked.

The girl nodded.

Olivia grasped the girl's hands. "But the bruises and your dresses."

"All from taking care of my animals, like I told ya."

Olivia shifted her feet. "You will come to me if you need anything at all? Yes?"

Susannah searched Olivia's face, then grinned. "Yes, ma'am." She let go and headed back to her house, then stopped and looked over her shoulder. "Miss Carmichael?"

"Yes, Susannah?"

"Thank you."

Olivia's face glowed with love for her student. She loved these kids like they were her own.

And in that moment, Luke wanted her to look at him the same way. "There's been a complete misunderstanding. I hope you can forgive me," he whispered.

Thirty-Seven

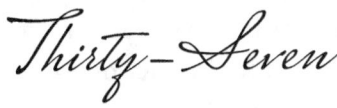

Why do men think women are not strong enough? Or wise enough? Men think they can say words to appease us and then move on. But actions are far more powerful than words. Something I've learned a lot about since I've moved west.

—From the journal of Olivia Carmichael

Olivia heard Luke's words, but didn't know how to respond, so she waited till Susannah walked far enough away, sighed, then turned to face Luke. *Mr. Taylor.*

"Please don't run. I have much to tell you," he pleaded.

Why would she want to hear about his new wife and their life together? "Why are you here?"

He blinked. "Will you hear me out?" His gaze drove into hers. "Please?"

She shook her head. "I can't, and I won't. You shouldn't be here. You have to stop following me. I have a job I love and want to keep."

He stared silently, hurt in his eyes.

She narrowed her eyes. Were his feelings truly engaged?

He pinched his lips before stepping closer. "The situation is not at all what you think." He let out a large huff, his warm breath fanning over her. "Olivia, I'm sorry for confusing you. I've been confused too."

She frowned. "It's clear where things stood between us. You have a mail-order bride here. Now." Her face heated. "Not that you made a declaration or anything. We're friends."

"Are we?" His lips quirked.

She opened her mouth, but he placed his finger against her lips. "Hear me out first, please?"

She searched his eyes, seeing sincerity in his gaze.

He hung his head and kicked a dirt clod with his boot. "Yes, Evelyn was my mail-order bride."

She pulled back as if slapped and pressed against warm horse flesh. His horse had her boxed in. Her gaze searched for an escape.

"We're not getting married, Olivia." A flash of embarrassment crossed his features. "Um ... we both agreed it would not work." His gaze intensified. "It was arranged before I even met you, and I did it only because the girls need a mother. But it was wrong of me not to tell you about her. And to be truly honest, I didn't want a mail-order bride. I thought it was necessary." His eyes glistened with tenderness. "I was so wrong. You are what I need."

Olivia heard his words, but her heart and mind refused to process them correctly.

The eager look on his face made her want to throw caution to the wind, but her fear of trusting and being hurt all over again kept her stock still.

She frowned. What was she supposed to say? Was this what *she* wanted?

"Let me make things clear. I want to marry *you*, instead."

Olivia stopped breathing and closed her eyes to keep from throwing her arms around his neck.

No declaration of love, no apology, just "I want to marry you."

Instead.

Her heart shattered further, if that was possible.

She flashed her eyes open and raised her chin, standing as tall as her five-foot-two inches made possible, using the most authoritative teacher voice she could muster. "What makes you think I want to get married. *Instead?*" Her feet led her away as fast as she could run.

He yelled her name, but the pounding in her ears drowned everything out except the desire to flee. She would not be his second choice. She would not be a pawn in his plans. She had her own plan, which never included getting married. If only ... if only ... she only considered because, well ... because he showed an interest in her, and she liked how he made her feel.

As she hustled toward the one-room schoolhouse and the room she lived in by herself, the truth shone crystal clear in her mind. Staying unmarried might've been the plan she made, but not the one her heart truly wanted.

LUKE HELD BACK, even though his heart wanted to give chase. Not what he wanted, but he had her answer. He had hurt her. Badly. And he couldn't think of a single way to undo any of the mistakes he'd made.

"I think you're the only one left who isn't mad at me, boy." Luke patted Admiral's neck and grabbed the pommel to mount.

After glancing back to make sure Susannah or her family

hadn't observed their interaction, he pulled the reigns and led Admiral in the direction Olivia ran. When the split in the road appeared, he stopped. Far ahead, a miniature dust storm circled around Olivia as she briskly moved toward the schoolhouse, feet stomping, arms swinging wildly at her sides, her hair flying loose behind her.

It was a beautiful sight.

Should he pursue? And tell her what exactly? Had he misread things? Ugly memories of a past rejection reared their head, taunting him. Maybe, there was more to Sarah leaving. Maybe he was undeserving of someone's love.

He shook his head. Even though this felt different, what if he asked again, and she still said no? His heart wouldn't stand the rebuff. All those patched holes around the organ would open again.

He waited till Olivia climbed the porch stairs and disappeared into her new room before heading back to the Martins' to collect the girls. Maybe she meant what she said about not wanting to marry, and she did prefer solitude over having a family.

Something deep inside, broke. Blocking out the pain, he focused on the even cadence of his horse's hooves clopping on the dirt. When he arrived, Caroline and Rose jumped from where they sat on the porch rockers and ran to greet him.

"Did you find Miss Carmichael?" Caroline asked.

"Yes, I found her." He swallowed.

"Did she find Susannah?"

"Yes, she did." How much should he tell them?

They grabbed and shook his arms. "Tell us! What happened?"

He kept his face devoid of emotions and gave them the facts. "So, as you see, both Susannah and Miss Carmichael are okay. Susannah probably won't be back at school again. She considers herself too old."

They looked around him. "Where is Miss Carmichael, then?"

The disappointment on their faces heightened his own. "She's back at the schoolhouse."

"Can we go see her?"

"No, I don't think that would be wise."

Chrissy Martin came out onto the porch. "Hi, Luke."

"Thank you, Chrissy, for watching the girls."

"No problem at all. Did you accomplish your task?" Her pointed question revealed the girls had told her his mission.

"As good as could be expected." He turned to the girls. "Time to get home. Miss Evelyn will have supper ready for us, and we don't want to be rude."

"I'm looking forward to meeting this Miss Evelyn. She seems to be a good addition to your family." Arthur had joined his wife on the porch and winked at Luke.

Luke was out of words, so he reached for the brim of his hat and nodded before securing Admiral to the wagon.

"Bye, Mrs. Martin." Both girls waved as they climbed in.

"Bye, girls. See you tomorrow."

He secured Admiral's straps, then set out for home. The girls murmured quietly. Or his thoughts were too loud to hear anything else. Neither his mail-order bride nor the one who stole his heart wanted to marry him.

IN THE QUIET of her small room, Olivia lit the single lamp. She paced back and forth, breathing in the wonderful fresh pine scent from the new wood while her nerves calmed. With no windows, the tiny space allowed her to hide her turmoil from the world.

Why were people horrible at being trustworthy?

Luke had surprised her in more ways than one. First, he appeared at Susannah's. Then he told her he wasn't marrying his mail-order bride, and he wanted to marry her, instead.

Instead! The nerve of that man. Would she always be an afterthought?

Who wanted to be tied to someone who couldn't make up his mind? She didn't. She wanted to know without any doubt she was loved and cared for. A certainty in that love.

Trust was a fragile thing. And hers had been broken by first her father, then Richard, then her so-called friends, and now Luke. Even Richard's defection hadn't wounded her so.

She sat, unlaced her boots and folded her legs under her skirt, then reached for her journal and pencil from the little table beside her bed. She flipped to a blank page. How should she start?

I really didn't want to see Luke again, but my heart still leaped. And now he says he's not marrying the person from the train, and he wants to marry me? I don't want to be disappointed. Disappointment hurts. All I have experienced in my life is disappointment.

She held her pencil still and let her mind flush out her thoughts. Her wanderings landed on something she heard in church.

Pastor William said we all fall short and at some point, those we love will disappoint us and we will disappoint others, but God never will. He is always there. Always waiting for us to ask for His help. I don't want to ask. I'm afraid to ask. What if nothing happens? Or the same thing happens? What if those I've come to care about in my new home turn their backs on me, and I'm all alone, once more? I'm afraid and don't want to be rejected again. But would it be worth the risk? Help me, God. Help me know what I should do?

Olivia blinked. When did she start talking to God like this? She flipped back a few pages. There. She asked for help when the students had to recite the poems they wrote. And they all did fine. And the one after when she asked for protection for Susannah, and Susannah was okay. She went back a few more pages and read an entry from two weeks ago about her students' behavior. And she hadn't had to pull the ruler out to dole out lashings once over the past week.

What if these wishes she wrote in her journal were actual prayers?

She flipped back farther in her journal, found on each page a plea or request she had made, and then reflected on the outcome. Some didn't happen necessarily in the way she asked specifically, but the situation was resolved in a better way.

She froze. No longer could she doubt God answered prayers. One just needed to ask.

How easy it was to not notice. To not see the small blessings when they occurred. If she hadn't written them, she would never have arrived at this moment.

She closed her book and placed it in her usual spot and laid out on her bed. God had helped her through some rough times, and she had to believe He would continue to do so in her future.

Thirty-Eight

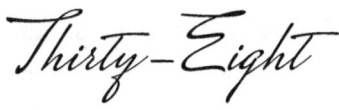

It's so challenging to not seek out Luke. The gossip mill had been all aflutter this past week about the Taylors' new housekeeper and Luke's foreman, Jimmy. That the men had things all wrong, and Luke's bride was not his bride after all. Why did I not allow him time to explain?

—From the journal of Olivia Carmichael

Throughout the week, Olivia gave all her attention to her students and the schoolhouse. She spent her waking hours cleaning slates, developing individual lesson plans for each pupil, and expending any excess energy during outside play time. She even volunteered to tutor anyone after school, if they were so inclined. Thankfully a few students accepted her offer and stayed behind every day.

She dropped into bed exhausted each night. Which was exactly what she needed.

Luke had attempted to speak to her both before and after school each day, but she stayed immersed in whatever task she was performing at the time, making things clear he shouldn't interrupt.

Caroline and Rose shared small snippets about their new housekeeper, even though Olivia pretended she wasn't interested. Something about new cooking and sewing tips. And possibly grooming tips, as they arrived at school each day with their hair styled differently.

The disappointment came swiftly. She hadn't realized how much she wanted to be the one to inspire the girls. Despite the fact she knew absolutely nothing about kitchen chores and had someone else style her hair her entire childhood. She should be happy for them, but she couldn't shake the idea she missed out on special memories with these girls.

Of course, amid the confusing emotions, questions settled in. Why did the men say the telegram was for Luke? And why, did Luke behave the way he did when they came to tell him? His actions could only mean he *was* waiting for a mail-order bride.

So then why did the gossip center around Jimmy and Evelyn spending afternoons reading the Bible together under the giant oak tree in front of the ranch house? And how they glanced at one another longingly.

Had Luke ordered a mail-order bride for Jimmy? And why had he said the word, *instead*.

After a week of trying to sort out the truth, she was more baffled than ever.

* * *

LUKE DROPPED the girls off at the house before wheeling the wagon into the barn. What should be his next move with Olivia? He'd made no progress to speak privately with her the entire week. And he didn't want to wait any longer. The madness brewing inside urged him to act.

Yet, as much as he wanted to, it was completely inappropriate to knock on her door. If she still stayed with the Martins or the Woodwards, well ... maybe.

But, no. She had to be independent and live on her own.

Was she okay? Did she need help with anything? Did she miss him like he missed her?

There was no doubt in his mind he cared for her. Deeply. Which, in the past would've sent him running. Now he wanted to run toward her and tell her.

And she wanted nothing to do with him.

He tilted his head back and groaned.

Admiral shifted.

"Whoa, boy. It's okay," he crooned while brushing him. "Who knew this heart of mine could feel this way?"

He now knew what he felt for Sarah was not romantic love. Nevertheless, his mother's request for the union on her deathbed and his sisters' excitement, encouraged his attachment to the idea of marriage to his friend.

He shook his head. How wrong he was.

When his ma died, and the responsibility for all of it—the ranch, his sisters, Sarah, his life—had him, at twenty-two-years-old, grappling for control somewhere. He could see that now.

So, on the day Ma died and after his sisters had finally gone to bed, Luke declared they'd get married the next day. But Sarah refused, which was so out of character for her.

Then she asked him to take a drive in the wagon.

He had said no at first, but she insisted.

They hadn't had a heart to heart at all. Not with taking care of Ma, the girls, the ranch, and being exhausted. Pretty much surviving. He figured she wanted privacy to talk. Boy, had he been wrong.

As Luke drove Sarah around the outskirts of town, rain poured from the nighttime sky. He had waited to listen to what she had to say. She opened her mouth to speak several times but couldn't get anything out. Not one who lacked for words before, Luke knew something was wrong.

"I'm not ready to be a mom yet," she had said in a quiet voice. "This is all too much, too fast, and I don't think I can do this. I'm too young for all this responsibility." He recalled her staring out into the darkness. "I want to see the world. I want to know what life is like beyond Washton, not be stuck here forever."

"So, you're telling me your promise to Ma meant nothing?" The pain in his chest increased when he asked her the question that came first to his mind.

"I never made that promise. *You* did. Marriage takes two people. I care deeply for you, Luke. I do love you. But not in a way a wife should love her husband." She hesitated, then spoke softly. "And, I still love your brother."

Luke shook his head of the painful memory. He sank to his knees, exhausted, not caring he was in the barn in the dirt and hay. At the time, he couldn't see her side of things through his raw and hurt emotions. Now, he did. He was thankful she had the courage to tell him before it was too late. Before they had ended up in a loveless marriage, full of resentment and regret.

He now knew his feelings for Sarah weren't love. In fact, she was correct that she never committed to the arrangement. Sarah had moved quietly around the room while he and his ma made all the plans. Plans which never included her own opinion.

He frowned. He had assumed, never once asking Sarah her

feelings about what Ma asked of them. No wonder she left. He had given her no other choice.

She had asked him to stop the wagon, and he complied, having no idea of her plans. She then jumped down and reached for her bag from the wagonbed, one he had no idea was there, looked at him, and walked away. From him and his sisters.

She might've been right, but at the time the only view of himself was he had failed. Failed to save his Pa and Thomas, failed to save Michael and Ma. Failed to follow through with Ma's last request and marry Sarah. And with a broken heart and bruised pride, he pushed further away from everyone, including God.

He sat back on his heels, reached for a piece of hay and ripped it apart.

He believed Sarah had betrayed him. Left when he needed her most. In a way, he had done the same to God. Left his faith, stopped trusting, and run away. Sarah didn't have to go, like Luke didn't have to build a wall around his heart, but she believed she didn't have a choice. To survive, Luke believed that too.

More empty spots in his heart fused together into some alignment as if joining on the same path. But still, one last piece remained missing.

His pulse leaped at the realization he didn't want to depend on himself anymore. He wanted to trust God fully. And he had this ... this urgency to start right now. He bowed his head.

"God, it's been a long time, but I feel Your presence. I know now You've been here all along. Thank You for carrying me through all this time. I'm sorry for my fear and my misguided trust. I pray if it is Your will, for a future with Olivia. Guide me to know what to do. Please help her to forgive me and to open her heart to trust both You

and me. Help me to do better by You. I need You. She needs You. We both need You. Amen."

Wetness penetrated Luke's knees and he opened his eyes. Heavy pounding pinged on the roof, while a light mist sprayed him in the face. A splash sounded, and he turned to see Jimmy in the doorway.

"There you are!" Jimmy's clipped voice grabbed Luke's full attention.

He stood. "What's wrong?"

"Haven't you noticed? It's pouring. And high tide."

Luke inwardly groaned. "Have you seen the river yet?" The river was the best indicator of what type of punch this storm would net out.

"The water has overflowed the riverbank near town."

A chill permeated his body as the last flood entered Luke's mind and the sight of his father and older brother being swept away by the rushing river. Luke knew his ranch sat far enough from the water to be safe. It was helping the others in town, which was situated near the river—that was dangerous.

"That's not unusual." His mind went to Olivia. "We built the schoolhouse high enough to withstand a large storm like this."

"Yes, but some figure, and I must agree, since Sacramento raised their sidewalks and left the lower levels of the buildings below, the water now has nowhere else to go. They've created a breakaway. Things might not go the way we planned."

The image of his pa and brother blurred into a picture of Olivia. Cold dread filled his body. He pivoted, pulled the saddle from the boards, then rushed toward Admiral, his movements quick and efficient from years of experience. "I have to go."

Jimmy placed a hand on Luke's arm. "It's too dangerous, Luke."

Luke threw it off. "I'm not going to sit around waiting

without knowing she's all right. Besides, if what you say is true, then Washton needs all the help we can give."

"Do you want me to ride with you?"

He shook his head. "No, stay here and keep Evelyn and the girls safe."

A slight smile crossed Jimmy's face.

Luke's own lips twitched, knowing Jimmy had eyes for Evelyn since the day she arrived. It wouldn't be long before his foreman became a happily married man. Something Luke hoped would happen to him soon too.

Yes, he wanted to spend the rest of his life happily married to Olivia.

But first, he needed to make sure she stayed safe. He pulled himself into the saddle, swung Admiral around, and galloped out of the yard, praying the entire ride to town.

Thirty-Nine

Rainstorms wash away all the dirt and grime and make things clean and fresh. If only my heart could be washed clean in the same way. Then my soul wouldn't hurt so much.

—From the journal of Olivia Carmichael

The thunderstorms Olivia experienced in Cincinnati came and went faster than one could brew tea, so she'd never known unrelenting rain such as this. The torrent of water pelted the roof, and the entire sky was covered in darkness. She shivered. With the dreary and damp weather, she wouldn't have known it was the middle of the afternoon if she hadn't just entered her room after closing the schoolhouse for the weekend.

The river water flowed fast, carrying broken tree limbs and personal belongings from upriver, all while creeping higher toward the bank. People said over and over they positioned the schoolhouse high enough, but the water kept rising, so she now questioned the truth of their words.

She couldn't see the river from her room, but she heard the waves hit the shore. Had it crested yet? Maybe she would be better served to wait out the storm in the schoolhouse, where she could see and escape out the front door if the water rose too high.

After pulling on her wet outerwear, she closed her door and hurried around to the front of the schoolhouse, thankful for the wraparound porch. A constant cascade poured over the edge in sheets, hitting the banister and splashing her in the face. As she reached the front door, she glanced at the river. Water spilled over the brim. She hoped the wooden slats the building sat on would hold. Sorrow invaded her heart at the thought of her beloved schoolhouse being washed away.

Her cold hand gripped the doorknob and opened the door. Once she was inside, the roar outside dulled to a lull of flowing water rushing by. A constant pinging banged on the roof, letting her know the storm wasn't waning yet.

She blew out her breath. The room felt secure. A slight dripping sound had her exploring the corner, where she noticed water pooled on the floor. She glanced at the ceiling and found wet spots where the wood was unable to keep out the deluge of water.

Her papers! She ran to her desk, and hurriedly stacked all the books and papers into a large pile and then grabbed an empty bucket and placed it on top. A second bucket was retrieved and placed by the stove, where another drip had started. She turned around and scanned the room for more leaks.

A flash of lightning lit the room. Thunder immediately followed, so loud the entire building shook.

Startled, Olivia dove under her desk.

Another burst of light along with loud thunder hit, shaking

the schoolhouse again. She wrapped her arms around herself. Should she stay or leave? Where would she go?

Thump.

She whimpered. Something hit the building. Is this what it meant to have her independence? Living through a gigantic storm all by herself? Other thumps banged the wall, one after the other. She had to do something. She couldn't stay here alone.

She crawled from under the desk and headed to the door. It was so dark, she couldn't see anything. She stood and put her hands out in front of her.

Halfway to the door, the thumping grew faster and louder. She froze.

Crash.

A glass window broke, a large tree limb floated in on a deluge of water.

Olivia screamed.

Glass shattered again as a second window broke. More water poured in. A cold sensation crept over Olivia's feet as water surrounded her.

Her beloved schoolhouse!

Boom. A flash of lightning lit the room with another pound of thunder immediately following. This time a second boom sounded right outside the window, followed by a cracking and creaking sound.

Crash.

Olivia threw her arms over her head and crouched low as glass shattered everywhere. The tree from outside must've fallen through the window. Rainwater and wind blew through the building, causing the temperature to drop quickly.

She raised her arm and glanced around to assess the damage. Water now flowed from the east to the west side of the building. The door for her to escape was on the far side.

She would die here, much like her parents did in their carriage when it fell into the river. Something bumped her legs and knocked them out from underneath her. She landed with a splash, the shock of the cold water causing her to cry out.

A minute later desks near her bobbed, then crashed into one another, sending one toward her. She had to move, now. "Oh, God. I don't want to die. Please help me," she cried as she pushed herself up and sloshed through the mini river flowing in the middle of her schoolhouse. The water continued to rise. Walking in a straight line was difficult. Her soaked clothing clung to her small frame and weighed her down. The third time she lost her balance, she fell into the freezing water. The frigid temperature sunk into her bones. She knew if she didn't reach the door soon, she would be swept away through the window along with her student's desks.

With one last effort, she closed her eyes, took a deep breath, then sprung forward on all fours, moving her knees and arms as fast as she could, praying the entire way. Water splashed on her face as she plowed through the waist-high depths. When she stretched her right arm out, she made contact with wood. She located the doorknob and pulled herself to a standing position. The momentum of the water pushed against the door, making it difficult to open. She yanked hard a few times. It finally gave way. The deluge from inside pushed at her legs as it found another exit point and merged with the chest high water on the porch.

A wave of water splashed all over her face. She sputtered the substance out of her mouth. Her hand reached to swipe her eyes, which stung when she opened them.

A book floated by. Then a gunny sack from the mill.

Before she could move, a broken fence post bobbed toward her, crashing into her hip. Pain lanced up her leg. She clung to the doorframe. A quiet voice echoed in her ear. *God never leaves us. You're never alone.*

All she could do was blindly trust those words. "Lord, help me."

* * *

NERVOUS ENERGY COURSED through Luke as he rode south. The river had crested in new places, and at this pace, Main Street, and other parts of Washton would be submerged. Jimmy was right. They were taking on all the water Sacramento deflected.

Which meant this would be a flood like no other.

Hopefully the schoolhouse would still be standing. He'd reach the schoolhouse first and pray it was high enough to withstand this type of torrent. As they drew closer, Admiral's hooves splashed through puddles, and the horse abruptly shifted away from the thick rushing water ahead.

"Whoa, there, boy!" Luke squeezed hard with his knees. Admiral had never shied from crossing rivers before, but animals had a sixth sense of understanding nature when man couldn't. Circling Admiral around, Luke studied the area looking for a safe place to cross.

A blood curdling scream echoed through the air.

"Olivia!" Luke immediately kicked his heels into Admiral and immersed them both into the cold, dirty water. The chill barely registered as he concentrated on staying in the saddle. Nothing would stop him from losing another person he cared for. Not a storm. Not a flood. Older, stronger, and more experienced than the last time, he would do all he could.

He found a dry patch which allowed horse and man to catch a breath before entering a new trail of gushing water.

He gasped as the schoolhouse came fully into sight.

A tree laid across one side, the glass windows broken, and

water surrounded the entire building. The new room they'd added on seemed in one piece but with no window, he had no way of knowing.

His heartbeat exploded in his chest as he pushed Admiral forward. "Oh, please, God, let her be all right." He grabbed his rope off his saddle and coiled it, ready for whatever came next.

Where should he look first?

Something rammed into his left foot as he drew closer, shoving both he and Admiral sideways. He squinted as he turned his face into the pelting rain. A desk! Floating in the water! The sight filled him with dread.

"Olivia!" he yelled.

He didn't hear a reply, but that wouldn't stop him. "Help, Lord," he cried out. "Help me know where to look."

"Help." A tiny cry came from the other side of the structure.

"Thank you, God!" Luke called out. "I'm coming, Olivia!" Energy surged through his veins. Carefully he drove Admiral in a zig-zag pattern, going wide to circumvent the strong current. He pushed his horse toward the porch, but the water was soon to Admiral's knees, making it difficult to move forward.

The horse slipped.

The current pushed them back.

Luke patted Admiral's neck with encouragement. "Come on boy, you can do it." He needed Admiral's strength to get closer. "God, please let me get to her in time, let her be okay ..." His words trailed off as he saw a small form clinging to the porch post.

* * *

With tired arms and numb legs, Olivia could barely hold on. The only reason she knew she was still alive was the rain pelting her face. If it wasn't for the belt hanging by the door, she would've floated away a while ago with the desks.

Once to the porch, she focused on one thing. Get to higher ground. Stay above the water. She had long enough to secure herself to the banister with the belt, but now it didn't matter. She couldn't move. Water lapped her head and filled her mouth whenever she tried to take a deep breath and yell out.

The porch had become a funnel, and she couldn't hang on much longer.

No one would come. The schoolhouse sat too far away for anyone to hear her cries.

She thought she had felt hopeless before.

Images of her new life flashed in her mind, and she focused on the cherished memories. The Martins, the Woodwards, all her students. Caroline. Rose. Luke. She closed her eyes and pictured him in the wagon with his sisters. On a horse. The feel of his arms around her when he taught her to shoot. Sitting tall in the first pew in church.

Church.

Her eyes opened. God! She was not alone. He was here with her and the reason she still held on. Why had it been so hard for her to trust Him before? It was all she could do at this point.

She had to cling to that faith as hard as she clung to this porch post. "Oh, God. Please hear my prayer. Help me. Help me know you. Help me to accept your love, God. Please love me and save me."

An urge to shout filled her. "Help!" Strength from within filled her. "Help!"

She heard a whiny. Her head leaned against the wood, but she could shift enough to see behind her.

And there she saw him. Her knight in shining armor.

Her heart lifted, even though the rest of her body couldn't move.

"Hold on," he yelled. She couldn't see, but the determination in his voice gave her confidence, strength, and courage to cling further.

"Can you give me your hand?"

The water splashed her face continuously, making the words difficult to speak. "I'm ... a ... fraid ... to ... arms ... weak."

"I'll get behind you, and you let go into me." he shouted.

She opened her lips to answer, but water filled her mouth. She coughed, forcing her hand to slip off the banister. Exhaustion overtook her as she hung from the post. Were her eyes open? She couldn't see or hear anything.

With one last smidgen of energy, she uttered one word. "B ... e ... l ... t."

Forty

How will I know, God, you are truly there?

—From the journal of Olivia Carmichael

Did she say belt?

Then he saw Olivia's body sag and his heart stopped. "Olivia!"

No response.

He jumped off Admiral, still clinging to the reins, and placed his feet on top of the banister, while he gripped the porch roof with his other hand. He fought for balance as water slammed into his legs. His position blocked the water from flowing into Olivia's body, which allowed him to take stock of the situation.

She was secured by something. What did she say? A belt! That's what she meant. "Smart girl."

Admiral huffed.

"Hang in there, boy. I've almost got her." He reached to unhook the belt. Olivia sputtered. He wanted to pull her close and tell her everything would be all right, but he had to get her away from the deluge first in order for both of them to survive.

Once unhooked, he tried to lift her, but the weight of her sodden skirts pulled her back. He growled in frustration as he tried again and again. But before he could lift her, she went limp.

They were out of time.

He pulled from somewhere deep inside and hefted her into the saddle.

She slumped forward across the horn but didn't fall off.

The water continued to push at his legs as he shifted his feet and repositioned his body. He leaped onto Admiral's back behind Olivia and squeezed his knees together. "Come on boy. Let's get out of here."

His arms circled Olivia, pulling her limp body tightly against him as he steered the reins. They ran alongside the tidal flow, and Luke leaned right to help balance. The water swirled at the stirrups. Admiral stumbled. "Hold on, boy. You can do it." His entire side drew close to the water. For a quick second, Luke figured they'd fall in, but the flowing waves actually held them up. Using the eddy to his advantage, he steered them out of the deepest part.

Once at higher ground, he slowed Admiral to a stop. He turned Olivia and placed his ear near her mouth. She was still breathing, praise God. He touched the rest of her body, her arms, shoulders, waist, making sure she wasn't hurt or bleeding. He knew it wasn't at all proper, but he didn't care. He didn't want to ever let her go. He awkwardly pulled out of his overcoat and draped the garment across her back hoping the heat between him and the inside would be enough until he got her back to the ranch.

The pouring rain eased to a light shower as they rode away from the river, but pools of water gathered everywhere. Not one business along Main Street was dry. His heart sank. The flood of 1862 flashed in his mind and the work involved to rebuild. This would be no different.

He clucked his tongue and Admiral headed home. Olivia stirred, and he gripped her tighter. "You're safe now. You can open your eyes, Olivia. You're no longer in danger."

A few seconds passed before she moved her head in response.

He had to get her out of these wet clothes. He hunched over and held her close, shielding her from any additional rain, while the continuous drizzle soaked his clothing now that he was no longer wearing his cover. Admiral moved at a slow pace, worn and weary.

The rain had fully stopped by the time his ranch came into view. He shouted, "Jimmy!"

Olivia stirred. He shifted to see her better. "Hey. Are you okay?" he asked.

She blinked and glanced around then frowned, causing her forehead to wrinkle. The most precious sight ever. "I think so." Her gaze met his. "I thought I would never see you again."

He gripped her arms. "I thought I wouldn't be fast enough to save you."

She sucked in a quick breath. "But you were."

He shook his head. "But I almost wasn't."

She placed her hand on his cheek. "You did."

He wrapped his arms around her. "I'm so glad you're safe."

She pulled back and searched his face. "Thank you. For coming for me. Even after I pushed you away." She gazed into his eyes, showing relief and something else.

He didn't dare hope for more. "I couldn't not come for you. I care too much for you."

Surprise crossed her face.

His heart thudded. "You may not believe me, but I love you, Olivia."

"But ... but ... but what about ..."

"I can explain more later, but trust me when I say I want to marry you. And my mail-order bride approves."

Admiral stopped. He lowered his lips to hers. Hers felt warm and trembling as he slowly kissed her, trying to communicate all his love into this one action. She didn't respond right away, but neither did she pull away. As her lips moved, timid and unsure, his heart soared.

She shivered.

"You're cold. Forgive me ..."

"No." She placed a shaking wet finger to his lips. "It's not that."

His brows furrowed as he looked at her intently. "Then what?"

She bit her lip. "I'm scared."

He held her close. "You are safe, Olivia. The water can't hurt you anymore. I won't let anything hurt you anymore."

She shook her head and mumbled. He leaned closer.

"It's not the flooding, Luke. Yes, the water scared me, but I knew God was with me. I *felt* Him, Luke. I never wanted to feel dependence on anyone again, but I had no choice, and God was there." She looked away. "But I couldn't have gotten to safety without you, either. I had to depend on you. And I told myself I would never depend on a man again. So I'm scared. All my planning, my arrangement with myself, my life as how I intended, needs to change. I don't want to live here on my own, but it's so hard for me to put my trust in others." She sobbed and buried her face into his chest.

His hold tightened. "I understand what you're saying." He chuckled. "In a way, I feel the same. I didn't want to lose my heart to anyone. To be close to someone. And then lose them. If something happened to you, I wouldn't survive. Which also means I can't live without you. I love you too much to let you go."

* * *

Olivia tucked her head into Luke's shoulder and pressed her face against his wet chest, allowing his words to sink in.

He loved her!

Even dripping wet from head to toe, her skirts heavy, and her hair plastered to her head.

She'd never sensed this type of love before. By both Luke and God. Could she say the words back?

Cheers and clapping had her lifting her head.

Half the town stood on Luke's ranch.

"It's about time, Luke," Caroline shouted.

"You two are made for each other," Chrissy's motherly tone rang into the darkness.

"What are the teacher's plans now?" Someone asked, whose voice Olivia couldn't recognize.

She glanced over at Luke, her face quite hot. "I have no plans, yet, to stop teaching for this schoolyear."

Luke grinned at her in the most loving and kind way possible. "I know now is not the best time to ask, but I refuse to wait any longer. Will you marry me?" He whispered conspiratorially, "We can work out the details, later."

She knew in her heart this was the right path. "Even the best plans need to change when God's plans are infinitely better. Yes, Luke, I'll marry you."

He gave a loud *whoop* then scooped her into his arms and dismounted. "You've made me the happiest of men, darling."

"I love you, Luke." Her heart nearly burst as the words tumbled out at last.

"I love you, too, Olivia." He placed his forehead to hers.

"See, I told you she would marry." James Chapman stood off to the side, arms crossed wearing a smug look on his face. "Now do you believe me when I say a man is the only option to teach?"

Olivia tucked her forehead to Luke's chest as she waited for Mr. Martin to concur with Mr. Chapman. A female spoken for was not allowed to teach. What would happen with her beloved schoolhouse and students? "We'll see, James. For now, you can help clean out the schoolhouse, which should take no more than a month or so."

James's smug look evaporated. "I'll clean the school, but then I will be the one to teach in it, like I should've from the beginning." He grumbled as he turned and walked inside the ranch house.

Olivia hesitantly raised her eyes at Luke.

"What?" he asked.

"What did you say about your mail-order bride?"

"Well ... that her plans have also been revised."

He bent and kissed her again. The sound of cheers fading away when she put her arms around him and kissed him back.

Epilogue

*Well, God. You have been here all along. And You knew what I
needed all along. I just needed to find You myself. And Luke? Well, I
found him, too, when I wasn't even looking. I've learned the best-
laid plans can go awry, but You turn them into good. Thank You for
better plans than I could ever have made myself.*

—From the journal of Olivia Carmichael

O livia threaded her arm through Luke's as they
headed up the hill to the schoolhouse to check on
the repairs. She leaned her head on his shoulder,
and he squeezed her hand.

His concern for her was endearing. After the flood, she had
spent a few days in bed resting, recovering from her ordeal,
thankful she didn't catch any severe ailments after being in the
cold water for so long.

Once her strength returned, she insisted she help with the
cleanup. Luke wouldn't let her go without being present
himself, so they slipped into a routine of sorts. He showed up

early in the morning, escorted her, and brought her back for the noon-day meal and to rest.

"You heard about the vote?" he asked.

"I did." The school board met and agreed to allow Olivia to finish the school year, even though she was betrothed to Luke. They wanted her to continue classes in the church starting next week since repairs will take longer on the schoolhouse.

"How does that make you feel?"

"Wanted. Appreciated. In Awe." The emotions were foreign to her, but she was grateful to experience them. Never would she question the Lord's plans. Instead, she would do her best in the situation, to serve without worry.

He bumped her arm. "The girls are excited. They didn't want to lose you as their teacher."

Olivia blew out a breath. She loved teaching and didn't want to give it up right away. The fact that the school board was allowing her to continue was a miracle. One that she would not squander. "I didn't want to stop either. You are okay with me working?"

He grinned. "Absolutely. It makes you happy, and you are good at it. There is no rush. Until everyone agrees it's time to find another teacher."

"I'm sure Mr. Chapman is not happy." The man had been more subdued since the flood, appearing every day to help haul away broken wood and glass and hammer together new planks provided by the mill. He hadn't said one word about him teaching, and that meant the world to her. He focused instead on the labor heavy work, day after day. Olivia had never seen him so disheveled. Yet he also seemed more at peace. Or maybe that was her own peace now that she no longer feared him taking away her job.

"I'm looking forward to all the extra time to court properly." Luke had already started calling on her when they weren't working at the schoolhouse. He was attentive, kind, and sweet in the plans he discussed with her about their future. A future she could've never prepared for yet was enthusiastic to experience.

She smiled at her future husband. "Thank you for your support and your patience and understanding. I am looking forward to our future together."

They arrived at the site, Will waving at them as they approached.

Luke paused and glanced down at her, "Sweetheart, our future has already begun."

A blur of color whooshed past as Bert mounted his stump to supervise the work.

Squawk!

THE END

Author's Note

When writing a historical novel, there are specific events that a writer wants to include. For my story to take place when it did, I had to take a bit of liberty with the timeline on some of these events to fit my story.

The Sacramento River did in fact flood the city of Sacramento several times and after the last one in 1862, they brought in thousands of tons of dirt to raise the street level (which took several years). Today, the original street level can be seen throughout Old Town under the boardwalks. When we toured with my son's 4th grade class, they reenacted a one-room schoolhouse experience in one of the buildings under the current city.

There truly was a town called Washington across the Sacramento River. And my fictional town of Washton is loosely based on this town. The actual town was created by a young widow with five children when she sold several lots of the ranchland to form a town (starting on Washington's birthday, and thus the name). It even had a post office for a few years before it burnt down. Unfortunately, the post office was never rebuilt. Its location across from Sacramento almost ensured the town's success, however a bridge built across the river in 1870 diverted all traffic away from the town. I chose to use the name Washton because I wanted to build a fictional town with a different outcome, but also because there is an existing small town called Washington further northeast of Sacramento.

There was an American Woman's Association founded by Catherine Beecher in 1852. The mission stated in the research I found was to recruit and train teachers for frontier schools and send women into the West to civilize the young. This is the school Olivia found in Cincinnati that trained her and sent her to Washton.

In my research it was said that the training courses included at the school were considered necessary because as soon as a young teacher set foot on the ground, some man would promptly woo her and make her his wife. This is why, again, I used some liberties with the timeline a bit, and why I had the mayor of Washton have Olivia sign a contract.

I went back and forth about the pencil Olivia would use to write in her journal. Should she write with ink and nib? Did pencils exist in 1869? From the research I could find, they did and so I decided it would be easier to store and reuse, than carrying around an ink bottle. They were costly and they made them last a long time. From the data I could find, the first American wooden pencil came to be in 1812. The first mechanical pencil was created in 1869.

If you'd like to learn more about old Sacramento, you can go to the website and look at their page on its history, https://www.oldsacramento.com/history. Taken from the website: *In the mid-1960s, a plan was set forth to redevelop the area and through it, the first historic district in the West was created. Today, with 53 historic buildings, Old Sacramento has more buildings of historic value condensed into its 28 acres than most areas of similar size in the West. Registered as a National and California Historic Landmark, the properties in the district are primarily owned by private owners, with individual businesses leasing shops and offices.*

My research turned up so much more information about early California, which I share on my website www.denisemcolby.com and blog, facebook https://www. facebook.com/denisemcolbywrites/ and Instagram https:// www.instagram.com/denisem.colby/posts.

Acknowledgments

First, I want to thank God for putting the story idea in my head while on a fourth-grade field trip to Sacramento with my oldest son. It was there while in the one-room schoolhouse that a seed was planted. And it was there, two years later, when I went with my second son on *his* fourth-grade trip, that the story idea was still brewing, along with new ideas that pushed me to take a stab at writing them out.

To my husband Ken who supported me without question and purchased my first writing group membership very early on. You had no idea what we were getting ourselves into. I appreciate you and I love you. And to Connor, Kyle, and Zach, for your unconditional support and encouragement. I kept going because I knew you were watching, and I wanted to show you that you could accomplish anything you put your mind to and to never give up on your goals and dreams.

To my sisters Pat & Suzanne, thank you for always being my cheerleaders in everything I do. Also, a shout out to my mom and dad who were both such encouragers my entire life. My mom shared books with me as a child (and then with my own children) that instilled a love a reading. The fact that I've written my own novel - she would've loved to have seen this book in print.

To my other mom & dad (my in-laws), thank you for always asking how my book was coming along and for celebrating every single little milestone with me. Your encouraging words were always what I needed to hear. I'm so excited to share this with you.

To my dearest friend Barb, thank you for going with me to my first writing meeting, my first conference, and the many, many tea meet-ups to help me write this book. You have been my biggest cheerleader. And to Kaycy, Tracy, Aimee, Lisa, Cori, Jen, the Dart Gang, Francesca and to the numerous other friends and family members who have cheered me on and believed in me, thank you! I am very blessed, indeed.

In case you haven't figured it out yet, I have been on this writing journey for a long time and there are many people who I have met in the writing world that I want to recognize.

To the many conferences, classes, and workshop teachers. I have learned so much along the way. This book is being published because of the time taken to teach a newbie writer who knew nothing about writing fiction.

A shoutout to the Yorba Linda Public Library Librarians who helped me track down historical books as I did my research. Finding research books is a fun part of this writing process that also generates way too many ideas and factual points we could never put in one novel.

To my dear writing friends who I have met on this journey. Many of you came alongside me during different stages of this book. Some of you have been by my side the entire time. I can't list everyone's name (so I'm organizing it by the groups I belong to), just know I'm truly thankful for all of you!

To all my OCRW friends (originally RWA OCC) and especially Elena Dillon, Kitty Bucholtz, Nancy Farrier, Debra Mullins, & Leslie Knowles. Early on, when I had no idea what I was doing, your patience and encouragement kept me going. I hear your cheers as I complete this final leg of this marathon and that means so much to me. I can't wait to collect my red rose with you all in June!

To my OC ACFW friends Kathleen Armstrong, Susan K. Beatty, Kathleen Robinson, Nancy Brashear, Marilyn Allison, Chautona Havig, and the rest of this wonderful group. Thank you for your enthusiasm, prayers, and encouragement. From the writing meetings to those conferences we served at together early on, you've been an integral part of this story's journey.

To my conference buddies I met through the SoCal Christian Writers Conference, Lori, Aurora, Kelly, Carol, and so many others, along with a special shout out to Kathleen Denly, whom I met at the first conference and became my first critique partner. I've learned a lot from you, and it's been so fun to celebrate your publishing success as well.

To my Novel Academy Huddle Group Becky Yauger, Becca Kinzer, CJ Meyerly, Wendy Galinetti, Lynn Watson, and Becky DePaulis. I love that we have cheered each other on for several years now and all have new chapters being written in our writing life.

And to my Faith, Hope, Love Christian Writers (FHLCW) online group and most especially my FHL critique group – Kimberly Keagan, Marie Wells Coutu, & Christina Rich – your encouragement and suggestions on everything means so much. To dive deep into this book and care about Luke and Olivia's story means the world to me. And it was so special to share with you the announcement of my Scrivenings Press Get Pubbed win when it was announced (and have you cheering so loudly, Kim!).

I also want to thank my new Scrivenings Press family and the warm welcome into a brand new to me group of writers I can learn from, and to my editors Regina Rudd Merrick and Linda Fulkerson. It's been so much fun to say I have deadlines!

And last, I want to thank *you*, dear reader, for being willing to pick up this book, and taking the time to read it. I hope you have found faith, hope, and love within these pages. And that you have enjoyed traveling along with Olivia and Luke on their journey to their happily ever after.

About the Author

Passionate about all types of stories—whether they are from songs, theatre, movies, or novels—Denise M. Colby loves history and constantly finds herself contemplating how it was to live in the 1800s. Combining her love of learning about history and reading, Denise writes Christian historical romance novels. Her first novel, *When Plans Go Awry*, is the first novel in her Best-laid Plans series.

Born and raised in Northern California, Denise moved to Southern California for college and to dance in the parades at Disneyland, where she met her husband thirty years ago. A mother to three boys and soon-to-be daughter-in-love, Denise loves to read, watch movies with her family, sing 80s and musical songs, tap dance, and spend date nights with her husband at 'The Happiest Place on Earth.' She treasures the written word and the messages that can be conveyed when certain words are strung together. An avid journal writer, Denise usually can be found with a pen and notepad whenever she's reading God's word. Every year, Denise chooses a word to focus on. She shares her learnings about that word throughout the year on the two blogs she writes for.

Visit Denise's website to sign up for her newsletter or connect with her on her social media. www.denisemcolby.com

You May Also Like ...

Seashells in My Pocket—by Terri Wangard

Unsung Stories of World War II—Book One

German-Brazilian Isabel Neumann delights in creating seashell art, but it's her mathematical ability that lands her a job at the American air base in Natal, northern Brazil during World War II. She doesn't need a calculator to determine the correct weights and balances for the Air Transport Command's cargo planes.

Daniel Lambert, an American transport pilot based at Natal, endures the taunts of combat pilots that he is "allergic to combat." His flying skills win him respect, however, and his friendship with Isabel deepens, even as a new source of trouble looms.

Isabel is caught in the crosshairs of a German saboteur who is obsessed with her. He insists that she belongs with him, and demands that she help him sabotage the Allied base. Her growing relationship with Daniel angers the Nazi, who will do anything to get rid of him. What will happen to Isabel if the madman captures her?

Get your copy here:

https://scrivenings.link/seashellsinmypocket

* * *

Of Faith and Dreams—by Tonya B. Ashley

Lost and Found series—Book One

When Van Buren, Arkansas, is inundated with Forty-Niners seeking to outfit themselves with horses before heading west, Justin Hogue sees it as the perfect opportunity to step out of his father's shadow to establish a horse ranch. The same influx of prospectors ushers in a competitive horse trader who wants him out of the way. Further complicating things, Justin is challenged with a new tenant at the Hogue family boardinghouse.

Eliza Dawn is an independent, headstrong seamstress who claims to follow the prospectors west to sell her garments. Justin believes she's hiding something. After all, a few dollars for shirts isn't worth the risk. So, he keeps his distance until a mysterious letter and an intriguing ring unite them in searching for an unknown prospector.

Can they find one man in a thousand before the gold expeditions leave town? What will put Justin's dreams at greater risk—conflict with the horse trader or Eliza Dawn's secrets?

Get your copy here:

https://scrivenings.link/offaithanddreams

* * *

Treasure and Trouble—by Betty Woods

Troubles of the Heart—Book One

Eugenia Hampton wants to be loved for who she is, not what she has. Her parents intend to see her married and cared for, but she's determined not to be a mere parlor decoration to show off some man's achievements. She wants a love match or no match.

Paul Stuart is tired of clashing with people over his abolitionist views. Especially with his father who is the overseer for Eugenia's father. He's saving money to move from Tennessee and buy a farm in

Illinois where he can live in peace with people who accept him and his ideas.

Paul rescues Eugenia after her horse throws her. They form a secret, forbidden friendship based on their common family problems. Neither of them expects their relationship to grow into love. When Eugenia's father selects a non-Christian man for her husband, she must choose between her known and comfortable life of luxury or a lifetime of love with Paul where little else will be certain.

Get your copy here:

https://scrivenings.link/treasureandtrouble